Praise for Debbie Macomber's Christmas stories

"*Call Me Mrs. Miracle* is an entertaining holiday story that will surely touch the heart… Best of all, readers will rediscover the magic of Christmas."

—*Bookreporter.com*

"[*There's Something About Christmas* is] a tale of romance in the lives of ordinary people, with a message that life is like a fruitcake: full of unexpected delights."

—*Publishers Weekly*

"*There's Something About Christmas* is a wonderfully funny, and at times heart-wrenching story of finding the right person to love at the most delightful time of year."

—*Times Record News* (Wichita Falls, Texas)

"Macomber once again demonstrates her impressive skills with characterization and her flair for humor."

—*RT Book Reviews* on *When Christmas Comes*

"[*When Christmas Comes*] is a sweetly satisfying, gently humorous story that celebrates the joy and love of the holiday season."

—*Booklist*

"A fast, frothy fantasy for those looking to add some romance to their holidays."

—*Publishers Weekly* on *The Snow Bride*

"*Where Angels Go*…should definitely get anyone in the mood for holiday cheer and warmth."

—*FreshFiction.com*

"*New York Times* bestselling author Debbie Macomber has written a delightful holiday story filled with romance, conflict and lots of humor."

—*BookReporter.com* on *The Christmas Basket*

Dear Friends,

Merry Christmas! I'm excited that two of my favorite holiday stories are being published together. *Call Me Mrs. Miracle* was written after the success of the Hallmark Channel adaptation of *Mrs. Miracle*, which ranked as their highest rated movie of 2009. *Call Me Mrs. Miracle*, also starring the talented Doris Roberts, again scored as the network's most viewed movie of the year.

The bonus story in this collection, *The Christmas Basket*, is another of my favorites. It won a RITA® Award, which is Romance Writers of America's highest award for excellence in writing. That's especially gratifying, because it was chosen by my peers. So you can see that both books signify high points in my writing career.

The holidays are a special time with our children and grandchildren, a time of gathering together, building memories, of laughter and fun. My wish is that these two stories will be part of your holiday enjoyment.

Merry Christmas!

Debbie Macomber

PS: You can reach me in a number of ways—through my webpage at debbiemacomber.com or on Facebook. Or if you wish, you can write to me at PO Box 1458, Port Orchard, WA 98366.

DEBBIE MACOMBER

Call Me Mrs. Miracle

MIRA

MIRA

Recycling programs for this product may not exist in your area.

ISBN-13: 978-0-7783-1848-4

Call Me Mrs. Miracle

Copyright © 2015 by Harlequin Books S.A.

The publisher acknowledges the copyright holder of the individual works as follows:

Call Me Mrs. Miracle
Copyright © 2010 by Debbie Macomber

The Christmas Basket
Copyright © 2002 by Debbie Macomber

For questions and comments about the quality of this book, please contact us at CustomerService@Harlequin.com.

www.MIRABooks.com

Printed in U.S.A.

Also by Debbie Macomber

Blossom Street Books

The Shop on Blossom Street
A Good Yarn
Susannah's Garden
Back on Blossom Street
Twenty Wishes
Summer on Blossom Street
Hannah's List
The Knitting Diaries
  "The Twenty-First Wish"
A Turn in the Road

Cedar Cove Books

16 Lighthouse Road
204 Rosewood Lane
311 Pelican Court
44 Cranberry Point
50 Harbor Street
6 Rainier Drive
74 Seaside Avenue
8 Sandpiper Way
92 Pacific Boulevard
1022 Evergreen Place
Christmas in Cedar Cove
  (*5-B Poppy Lane* and
  A Cedar Cove Christmas)
1105 Yakima Street
1225 Christmas Tree Lane

Dakota Series

Dakota Born
Dakota Home
Always Dakota
Buffalo Valley

The Manning Family

The Manning Sisters
The Manning Brides
The Manning Grooms

Christmas Books

A Gift to Last
On a Snowy Night
Home for the Holidays
Glad Tidings
Christmas Wishes
Small Town Christmas
When Christmas Comes
  (now retitled *Trading
  Christmas*)
*There's Something About
  Christmas*
Christmas Letters
The Perfect Christmas
Choir of Angels
  (*Shirley, Goodness and
  Mercy,*
  Those Christmas Angels and
  Where Angels Go)
Call Me Mrs. Miracle

Heart of Texas Series

VOLUME 1
  (*Lonesome Cowboy* and
  Texas Two-Step)
VOLUME 2
  (*Caroline's Child* and
  Dr. Texas)
VOLUME 3
  (*Nell's Cowboy* and
  Lone Star Baby)
Promise, Texas
Return to Promise

Midnight Sons

VOLUME 1
  (*Brides for Brothers* and
  The Marriage Risk)
VOLUME 2
  (*Daddy's Little Helper* and
  Because of the Baby)
VOLUME 3
  (*Falling for Him,*
  Ending in Marriage and
  Midnight Sons and Daughters)

This Matter of Marriage
Montana
Thursdays at Eight
Between Friends
Changing Habits
Married in Seattle
  (*First Comes Marriage* and
  Wanted: Perfect Partner)
Right Next Door
  (*Father's Day* and
  The Courtship of Carol Sommars)
Wyoming Brides
  (*Denim and Diamonds* and
  The Wyoming Kid)
Fairy Tale Weddings
  (*Cindy and the Prince* and
  Some Kind of Wonderful)
The Man You'll Marry
  (*The First Man You Meet* and
  The Man You'll Marry)
Orchard Valley Grooms
  (*Valerie* and *Stephanie*)
Orchard Valley Brides
  (*Norah* and *Lone Star Lovin'*)
The Sooner the Better
An Engagement in Seattle
  (*Groom Wanted* and
  Bride Wanted)
Out of the Rain
  (*Marriage Wanted* and
  Laughter in the Rain)
Learning to Love
  (*Sugar and Spice* and *Love by Degree*)
You…Again
  (*Baby Blessed* and
  Yesterday Once More)

The Unexpected Husband
  (*Jury of His Peers* and
  Any Sunday)
Three Brides, No Groom
Love in Plain Sight
  (*Love 'n' Marriage* and
  Almost an Angel)
I Left My Heart
  (*A Friend or Two* and
  No Competition)
Marriage Between Friends
  (*White Lace and Promises* and
  Friends—and Then Some)
A Man's Heart
  (*The Way to a Man's Heart*
  and *Hasty Wedding*)
North to Alaska
  (*That Wintry Feeling* and
  Borrowed Dreams)
On a Clear Day
  (*Starlight* and
  Promise Me Forever)
To Love and Protect
  (*Shadow Chasing* and
  For All My Tomorrows)
Home in Seattle
  (*The Playboy and the Widow*
  and *Fallen Angel*)
Together Again
  (*The Trouble with Caasi* and
  Reflections of Yesterday)
The Reluctant Groom
  (*All Things Considered*
  and *Almost Paradise*)
A Real Prince
  (*The Bachelor Prince*
  and *Yesterday's Hero*)
Private Paradise in
  (*That Summer Place*)

Debbie Macomber's
  Cedar Cove Cookbook
Debbie Macomber's
  Christmas Cookbook

Call Me Mrs. Miracle

9

The Christmas Basket

195

Call Me Mrs. Miracle

To

Dan and Sally Wigutow

and

Caroline Moore

in appreciation for bringing Mrs. Miracle to life

One

NEED A NEW LIFE? GOD TAKES TRADE-INS.

—MRS. MIRACLE

Jake Finley waited impatiently to be ushered into his father's executive office—the office that would one day be his. The thought of eventually stepping into J. R. Finley's shoes excited him. Even though he'd slowly been working his way through the ranks, he'd be the first to admit he still had a lot to learn. However, he was willing to do whatever it took to prove himself.

Finley's was the last of the family-owned department stores in New York City. His great-grandfather had begun the small mercantile on East 34th Street more than seventy years earlier. In the decades since, succeeding Finleys had opened branches in the other boroughs and then in nearby towns. Eventually the chain had spread up and down the East Coast.

"Your father will see you now," Mrs. Coffey said. Dora Coffey had served as J.R.'s executive assistant for at least twenty-five years and knew as much about the company as Jake did—maybe more. He hoped that when the time came she'd stay on, although she had to be close to retirement age.

"Thank you." He walked into the large office with its panoramic view of the Manhattan skyline. He'd lived in the city all his life, but this view never failed to stir him, never failed to lift his heart. No place on earth was more enchanting than New York in December. He could see a light snow drifting down, and the city appeared even more magical through that delicate veil.

Jacob R. Finley, however, wasn't looking at the view. His gaze remained focused on the computer screen. And his frown told Jake everything he needed to know.

He cleared his throat, intending to catch J.R.'s attention, although he suspected that his father was well aware of his presence. "You asked to see me?" he said. Now that he was here, he had a fairly good idea what had initiated this summons. Jake had hoped it wouldn't happen quite so soon, but he should've guessed Mike Scott would go running to his father at the first opportunity. Unfortunately, Jake hadn't had enough time to prove that he was right—and Mike was wrong.

"How many of those SuperRobot toys did you order?" J.R. demanded, getting straight to the point. His father had never been one to lead gently into a subject. "Intellytron," he added scornfully.

"Also known as Telly," Jake said in a mild voice.

"How many?"

"Five hundred." As if J.R. didn't know.

"What?"

Jake struggled not to flinch at his father's angry tone, which was something he rarely heard. They had a good relationship, but until now, Jake hadn't defied one of his father's experienced buyers.

"For how many stores?"

"Just here."

J.R.'s brow relaxed, but only slightly. "Do you realize those things retail for two hundred and fifty dollars apiece?"

J.R. knew the answer to that as well as Jake did. "Yes."

His father stood and walked over to the window, pacing back and forth with long, vigorous strides. Although in his early sixties, J.R. was in excellent shape. Tall and lean, like Jake himself, he had dark hair streaked with gray and his features were well-defined. No one could doubt that they were father and son. J.R. whirled around, hands linked behind him. "Did you clear the order with...anyone?"

Jake was as straightforward as his father. "No."

"Any particular reason you went over Scott's head?"

Jake had a very good reason. "We discussed it. He didn't agree, but I felt this was the right thing to do." Mike Scott had wanted to bring a maximum of fifty robots into the Manhattan location. Jake had tried to persuade him, but Mike wasn't interested in listening to speculation or taking what he saw as a risk—one that had the potential of leaving them with a huge overstock. He relied on cold, hard figures and years of purchasing experience. When their discussion was over, Mike still refused to go against what he considered his own better judgment. Jake continued to argue, presenting internet research and what his gut was telling him about this toy. When he'd finished, Mike Scott had countered with a list of reasons why fifty units per store would be adequate. *More* than adequate, in his opinion. While Jake couldn't disagree with the other man's logic, he had a strong hunch that the much larger order was worth the risk.

"You *felt* it was right?" his father repeated in a scathing voice. "Mike Scott told me we'd be fortunate to sell fifty in each store, yet you, with your vast experience of two months in the toy department, decided the Manhattan store needed ten times that number."

Jake didn't have anything to add.

"I don't suppose you happened to notice that there's been

a downturn in the economy? Parents don't *have* two hundred and fifty bucks for a toy. Not when a lot of families are pinching pennies."

"You made me manager of the toy department." Jake wasn't stupid or reckless. "I'm convinced we'll sell those robots before Christmas." As manager, it was his responsibility—and his right—to order as he deemed fit. And if that meant overriding a buyer's decision—well, he could live with that.

"You think you can sell *all* five hundred of those robots?" Skepticism weighted each word. "In two weeks?"

"Yes." Jake had to work hard to maintain his air of confidence. Still he held firm.

His father took a moment to consider Jake's answer, walking a full circle around his desk as he did. "As of this morning, how many units have you sold?"

That was an uncomfortable question and Jake glanced down at the floor. "Three."

"Three." J.R. shook his head and stalked to the far side of the room, then back again as if debating how to address the situation. "So what you're saying is that our storeroom has four hundred and ninety-seven expensive SuperRobots clogging it up?"

"They're going to sell, Dad."

"It hasn't happened yet, though, has it?"

"No, but I believe the robot's going to be the hottest toy of the season. I've done the research—this is the toy kids are talking about."

"Maybe, but let me remind you, *kids* aren't our customers. Their parents are. Which is why no one else in the industry shares your opinion."

"I know it's a risk, Dad, but it's a calculated one. Have faith."

His father snorted harshly at the word *faith*. "My faith died along with your mother and sister," he snapped.

Involuntarily Jake's eyes sought out the photograph of his mother and sister. Both had been killed in a freak car accident on Christmas Eve twenty-one years ago. Neither Jake nor his father had celebrated Christmas since that tragic night. Ironically, the holiday season was what kept Finley's in the black financially. Without the three-month Christmas shopping craze, the department-store chain would be out of business.

Because of the accident, Jake and his father ignored anything to do with Christmas in their personal lives. Every December twenty-fourth, soon after the store closed, the two of them got on a plane and flew to Saint John in the Virgin Islands. From the time Jake was twelve, there hadn't been a Christmas tree or presents or anything else that would remind him of the holiday. Except, of course, at the store…

"Trust me in this, Dad," Jake pleaded. "Telly the Super-Robot will be the biggest seller of the season, and pretty soon Finley's will be the only store in Manhattan where people can find them."

His father reached for a pen and rolled it between his fingers as he mulled over Jake's words. "I put you in charge of the toy department because I thought it would be a valuable experience for you. One day you'll sit in this chair. The fate of the company will rest in your hands."

His father wasn't telling him anything Jake didn't already know.

"If the toy department doesn't show a profit because you went over Mike Scott's head, then you'll have a lot to answer for." He locked eyes with Jake. "Do I make myself clear?"

Jake nodded. If the toy department reported a loss as a result of his judgment, his father would question Jake's readiness to take over the company.

"Got it," Jake assured his father.

"Good. I want a report on the sale of that robot every week until Christmas."

"You'll have it," Jake promised. He turned to leave.

"I hope you're right about this toy, son," J.R. said as Jake opened the office door. "You've taken a big risk. I hope it pays off."

He wasn't the only one. Still, Jake believed. He'd counted on having proof that the robots were selling by the time his father learned what he'd done. Black Friday, the day after Thanksgiving, which was generally the biggest shopping day of the year, had been a major disappointment. He'd fantasized watching the robots fly off the shelves.

It hadn't happened.

Although they'd been prominently displayed, just one of the expensive toys had sold. He supposed his father had a point; in a faltering economy, people were evaluating their Christmas budgets, so toys, especially expensive ones, had taken a hit. Children might want the robots but it was their parents who did the buying.

Jake's head throbbed as he made his way to the toy department. In his rush to get to the store that morning, he'd skipped his usual stop at a nearby Starbucks. He needed his caffeine fix.

"Welcome to Finley's. May I be of assistance?" an older woman asked him. The store badge pinned prominently on her neat gray cardigan told him her name was Mrs. Emily Miracle. Her smile was cheerful and engaging. She must be the new sales assistant Human Resources had been promising him—but she simply wouldn't do. Good grief, what were they thinking up in HR? Sales in the toy department could be brisk, demanding hours of standing, not to mention dealing with cranky kids and short-tempered parents. He needed someone young. Energetic.

"What can I show you?" the woman asked.

Jake blinked, taken aback by her question. "I beg your pardon?"

"Are you shopping for one of your children?"

"Well, no. I—"

She didn't allow him to finish and steered him toward the center aisle. "We have an excellent selection of toys for any age group. If you're looking for suggestions, I'd be more than happy to help."

She seemed completely oblivious to the fact that he was the department manager—and therefore her boss. "Excuse me, Mrs...." He glanced at her name tag a second time. "Mrs. Miracle."

"Actually, it's Merkle."

"The badge says Miracle."

"Right," she said, looking a bit chagrined. "HR made a mistake, but I don't mind. You can call me Mrs. Miracle."

Speaking of miracles... If ever Jake needed one, it was now. Those robots *had* to sell. His entire future with the company could depend on this toy.

"I'd be more than happy to assist you," Mrs. Miracle said again, breaking into his thoughts.

"I'm Jake Finley."

"Pleased to meet you. Do you have a son or a daughter?" she asked.

"This is *Finley's* Department Store," he said pointedly.

Apparently this new employee had yet to make the connection, which left Jake wondering exactly where HR found their seasonal help. There had to be someone more capable than this woman.

"Finley," Mrs. Miracle repeated slowly. "Jacob Robert is your father, then?"

"Yes," he said, frowning. Only family and close friends knew his father's middle name.

Her eyes brightened, and a smile slid into place. "Ahh," she said knowingly.

"You're acquainted with my father?" That could explain why she'd been hired. Maybe she had some connection to his family he knew nothing about.

"No, no, not directly, but I *have* heard a great deal about him."

So had half the population on the East Coast. "I'm the manager here in the toy department," he told her. He clipped on his badge as he spoke, realizing he'd stuck it in his pocket. The badge said simply "Manager," without including his name, since his policy was to be as anonymous as possible, to be known by his role, not his relationship to the owner.

"The manager. Yes," she said, nodding happily. "This works out beautifully."

"What does?" Her comments struck him as odd.

"Oh, nothing," she returned with the same smile.

She certainly looked pleased with herself, although Jake couldn't imagine why. He doubted she'd last a week. He'd see about getting her transferred to a more suitable department for someone her age. Oh, he'd be subtle about it. He had no desire to risk a discrimination suit.

Jake examined the robot display, hoping that while he'd been gone another one might have sold. But if that was the case, he didn't see any evidence of it.

"Have you had your morning coffee?" Mrs. Miracle asked.

"No," he muttered. His head throbbed, reminding him of his craving for caffeine.

"It seems quiet here at the moment. Why don't you take your break?" she suggested. "The other sales associate and I can handle anything that comes along."

Jake hesitated.

"Go on," she urged. "Everyone needs their morning coffee."

"You go," he said. He was, after all, the department manager, so he should be the last to leave.

"Oh, heavens, no. I just finished a cup." Looking around, she gestured toward the empty aisles. "It's slow right now but it's sure to pick up later, don't you think?"

She was right. In another half hour or so, he might not get a chance. His gaze rested on the robots and he pointed in their direction. "Do what you can to interest shoppers in those."

"Telly the SuperRobot?" she said. Not waiting for his reply, she added, "You won't have any worries there. They're going to be the hottest item this Christmas."

Jake felt a surge of excitement. "You heard that?"

"No…" she answered thoughtfully.

"Then you must've seen a news report." Jake had been waiting for exactly this kind of confirmation. He'd played a hunch, taken a chance, and in his heart of hearts felt it had been a good decision. But he had four hundred and ninety-seven of these robots on his hands. If his projections didn't pan out, it would take a long time—like maybe forever—to live it down.

"Coffee," Mrs. Miracle said, without explaining why she was so sure of the robot's success.

Jake checked his watch, then nodded. "I'll be back soon."

"Take whatever time you need."

Jake thanked her and hurriedly left, stopping by HR on his way out. The head of the department, Gloria Palmer, glanced up when Jake entered the office. "I've got a new woman on the floor this morning. Emily Miracle," he said.

Gloria frowned. "Miracle?" She tapped some keys on her computer and looked back at Jake. "I don't show anyone with that name working in your department."

Jake remembered that Emily Miracle had said there'd been

an error on her name tag. He rubbed his hand across his fore-head, momentarily closing his eyes as he tried to remember the name she'd mentioned. "It starts with an *M*—McKinsey, Merk, something like that."

Gloria's phone rang and she reached for it, holding it be-tween her shoulder and ear as her fingers flew across the key-board. She tried to divide her attention between Jake and the person on the line. Catching Jake's eye, she motioned toward the computer screen, shrugged and shook her head.

Jake raised his hand and mouthed, "I'll catch you later."

Gloria nodded and returned her attention to the caller. Clearly she had more pressing issues to attend to just then. Jake would seek her out later that afternoon and suggest Mrs. Mira-cle be switched to another department. A less demanding one.

As he rushed out the door onto Thirty-Fourth and headed into the still-falling snow, he decided it would be only fair to give the older woman a chance. If she managed to sell one of the robots while he collected his morning cup of java, he'd consider keeping her. And if she managed to sell *two,* she'd be living up to her name!

Two

IF GOD IS YOUR COPILOT, TRADE PLACES.

—MRS. MIRACLE

Friday morning, and Holly Larson was right on schedule—even a few minutes ahead. This was a vast improvement over the past two months, ever since her eight-year-old
nephew, Gabe, had come to live with her. It'd taken effort
on both their parts to make this arrangement work. Mickey,
Holly's brother, had been called up by the National Guard
and sent to Afghanistan for the next fifteen months. He was a
widower, and with her parents doing volunteer medical work
in Haiti, the only option for Gabe was to move in with Holly,
who lived in a small Brooklyn apartment. Fortunately, she'd
been able to turn her minuscule home office into a bedroom
for Gabe.

They were doing okay, but it hadn't been easy. Never having spent much time with children Gabe's age, the biggest ad-
justment had been Holly's—in her opinion, anyway.

Gabe might not agree, however. He didn't think sun-dried
tomatoes with fresh mozzarella cheese was a special dinner.
He turned up his nose and refused even one bite. So she was
learning. Boxed macaroni and cheese suited him just fine, al-

though she couldn't tolerate the stuff. At least it was cheap. Adding food for a growing boy to her already strained budget had been a challenge. Mickey, who was the manager of a large grocery store in his civilian life, sent what he could but he had his own financial difficulties; she knew he was still paying off his wife's medical bills and funeral expenses. And he had a mortgage to maintain on his Trenton, New Jersey, home. Poor Gabe. The little boy had lost his mother when he was an infant. Now his father was gone, too. Holly considered herself a poor replacement for either parent, let alone both, although she was giving it her best shot.

Since she had a few minutes to spare before she was due at the office, she hurried into Starbucks to reward herself with her favorite latte. It'd been two weeks since she'd had one. A hot, freshly brewed latte was an extravagance these days, so she only bought them occasionally.

Getting Gabe to school and then hurrying to the office was as difficult as collecting him from the after-school facility at the end of the day. Lindy Lee, her boss, hadn't taken kindly to Holly's rushing out the instant the clock struck five. But the child-care center at Gabe's school charged by the minute when she was late. *By the minute.*

Stepping out of the cold into the warmth of the coffee shop, Holly breathed in the pungent scent of fresh coffee. A cheery evergreen swag was draped across the display case. She dared not look because she had a weakness for cranberry scones. She missed her morning ritual of a latte and a scone almost as much as she did her independence. But giving it up was a small sacrifice if it meant she could help her brother and Gabe. Not only that, she'd come to adore her young nephew and, despite everything, knew she'd miss him when her brother returned.

The line moved quickly, and she placed her order for a skinny latte with vanilla flavoring. The man behind her ordered a large coffee. He smiled at her and Holly smiled back. She'd seen him in this Starbucks before, although they'd never spoken.

"Merry Christmas," she said.

"Same to you."

The girl at the cash register told Holly her total and she opened her purse to pay. That was when she remembered—she'd given the last of her cash to Gabe for lunch money. It seemed ridiculous to use a credit card for such a small amount, but she didn't have any choice. She took out her card and handed it to the barista. The young woman slid it through the machine, then leaned forward and whispered, "It's been declined."

Hot embarrassment reddened her face. She'd maxed out her card the month before but thought her payment would've been credited by now. Scrambling, she searched for coins in the bottom of her purse. It didn't take her long to realize she didn't have nearly enough change to cover the latte. "I have a debit card in here someplace," she muttered, grabbing her card case again.

"Excuse me." The good-looking man behind her pulled his wallet from his hip pocket.

"I'm... I'm sorry," she whispered, unable to meet his eyes. This was embarrassing, humiliating, downright mortifying.

"Allow me to pay for your latte," he said.

Holly sent him a shocked look. "You don't need to do that."

The woman standing behind him frowned impatiently at Holly. "If I'm going to get to work on time, he does."

"Oh, sorry."

Not waiting for her to agree, the stranger stepped forward and paid for both her latte and his coffee.

"Thank you," she said in a low, strangled voice.

"I'll consider it my good deed for the day."

"I'll pay for your coffee the next time I see you."

He grinned. "You've got a deal." He moved down to the

end of the counter, where she went to wait for her latte. "I'm Jake Finley."

"Holly Larson." She extended her hand.

"Holly," he repeated.

"People assume I was born around Christmas but I wasn't. Actually, I was born in June and named after my mother's favorite aunt," she said. She didn't know why she'd blurted out such ridiculous information. Perhaps because she still felt embarrassed and was trying to disguise her chagrin with conversation. "I do love Christmas, though, don't you?"

"Not particularly." Frowning, he glanced at his watch. "I've got to get back to work."

"Oh, sure. Thank you again." He'd been thoughtful and generous.

"See you soon," Jake said as he turned toward the door.

"I owe you," she said. "I won't forget."

He smiled at her. "I hope I'll run into you again."

"That would be great." She meant it, and next time she'd make sure she had enough cash to treat him. She felt a glow of pleasure as Jake left Starbucks.

Holly stopped to calculate—it'd been more than three months since her last date. That was pitiful! Three months. Nuns had a more active social life than she did.

Her last relationship had been with Bill Carter. For a while it had seemed promising. As a divorced father, Bill was protective and caring toward his young son. Holly had only met Billy once. Unfortunately, the trip to the Central Park Zoo hadn't gone well. Billy had been whiny and overtired, and Bill had seemed to want *her* to deal with the boy. She'd tried but Billy didn't know her and she didn't know him, and the entire outing had been strained and uncomfortable. Holly had tried—unsuccessfully—to make the trip as much fun as possible. Shortly thereafter, Bill called to tell her their relationship wasn't "working" for him. He'd made a point of letting her know he was interested in finding someone more "suitable" for his son because he didn't feel she'd make a good mother. His words had stung.

Holly hadn't argued. Really, how could she? Her one experience with Billy had been a disaster. Then, just a month after Bill's heartless comment, Gabe had entered her life. These days she was more inclined to agree with Bill's assessment of her parenting skills. She didn't seem to have what it took to raise a child, which deeply concerned her.

Things were getting easier with Gabe, but progress had been slow, and it didn't help that her nephew seemed to sense her unease. She had a lot to learn about being an effective and nurturing parent.

Dating Bill had been enjoyable enough, but there'd never been much chemistry between them, so not seeing him wasn't a huge loss. She categorized it as more of a disappointment. A letdown. His parting words, however, had left her with doubts and regrets.

Carrying her latte, Holly walked the three blocks to the office. She actually arrived a minute early. Working as an assistant to a fashion designer sounded glamorous but it wasn't. She didn't get to take home designer purses for a fraction of their retail price—except for the knockoff versions she could buy on the street—or acquire fashion-model hand-me-downs.

She was paid a pittance and had become the go-to person for practically everyone on staff, and that added up to at least forty people. Her boss, Lindy Lee, was often unreasonable. Unfortunately, most of the time it was Holly's job to make sure that whatever Lindy wanted actually happened. Lindy wasn't much older than Holly, but she was well connected in the fashion world and had quickly risen to the top. Because her work as a designer of upscale women's sportswear was in high demand, Lindy Lee frequently worked under impossible deadlines. One thing was certain; she had no tolerance for the fact that Holly now had to stick to her official nine-to-five schedule, which meant her job as Lindy Lee's assistant might be in jeopardy. She'd explained the situation with Gabe, but her boss didn't care about Holly's problems at home.

Rushing to her desk, Holly set the latte down, shrugged off her coat and readied herself for the day. She was responsible for decorating the office for Christmas, and so far, there just hadn't been time. On Saturday she'd bring Gabe into the office and the two of them would get it done. That meant her own apartment would have to wait, but...oh, well.

Despite her boss's complaints about one thing or another, Holly's smile stayed in place all morning. A kind deed by a virtual stranger buffered her from four hours of commands, criticism and complaints.

Jack...no, Jake. He'd said his name was Jake, and he was cute, too. Maybe *handsome* was a more accurate description. Classically handsome, like those 1940s movie stars in the old films she loved. Tall, nicely trimmed dark hair, broad shoulders, expressive eyes and...probably married. She'd been too shocked by his generosity to see whether he had a wedding band. Yeah, he was probably taken. Par for the course, she thought a little glumly. Holly was thirty, but being single at that age wasn't uncommon among her friends. Her parents seemed more worried about it than she was.

Most of her girlfriends didn't even *think* about settling down until after they turned thirty. Holly knew she wanted a husband and eventually a family. What she hadn't expected was becoming a sole parent to Gabe. This time with her nephew was like a dress rehearsal for being a mother, her friends told her. Unfortunately, there weren't any lines to memorize and the script changed almost every day.

At lunch she heated her Cup-a-Soup in the microwave and logged on to the internet to check for messages from Mickey. Her brother kept in touch with Gabe every day and sent her a quick note whenever he could. Sure enough, there was an email waiting for her.

From: "Lieutenant Mickey Larson" <larsonmichael@goarmy.com>
To: "Holly Larson" <hollylarson@msm.com>
Sent: December 10
Subject: Gabe's email

Hi, sis,
Gabe's last note to me was hilarious. What's this about you making him put down the toilet seat? He thinks girls should do it themselves. This is what happens when men live together. The seat's perpetually up.

Has he told you what he wants for Christmas yet? He generally mentions a toy before now, but he's been suspiciously quiet about it this year. Let me know when he drops his hints.

I wish I could be with you both, but that's out of the question. Next year for sure.

I know it's been rough on you having to fit Gabe into your apartment and your life, but I have no idea what I would've done without you.

By the way, I heard from Mom and Dad. The dental clinic Dad set up is going well. Who'd have guessed our parents would be doing volunteer work after retirement? They send their love...but now that I think about it, you got the same email as me, didn't you? They both sound happy but really busy. Mom was concerned about you taking Gabe, but she seems reassured now.

Well, I better get some shut-eye. Not to worry—I reminded Gabe that when he's staying at a house with a woman living in it, the correct thing to do is put down the toilet seat.

Check in with you later.

Thank you again for everything.

Love,
Mickey

Holly read the message twice, then sent him a note. She'd always been close to her brother and admired him for picking up the pieces of his life after Sally died of a rare blood disease. Gabe hadn't even been a year old. Holly had a lot more respect for the demands of parenthood—and especially single parenthood—now that Gabe lived with her.

At five o'clock, she was out the door. Lindy Lee threw her an evil look, which Holly pretended not to see. She caught the subway and had to stand, holding tight to one of the poles, for the whole rush-hour ride into Brooklyn.

As she was lurched and jolted on the train, her mind wandered back to Mickey's email. Gabe hadn't said anything about Christmas to her, either. And yet he had to know that the holidays were almost upon them; all the decorations in the neighborhood and the ads on TV made it hard to miss. For the first time in his life, Gabe wouldn't be spending Christmas with his father and grandparents. This year, there'd be just the two of them. Maybe he'd rather not celebrate until his father came home, she thought. That didn't seem right, though. Holly was determined to make this the best Christmas possible.

Not once had Gabe told her what he wanted. She wondered whether she should ask him, maybe encourage him to write Santa a letter—did he still believe in Santa?—or try to guess what he might like. Her other question was what she could buy on a limited income. A toy? She knew next to nothing about toys, especially the kind that would intrigue an eight-year-old boy. She felt besieged by even more insecurities.

She stepped off the subway, climbed the stairs to the street and hurried to Gabe's school, which housed the after-hours activity program set up for working parents. At least it wasn't snowing anymore. Which was a good thing, since she'd forgotten to make Gabe wear his boots that morning.

What happened the first day she'd gone to collect Gabe still made her cringe. She'd been thirty-two minutes late. The financial penalty was steep and cut into her carefully planned budget, but that didn't bother her nearly as much as the look on Gabe's face.

He must have assumed she'd abandoned him. His haunted expression brought her to the edge of tears every time she thought about it. That was the same night she'd prepared her favorite dinner for him—another disaster. Now she knew better and kept an unending supply of hot dogs—God help them both—plus boxes of macaroni and cheese. He'd deign to eat carrot sticks and bananas, but those were his only concessions, no matter how much she talked about balanced nutrition. He found it hilarious to claim that the relish he slathered on his hot dogs was a "vegetable."

She waited by the row of hooks, each marked with a child's name. Gabe ran over the instant he saw her, his face bright with excitement. "I made a new friend!"

"That's great." Thankfully Gabe appeared to have adjusted well to his new school and teacher.

"Billy!" he called. "Come and meet my aunt Holly."

Holly's smile froze. This wasn't just any Billy. It was Bill Carter, Junior, son of the man who'd broken up with her three months earlier.

"Hello, Billy," she said, wondering if he'd recognize her.

The boy gazed up at her quizzically. Apparently he didn't. Or maybe he did remember her but wasn't sure when they'd met. Either way, Holly was relieved.

"Can I go over to Billy's house?" Gabe asked. The two boys linked arms like long-lost brothers.

"Ah, when?" she hedged. Seeing Bill again would be difficult. Holly wasn't eager to talk to the man who'd dumped her—especially considering why. It would be uncomfortable for both of them.

"I want him to come tonight," Billy said. "My dad's making sloppy joes. And we've got marshmallow ice cream for dessert."

"Well..." Her meals could hardly compete with that—not if you were an eight-year-old boy. Personally, Holly couldn't think of a less appetizing combination.

Before she could come up with a response, Gabe tugged at her sleeve. "Billy doesn't have a mom, either," he told her.

"I have a mom," Billy countered, "only she doesn't live with us anymore."

"My mother's in heaven with the angels," Gabe said. "I live with my dad, too, 'cept he's in Afghanistan now."

"So that's why you're staying with your aunt Holly." Billy nodded.

"Yeah." Gabe reached for his jacket and backpack.

"I'm sorry, Billy," she finally managed to say, "but Gabe and I already have plans for tonight."

Gabe whirled around. "We do?"

"We're going shopping," she said, thinking on her feet.

Gabe scowled and crossed his arms. "I hate shopping."

"You won't this time," she promised and helped him put on his winter jacket, along with his hat and mitts.

"Yes, I will," Gabe insisted, his head lowered.

"You and Billy can have a playdate later," she said, forcing herself to speak cheerfully.

"When?" Billy asked, unwilling to let the matter drop.

"How about next week?" She'd call or email Bill so it wouldn't come as a big shock when she showed up on his doorstep.

"Okay," Billy agreed.

"That suit you?" Holly asked Gabe. She wanted to leave *now,* just in case Bill was picking up his son today. She recalled that their housekeeper usually did this—but why take chances? Bill was the very last person she wanted to see.

Gabe shrugged, unhappy with the compromise. He let her take his hand as they left the school, but as soon as they were outdoors, he promptly snatched it away.

"Where are we going shopping?" he asked, still pouting as they headed in the opposite direction of her apartment building. The streetlights glowed and she saw Christmas decorations in apartment windows—wreaths, small potted trees and strings of colored lights. So far Holly hadn't done anything. Perhaps this weekend she'd find time to put up their tree— after she'd finished decorating the office, of course.

"I thought we'd go see Santa this evening," Holly announced.

"Santa?" He raised his head and eyed her speculatively.

"Would you like that?"

Gabe seemed to need a moment to consider the question. "I guess."

Holly assumed he was past the age of believing in Santa but wasn't quite ready to admit it, for fear of losing out on extra gifts. Still, she didn't feel she could ask him. "I want you to hold my hand while we're on the subway, okay?"

"Okay," he said in a grumpy voice.

They'd go to Finley's, she decided. She knew for sure that the store had a Santa. Besides, she wanted to look at the windows with their festive scenes and moving parts. Even in his current mood, Gabe would enjoy them, Holly thought. And so would she.

Three

EXERCISE DAILY—WALK WITH THE LORD.

—MRS. MIRACLE

It was the second Friday in December and the streets were crowded with shoppers and tourists. As they left the subway, Holly kept a close watch on Gabe, terrified of becoming separated. She heaved a sigh of relief when they reached Finley's Department Store. The big display windows in the front of the fourteen-story structure were cleverly decorated. One showed a Santa's workshop scene, including animated elves wielding hammers and saws. Another was a mirrored pond that had teddy bears skating around and around. Still another, the window closest to the doors, featured a huge Christmas tree, circled by a toy train running on its own miniature track. The boxcars were filled with gaily wrapped gifts.

With the crowds pressing against them, Gabe and Holly moved from window to window, stopping at the final one. "Isn't that a great train set?" she asked.

Gabe nodded.

"Would you like one of those for Christmas?" she murmured. "You could ask Santa."

Gabe glanced up at her. "There's something else I want more."

"Okay, you can tell Santa that," she said.

They headed into the store, and had difficulty getting through the revolving doors, crushed in with other shoppers. "Can we go home and have dinner when we're done seeing Santa?" Gabe asked.

"Of course. What would you like?"

If he said hot dogs or macaroni and cheese Holly promised herself she wouldn't scream.

"Mashed potatoes with gravy and meat loaf with lots of ketchup."

That would take a certain amount of effort but was definitely something she could do. "You got it."

Gabe cast her one of his rare smiles, and Holly placed her hand on his shoulder. This was progress.

The ground floor of Finley's was crammed. The men's department was to the right and the cosmetics and perfume counters directly ahead. Holly inched her way forward, Gabe close by her side.

"We need to get to the escalator," she told him, steering the boy in that direction. She hoped that once they got up to the third floor, the crowds would have thinned out, at least a little.

"Okay." He voluntarily slipped his hand in hers.

More progress. Visiting Santa had clearly been a stroke of genius on her part.

Her guess about the crowds was accurate. When they reached the third floor Holly felt she could breathe again. If it wasn't for Gabe, she wouldn't come within ten miles of Thirty-Fourth on a Friday night in December.

"Santa's over there," Gabe said, pointing.

The kid obviously had Santa Claus radar. Several spry elves in green tights and pointy hats surrounded the jolly old man in the red suit. This guy was good, too. His full white beard was real. He must've just gotten off break because he wore a huge smile.

The visit to Santa was free but for an extra twenty dollars, she could buy a picture. They'd stopped at an ATM on their way to the subway and she'd gotten cash. Although she couldn't help feeling a twinge at spending the money, a photo of Gabe with Santa would be the perfect Christmas gift for Mickey.

The line moved quickly. Gabe seemed excited and happy, chattering away about this and that, and his mood infected Holly. She hadn't felt much like Christmas until now. Classic carols rang through the store and soon Holly was humming along.

When it was Gabe's turn, he hopped onto Santa's knee as if the two of them were old friends.

"Hello there, young man," Santa said, adding a "Ho, ho, ho."

"Hello." Gabe looked him square in the eyes.

"And what would you like Santa to bring you?" the jolly old fellow inquired.

Her nephew didn't hesitate. "All I want for Christmas is Telly the SuperRobot."

What in heaven's name was that? A robot? Even without checking, Holly knew this wasn't going to be a cheap toy. A train set—a small one—she could manage, but an electronic toy was probably out of her price range.

"Very well, young man, Santa will see what he can do. Anything else you're interested in?"

"A train set," Gabe said, his eyes serious. "But I *really* want Intellytron."

"Intellytron," Holly muttered to herself.

Santa gestured at the camera. "Now smile big for me, and your mom can collect the photograph in five minutes."

"Okay." Gabe gave Santa a huge smile, then slid off his knee so the next child in line could have a turn. It took Holly a moment to realize that Gabe hadn't corrected Santa about who she was.

Holly went around to the counter behind Santa's chair to wait for the photograph, accompanied by Gabe.

"I don't know where Santa will find one of those robots," she said, trying to get as much information as she could.

"All the stores have them," Gabe assured her. "Billy wants an Intellytron, too."

So she could blame Billy for this sudden desire. But since this was the only toy Gabe wanted, she'd do her best to make sure that Intellytron the SuperRobot would be wrapped and under the tree Christmas morning.

"Maybe I should see what this robot friend of yours looks like," she suggested. A huge sign pointing to the toy department was strategically placed near Santa's residence. This, Holly felt certain, was no coincidence.

"Toys are this way," Gabe said, leading her by the hand.

Holly dutifully followed. "What if they don't have the robot?" she asked.

"They will," he said with sublime confidence.

"But what if they don't?"

Gabe frowned and then tilted his chin at a thoughtful angle. "Can Santa bring my dad home?"

Holly's heart sank. "Not this year, sweetheart."

"Then all I really want is my robot."

She'd been afraid of that.

They entered the toy department and were met by a grandmotherly woman with a name badge that identified her as Mrs. Emily Miracle.

"Why, hello there," the woman greeted Gabe with a smile. Gabe immediately smiled back at her. "Hello."

"I see you've been to visit Santa." She nodded at the photo Holly was holding.

"Yup," Gabe said happily. "He was nice."

"Did you tell Santa what you want for Christmas?"

"Intellytron the SuperRobot," he replied.

"Telly is a wonderful toy. Let me show you one."

"Please," Holly said, hoping against hope that the robot was reasonably priced. If fate was truly with her, it would also be on sale.

Mrs. Miracle took them to a display on the other side of the department, directly across from the elevator. The robots would be the first toys seen by those stepping off. She wondered why they weren't by the escalator, but then it dawned on her. Mothers with young children usually came up via elevator. The manager of this department was no dummy.

"Look!" Gabe said, his eyes huge. "It's Telly! He's here. I told you he would be. Isn't he the best *ever?*"

"Would you like to see how he works?" the grandmotherly saleswoman asked.

"Yes, please."

Holly was impressed by Gabe's politeness, which she'd never seen to quite this degree. Well, it was December, and this was the one toy he wanted more than any other. The saleswoman took down the display model and started to demonstrate it when a male voice caught Holly's attention.

"Hello again."

She turned to face Jake, the man she'd met in Starbucks that morning. For a moment she couldn't speak. Eventually she croaked out a subdued hello.

He looked curiously at Gabe. "Your son?"

"My nephew," she said, recovering her voice. "Gabe's living with me for the next year while his father's in Afghanistan."

"Nephew," he repeated, and his eyes sparked with renewed interest.

"I brought Gabe here to visit Santa and he said that what he wants for Christmas is Intellytron the SuperRobot."

"An excellent choice. Would you like me to wrap one for you now?"

"Ah…" Holly paused. "I need to know how much they are first." Just looking at the toy told her she wasn't getting off cheap.

"Two hundred and fifty dollars."

Holly's hand flew to her heart. "*How* much?"

"Two hundred and fifty dollars."

"Oh." She swallowed. "Will there be a sale on these later? A big sale?"

Jake shook his head. "I doubt it."

"Oh," she said again.

Jake seemed disappointed, too.

Holly bit her lip. This was the only gift Gabe had requested. He'd indicated mild interest in a train set, but that was more at her instigation. Watching his eyes light up as the robot maneuvered itself down the aisle filled her with a sense of delight. He loved this toy and it would mean so much to him. "I get my Christmas bonus at the end of next week. Will you still have the robot then?" Never mind that Lindy Lee might be less than generous this year….

"We should have plenty," Jake told her.

"Thank goodness," Holly said gratefully.

"We've sold a number today, but I brought in a large supply so you shouldn't have anything to worry about."

"Wonderful." She could hardly wait for Gabe to unwrap this special gift Christmas morning. Tonight, the spirit of

Christmas had finally begun to take root in her own heart. Seeing the joy of the season in Gabe's eyes helped her accept that this year would be different but could still be good. Although she and Gabe were separated from their family, she intended to make it a Christmas the two of them would always remember.

"I want to thank you again for buying my latte this morning," she said to Jake. She was about to suggest she pay him back, because she had the cash now, but hesitated, hoping for the opportunity to return the favor and spend more time with him.

"Like I said, it was my good deed for the day."

"Do you often purchase a complete stranger a cup of coffee?"

"You're the first."

She laughed. "Then I'm doubly honored."

"Aunt Holly, did you see? Did you see Telly move?" Gabe asked, dashing to her side. "He can talk, too!"

She'd been so involved in chatting with Jake that she'd missed most of the demonstration. Other children had come over to the aisle, drawn by the robot's activities; in fact, a small crowd had formed to watch. Several boys Gabe's age were tugging at their parents' arms.

"We'll have to see what Santa brings," Holly told him.

"He'll bring me Telly, won't he?"

Holly shrugged, pretending nonchalance. "We'll have to wait and see."

"How many days until Christmas?" Gabe asked eagerly.

"Today's the tenth, so…fifteen days."

"That long?" He dragged out the words as if he could barely hang on all those weeks.

"The time will fly by, Gabe. I promise."

"Excuse me," Jake said as he turned to answer a customer's

question. Her query was about the price of the robot, and the woman had nearly the same reaction as Holly. Two hundred and fifty dollars! A lot of money for a toy. Still, in Gabe's case it would be worth it.

Mrs. Miracle brought out the display robot to demonstrate again, and Gabe and a second youngster watched with rapt attention. The older woman was a marvel, a natural with children.

"So, you're the manager here," Holly said once Jake was free.

He nodded. "How'd you guess?" he asked with a grin.

"Your badge, among other things." She smiled back at him. "I was just thinking how smart you were to place Santa next to the toy section."

"That wasn't my idea," Jake said. "Santa's been in that location for years."

"What about the Intellytron display across from the elevator?"

"Now that *was* my idea."

"I thought as much."

Jake seemed pleased that she'd noticed. "I'm hoping it really takes off."

"Well, if Gabe's interest is any indication, I'm sure it will."

He seemed to appreciate her vote of confidence.

"Look!" Gabe said, grabbing Holly's hand. He pointed to a couple who were removing a boxed unit of Intellytron from the display. "My robot will still be here by Christmas, won't he?"

"Absolutely," she assured him.

Jake winked at her as Mrs. Miracle led the young couple toward the cash register.

"Hiring Mrs. Miracle was a smart move, too," she said.

"Oh, I can't really take credit for that," Jake responded.

"Well, you're lucky, then. She's exactly right for the toy department. It's like having someone's grandmother here. She's helping parents fulfill all their children's Christmas wishes."

Jake glanced at the older woman, then slowly nodded. "I guess so," he said, sounding a bit uncertain.

"Haven't you seen the way kids immediately take to her?" Holly asked.

"Not only can't I take credit for her being here, it's actually a mistake."

"A mistake," Holly echoed. "You're joking! She's *perfect*. It wouldn't surprise me if you sold out the whole toy department with her working here."

"Really?" He said this as if Holly had given him something to think about.

"I love her name, too. Mrs. Miracle—it has such a nice Christmas sound."

"That's a mistake, as well. Her name's not really Miracle. HR spelled it wrong on her badge, and I asked that it be corrected."

"Oh, let her keep the badge," Holly urged. "Mrs. Miracle. It couldn't be more appropriate."

Jake nodded again. "Perhaps you're right."

Mrs. Miracle finished the sale and joined them. "Very nice meeting you, Gabe and Holly," she said warmly.

Holly didn't remember giving the older woman her name. Gabe must have mentioned it.

"You, too, Emily," she said.

"Oh, please," she said with a charming smile. "Just call me Mrs. Miracle."

"Okay," Gabe piped up. "We will."

Four

"I thought we'd bake cookies today," Holly said on Saturday morning as Gabe sat at the kitchen counter eating his breakfast cereal. When he didn't think she was looking, he picked up the bowl and slurped what was left of his milk.

"Cookies?" Gabe said, frowning. "Can't we just buy them?"

"We could," Holly answered, "but I figured it would be fun to bake them ourselves."

Gabe didn't seem convinced. "Dad and I always got ours at the store. We never had to *work* to get them."

"But it's fun," Holly insisted, unwilling to give up quite so easily. "You can roll out the dough. I even have special cookie cutters. After the cookies are baked and they've cooled down, we can frost and decorate them." She'd hoped this Christmas tradition would appeal to Gabe.

He slid down from his chair and carried his bowl to the dishwasher. "Can I go on the computer?"

"Sure." Holly made an effort to hide her disappointment. She'd really hoped the two of them would bond while they were baking Christmas cookies. Later, she intended to go into the office and put up decorations—with Gabe's help. She wanted that to be fun for him, too.

Gabe moved to the alcove between the kitchen and small living room with its sofa and television. Holly was astonished at how adept the eight-year-old was on the computer. While he logged on, she brought out the eggs and flour and the rest of the ingredients for sugar cookies and set them on the kitchen counter.

Gabe obviously didn't realize she could see the computer screen from her position. She was pleased that he was writing his father a note.

From: "Gabe Larson" <gabelarson@msm.com>
To: "Lieutenant Mickey Larson" <larsonmichael@goarmy.com>
Sent: December 11
Subject: Cookies

Hi, Dad,
Guess what? Aunt Holly wants me to bake cookies. Doesn't she know I'm a BOY? Boys don't bake cookies. It's bad enough that I have to put the toilet seat down for her. I hope you get home soon because I'm afraid she's going to turn me into a girl!
Gabe

Holly tried to conceal her smile. "Would you like to go into the city this afternoon?" she asked as she added the butter she'd cubed to the sugar in the mixing bowl.

Gabe turned around to look at her. "You aren't going to make me go shopping, are you?"

"No. I'll take you to my office. Wouldn't you like that?"

"Yes," he said halfheartedly.

"I have to put up a few decorations. You can help me."

"Okay." Again he showed a decided lack of enthusiasm.

"The Rockefeller Center Christmas tree is up," she told him next.

Now that caught his interest. "Can we go ice-skating?"

"Ah…" Holly had never gone skating. "Maybe another time, okay?"

Gabe shrugged. "Okay. I bet Billy and his dad will take me."

The kid had no idea how much that comment irritated her. However, Holly knew she had to be an adult about it. She hadn't phoned Bill to discuss the fact that his son and her nephew were friends. She would, though, in order to arrange a playdate for the two boys.

"I thought we'd leave after lunch," she said, resuming their original conversation.

"Okay." Gabe returned to the computer and was soon involved in a game featuring beasts in some alien kingdom. Whatever it was held his attention for the next ten minutes.

Using the electric mixer, Holly blended the sugar, butter and eggs and was about to add the dry ingredients when Gabe climbed up on the stool beside her.

"I've never seen anyone make cookies before," he said.

"You can watch if you want." She made an effort to sound matter-of-fact, not revealing how pleased she was at his interest.

"When we go into the city, would it be all right if we went to Finley's?" he asked.

Holly looked up. "I suppose so. Any particular reason?"

He stared at her as if it should be obvious. "I want to see Telly. He can do all kinds of tricks and stuff, and maybe Mrs. Miracle will be there."

"Oh."

"Mrs. Miracle said I could stop by anytime I want and she'd let me work the controls. She said they don't normally let kids play with the toys but she'd make an exception." He drew in a deep breath. "What's an 'exception'?"

"It means she'll allow you to do it even though other people can't."

"That's what I thought." He leaned forward and braced his elbows on the counter, nodding solemnly at this evidence of his elevated status—at least in Mrs. Miracle's view.

As soon as the dough was mixed, Holly covered it with plastic wrap and put it inside the refrigerator to chill. When she'd finished, she cleaned off the kitchen counter. "You want to lick the beaters?" she asked.

Gabe straightened and looked skeptically at the mixer. "You can do that?"

"Sure. That's one of the best parts of baking cookies."

"Okay."

She handed him one beater and took the second herself.

Gabe's eyes widened after his first lick. "Hey, this tastes *good*."

"Told you," she said with a smug smile.

"Why can't we just eat the dough? Why ruin cookies by baking 'em?"

"Well, they're not cookies unless you bake them."

"Oh."

Her response seemed to satisfy him.

"I'm going to roll the dough out in a few minutes. Would you help me decide which cookie cutters to use?"

"I guess." Gabe didn't display a lot of enthusiasm at the request.

Holly stood on tiptoe to take down the plastic bag she kept on the upper kitchen shelf. "Your grandma Larson gave these to me last year. When your dad and I were your age, we used to make sugar cookies."

Gabe sat up straighter. "You mean my dad baked cookies?"

"Every Christmas. After we decorated them, we chose special people to give them to."

Gabe was always interested in learning facts about Mickey. Every night he asked Holly to tell him a story about his father as a boy. She'd run out of stories, but it didn't matter; Gabe liked hearing them again and again.

"You gave the cookies to special people? Like who?"

"Well…" Holly had to think about that. "Once I brought a plate of cookies to my Sunday school teacher and one year—" she paused and smiled "—I was twelve and had a crush on a boy in my class, so I brought the cookies to school for him."

"Who'd my dad give the cookies to?"

"I don't remember. You'll have to ask him."

"I will." Gabe propped his chin on one hand. "Can I take a plate of cookies to Mrs. Miracle?"

Holly was about to tell him that would be a wonderful idea, then hesitated. "The problem is, if I baked the cookies and decorated them, they'd be from me and not from you."

Gabe frowned. "I could help with cutting them out and stuff. You won't tell anyone, will you?"

"Not if you don't want me to."

"I don't want any of my friends to think I'm a sissy."

She crossed her heart. "I promise not to say a word."

"Okay, then, I'll do it." Gabe dug into the bag of cookie cutters and made his selections, removing the Christmas tree, the star and several others. Then, as if a thought had suddenly struck him, he pointed at her apron. "I don't have to put on one of those, do I?"

"You don't like my apron?"

"They're okay for girls, but not boys."

"You don't have to wear one if you'd rather not."

He shook his head adamantly.

"But you might get flour on your clothes, and your friends

would guess you were baking." This was a clever argument, if she did say so herself.

Gabe nibbled on his lower lip, apparently undecided. "Then I'll change clothes. I'm not wearing any girlie apron."

"That's fine," Holly said, grinning.

The rest of the morning was spent baking and decorating cookies. Once he got started, Gabe appeared to enjoy himself. He frosted the Christmas tree with green icing and sprinkled red sugar over it.

Then, with a sideways glance at Holly, he promptly ate the cookie. She let him assume she hadn't noticed.

"Who are you giving your cookies to?" Gabe asked.

Actually, Holly hadn't thought about it. "I'm not sure." A heartbeat later, the decision was made. "Jake."

"The man in the toy department at Finley's?"

Holly nodded. "He did something kind for me on Friday. He bought my coffee."

Gabe cocked his head. "Is he your boyfriend?"

"Oh, no. But he's very nice and I want to repay him." She got two plastic plates and, together, they arranged the cookies. Holly bundled each plate in green-tinted cellophane wrap and added silver bows for a festive look.

"You ready to head into town?" she asked.

Gabe raced into his bedroom for his coat, hat and mittens. "I'm ready."

"Me, too." The truth was, Holly felt excited about seeing Jake again. Of course, there was always the possibility that he wouldn't be working today—but she had to admit she hoped he was. Her reaction surprised her; since Bill had broken off their relationship she'd been reluctant to even consider dating someone new.

Meeting Jake had been an unexpected bonus. He'd been so— She stopped abruptly. Here she was, doing it again. Jake

had paid for her coffee. He was obviously a generous man...
or he might've been in a rush to get back to the store. Either way, he'd been kind to her. But that didn't mean he was
attracted to her. In reality it meant nada. Zilch. Zip. Gazing
down at the plate of cookies, Holly felt she might be pushing this too far.

"Aunt Holly?"

She looked at her nephew, who was staring quizzically at
her. "Is something wrong?" he asked.

"Oh, sorry... No, nothing's wrong. I was just thinking
maybe I should give these cookies to someone else."

"How come?"

"I... I don't know."

"Give them to Jake," Gabe said without a second's doubt.
"Didn't you say he bought your coffee?"

"He did." Gabe was right. The cookies were simply a way
of thanking him. That was all. She was returning a kindness.
With her quandary settled, they walked over to the subway
station.

When they arrived at Finley's, the streets and the store were
even more crowded than they'd been the night before. Again
Holly kept a close eye on her nephew. She'd made a contin-
gency plan—if they did happen to get separated, they were
to meet in the toy department by the robots.

They rode up on the escalator, after braving the cosmetics aisles, with staff handing out perfume samples. Gabe held
his nose, but Holly was delighted to accept several tiny vials
of perfume. When they finally reached the toy department,
it was far busier than it had been the previous evening. Both
Gabe and Holly studied the display of robots. There did seem
to be fewer of the large boxes, but Jake had assured her there'd
be plenty left by the time she received her Christmas bonus.
She sincerely hoped that was true.

The moment Gabe saw Mrs. Miracle, he rushed to her side. "We made you sugar cookies," he said, giving her the plate.

"Oh, my, these are lovely." The grandmotherly woman smiled. "They look good enough to eat."

"You *are* supposed to eat them," Gabe said with a giggle.

"And I will." She bent down and hugged the boy. "Thank you so much."

Gabe whispered, "Don't tell anyone, but I helped Aunt Holly make them."

Holly was standing close enough to hear him and exchanged a smile with Mrs. Miracle.

"You should be proud of that," Mrs. Miracle said as she led him toward the Intellytron display, holding the plate of cookies aloft. "Lots of men cook. You should have your aunt Holly turn on the Food Network so you see for yourself."

"Men bake cookies?"

"Oh, my, yes," she told him. "Now that you're here, why don't we go and show these other children how to work this special robot. You can be my assistant."

"Can I?" Wide-eyed, Gabe looked at Holly for permission.

She nodded, and Mrs. Miracle and Gabe went to the other side of the toy department. Holly noticed that Jake was busy with customers, so she wandered down a randomly chosen aisle, examining the Barbie dolls and all their accoutrements. She felt a bit foolish carrying a plate of decorated cookies.

As soon as he was free, Jake made a beeline toward her. "Hi," he said. "I didn't expect to see you again so soon."

"Hi." Looking away, she tried to explain the reason for her visit. "Gabe wanted to check out his robot again. After that, we're going to my office and then Rockefeller Center to see the Christmas tree…but we decided to come here first." The words tumbled out so quickly she wondered if he'd understood a thing she'd said.

He glanced at the cookies.

"These are for you," she said, shoving the plate in his direction. "Sugar cookies. In appreciation for my latte."

"Homemade sugar cookies," he murmured as if he'd never seen anything like them before.

He continued to stare at the plate for an awkward moment. Holly was afraid she'd committed a social faux pas.

"My mother used to bake sugar cookies every Christmas," Jake finally said. His eyes narrowed, and the memory seemed to bring him pain.

Holly had the absurd notion that she should apologize.

"I remember the star and the bell." He spoke in a low voice, as though transported through the years. "Oh, and look, that one's a reindeer, and of course the Christmas tree with the little cinnamon candies as ornaments."

"Gabe actually decorated that one," she said.

He looked up and his smile banished all doubt. "Thank you, Holly."

"You're welcome, Jake."

"Excuse me." A woman spoke from behind Holly. "Is there someone here who could show me the electronic games?"

Jake seemed reluctant to leave her, and Holly was loath to see him go. "I'll be happy to help you," he said. He set the cookies behind the counter and escorted the woman to another section of the department.

Holly moved to the area where Gabe and Mrs. Miracle were demonstrating Intellytron. A small crowd had gathered, and Gabe's face shone with happiness as he put the robot through its paces. In all the weeks her nephew had lived with her, she'd never seen him so excited, so fully engaged. She knew Gabe wanted this toy for Christmas; what Holly hadn't understood until this very second was just how much it meant to him.

Regardless of the cost, Holly intended to get her nephew that robot.

Holiday Sugar Cookies

(from *Debbie Macomber's Cedar Cove Cookbook*)

This foolproof sugar cookie recipe makes a sturdy, sweet treat that's a perfect gift or a great addition to a holiday cookie platter.

2 cups (4 sticks) unsalted butter, at room temperature
2 cups brown sugar
2 large eggs
2 teaspoons vanilla extract or grated lemon peel
6 cups all-purpose flour, plus extra for rolling
2 teaspoons baking powder
1 teaspoon salt

1. In a large bowl with electric mixer on medium speed, cream butter and sugar until light and fluffy. Add eggs and vanilla; beat until combined.

2. In a separate bowl, combine flour, baking powder and salt. Reduce mixer speed to low; beat in flour mixture just until combined. Shape dough into two disks; wrap and refrigerate at least 2 hours or up to overnight.

3. Preheat oven to 350ºF. Line baking sheets with parchment paper. Remove 1 dough disk from the refrigerator. Cut disk in half; cover remaining half. On a lightly floured surface with floured rolling pin, roll dough 1/4-inch thick. Using cookie cutters, cut dough into as many cookies as possible; reserve trimmings for rerolling.

4. Place cookies on prepared sheets about 1 inch apart. Bake 10 to 12 minutes (depending on the size of cookies) until pale gold. Transfer to wire rack to cool. Repeat with remaining dough and rerolled scraps.

Tip: Decorate baked cookies with prepared frosting or sprinkle unbaked cookies with colored sugars before putting them in the oven.

Makes about 48 cookies.

Five

PEOPLE ARE LIKE TEA BAGS—YOU HAVE TO DROP THEM IN
HOT WATER BEFORE YOU KNOW HOW STRONG THEY ARE.

—MRS. MIRACLE

"Sugar cookies," Jake said to himself. A rush of memories warmed him. Memories of his mother and sister at Christmas. Spicy scents in the air—cinnamon and ginger and cloves. Those sensory memories had been so deeply buried, he'd all but forgotten them.

"We sold three of the SuperRobots this afternoon," Mrs. Miracle said, breaking into his thoughts.

Just three? Jake felt a sense of dread. He'd need to sell a lot more than three a day to unload the five hundred robots he'd ordered. He checked the computer, which instantly gave him the total number sold since Black Friday. When he saw the screen, his heart sank down to his shoes. This wasn't good. Not good at all. Jake had made a bold decision, hoping to prove himself to his father, and he was about to fall flat on his face.

"I'll be leaving for the night," Mrs. Miracle announced. "Karen—" the other sales associate "—is already gone."

He glanced at his watch. Five after nine. "By all means. You've put in a full day."

"So have you."

As the owner's son, Jake was expected to stay late. He wouldn't ask anything of his staff that he wasn't willing to do himself. That had been drilled into him by his father, who lived by the same rules.

"It's a lovely night for a walk in the park, don't you think?" the older woman said wistfully.

Jake lived directly across from Central Park. He often jogged through the grounds during the summer months, but winter was a different story.

Mrs. Miracle patted him on the back. "I appreciate that you let me stay here in the toy department," she said.

Jake turned to look at her. He hadn't said anything to the older woman about getting her transferred. He couldn't imagine HR had, either. He wondered how she'd found out about his sudden decision to keep her with him. Actually, it'd been Holly's comment about having a grandmotherly figure around that had influenced him. That, and Emily's obvious rapport with children.

"Good night, Mrs. Miracle," he said.

"Good night, Mr. Finley. Oh, and I don't think you need to worry about that robot," she said. "It's going to do very well. Mark my words."

Now it appeared the woman was a mind reader, too.

"I hope you're right," he murmured.

"I am," she said, reaching for her purse. "And remember, this is a lovely evening for a stroll through the park. It's an excellent way to clear your head of worries."

Again, she'd caught him unawares. Jake had no idea he could be so easily read. Good thing he didn't play high-stakes poker. That thought amused him as he finished up for the day and left the store.

He was grateful not to run into his father because J.R. would certainly question him about those robots. No doubt his father already knew the dismal truth; the click of a computer key would show him everything.

When Jake reached his apartment, he was hungry and restless. He unwrapped the plate of cookies and quickly ate two. If this wasn't his mother's recipe, then it was a very similar one. They tasted the same as the cookies he recalled from his childhood.

Standing by the picture window that overlooked the park, he remembered the Christmas his mother and sister had been killed. The shock and pain of it seemed as fresh now as it'd been all those years ago. No wonder his father still refused to celebrate the holiday. Jake couldn't, either.

When he looked out, he noticed how brightly lit the park was. Horse-drawn carriages clattered past, and although he couldn't hear the clopping of the horses' hooves, it sounded in his mind as clearly as if he'd been out on the street. He suddenly saw himself with his parents and his sister, all huddled under a blanket in a carriage. The horse had been named Silver, he remembered, and the snow had drifted softly down. That was almost twenty-one years ago, the winter they'd died, and he hadn't taken a carriage ride since.

Mrs. Miracle had suggested he go for a walk that evening. An odd idea, he thought, especially after a long day spent dealing with harried shoppers. The last thing he'd normally want to do was spend even more time on his feet. And yet he felt irresistibly attracted to the park. The cheerful lights, the elegant carriages, the man on the corner selling roasted chestnuts, drew him like a kid to a Christmas tree.

None of this made any sense. He was exhausted, doubting himself and his judgment, entangled in memories he'd rather ignore. Perhaps a swift walk would chase away the demons that hounded him.

Putting on his coat, he wrapped the cashmere scarf around

his neck. George, the building doorman, opened the front door and, hunching his shoulders against the wind, Jake hurried across the street.

"Aunt Holly, can we buy hot chestnuts?"

The young boy's voice immediately caught Jake's attention. He turned abruptly and came face-to-face with Holly Larson. The fourth time in less than twenty-four hours.

"Jake!"

"Holly."

They stared at each other, both apparently too shocked to speak.

She found her voice first. "What are you doing here?"

He pointed to the apartment building on the other side of the street. "I live over there. What are you doing here this late?"

"How late *is* it?"

He checked his watch. "Twenty to ten."

"Ten!" she cried. "You've got to be kidding. I had no idea it was so late. Hurry up, Gabe, it's time we got to the subway."

"Can we buy some chestnuts first?" he asked, gazing longingly at the vendor's cart.

"Not now. Come on, we have to go."

"I've never had roasted chestnuts before," the boy complained.

"Neither have I," Jake said, although that wasn't strictly true, and stepped up to the vendor. "Three, please."

"Jake, you shouldn't."

"Oh, come on, it'll be fun." He paid for the chestnuts, then handed bags to Holly and Gabe.

"I'm not sure how we got this far north," Holly said, walking close to his side as the three of them strolled down the street, eating chestnuts. "Gabe wanted to see the carriages in the park."

"Lindy told me about them." Gabe spoke with his mouth full. "Lindy Lee."

"Lindy Lee's my boss," Holly explained. "The designer."

Jake knew who she was, impressed that Holly worked for such a respected industry name.

"We went into Holly's office to decorate for Christmas, and Lindy was there and she let me put up stuff around her desk. That's when she told me about the horses in the park," Gabe said.

"Did you go for a ride?" Jake asked.

Gabe shook his head sadly. "Aunt Holly said it costs a lot of money."

"It is expensive," Jake agreed. "But sometimes you can make a deal with the driver. Do you want me to try?"

"Yeah!" Gabe said excitedly. "I've never been in a carriage before—not even once."

"Jake, no," Holly whispered, and laid a restraining hand on his arm. "I should get him home and in bed."

"Aunt Holly, *please!*" The eight-year-old's plaintive cry rang out. "It's Saturday."

"You're turning down a carriage ride?" Jake asked. He saw the dreamy look that came over Holly as a carriage rolled past—a white carriage drawn by a midnight-black horse. "Have you ever been on one?"

"No…"

"Then that settles it. The three of us are going." Several carriages had lined up along the street. Jake walked over to the first one and asked his price, which he willingly paid. All that talk about negotiating had been just that—talk. This was the perfect end to a magical day. Magical because of a plate of silly sugar cookies. Magical because of Holly and Gabe. Magical because of Christmas, reluctant though he was to admit it.

He helped Holly up into the carriage. When she was seated,

he lifted Gabe so the boy could climb aboard, too. Finally he hoisted himself onto the bench across from Holly and Gabe. They shared a thick fuzzy blanket.

"This is great," Gabe exclaimed. "I can hardly wait to tell my dad."

Holly smiled delightedly. "I'm surprised he's still awake," she said. "We've been on the go for hours."

"There's nothing like seeing Christmas through the eyes of a child, is there?"

"Nothing."

"Reminds me of when I was a kid…"

The carriage moved into Central Park and, even at this hour, the place was alive with activity.

"Oh, look, Gabe," Holly said, pointing at the carousel. She wrapped her arm around the boy, who snuggled closer. "We'll go on the carousel this spring."

He nodded sleepily. The ride lasted about thirty minutes, and by the time they returned to the park entrance, Gabe's eyes had drifted shut.

"I was afraid this would happen," Holly whispered.

"We'll go to my apartment, and I'll contact a car service to get you home."

Holly shook her head. "I…appreciate that, but we'll take the subway."

"Nonsense," Jake said.

"Jake, I can't afford a car service."

"It's on me."

"No." She shook her head again. "I can't let you do that."

"You can and you will. If I hadn't insisted on the carriage ride, you'd have been home by now."

She looked as if she wanted to argue more but changed her mind. "Then I'll graciously accept and say thank-you. It's been a magical evening."

Magical. The same word he'd used himself. He leaped down, helped her and Gabe out, then carried Gabe across the street. The doorman held the door for them.

"Evening, Mr. Finley."

"Evening, George."

Holly followed him onto the elevator. When they reached the tenth floor and the doors glided open, he led the way down the hall to his apartment. He had to shift the boy in his arms to get his key in the lock.

Once inside Holly looked around her, eyes wide. By New York standards, his apartment was huge. His father had lived in it for fifteen years before moving to a different place. This apartment had suited Jake, so he'd taken it over.

"I see you're like me. I haven't had time to decorate for Christmas, either," she finally said. "I was so late getting the office done that I had to come in on a Saturday to do it."

"I don't decorate for the holidays," he said without explaining the reasons. He knew he probably sounded a little brusque; he hadn't meant to.

"I suppose you get enough of that working for the store."

He nodded, again avoiding an explanation. He laid a sleeping Gabe on the sofa.

"I'll see how long we'll have to wait for a car," he said. The number was on speed dial; he used it often, since he didn't own a car himself. In midtown Manhattan car ownership could be more of a liability than a benefit. He watched Holly walk over to the picture window and gaze outside. Apparently she found the scene as mesmerizing as he had earlier. Although he made every effort to ignore Christmas, it stared back at him from the street, the city, the park. New York was always intensely alive but never more so than in December.

The call connected with the dispatcher. "How may I help you?"

Jake identified himself and gave his account number and address, and was assured a car would be there in fifteen minutes.

"I'll ride with you," Jake told her when he'd hung up the phone.

His offer appeared to surprise her. "You don't need to do that."

"True, but I'd like to," he said with a smile.

She smiled shyly back. "I'd like it, too." Walking away from the window, she sighed. "I don't understand why, but I feel like I've known you for ages."

"I feel the same way."

"Was it only yesterday morning that you paid for my latte?"

"You were a damsel in distress."

"And you were my knight in shining armor," she said warmly. "You're still in character this evening."

He sensed that she wanted to change the subject because she turned away from him, resting her gaze on something across the room. "You know, you have the ideal spot for a Christmas tree in that corner," she said.

"I haven't celebrated Christmas in more than twenty years," Jake blurted out, shocking himself even more than Holly.

"I beg your pardon?"

Jake went back into the kitchen and found that his throat had gone dry and his hands sweaty. He never talked about his mother and sister. Not with anyone. Including his father.

"You don't believe in Christmas?" she asked, trailing after him. "What about Hanukkah?"

"Neither." He'd dug himself into a hole and the only way out was to explain. "My mother and sister were killed on Christmas Eve twenty-one years ago. A freak car accident that happened in the middle of a snowstorm, when two taxis collided."

"Oh, Jake. I'm so sorry."

"Dad and I agreed to forget about Christmas from that point forward."

Holly moved to his side. She didn't say a word and he was grateful. When people learned of the tragedy—almost always from someone other than him—they rarely knew what to say or how to react. It was an uncomfortable situation and still painful; he usually mumbled some remark about how long ago the accident had been and then tried to put it out of his mind. But he *couldn't,* any more than his father could.

Holly slid her arms around him and simply laid her head against his chest. For a moment, Jake stood unmoving as she held him. Then he placed his own arms around her. It felt as though she was an anchor, securing him in an unsteady sea. He needed her. *Wanted* her. Before he fully realized what he was doing, he lifted her head and lowered his mouth to hers.

The kiss was filled with urgency and need. She slipped her arms around his neck, and her touch had a powerful effect on him.

He tangled his fingers in her dark shoulder-length hair and brought his mouth to hers a second time. Soon they were so involved in each other that it took him far longer than it should to hear the ringing of his phone.

He broke away in order to answer; as he suspected, the car was downstairs, waiting. When he told Holly, she immediately put on her coat. Gabe continued to sleep as Jake scooped him up, holding the boy carefully in both arms.

George opened the lobby door for them. Holly slid into the vehicle first, and then as Jake started to hand her the boy, he noticed a movement on the other side of the street.

"Jake?" Holly called from the car. "Please, there's no need for you to come. You've been so kind already."

"I want to see you safely home," he said as he stared across the street. For just an instant—it must have been his imagination—he was sure he'd seen Emily Merkle, better known as Mrs. Miracle.

Six

The phone rang just as Holly and Gabe walked into the apartment after church the next morning. For one wild second Holly thought it might be Jake.

Or rather, *hoped* it was Jake.

Although she'd been dead on her feet by the time they got to Brooklyn, she couldn't sleep. She'd lain awake for hours, thinking about the kisses they'd shared, replaying every minute of their time together. All of this was so unexpected and yet so welcome. Jake was—

"Hello," she said, sounding breathless with anticipation.

"What's this I hear about you turning my son into a girl?"

"Mickey!" Her brother's voice was as clear as if he were in the next room. He tried to phone on a regular basis, but it wasn't easy. The most reliable form of communication had proved to be email.

"So you're baking cookies with my son, are you?" he teased.

"We had a blast." Gabe was leaping up and down, eager to speak to his father. "Here, I'll let Gabe tell you about it himself." She passed the phone to her nephew, who immediately grabbed it.

"Dad! Dad, guess what? I went to Aunt Holly's office to help her decorate and then she took me to see the big tree at Rockefeller Center and we watched the skaters and had hot chocolate and then we walked to Central Park and had hot dogs for dinner, and, oh, we went to see Mrs. Miracle. I helped Aunt Holly roll out cookies and…" He paused for breath.

Evidently Mickey took the opportunity to ask a few questions, because Gabe nodded a couple of times.

"Mrs. Miracle is the lady in the toy department at Finley's," he said.

He was silent for a few seconds.

"She's really nice," Gabe continued. "She reminds me of Grandma Larson. I gave her a plate of cookies, and Aunt Holly gave cookies to Jake." Silence again, followed by "He's Aunt Holly's new boyfriend and he's really, really nice."

"Maybe I should talk to your father now," Holly inserted, wishing Gabe hadn't been so quick to mention Jake's name.

Gabe clutched the receiver in both hands and turned his back, unwilling to relinquish the phone.

"Jake took us on a carriage ride in Central Park and then…" Gabe stopped talking for a few seconds. "I don't know what happened after that 'cause I fell asleep."

Mickey was asking something else, and although Holly strained to hear what it was, she couldn't.

Whatever his question, Gabe responded by glancing at Holly, grinning widely and saying, "Oh, yeah."

"Are you two talking about me?" she demanded, half laughing and half annoyed.

She was ignored. Apparently Gabe felt there was a lot to tell his father, because he cupped his hand around the mouthpiece and whispered loudly, "I think they *kissed*."

"Gabe!" she protested. If she wanted her brother to know this, she'd tell him herself.

"Okay," Gabe said, nodding. He held out the phone to her. "Dad wants to talk to you."

Holly took it from him and glared down at her nephew.

"So I hear you've found a new love interest," Mickey said in the same tone he'd used to tease her when they were teenagers.

"Oh, stop. Jake and I hardly know each other."

"How'd you meet?"

"At Starbucks. Mickey, please, it's nothing. I only met him on Friday." It felt longer than two days, but this was far too soon to even suggest they were in a relationship.

"Gabe doesn't seem to feel that's a problem."

"Okay, so I took Jake a plate of cookies like Gabe said—it was just a thank-you for buying me a coffee—and…and we happened to run into him last evening in Central Park. It's no big deal. He's a nice person and, well…like I said, we've just met."

"But it looks promising," her brother added.

Holly hated to acknowledge how true that was. Joy and anticipation had surged through her from the moment she and Jake kissed. Still, she was afraid to admit this to her brother—and, for that matter, afraid to admit it to herself. "It's too soon to say that yet."

"Ah, so you're still hung up on Bill?"

Was she? Holly didn't think so. If Bill had ended the relationship by telling her the chemistry just wasn't there, she could've accepted that. Instead, he'd left her with serious doubts regarding her parenting abilities.

"Is that it?" Mickey pressed.

"No," she said. "Not at all. Bill and I weren't really meant to be together. I think we both realized that early on, only neither of us was ready to be honest about it."

"Mmm." Mickey made a sound of agreement. "Things are going better with Gabe, aren't they?"

"Much better."

"Good."

"He's adjusting and so am I." This past week seemed to have been a turning point. They were more at ease with each other. Gabe had made new friends and was getting used to life without his father—and with her. She knew she insisted on rules Mickey didn't bother with—like making their beds every morning, drinking milk with breakfast and, of course, putting the toilet seat down. But Gabe hardly complained at all anymore.

"What was it he told Santa he wanted for Christmas?" Mickey asked.

"So he emailed you about the visit with Santa, did he?"

"Yup, he sent the email right after he got home. He seemed quite excited."

"It's Intellytron the SuperRobot."

At her reference to the toy, Gabe's eyes lit up and he nodded vigorously.

"We found them in Finley's Department Store. Mrs. Miracle, the woman Gabe mentioned, works there...and Jake does, too."

"Didn't Gabe tell me Jake's name is Finley?" Mickey asked. "He said he heard Mrs. Miracle call him that—Mr. Finley. Is he related to the guy who owns the store?"

"Y-e-s." How dense could she be? Holly felt like slapping her forehead. She'd known his name was Finley from the beginning and it hadn't meant a thing to her. But now...now she realized Jake was probably related to the Finley family—was possibly even the owner's son. No wonder he could afford to live where he did. He hadn't given the price of the carriage ride or the car service a second thought, either.

She had the sudden, awful feeling that she was swimming in treacherous waters and there wasn't a life preserver in sight.

"Holly?"

"I... I think he must be." She'd been so caught up in her juvenile fantasies, based on the coincidence of their meetings, that she hadn't paid attention to anything else.

"You sound like this is shocking news."

"I hadn't put two and two together," she confessed.

"And now you're scared."

"I guess I am."

"Don't be. He puts his pants on one leg at a time like everyone else, if you'll pardon the cliché. He's just a guy."

"Right."

"You don't seem too sure of that."

Holly wasn't. A chill had overtaken her and she hugged herself with one arm. "I need to think about this."

"While you're thinking, tell me more about this robot that's got my son so excited."

"It's expensive."

"How...expensive?"

Holly heard the hesitation in her brother's voice. He had his own financial problems. "Don't worry—I've got it. This is on me."

"You're sure about that?"

"Positive." The Christmas bonus checks were due the following Friday. If all went well, hers should cover the price of the toy with enough left over for a really special Christmas dinner.

Christmas.

When she woke that morning, still warm under the covers, Holly's first thought had been of Jake. She'd had the craziest idea that...well, it was out of the question now.

What Jake had confided about his mother and sister had

nearly broken her heart. The tragedy had not only robbed him of his mother and sibling, it had destroyed his pleasure in Christmas. Holly had hoped to change that, but the mere notion seemed ridiculous now. She'd actually planned to invite Jake to spend Christmas Day with her and Gabe. She knew now that he'd never accept. He was a Finley, after all, a man whose background was vastly different from her own.

Half-asleep, she'd pictured the three of them sitting around her table, a lovely golden-brown turkey with sage stuffing resting in the center. She'd imagined Christmas music playing and the tree lights blinking merrily, enhancing the celebratory mood. She couldn't believe she'd even considered such a thing, knowing what she did now.

"I have a Christmas surprise coming your way," Mickey said. "I'm just hoping it arrives in time for the holidays."

"It doesn't matter," she assured her brother, dragging her thoughts away from Jake. She focused on her brother and nephew—which was exactly what she intended to do from this point forward. She needed to forget this romantic fantasy she'd invented within a day of meeting Jake Finley.

"I can guarantee Gabe will like it and so will you," Mickey was saying.

Holly couldn't begin to guess what Mickey might have purchased in Afghanistan for Christmas, but then her brother had always been full of surprises. He'd probably ordered something over the internet, she decided.

"Mom and Dad mailed us a package, as well," she told him. "The box got here this week."

"From Haiti? What would they be sending?"

"I don't have a clue," she said. Once the tree was up she'd arrange the gifts underneath it.

"You're going to wait until Christmas morning, aren't you?" he asked. "Don't open anything before that."

"Of course we'll wait." Even as kids, they'd managed not to peek at their gifts.

Mickey laughed, then grew serious. "This won't be an ordinary Christmas, will it?"

Holly hadn't dwelled on not being with her parents. Her father, a retired dentist, and her mother, a retired nurse, had offered their services in a health clinic for twelve months after the devastating earthquake. They'd been happy about the idea of giving back, and Holly had been happy for them. This Christmas was supposed to be Mickey, Gabe and her for the holidays—and then Mickey's National Guard unit had been called up and he'd left to serve his country.

"It could be worse," she said, and her thoughts involuntarily went to Jake and his father, who refused to celebrate Christmas at all.

"Next year everything will be different," Mickey told her.

"Yes, it will," she agreed.

Her brother spoke to Gabe for a few more minutes and then said goodbye. Gabe was pensive after the conversation with his father and so was Holly, but for different reasons.

"How about toasted cheese sandwiches and tomato soup for lunch?" she suggested, hoping to lighten the mood. "That was your dad's and my favorite Sunday lunch when we were growing up."

Gabe looked at her suspiciously. "What kind of cheese?"

Holly shrugged. "Regular cheese?" By that she meant the plastic-wrapped slices, Gabe's idea of cheese.

"You won't use any of that buffalo stuff, will you?"

She grinned. "Buffalo mozzarella. Nope, this is plain old sliced regular cheese in a package."

"Okay, as long as the soup comes from a can. That's the way Dad made it and that's how I like it."

"You got it," she said, and moved into the kitchen.

Gabe sat on a stool and watched her work, leaning his elbows on the kitchen counter. Holly wasn't fooled by his intent expression. He wasn't interested in spending time with her; he was keeping a close eye on their lunch in case she tried to slip in a foreign ingredient. After a moment he released a deep sigh.

"What's that about?" she asked.

"I miss my dad."

"I know you do, sweetheart. I miss him, too."

"And Grandma and Grandpa."

"And they miss us."

Gabe nodded. "It's not so bad living with you. I thought it was at first, but you're okay."

"Thanks." She hid a smile and set a piece of buttered bread on the heated griddle, then carefully placed a slice of processed cheese on top before adding the second piece of bread. She planned to have a plain cheese sandwich herself—one with *real* cheese.

Obviously satisfied that she was preparing his lunch according to his specifications, Gabe clambered off the stool. "Can we go to the movies this afternoon?"

"Maybe." She had to be careful with her entertainment budget, especially since there were additional expenses coming up this month. "It might be better if we got a video."

"Can I invite a friend over?"

She hesitated a moment, afraid he might want to ask his new friend, Billy.

"Sure," she said. "How about Jonathan Krantz?" Jonathan was another eight-year-old who lived in the building, and Caroline, his mother, sometimes babysat for her.

That was acceptable to Gabe.

After lunch they walked down to the neighborhood video store, found a movie they could both agree on and then asked Jonathan to join them.

Holly did her best to pay attention to the movie; however, her mind had a will of its own. No matter how hard she tried, all she could think about was Jake. He didn't phone and that was just as well. She wasn't sure what she would've said if he had.

Then again, he hadn't asked for her phone number. Still, he could get it easily enough if he wanted....

Late Sunday night, after Gabe was asleep, Holly went on the computer and did a bit of research. Sure enough, Jake was related to the owner. Not only that, he was the son and heir.

Monday morning, Holly dropped Gabe off at school and took the subway into Manhattan. As she walked past Starbucks, she felt a twinge of longing—for more than just the coffee they served. This was where she'd met Jake. Jake Finley.

As she walked briskly past Starbucks, the door flew open and Jake Finley dashed out, calling her name.

Holly pretended not to hear.

"Holly!" he shouted, running after her. "Wait up!"

Seven

COINCIDENCE IS WHEN GOD CHOOSES
TO REMAIN ANONYMOUS.

—MRS. MIRACLE

"Wait up!" Jake called. Holly acted as if she hadn't heard him. Jake knew better. She was clearly upset about something, although he couldn't figure out what. His mind raced with possibilities, but he couldn't come up with a single one that made sense.

Finally she turned around.

Jake relaxed. Just seeing her again brought him a feeling of happiness he couldn't define. He barely knew Holly Larson, yet he hadn't been able to forget her. She was constantly in his thoughts, constantly with him, and perhaps the most puzzling of all was the *rightness* he felt in her presence. He couldn't think of any other way to describe it.

Jake had resisted the urge to contact her on Sunday, afraid of coming on too strong. They'd seen quite a bit of each other in the past few days, seemingly thrown together by fate. Coincidence? He supposed so, and yet... It was as though a providential hand was behind all this. Admittedly that sounded fanciful, even melodramatic. Nevertheless, four chance meetings in quick succession was hard to explain.

With someone else, a different kind of woman, Jake might have suspected these meetings had been contrived, and certainly this morning's was pure manipulation on his part. He'd hoped to run into her casually. But he hadn't expected to see Holly walk directly past the coffee shop. He couldn't allow this opportunity to pass.

She looked up at him expectantly; she didn't say anything.

"Good morning," he said, unsure of her mood.

"Hi." She just missed making eye contact.

He felt her reluctance and frowned, unable to fathom what he might have done to upset her. "What's wrong?" he asked.

"Nothing."

"Then why won't you look at me?"

The question forced her to raise her eyes and meet his. She held his gaze for only a fraction of a second before glancing away.

The traffic light changed and, side by side, they crossed the street.

"I'd like to take you to dinner," he said. He'd decided that if he invited her out on a real date they could straighten out the problem, whatever it was.

"When?"

At least she hadn't turned him down flat. That was encouraging. "Whenever you say." He'd rearrange his schedule if necessary. "Tonight? Tomorrow? I'm free every evening. Or I can be." He wanted it understood that he wasn't involved with anyone else. In fact, he hadn't been in a serious relationship in years.

His primary goal for the past decade had been to learn the retail business from the ground up, and as a result his social life had suffered. He worked long hours and that had taken a toll on his relationships. After his last breakup, which was in… Jake had to stop and think. June, he remembered. Had it really been that long? At any rate, Judith had told him it was over before they'd really begun.

At the time he'd felt bad, but agreed it was probably for the best. Funny how easily he could let go of a woman with hardly a pause after just four weeks. Judith had been attractive, successful, intelligent, but there'd been no real connection between them. The thought of letting Holly walk out of his life was a completely different scenario, one that filled him with dread.

All he could think about on Sunday was when he'd see her again. His pride had influenced his decision not to call her; he didn't want her to know how important she'd become to him in such a short time. Despite that, he'd gone to Starbucks first thing this morning.

"Tonight?" she repeated, referring to his dinner invitation. "You mean this evening?"

"Sure," he said with a shrug. "I'm available Tuesday night if that's better for you."

She hesitated, as if considering his offer. "Thanks, but I don't have anyone to look after Gabe."

"I could bring us dinner." He wasn't willing to give up that quickly.

Her eyes narrowed. "Why are you trying so hard?"

"Why are you inventing excuses not to see me?"

He didn't understand her reluctance. Saturday, when he'd dropped her off at her Brooklyn apartment and kissed her good-night, she'd practically melted in his arms. Now she couldn't get away from him fast enough.

Holly stared down at the sidewalk. People hurried past them and around them. They stood like boulders in the middle of a fast-moving stream, neither of them moving, neither talking.

"I... I didn't know who you were," she eventually admitted. "Not until later."

"I told you my name's Jake Finley." He didn't pretend not to understand what she meant. This wasn't the first time his family name had intimidated someone. He just hadn't expected that sort of reaction from Holly. He'd assumed she knew, and that was part of her charm because it hadn't mattered to her.

"I know you did," she countered swiftly. "And I feel stupid for not connecting the dots."

He stiffened. "And my name bothers you?"

"Not really," she said, and her gaze locked with his before she slowly lowered her lashes. "I guess it does, but not for the reasons you're assuming."

"What exactly am I assuming?" he asked.

"That I'd use you."

"For what?" he demanded.

"Well, for one thing, that robot toy. We both know how badly Gabe wants it for Christmas and it's expensive and you might think I…"

"*What* would I think?" he asked forcefully when she didn't complete her sentence.

"That I'd want you to get me the toy."

"Would you ask me to do that?" If she did, he'd gladly purchase it—retail price—on her behalf.

"No. Never." Her eyes flared with the intensity of her response. She started to leave and Jake followed.

"Then it's a moot point." He began to walk, carefully matching his longer stride to her shorter one. "Under no circumstances will I purchase that toy for you. Agreed?"

"Agreed," she said.

"Anything else?"

Holly looked at him and then away. "I don't come from a powerful family or know famous people or—"

"Do you think I care?"

"No, but if you did, you'd be plain out of luck."

He smiled. "That's fine with me."

"Okay," she said, stopping abruptly. "Can you explain why you want to see me?"

Jake wished he had a logical response. He felt drawn to her in ways he hadn't with other women. "I can't say for sure, but deep down I feel that if we were to walk away from each other right now, I'd regret it."

"You do?" she asked softly, and pressed her hand to her heart. "Jake, I feel the same way. What's happening to us?"

He didn't have an answer. "I don't know." But he definitely felt it, and that feeling intensified with each meeting.

They started walking again. "So, can I see you tonight?" he asked. That was important, necessary.

Her face fell. "I wasn't making it up, about not having anyone to take care of Gabe. If you were serious about bringing us dinner..."

"I was."

Her face brightened. "Then that would work out perfectly."

"Do you like take-out Chinese?" he asked, thinking Gabe would enjoy it, as well.

"Love it."

"Me, too, but you'll have to use chopsticks."

"Okay, I'll give it a try."

"Great." Jake breathed easier. Everything was falling into place, just the way he'd hoped it would. He glanced at his watch and grimaced. He was late for work. He hoped Karen or Mrs. Miracle had covered for him.

Retreating now, taking two steps backward, he called out to Holly, "Six-thirty? At your place?"

She nodded eagerly. "Yes. And thank you, Jake, thank you so much."

He raised his hand. "See you tonight."

"Tonight," she echoed, and they both turned and hurried off to their respective jobs.

Jake's step was noticeably lighter as he rushed toward the department store. By the time he arrived, ten minutes later than usual, he was breathless. He'd just clocked in and headed for the elevator when his father stopped him, wearing a frown that told him J.R. wasn't happy.

"Are you keeping bankers' hours these days?"

"No," Jake told him. "I had an appointment." A slight stretch of the truth.

"I was looking for you."

"Any particular reason?" Jake asked. He'd bet his lunch break this sudden interest in the toy department had to do with those robots.

His father surprised him, however, with a completely different question. "I heard from HR that you requested a transfer for one of the seasonal staff...."

"Mrs. Miracle."

"Who? No, that wasn't the name."

"No, it's Merkle or Michaels or something like that. The name badge mistakenly says Miracle, and she insisted that's what we call her."

His father seemed confused, which was fine with Jake. He felt he was being rather clever to keep J.R.'s attention away from the robots.

J.R. ignored the comment. "You asked for this Mrs. Miracle or whoever she is to be transferred and then you changed your mind. Do I understand correctly?"

"Yes. After I made the initial request, I realized she was a good fit for the department—a grandmotherly figure who relates well to kids *and* parents. She adds exactly the right touch."

"I see," his father murmured. "Okay, whatever you decide is fine."

That was generous, seeing that *he* was the department head, Jake mused with more affection than sarcasm.

"While I have you, tell me, how are sales of that expensive robot going?"

Jake wasn't fooled. His father already knew the answer to that. "Sales are picking up. We sold a total of twenty-five over the weekend."

"Twenty-five," his father said slowly. "There're still a lot of robots left in the storeroom, though, aren't there?"

"Yes," Jake admitted.

"That's what I thought."

He made some additional remark Jake couldn't quite grasp, but it didn't sound like something he wanted to hear, anyway, so he didn't ask J.R. to repeat it.

As he entered the toy department, clipping on his "Manager" badge, Jake was glad to see Mrs. Miracle on duty.

"Good morning, Mr. Finley," she said, looking pleased with herself.

"Good morning. I apologize for being late—"

"No problem. I sold two Intellytrons this morning."

"Already?" This was encouraging news and improved his workday almost before it had started. "That's wonderful!"

"They seem to be catching on."

The phone rang just then, and Jake stepped behind the counter to answer. The woman at the other end of the line was looking for Intellytron and sighed with audible relief when Jake assured her he had plenty in stock. She asked that he hold one for her.

"I'll be happy to," Jake said. He found Mrs. Miracle watching him, smiling, when he ended the conversation. "I think you might be right," he said. "That was a woman calling about Intellytron. She sounded excited when I told her we've got them."

Mrs. Miracle rubbed her palms together. "I knew it." The morning lull was about to end; in another half hour, the store would explode with customers. Since toys were on the third floor, it took time for shoppers to drift up the escalators and elevators, so they still had a few minutes of relative peace. Jake decided to take advantage of it by questioning his rather unusual employee.

"I thought I saw you on Saturday night," he commented in a nonchalant voice, watching her closely.

"Me?" she asked.

Jake noted that she looked a bit sheepish. "Did you happen to take a walk around Central Park around ten or ten-thirty?"

"My heavens, no! After spending all day on my feet, the last thing I'd do is wander aimlessly around Central Park. At that time of night, no less." Her expression turned serious. "What makes you ask?"

"I could've sworn that was you I saw across from the park."

She laughed as though the question was ludicrous. "You're joking, aren't you?"

"No." Jake grew even more suspicious. Her nervous reaction seemed to imply that she wasn't being completely truthful. "Don't you remember? You suggested I take a stroll through the park."

"I said that?"

"You did," he insisted. He wasn't about to be dismissed quite this easily. "You said it would help clear my head."

"After a long day at work? My goodness, what was I thinking?"

Jake figured the question was rhetorical, so he didn't respond. "I met Holly Larson and her nephew there," he told her.

"My, that was a nice coincidence, wasn't it?"

"Very nice," he agreed.

"Are you seeing her again?" the older woman asked.

"Yes, as a matter of fact, I am." He didn't share any details. The less she knew about his personal life, the better. Mrs. Miracle might appear to be an innocent senior citizen, but he had his doubts. Not that he suspected anything underhanded or nefarious. She seemed... Jake couldn't come up with the right word. He liked Mrs. Miracle and she was an excellent employee, a natural saleswoman. And yet... He didn't really know much about her.

And what he did know didn't seem to add up.

Eight

Holly felt as if she was walking on air the rest of the way into the office. It didn't matter how rotten her day turned out to be; no one was going to ruin it after her conversation with Jake.

She'd spent a miserable Sunday and had worked herself into a state after she'd discovered Jake's position with the department store. Son and heir. Now, having talked to him, she realized her concerns were irrelevant. Okay, so his family was rich and influential; that didn't define him or say anything about the person he really was.

The question that, inevitably, kept going around and around in her mind was why someone like Jake Finley would be interested in *her*. The reality was that he could have his pick of women. To further complicate the situation, she was taking care of Gabe. Lots of men would see her nephew as an encumbrance. Apparently not Jake.

Holly was happy they'd gotten this settled. She felt reassured about his interest—and about the fact that he'd promised not to purchase the robot for her. Mickey had offered, too, but she knew he was financially strapped. Besides, getting Gabe this toy for Christmas—as *her* gift to him—was important to Holly.

She couldn't entirely explain why. Maybe because of Bill's implication that she wasn't good with kids. She had something to prove—if not to Bill or Mickey or even Jake, she had to prove it to herself. Nothing was going to keep her from making this the best possible Christmas for Gabe.

Holly entered her cubicle outside Lindy Lee's office and hung up her coat. She'd been surprised to find her boss in the office on Saturday afternoon and had tried to keep Gabe occupied so he wouldn't pester her. Unfortunately, Holly's efforts hadn't worked. She'd caught Gabe with Lindy Lee twice. One look made her suspect Lindy didn't really appreciate the intrusion. As soon as they'd finished putting up the decorations, Holly had dragged Gabe out with her. But this morning, as she looked around the office, she was pleased with her work. The bright red bulbs that hung outside her cubicle created an air of festivity. She couldn't help it—she started singing "Jingle Bells."

"Where is that file?" Lindy Lee shouted. She was obviously in her usual Monday-morning bad mood. Her employer was sorting through her in-basket, cursing impatiently under her breath.

Of course, Lindy Lee didn't mention *which* file she needed. But deciphering vague demands was all part and parcel of Holly's job. And fortunately she had a pretty good idea which one her boss required.

Walking into Lindy Lee's office, Holly reached across the top of the desk, picked up a file and handed it to her.

Lindy Lee growled something back, opened the file and then smiled. "Thank you."

"You're welcome," Holly said cheerfully.

The designer eyed her suspiciously. "What are *you* so happy about?" she asked.

"Nothing... I met up with a friend this morning, that's all."

"I take it this *friend* is a man."

Holly nodded. "A very special man."

"Honey, don't believe it." She laughed as though to say Holly had a lot to learn about the opposite sex. "Men will break your heart before breakfast and flush it down the toilet just for fun."

Holly didn't bother to explain about Jake. Lindy Lee's experience with men might be far more extensive than her own, but it was obviously different. Jake would never do anything to hurt her; she was sure of it. Besides, Lindy Lee socialized in different circles—Jake's circles, she realized with a start. Still, Holly couldn't make herself believe Jake was the kind of man who'd mislead her. Even though they'd known each other so briefly, every instinct she had told her she could trust him, and she did.

No irrational demand or bad temper was going to spoil her day, Holly decided. Because that evening she was seeing Jake.

Holly guessed wrong. Her day was ruined.

Early that afternoon she slipped back into her cubicle after delivering Lindy Lee's latest sketches to the tech department, where they'd be translated into patterns, which would then be sewn up as samples. Lindy was talking to the bookkeeper and apparently neither one noticed that she'd returned.

Holly hadn't intended to listen in on the conversation, but it would've been impossible not to with Lindy Lee's office door wide-open. In Holly's opinion, if Lindy wanted to keep the conversation private, then it was up to her to close the door.

"Christmas bonuses are due this Friday," Marsha, the bookkeeper, reminded their boss.

"Due." Lindy Lee pounced on the word. "Since when is a

bonus *due?* It's my understanding that a bonus is exactly that— a bonus—an extra that's distributed at my discretion."

"Well, yes, but you've given us one every year since you went out on your own."

"That's because I could afford to."

"You've had a decent year," Marsha said calmly.

Holly wanted to stand and cheer. Marsha was right; profits were steady despite the economy. The staff had worked hard, although their employer took them for granted. Lindy Lee didn't appear to notice or value the team who backed her both personally and professionally. More times than she cared to count, Holly had dropped off and picked up Lindy's dry cleaning or run errands for her. She often went above and beyond anything listed in her job description.

Not once had she complained. The way Holly figured it, her main task was to give Lindy Lee the freedom to be creative and do what she did best and that was design clothes.

"A *decent* year, perhaps," Lindy Lee repeated. "But not a stellar one."

"True," Marsha agreed. "But you're holding your own in a terrible economy."

"All right, I'll reconsider." Lindy Lee walked over to the window, her back to Holly. Not wanting to be caught listening, Holly quietly stood. There was plenty to do away from her desk—like filing. Clutching a sheaf of documents, she held her breath as she waited for Lindy's decision.

"Everyone gets the same bonus as last year," Lindy Lee said with a beleaguered sigh.

Holly released her breath.

"Everyone except Holly Larson."

Her heart seemed to stop.

"Why not Holly?" Marsha asked.

"She doesn't deserve it," Lindy Lee said flippantly. "She's

out of the office at the stroke of five and she's been late for work a number of mornings, as well."

The bookkeeper was quick to defend Holly. "Yes, but she's looking after her nephew while her brother's in Afghanistan. This hasn't been easy for her, you know."

Lindy Lee whirled around and Holly moved from her line of vision in the nick of time. She flattened herself against the wall and continued to listen.

"Yes, yes, I met the boy this weekend. She brought him on Saturday when she came in to decorate."

"On her own time," Marsha said pointedly.

"True, but if she managed her time better, Holly could've done it earlier. As it is, the decorations are up much later than in previous years. If I was giving out bleeding-heart awards this Christmas, I'd make sure Holly got one. No, I won't change my mind," she snapped as Marsha began to protest. "A bonus is a bonus, and as far as I'm concerned Holly doesn't deserve one. It's about merit, you know, and going the extra mile, and she hasn't done that."

Holly gasped.

"But—"

"I've made my decision."

Marsha didn't argue further.

Holly didn't blame her. The bookkeeper had tried. Holly felt tears well up but blinked them away. She was a good employee; she worked hard. While Lindy Lee was correct—these days she *did* leave the office on time—there'd been many a night earlier in the year when she'd stayed late without being asked. She'd often gone that extra mile for her employer. Yet all Lindy seemed to remember was the past three months.

She felt sick to her stomach. So there'd be no bonus for her. Although the amount of money wasn't substantial—maybe five hundred dollars—it would've made all the difference.

But somehow, she promised herself, she'd find a way to buy Gabe his special Christmas toy.

Even though she was distracted by her financial worries, Holly managed to enjoy dinner with Jake and Gabe that evening. Jake brought chopsticks along with their take-out Chinese—an order large enough to feed a family of eight. Several of the dishes were new to Holly. He'd chosen moo shu pork and shrimp in lobster sauce, plus barbecue pork, egg rolls, fried rice and almond fried chicken.

Gabe loved every minute of their time with Jake. As he so eloquently said, "It's nice being around a guy."

"I don't know," Jake commented as he slipped his arm around Holly's waist. "Women aren't so bad."

Gabe considered his comment carefully. "Aunt Holly's okay, I guess."

"You *guess*," she sputtered. Using her chopsticks she removed the last bit of almond fried chicken from her nephew's plate.

"Hey, that was mine," Gabe cried.

"That's what you get for criticizing women," Holly told him, and then, to prove her point, she reached for his fried dumpling, too. In retaliation, Gabe reached across for her egg roll, dropping it on the table.

Jake immediately retrieved it and stuck one end in his mouth. "Five-second rule," he said just before he bit down.

When they'd finished, they cleared the table and settled down in front of the television.

As Jake flipped through the channels, Gabe asked, "When are we gonna put up the Christmas tree?"

"This week," Holly told him. She'd need to budget carefully now that she wasn't going to get her bonus. The tree— she'd hoped to buy a real one—was an added expense she'd planned to cover with the extra money. This year she'd have to resort to the small artificial tree she'd stuck in the back of her coat closet.

The news that she wouldn't be receiving the bonus was devastating. Holly's first instinct had been to strike back. If everyone else was getting a bonus, it didn't seem fair that she wasn't. Still, Lindy Lee had a point. Holly hadn't been as dedicated to her job since Gabe came into her life. She had other responsibilities now.

That afternoon she'd toyed with the idea of looking for a new job. She could walk out—that would show Lindy Lee. Reason quickly asserted itself. She couldn't leave her job and survive financially. It could take her months to find a new one. And although this was an entry-level position, the chance to advance in the fashion world was an inducement she simply couldn't reject that easily. She'd made friends at the office, too. Friends like Marsha, who'd willingly defended her to their employer.

Besides, if she left her job, there'd be dozens who'd leap at the opportunity to take her place. No, Holly would swallow her disappointment and ride this out until Mickey returned. Next Christmas would be different.

"Can Jake help decorate the Christmas tree?" Gabe asked.

Jake was sitting next to her and Holly felt him tense. His face was pale, his expression shocked.

"Jake." Holly said his name softly and laid her hand on his forearm. "Are you okay?"

"Sure. Sorry, no decorating trees for me this year," he said in an offhand way.

"Why not?" Gabe pressed. "It's really fun. Aunt Holly said she'd make popcorn and we'd have cider. She has some ornaments from when she and my dad were kids. She won't let me see them until we put up the tree. It'll be lots of fun." His young face pleaded with Jake to reconsider.

Holly gently placed her hand on her nephew's shoulder. "Jake said another time," she reminded him. Jake hadn't participated in any of the usual Christmas traditions or activities in more than twenty years, ever since he'd lost his mother and sister.

"But there won't be another time," her nephew sulked. "I'll be with my dad next year."

"Jake's busy," Holly said, offering yet another excuse.

"Sorry to let you down, buddy," Jake told Gabe. "We'll do something else, all right?"

Gabe shrugged, his head hanging. "Okay."

"How about if I take you ice-skating at Rockefeller Center? Would you like that?"

"Wow!" In his excitement, Gabe propelled himself off the sofa and landed with a thud on the living room carpet. "I wanted to go skating last Saturday but Aunt Holly doesn't know how."

"She's a girl," Jake said in a stage whisper. Then he looked at her and grinned boyishly. "Frankly, I'm glad of it."

"As you should be," she returned under her breath.

"When can we go?" Gabe wasn't letting this opportunity slip through his fingers. He wanted to nail down the date as soon as possible. "I took skating lessons last winter," he said proudly.

Jake hesitated. "I'll need to get back to you once I see how everything goes at the store. It's the Christmas season, you know, so we might have to wait until the first week of the new year. How about Sunday the second?"

"That *long?*"

"Yes, but then I'll have more time to show you some classic moves. Deal?"

Gabe considered this compromise and finally nodded. "Deal." They clenched their fists and bumped them together to seal the bargain.

The three of them sat side by side and watched a rerun of *Everybody Loves Raymond* for the next half hour. Jake was beside her, his arm around her shoulders. Gabe sat to her left with his feet tucked beneath him.

When the program ended, Gabe turned to Jake. "Do you want me to leave the room so you can kiss my aunt Holly?"

"Gabe!" Holly's cheeks were warm with embarrassment.

"What makes you suggest that?" Jake asked the boy.

Gabe stood in the center of the room. "My dad emailed and said if you came to the apartment, I should dis–discreetly leave for a few minutes, only I don't know what that word means. I think it means you want to kiss Aunt Holly without me watching. Right?"

Jake nodded solemnly. "Something like that."

"I thought so. Okay, I'm going to go and get ready for bed." He enunciated each word as if reading a line of dialogue from an unfamiliar play.

Jake winked at Holly. "Pucker up, sweetheart," he said, doing a recognizable imitation of Humphrey Bogart.

Holly rolled her eyes and clasped her hands prayerfully. "Ah, sweet romance."

As soon as the bedroom door closed, Jake pulled her into his arms. The kiss was everything she'd remembered and more. They kissed repeatedly until Gabe came back and stood in front of them. He cleared his throat.

"Should I go away again?" he asked.

"No, that's fine," Holly said. She had trouble speaking.

"Your timing is perfect," Jake assured the boy.

Jake left shortly after that, and once she'd let him out of the apartment, Holly leaned against the door, still a little breathless. Being with Jake was very nice, indeed, but she had something else on her mind at the moment—Intellytron the SuperRobot and how she was going to afford one before Christmas.

Nine

It's hard to stumble when you're down on your knees.

—Shirley, Goodness and Mercy,
friends of Mrs. Miracle

Holly gave the situation regarding Gabe and the robot careful thought during the sleepless night that followed their dinner. She'd asked Jake about it when Gabe was out of earshot.

"There are still plenty left," he'd told her.

"But they're selling, aren't they?"

"Yes, sales are picking up."

That was good for him but unsettling for her. If she couldn't afford to pay for the robot until closer to Christmas, then she'd need to make a small deposit and put one on layaway now. She didn't know if Finley's offered that option; not many stores did anymore. She'd have to check with Jake. She dared not take a chance that Intellytron would sell out before she had the cash.

While she was dead set against letting Jake purchase the robot for her, she hoped he'd be willing to put one aside, even if layaway wasn't a current practice at higher-end department stores. If she made their lunches, cut back on groceries and bought only what was absolutely necessary, she should be able to pay cash for the robot just before Christmas.

Tuesday morning she packed a hard-boiled egg and an apple for lunch. For Gabe she prepared a peanut butter and jelly sandwich, adding an apple for him, too, plus the last of the sugar cookies. Gabe hadn't been happy to take a packed lunch. He much preferred to buy his meal with his friends. But it was so much cheaper for him to bring it—and, at this point, necessary, although of course she couldn't tell him why. The leftover Chinese food figured into her money-saving calculations, too. It would make a great dinner.

On her lunch hour, after she'd eaten her apple and boiled egg, Holly hurried to Finley's to talk to Jake. She'd been uneasy from the moment she'd learned she wasn't getting a Christmas bonus. She wouldn't relax until she knew the SuperRobot would still be available the following week.

Unfortunately, Jake wasn't in the toy department.

"He's not here?" Holly asked Mrs. Miracle, unable to hide her disappointment.

"He's with his father just now," the older woman told her, and then frowned. "I do hope the meeting goes smoothly. It can be difficult to read the senior Mr. Finley sometimes. But I have faith that all will end well." Her eyes twinkled as she spoke.

Holly hoped she'd explain, and Mrs. Miracle obliged.

"In case you didn't hear, Jake went over the department buyer's head when he ordered those extra robots," she confided, "and that's caused some difficulty with his father. J. R. Finley has a real stubborn streak."

Mrs. Miracle seemed very well-informed about the relationship between Jake and his father. "The robots are selling, though. Isn't that right?" she asked, again torn between pleasure at Jake's success and worry about laying her hands on one of the toys. The display appeared to be much smaller than last week.

"Thankfully, yes," Mrs. Miracle told her. "Jake took quite a risk, you know?"

Holly shook her head.

"Jake tried to talk Mike Scott into ordering more of the robots, but Mike refused to listen, so Jake did what he felt was best." Her expression sobered. "His father was not pleased, to put it mildly."

"But you said they're selling."

"Oh, yes. We sold another twenty-five over the weekend and double that on Monday." She nodded sagely. "I can only assume J.R. is feeling somewhat reassured."

"That's great." Holly meant it, but a shiver of dread went through her.

"Several of our competitors have already sold out," Mrs. Miracle said with a gleeful smile.

"That's terrific news." And it was—for Finley's. Parents searching for the toy would now flock to one of the few department stores in town with enough inventory to meet demand.

"How's Gabe?" Mrs. Miracle asked, changing the subject.

"He's doing fine." Holly chewed her lip, her thoughts still on the robot. "Seeing how well the robot's selling, would it be possible for me to set one aside on a layaway plan?"

The older woman's smile faded. "Oh, dear, the store doesn't have a layaway option. They haven't in years. Is that going to be a problem for you?"

Holly wasn't surprised that layaway was no longer offered, but she figured it was worth asking. Holly clutched her purse. "I... I don't know." Her mind spinning, she looked hopefully at the older woman. "Do you think you could hold one of the robots for me?" She hated to make that kind of request, but with her credit card temporarily out of commission and no layaway plan, she didn't have any other choice. The payment she'd made on her card would've been processed by now, but she didn't dare risk a purchase as big as this.

"Oh, dear, I'm really not sure."

"Could you ask Jake for me?" Holly inquired. She'd do it herself if he was there.

"Of course. I just don't think I could go against store policy, being seasonal staff and all."

"I wouldn't want you to do that, Mrs. Miracle."

"However, I'm positive Jake would be happy to help if he can." She leaned closer and lowered her voice. "He's rather sweet on you."

Sweet? That was a nice, old-fashioned word. "He's been wonderful to me and Gabe."

"So I understand. Didn't he bring you dinner last night?"

Holly wondered how Mrs. Miracle knew about that, unless Jake had mentioned it. No reason not to, she supposed. "Yes, and it was a lovely evening," she said. The only disappointment had come when Gabe asked him to help decorate the tree and Jake refused. The mere suggestion had distressed him. She hadn't realized that the trauma of those family deaths was as intense and painful as if the accident had just happened. If it was this traumatic for Jake, Holly could only imagine what it was like for his father.

"Did you know Jake and his father leave New York every Christmas Eve?" Mrs. Miracle whispered.

It was as if the older woman had been reading her mind. "I beg your pardon?"

"Jake and his father leave New York every Christmas Eve," she repeated.

Holly hadn't known this and wasn't sure what to say.

"Isn't that a shame?"

Holly shrugged. "Everyone deals with grief differently," she murmured. Her brother handled the loss of his wife with composure and resolve. That was his personality. Practical. Responsible. As he'd said himself, he couldn't fall apart; he had a boy to raise.

Sally had been sick for a long while, giving Mickey time to prepare for the inevitable—at least to the extent anyone can. He'd loved Sally and missed her terribly, especially in the beginning. Yet he'd gone on with his life, determined to be a good father.

Perhaps the difference was that for the Finleys, the deaths had come suddenly, without warning. The family had awakened the morning of Christmas Eve, excited about the holiday. There'd been no indication that by the end of the day tragedy would befall them. The shock, the grief, the complete unexpectedness of the accident, had remained an unhealed wound all these years.

"He needs you," Mrs. Miracle said.

"Me?" Holly responded with a short laugh. "We barely know each other."

"Really?"

"We met last week, remember?"

"Last week," she echoed, with that same twinkle in her eye. "But you like him, don't you?"

"Yes, I guess I do," Holly admitted.

"You should invite him for a home-cooked dinner."

Funny, Holly had been thinking exactly that. She'd wait, not wanting to appear too eager—although heaven knew that was how she felt. And of course there was the problem of her finances....

"I'd like to have Jake over," she began. "He—"

"Did I hear someone mention my name?" Jake said from behind her.

"Jake!" She turned to face him as his assistant moved away to help a young couple who'd approached the department. From the corner of her eye, Holly saw that the husband and wife Mrs. Miracle had greeted were pointing at the Super-Robot. Mrs. Miracle picked up a box and walked over to the cash register to ring up the sale.

"Holly?" Jake asked.

"I need to put Intellytron on layaway but Mrs. Miracle told me you don't do that," she said in a rush.

"Sorry, no. I thought you were going to use your Christmas bonus to purchase the robot this week."

"I'm not getting one," she blurted out. She was close to tears, which embarrassed her.

"Listen, I'll buy the robot for Gabe and—"

"No," she broke in. "We already talked about that, remember? I won't let you."

"Why not?"

"Because... I just won't. Let's leave it at that."

He frowned but reluctantly agreed. "Okay, if that's the way you want it."

"That's the way it has to be."

"At least let me hold one for you," Jake said before she could compose herself enough to ask.

"You can do that?"

Jake nodded. "Sure. I'll set one aside right away and put your name on it. I'll tell everyone on staff that it isn't to be sold. How does that sound?"

She closed her eyes as relief washed over her. "Thank you. That would be perfect."

"Are you all right now?" He placed his hand on her shoulder in a comforting gesture.

"I'm fine. I apologize if I seem unreasonable."

"I understand."

"You do?" Holly wasn't convinced she could explain it herself. She just knew she had to do this. For Gabe, for Mickey... and for herself. The robot had become more than a toy. It was a symbol of her commitment to her nephew and her desire to give him the Christmas he deserved.

She saw that the department was busy and she was keeping Jake from his customers. "I have to get back to the office," she said.

He grinned. "Next time maybe you could stay longer."

Holly smiled back. "Next time I will."

"I'll call you. You're in the phone directory?"

She nodded, hoping she'd hear from him soon. "See you, Jake."

"See you, Holly."

As she walked toward the elevator, Mrs. Miracle joined her. "Mr. Finley suggested I take my lunch hour now," she said as they stepped into the empty car together. "What I feel like having is fried chicken."

"Fried chicken," Holly echoed. "My mother, who was born and raised in the South, has a special family recipe but she hasn't made it in years. I can't even remember the last time we ate fried chicken." In this age of heart-healthy diets, her mother had focused on lean, low-carb meals.

"A special recipe?" Mrs. Miracle murmured. "I'll bet it was good."

"The best." Now that she thought about it, Holly figured she might have a copy in her kitchen. "Mom put together a book of family recipes for me when I left home. I wonder if she included that one." Fried chicken was the ultimate comfort food and would make a wonderful dinner when she invited Jake over—sometime in the new year.

"She probably did. That sounds just like her."

"You know my mother?" Holly asked, surprised.

"No…no, but having met you, I know she must be a very considerate woman, someone who cares about family and traditions."

What a lovely compliment. The kind words helped take the sting out of her employer's refusal to give Holly a Christmas bonus. Lindy Lee was a modern-day Scrooge as far as Holly was concerned.

That evening, as dinner heated in the microwave, Holly searched through her kitchen drawers for the notebook where her mother had written various recipes passed down through her family.

"What would you think of homemade fried chicken for Christmas?" Holly asked Gabe. It wasn't the traditional dinner but roast turkey with all the fixings was out of her budget now. If Gabe considered her fried chicken a success, she'd serve it again when Jake came over.

"I've had take-out chicken. Is that the same?"

"The same?" she repeated incredulously. "Not even close!"

"Then I've never had it." He shrugged. "If it's not frozen or out of a can Dad doesn't know how to make it," Gabe said. "Except for macaroni and cheese in the box." He sat down at the computer and logged on to the internet, preparing to send an email to his father, as he did every night. He hadn't typed more than a few words when he turned and looked at Holly. "What's for dinner tonight?"

"Leftover Chinese. You okay with that?"

"Sure." Gabe returned to the computer screen.

Ten minutes later, he asked, "Can you invite Jake for Christmas dinner?"

"He won't be able to come."

"Why not?"

"He's going away for Christmas."

Gabe was off the internet and playing one of his games, jerking the game stick left and right as he battled aliens. "Why?"

"You'll have to ask him."

"I will." Apparently he'd won the battle because he let go of the stick and faced her. "You're going to see him again, right? You want to, don't you?"

Even an eight-year-old boy could easily see through her. "I hope so."

"Me, too," Gabe said, then added, "Billy wants me to come over after school on Friday. I can go, can't I?" He regarded her hopefully.

The boys had obviously remained friends. "I'll clear it with his dad first." Holly had been meaning to talk to Bill before this. She'd make a point of doing it soon, although she wasn't looking forward to contacting him.

The good news was that she'd found the recipe in her mother's book.

(from *Debbie Macomber's Cedar Cove Cookbook*)

The key to crisp fried chicken is cooking at a high temperature. Stick a candy or deep-frying thermometer in the chicken as you fry to make sure the oil temperature remains between 250° and 300°F.

1 whole chicken (about 3 1/2 pounds), cut into 10 pieces
1 quart buttermilk
2 tablespoons Tabasco or other hot sauce
2 cups all-purpose flour
Salt and pepper, to taste
2 large eggs
1 teaspoon baking powder
1/2 teaspoon baking soda
Vegetable oil or shortening

1. Rinse chicken. In a large bowl or resealable plastic bag, combine buttermilk and Tabasco. Add chicken pieces, turn to coat. Refrigerate, covered, for at least 8 hours and up to 16, turning the pieces occasionally. Remove chicken from buttermilk; shake off excess. Arrange in a single layer on large wire rack set over rimmed baking sheet. Refrigerate, uncovered, for 2 hours.

2. Measure flour into large shallow dish; whisk in some salt and pepper. In a medium bowl, beat eggs, baking powder and baking soda. Working in batches of 3, drop chicken pieces in flour and shake dish to coat. Shake excess flour from each piece. Using tongs, dip chicken pieces into egg mixture, turning to coat well and allowing excess to drip off. Return chicken pieces to flour; coat again, shake off excess and set on wire rack.

3. Preheat oven to 200°F. Set oven rack to middle position. Set another wire rack over a rimmed baking sheet, and place in oven. Line a large plate with paper towels. Pour

oil about 1/2 inch up the side of a large, heavy skillet. Place skillet over high heat; let pan warm until oil shimmers.

4. Place half of chicken, skin-side down, in hot oil. Reduce heat to medium and fry 8 minutes, until deep golden brown. Turn chicken pieces; cook an additional eight minutes, turning to fry evenly on all sides. Using tongs, transfer chicken to paper towel–lined plate. After draining, transfer chicken to wire rack in oven. Fry remaining chicken, transferring pieces to paper towel–lined plate to drain, then to wire rack in oven to keep warm.

Serves 4 to 6.

Ten

MAY YOU LIVE ALL THE DAYS OF YOUR LIFE.

—MRS. MIRACLE

Emily Merkle smiled to herself. This latest assignment was going well. She enjoyed the ones that took place during the Christmas season most of all. She hadn't expected the romance between Jake and Holly to develop quite this quickly, so that was a bonus. Those two were very good together— and good for each other.

She attached her name badge to her sweater and hung her purse in the employee locker, then headed up to the toy department. She'd grown fond of Jake Finley. He was a kind-hearted young man, a bit reserved, to be sure, but willing to take a risk he believed in. The robots were one example of that, his pursuit of Holly another.

Walking toward the elevator, she saw J. R. Finley, who'd just come into the hallway. He stopped, and his eyes automatically went to her badge.

"Mrs. Miracle," he said thoughtfully. He seemed to be mulling over where he'd heard it before.

"Mr. Finley," she said in the same thoughtful tone.

"To the best of my recollection, we don't have an employee here at Finley's named Miracle."

Emily was about to identify herself, but before she could, J.R. continued.

"I pride myself on knowing the name of every employee at the Thirty-Fourth Street Finley's. Including seasonal staff." He narrowed his eyes. "Just a minute. I remember my son mentioning you earlier."

"The name is Merkle," Emily told him. "Emily Merkle."

Finley shook his head. "Can't say I'm familiar with that name, either."

"If you check with HR, I'm sure—"

"You're working with my son in the toy department, aren't you?" he said abruptly.

Emily frowned. "Are you always this rude, or are you making an exception in my case?"

He blinked twice.

He was used to everyone kowtowing to him. Well, *she* wouldn't do it.

"I beg your pardon?"

Emily met his look boldly. "I was saying something, young man."

J.R.'s head reared back and he released a howl of laughter. "*Young* man? My dear woman, it's been a long time since anyone referred to me as young."

Compared to her, he was practically in diapers. "That's beside the point."

He seemed confused.

"As I was saying," Emily continued politely, "if you care to check with HR, you'll find that I was hired last week as seasonal help."

"Only last week?" J.R. smiled at her. "That explains it, then."

"It does, indeed." She started down the hallway and was surprised when J.R. kept pace with her.

"You *are* working with my son, correct?"

"Yes. The toy department is extremely busy this time of year, as you well know." She glanced pointedly at her watch, wanting him to realize she should be on the floor that very moment.

"My son made a huge error in judgment by ordering five hundred of those expensive robots."

She was puzzled by his willingness to discuss business—and family—matters with a short-term employee. But she couldn't let his comment go unchallenged. "You think so, do you?" she asked mildly.

He gave her a startled look, as if no one had dared question his opinion before. "I know so," he insisted.

Emily was curious as to why he felt Jake was wrong and he was right. "Please tell me why you're so convinced your son's about to fail."

"Good grief, woman—"

"Call me Mrs. Miracle."

"Fine, Mrs. Miracle. Do you realize exactly how many of these… Intellytromps he needs to sell by Christmas? That's less than two weeks from now. It'll never happen."

"They're Intelly*trons*."

"Tromps, trons, whatever. They won't sell. Mark my words. It would take a miracle." He grinned broadly, obviously thinking himself very clever.

"You called?" she said, and laughed.

J.R. apparently didn't like the fact that she'd responded to his joke with one of her own. Instead of laughing, he scowled.

"Never mind," she said with a sigh. "I just wish you had more faith in your son."

He quickly took offense. "My son is my concern."

"He *is* your concern," she agreed. "And your future. So it's time you trusted his judgment."

She'd really ruffled his feathers now. He grew red in the face and puffed up like an angry rooster, his chest expanding. "Now listen here. I won't have an employee talking to me as if I'm some messenger boy."

Emily stood her ground. "Someone needs to tell you the truth and it might as well be me."

"Is that so?"

He sounded like a third-grader exchanging insults on the playground.

"You need to give your son a bit of leeway to make his own mistakes instead of second-guessing all his decisions."

He opened and closed his mouth as if he couldn't speak fast enough to say what was on his mind. He thrust out one hand. "Your badge."

So he intended to fire her. "You don't want to do that," she told him calmly.

"I will not have an insubordinate employee working in my store!"

"I'm temporary help," she reminded him. "I'll be gone soon enough."

"I expect you gone *today*."

"Sorry, I'm afraid that would be impossible. You'll need to reconsider."

Once again he couldn't seem to speak. "Are...are you refusing to leave the premises?" he finally managed to sputter.

"Jacob Robert, settle down. You've always had a problem with your temper, haven't you? Now, take a deep breath and listen to me. You do not want to fire me this close to Christmas."

"Are you threatening me?" he growled. "And how do you know my middle name?"

"Not in the least," she said, answering his first question and ignoring his second.

"I'm calling Security and having you escorted from the building. Your check will be mailed to you."

"Security?" The image of two beefy security guards lifting her by the arms and marching her outside was so comical it made Emily laugh.

That seemed to infuriate him even more. "Do you find this humorous?"

"Frankly, yes." She wouldn't lie; the man was insufferable. Oh, heavens, she did have her work cut out for her. "Now, if you'll excuse me, your son needs my help."

His jaw sagged as she scurried past him and walked quickly to the elevator.

As she suspected, the toy department was in chaos. Poor Jake was run ragged—thanks, in part, to his father, who'd taken too much pleasure in making her late for her shift. That man was about to meet his match. Emily Merkle was not going to let one overstuffed, pigheaded man stand in the way of her mission.

She'd been on the floor for thirty minutes or so when J.R. unexpectedly showed up. When he saw how busy the department was, he did a double take.

"Don't stand there gawking," Emily said as she marched past him, leading a customer to the cash register. Brenda and Karen, also on duty, were bustling around, answering questions, ringing up sales, demonstrating toys.

He stared at her blankly.

"Help," she told him. "We could use an extra pair of hands, in case you hadn't noticed."

"Ah…" He froze, as if he didn't know where to start.

"That couple over there," Emily said, pointing in the direction of the board games. "They have a three-year-old and a six-year-old and they're looking for suggestions. Give them a few."

"Ah…"

"Don't just stand there with your mouth hanging open," she ordered. "Get to work!"

To his credit, J.R. rolled up his sleeves and dug in. J. R. Finley might know the name of every employee in his store—with minor exceptions, of course—but he was in way over his head when it came to recommending board games. To *her* credit, Emily kept her mouth shut.

At four o'clock there was a slight lull. "Dad," Jake greeted his father. "What brings you down here?"

J.R. squinted at Emily but didn't answer.

"Whatever it was, I'm grateful." He turned to Emily. "How many Intellytrons did we sell this afternoon?"

"Sixteen."

"Fabulous!" Jake couldn't conceal his excitement.

His father, however, looked as though he needed to sit down, put up his feet and have a cup of hot tea. In Emily's view, it would do the man good to work the floor once in a while. He might actually learn something that way.

"I came to talk to you about this woman." J.R. stabbed a menacing finger at Emily.

"Ah, you mean Mrs. Miracle," Jake said fondly. "She's a wonder, isn't she?"

"She's a nuisance," J.R. snapped. "I want her fired."

Jake laughed, which was clearly the opposite reaction of what his father expected.

"This is not a joke."

"Yes, it is," Jake insisted. "Didn't you see what a madhouse this place was? It's like that every day now. I can't afford to lose Mrs. Miracle."

Emily sauntered over to J.R.'s side and whispered saucily, "Told you so."

He shook his finger. "I don't care if I have to work this department on my own," he yelled, "I will not tolerate insubordination."

"Excuse me, Dad, I've got another customer."

"I do, too," Emily said. "But you can keep standing there for a while. You make a nice fixture."

A kid of about five stepped in front of J.R. and stared up at him. "Is that a trick, mister?"

J.R. lowered his arms. "What, son?"

The boy was completely enthralled. "The way you get your cheeks to puff out like that."

Difficult though it was, Emily managed not to laugh. The boy was quite observant. J.R. had the puffing of cheeks down to an art form.

Jake finished with his customer and hurried back to his father. "Dad, I am *not* firing Mrs. Miracle."

"No, you're not. I am," J.R. said. "It will give me great pleasure to make sure she never works in this store again."

"What did she do that was so terrible?" Jake demanded.

"She insulted me and meddled in my personal affairs," his father burst out.

"How?" Jake asked, calm and collected. He was the perfect contrast to his father, who waved both arms wildly and spoke loudly enough to attract attention from every corner of the third floor.

When J.R. didn't answer, Jake shrugged and said, "Sorry, Dad, I need her."

Emily smiled ever so sweetly.

"She's out of here," J.R. roared, making a chopping motion with his arm. She thought he resembled an umpire signaling a strikeout.

Jake shook his head. "She's our best sales associate by a mile, so if she goes, we might as well close down the entire department. You wouldn't want that, would you, Dad?"

J.R. hesitated.

"And if we close the department, you won't have a chance to prove how wrong I was by ordering five hundred Intellytrons," he said, as if that should be sufficient inducement to keep her on staff.

Emily suspected J.R. wanted Jake to fall flat on his face over this robot. He'd pay a high price for being right—and, as a matter of fact, he was dead wrong. She'd seen for herself how popular the toy was. She'd hoped it would be and had done her best to sell it. However, after the past twenty-four hours, she didn't need to try very hard; the toy sold itself. Apparently, its sudden popularity had begun like so many trends, on the West Coast. Now, the moment someone heard that Finley's still had robots in stock, they dashed over. Then they couldn't whip out their credit cards fast enough.

"I'd better stay," Emily murmured to Jake. "As much as I'd like to walk away right now, I wouldn't give your father the satisfaction."

J.R. stomped his foot.

"Are you having a temper tantrum?" she asked sweetly.

Jake only laughed. "Dad, I think it might be best if you went back to your office now. Or you could go home."

"This is *my* store and I'll stay anywhere I darn well please."

Jake leaned closer to his father and whispered, "You're scaring off my customers."

"Oh, sorry."

"We want customers, don't we, Dad? Isn't that the whole idea?"

"Don't get smart with me," J.R. muttered.

"Yes, Dad." Jake winked at Emily, who winked back.

J.R. must have caught sight of what they were doing. "What's that about?"

"What?" Emily asked, again the picture of politeness.

"What?" Jake echoed.

Seeing that he'd forfeited even the pretense of control, J.R. sighed. "Forget it."

"I can stay on, then?" Emily asked the store owner.

"Why ask me? I seem to have lost complete control of this company to a man I no longer recognize—my son." With that he marched toward the elevator that would deliver him to his private office on the fourteenth floor.

Eleven

PEOPLE ARE FUNNY. THEY WANT THE FRONT OF THE BUS,
THE MIDDLE OF THE ROAD AND THE BACK OF THE CHURCH.

—MRS. MIRACLE

Holly knew she couldn't postpone calling Bill Carter, since the boys wanted to get together two days from now. It would be petty to allow her awkward relationship with Bill to stand in the way of her nephew being friends with his son.

The problem was how to approach him. She waited until Gabe was in bed on Wednesday night. Then she drew in a deep breath and looked up Bill's home number, which she'd made a point of erasing from her mind—and her phone. She hated feeling nervous about this. It was a courtesy call and nothing more.

Bill picked up on the fourth ring, when she was about to hang up, almost relieved he hadn't answered. Then all of a sudden, she heard, "Hello."

"Bill, it's Holly."

"Do you realize what time it is?"

"Uh, yes… It's nine-thirty. Am I calling too late?"

He didn't respond immediately. "I know why you're call-ing and I—"

"You do?" So all this angst had been for nothing. She should've noticed earlier how silly she was being, how badly she'd overreacted.

"It's about Tiffany, isn't it?"

"No...who's Tiffany?"

"You mean you *don't* know?"

Obviously she didn't. "Sorry, I think we're talking at cross-purposes here. I don't know any Tiffany—well, other than the one I met through work. I'm calling about Billy."

"My son?"

He sounded both relieved and worried, which confused Holly. "Listen, can we start over?" she asked.

"It's too late for that."

Just how obtuse *was* the man? "I don't mean our relationship, Bill. I was referring to our conversation."

"Just tell me why you called," he said, with more than a hint of impatience.

"I'm trying to, but you keep interrupting me. This isn't an easy phone call for me and your attitude's not helping." If Bill was a decent human being, he should understand this was difficult and appreciate the courage it had taken her to contact him. The fact that he didn't angered her. "No wonder the two of us aren't dating anymore," she muttered.

"Okay, fine. But what's that got to do with my son?"

She sighed loudly. "Since you haven't worked it out for yourself, I'll tell you. Billy and Gabe have become friends."

"Yeah? So what?"

"Well, I—" Before she could answer his rudely phrased question, he broke in.

"Wait a minute," he said suspiciously. "How do you know my son's friends with this kid?"

The way he said it practically implied that Holly had been

stalking his son. "That's the most ridiculous question I've ever heard! I know because Gabe's my nephew."

"So?"

"So Billy wants Gabe to come home with him after school on Friday."

"Fine. And this concerns you how?"

"I thought I should tell you we're related."

"That still doesn't explain why you're calling. Shouldn't Gabe's parents clear this with me? Not you."

Holly gritted her teeth at his offensive tone. What she'd ever seen in this man was completely lost on her now. At the moment, she was grateful he'd broken it off.

"I have custody of Gabe," she said calmly. She didn't feel like describing how that had come about; it was none of his business—and besides, she wanted to keep the conversation as short as possible.

"*You* have custody?"

The question grated on her nerves. "Yes, *me,* and it's working out very nicely, I might add."

"Ah…" Bill apparently hadn't figured out yet how to react.

Holly had no intention of allowing him to make any more derogatory comments about her mothering skills. She launched right into her question, not giving him a chance to say much of anything. "Is it still okay if Gabe comes to your house after school?"

"Uh, sure."

"Do you have the same housekeeper looking after Billy as before?"

The suspicious voice was back. "Why do you ask?"

"Because I don't want Gabe visiting Billy if there isn't any adult supervision." The after-school program only went until five-thirty, and Bill was often home much later than that, which meant the part-time housekeeper picked the boy up and then stayed at the apartment to supervise him.

"Oh, yeah, Mrs. Henry still looks after Billy from five-thirty to seven, except for the nights I have social engagements. Then she stays until I get home."

He seemed to delight in letting her know—in what he probably thought was a subtle fashion—that he'd started dating again. Well, she had social engagements, too, even if they mostly involved going out with friends, but was mature enough not to mention it. Let him think what he liked.

Holly waited a moment, hoping he'd realize how juvenile his reaction had been. "Talking civilly isn't so hard, is it?" she asked.

"No," he agreed.

"Great. Now that's settled, what time would you like me to pick Gabe up?"

"You'll pick him up?"

"Would you rather bring him back to my apartment?" That certainly made it easier for her. Maybe he didn't want Holly showing up at his house, but if so, she didn't care enough to be offended.

"I can do that," he said.

"Fine."

"Fine," he echoed.

"What time should I expect you?"

"Seven-thirty, I guess."

"I'll be here."

She was about to disconnect when Bill's soft chuckle caught her off guard. "So Gabe's your nephew, huh?"

"I already told you that."

"You did. His last name's Larson?"

"Yes, Gabe Larson." She didn't see the humor in this. "I

apologize for calling so late, but I thought it would be best if you and I talked when Gabe was in bed."

"Did you think I'd refuse to let the two boys be friends?"

"I wasn't sure. Our last conversation wasn't very pleasant and, well, it seemed better to ask."

"I'm glad you did."

She was glad to hear that because he sure hadn't acted like it.

Holly met Jake for lunch on Thursday. He'd called her at the office that morning and suggested a nearby restaurant; thankfully he'd insisted on buying. She might've sounded a bit too eager to accept, because she was sick of making do with leftovers. By cutting back, packing lunches and not spending a penny more than necessary Holly had managed to save seventy-five dollars toward the robot. According to her calculations, she'd have the funds to make the purchase but it would be close. Every cent counted.

Jake had arrived at the restaurant before her and secured a booth. "Hi," he said with a smile when she slid in across from him.

"Hi. This is nice. Thanks so much." She reached for the menu and quickly scanned the day's specials. She was so hungry, Jake would be fortunate if she could limit her selection to one entrée. As it was, she ordered a cup of wild-mushroom soup, half a turkey sandwich with salad and a slice of apple pie à la mode for dessert.

Jake didn't seem to mind.

"That was delicious," she said as she sat back half an hour later and pressed her hands over her stomach. "I probably ate twice as much as any other woman you've ever gone out with."

"It's a relief to be with someone who isn't constantly worried about her weight."

"I do watch my calories but I've been doing without break-fast, and lunches have been pretty skimpy and—"

"No breakfast?"

"That's not entirely accurate. I have breakfast, sort of. Just not much."

"And the reason is?"

Holly wished she'd kept her mouth shut. She pretended not to hear his question and glanced at her watch instead. "Oh, it's almost one. I should get back to work."

"Holly." Jake wasn't easily distracted. "Answer the question."

Her shoulders sagged. "I really do need to go."

"You're going without breakfast to save money for the robot, aren't you?"

"Sorry, I have to run." She slid out of the booth and grabbed her coat and purse. "Oh, before I forget. Gabe wanted me to invite you to come and watch us decorate our Christmas tree tomorrow night, if you can. He'll be at a friend's place and won't get home until seven-thirty."

He hesitated, and Holly knew why. "I won't be able to leave the store until at least nine," he said.

"I let Gabe stay up until ten on Friday and Saturday nights."

He hesitated again. Holly hadn't forgotten his reaction when Gabe had first mentioned decorating for Christmas. She knew that, like his father, he ignored the holiday—apart from being surrounded by all that bright and shiny yuletide evidence at the store. Perhaps it was selfish of her, but she wanted to show him the joy of Christmas, prove that not all his Christmas memories were bad. She was convinced there must be happy remembrances, too, and she hoped to revive those so he could let go of the past. Holly held her breath as she waited for his response.

Jake stared into the distance for what seemed like a long time before he said, "Okay, I'll come."

Her breath whooshed out in relief and she gave him her brightest, happiest smile. "Thank you, Jake." She finished putting on her coat, hoping he understood how much she appreciated his decision.

"Can we do this again?" he asked. "It's been crazy in the toy department. Mrs. Miracle insisted I take my lunch break early—and she said I should invite you. I need to get back to work, but I wanted to see you."

"I wanted to see you, too."

They left the restaurant together and went their separate ways. Holly's spirits were high. She'd cleared the air with Bill as much as possible, and Gabe had been excited to learn he'd be able to go to his friend's house on Friday.

When she returned to work, she found her boss on the phone, talking in her usual emphatic manner. Despite the fact that Holly wouldn't be receiving a Christmas bonus, she'd tried not to let that influence her job performance.

As soon as Lindy Lee saw her, she waved one arm to get her attention.

Holly stepped into her employer's office. "You're back late from lunch," Lindy said as she slammed down the phone.

"I have an hour lunch," Holly reminded her. She rarely took that long and often ate at her desk. Taking the full time allotted her was the exception rather than the rule.

"It's one-fifteen," Lindy Lee said pointedly, tapping her index finger against her wristwatch.

"And I left the office at twelve-thirty. Technically I still have fifteen minutes." Holly could see that she might have said more than necessary and decided it would be best to stop while she was ahead. "Is there something you need me to do?" she asked.

Frowning, Lindy handed her a thick file folder. "I need you to get these sketches over to Design."

"Right away." She took the folder and hurried out of the office, catching the elevator to the sixth floor. As she entered the design department she caught sight of one of the models regularly hired by the company. Tiffani White was tall, slim and elegant and she possessed about as perfect a body as one could hope to have. She was a favorite of Lindy Lee's and no wonder. The model showed Lindy's creations to their peak potential.

Tiffani saw Holly and blinked, as if she had trouble placing her, which was odd. They'd spent a fair amount of time together, since Holly had been backstage at several runway events with her.

"Lindy Lee asked me to deliver these sketches," she said to the head of the technical department. She turned to Tiffani.

"Hi, Tiff," she said casually.

"Hi." The model smiled—a smile that didn't quite reach her eyes.

Holly smiled back, but there was something strange going on. Tiffani had always been friendly. They'd even had coffee together now and then. Once, nearly a year ago when she'd been dating Bill, they'd run into Tiffani and—

Just a minute!

Thoughts and memories collided inside Holly's head. The conversation with Bill the night before played back in her mind. He'd made an unusual comment when they'd first spoken, mentioning the name Tiffany—or rather, Tiffani, with an *i*. The pieces were falling into place....

"Tiffani," Holly said. "I talked to Bill the other night."

"You did?"

"Yes, and your name came up."

The model brought one beautifully manicured hand to her mouth. "It did? Then you know?"

"Well, not everything."

"I wanted him to tell you before now, but Bill said it wasn't really any of your business. I told him that sometimes we see each other at work and it would make things better for me if you knew."

"So the two of you are...dating?"

"Actually we're...talking about marriage."

Marriage. Bill was planning to *marry* Tiffani? This didn't make sense. The model was about the least motherly woman Holly had ever met; she'd even told Holly she didn't like children. And she'd demonstrated it, too. They'd had a shoot earlier in the year with a couple of child models and Tiffani had been difficult and cranky all day. She'd made it clear that she didn't enjoy being around kids.

Holly wondered if Bill had any idea of the other woman's feelings. Probably not, she thought uncharitably. All he saw was Tiffani's perfect body and how good she looked on his arm.

In some ways, she had to concede, Bill and Tiffani were a good match. Bill had his own graphic design business and often hosted clients. Tiffani would do well entertaining, but Holly suspected she didn't have a lot to offer as a stepmother to Billy.

Yet that'd been the excuse Bill had used when he'd broken off *their* relationship.

That was exactly what it'd been. An excuse, and a convenient one. He'd wanted Holly out of his life and he didn't care how badly he hurt her to make that happen. Granted, the relationship would've ended anyway, but in the process of hastening its demise, he'd damaged her confidence—in herself and in her maternal instincts.

Bill Carter was a jerk, no question about it. Tiffani was welcome to him.

Twelve

"Can I go see Telly the robot after school?" Gabe asked as Holly walked him to school Monday morning.

"Not today," she said, stepping up her speed so she'd make it to work on time. The last thing she needed was to show up late. As it was, Gabe would get out of school at eleven-thirty this morning for winter break, and there was no after-school care today. Thankfully her neighbor Caroline Krantz had children of her own, including a son, Jonathan, who was Gabe's age, and Gabe enjoyed going there. Today, however, he obviously had a different agenda.

"But it's been so *long* since I saw him and I want—"

"I know. I'm sorry, Gabe. But Christmas will be here soon," she said, cutting him off.

"Do you think Santa's going to bring me my robot?"

"We won't find out until Christmas, will we?" she said, ushering him along. At the school, she bent down and kissed his cheek. "Remember, you're going to Mrs. Krantz's house with Jonathan after school."

"Yeah," he said, kicking at the sidewalk with the toe of his boot.

"Call me at the office when you get there, okay?"

"Okay."

Holly watched him walk into the building and then half ran to the subway station.

She was jostled by the crowd and once again had to stand, clutching the pole as she rode into the city. Her weekend had been everything she'd hoped for. Jake had stopped by on Friday night, arriving later than expected. She'd assembled the small artificial tree, which she'd bought years before; she would've preferred a real one but didn't want to spend the money this year. Then she'd draped it with lights, and she and Gabe had carefully arranged the ornaments. They were almost done by the time Jake came over, and Gabe insisted that he place the angel on top of the tree. Holly wasn't sure how he'd react to that request. At first he'd hesitated until she explained it was an honor and that it meant a lot to Gabe. Then he reluctantly set the angel on the tree.

Maybe it wasn't up to her to change—or try to change—his feelings about Christmas, but she hoped to coax him by creating new memories and by reminding him of happy ones from his own childhood.

On Friday, after school and his playdate with Billy, Gabe had been exhausted by ten o'clock. Holly tucked him in, and then she and Jake had cuddled and kissed in front of the television. She couldn't remember what TV program they'd started to watch because they were soon more focused on each other than on the TV.

Thinking about Friday night with Jake made her tingle with excitement and anticipation. Bill could have his Tiffani.

Holly would rather be with Jake. Their relationship held such promise....

Unfortunately, Jake was so busy at the store on Saturday that a couple of quick phone calls had to suffice. On Sunday evening he came to the apartment, bringing a take-out pizza and a bottle of lovely, smooth merlot—the best wine she'd had in ages. Jake had been full of tales about the store, and especially how well Intellytron was now selling. Rumor had it that Finley's was the only place in Manhattan that had the robot available, and customers had flooded the store, many of them going straight from Santa's throne to the toy department. No one else had guessed that Intellytron would be one of the hottest retail trends of the season.

While Holly was thrilled for Jake, she was still concerned that there wouldn't be any left once she could afford to make the purchase. Jake had again assured her she didn't need to worry; he'd put one aside for Gabe. It was safely hidden away in the back of the storeroom, with a note that said it wasn't to be sold.

Holly dashed into the office just in time. She saw Lindy Lee glance at her watch but Holly knew she had three minutes to spare. While Lindy Lee might not appreciate her new work habits, she was well within the bounds of what was required. Before Gabe's advent into her life, she'd often arrived early and stayed late. That wasn't possible now, and she was paying the price for her earlier generosity, which Lindy Lee had quickly taken for granted. Still, she enjoyed her job and believed she was a credit to her employer, even if Lindy didn't agree.

"Good morning," she said to her boss, sounding more cheerful than she felt. Holly was determined not to allow Lindy Lee's attitude to affect her day.

At noon, Holly began to check her watch every few minutes. She kept her cell phone on her desk, ready to receive Gabe's call. He should be phoning any time now; school was out, and he'd be going home with Jonathan. At twelve-thirty Holly started to worry. Gabe should be at the Krantzes'. Why hadn't he called? She felt too anxious to eat the crackers and cheese she'd brought, too anxious to do anything productive. She'd give him until one-fifteen and then she'd call.

At one-thirteen, her cell phone chirped, and she recognized the Krantzes' number. Holly heaved a grateful sigh. "Hello," she said.

"Holly?" It was Caroline.

"Oh, hi. Did everything go as scheduled? Did Gabe and Jonathan walk home from school together?"

"Well, that's the reason I'm phoning. Gabe didn't come home with Jonathan."

A chill raced down her spine. "What do you mean?"

"He told Jonathan there was something he needed to do first, so Jonathan came home by himself. I... I feel really bad about this."

"Where is he?" Holly asked, struggling not to panic.

"That's just it. I don't know."

There was a huge knot in Holly's chest, and she found it difficult to breathe. How could she tell her brother that Gabe had gone missing?

Panicked thoughts surged through her mind. He'd been abducted, kidnapped, held for ransom. Or even worse, simply taken, never to be seen or heard from again.

"I'll call you if I hear anything," Caroline told her. "I'd go look myself but I can't leave the children. If he's not here in an hour, we'll reassess, call the police. In the meantime, I'll phone some of the other kids' parents."

"Yes… Thank you." Holly disconnected the line, her cell phone clenched in her fist.

"Holly?" Lindy Lee asked, staring at her. "What's wrong?"

Holly didn't realize she'd bolted to her feet. She felt herself swaying and wondered if she was going to faint. "My—my nephew's missing."

"Missing," Lindy Lee repeated. "What do you mean, missing?"

"He didn't show up at the sitter's house after school."

Lindy Lee looked at her watch. "It's a bit early for him to be out of school, isn't it?"

"No, not today," she said, panic making her sound curt. She was torn by indecision. Her first inclination was to contact the police immediately, not to wait another hour as Caroline had suggested. They should start a neighborhood search. Ask questions.

She wondered crazily if she should get his picture to the authorities so they could place it on milk cartons all across America.

Her cell phone chirped again and she nearly dropped it in her rush to answer.

"Yes?" she blurted out.

"Holly, it's Jake."

"I don't have time to talk now. Gabe's missing and we've got to contact the police and get a search organized and—"

"Gabe's with me," Jake interrupted.

She sank into her chair, weak with relief. "He's with you?"

"Yes. He came into the city."

"On his own?" This was unbelievable!

"Yup."

"You mean to say he walked from school to the subway station, took the train and then walked to Finley's by *himself*?" It seemed almost impossible to comprehend. She held her head in one hand and leaned back in her chair, eyes closed. She remembered what he'd said that morning, about wanting to see the robot, but she'd had no idea he'd actually try to do it.

"Would you like to talk to him?" Jake was asking.

"Please."

"Aunt Holly?" Gabe's voice was small and meek.

"So," she said, releasing a long sigh. Although the urge to lambaste him was nearly overwhelming, she resisted. "You didn't walk home with Jonathan the way you were supposed to?"

"No."

"Can you tell me why?"

"Because…"

"Because *what?*"

"I wanted to see Intellytron again and you said we couldn't and I thought, well, I know you have to work and everything, but I could come by myself, so I did. I remembered to take the green line and then I walked from the subway station." Despite the fact that he was obviously in trouble, there was a hint of pride in his voice.

Gabe had traveled into the city on his own just to see his favorite toy. The possibility hadn't even occurred to her. Holly suppressed the urge to break into sobs.

"I'm coming to get you right this minute," she declared. "Stay with Jake and Mrs. Miracle, and I'll be there as soon as I can. Now put Jake back on the phone."

His voice, strong and clear, came through a moment later. "Holly, it's Jake."

"I'm on my way."

"He'll be fine until you get here," he said.

"Thank you, thank you so much." This time, the urge to weep nearly overcame her.

"Everything's fine. Relax."

"I'm trying." She closed her cell, then looked up to see her boss standing in front of her desk.

"I take it you've located the little scoundrel?"

Holly nodded. "He came into the city on his own. Would it be okay if I brought him to the office for the rest of the day?" Taking him back to Brooklyn would be time-consuming and Lindy Lee would no doubt dock her pay. Holly needed every penny of her next paycheck. "I promise he won't make a sound."

Lindy Lee considered the request, then slowly nodded. "I enjoyed meeting Gabe that Saturday.... I wouldn't mind seeing him again."

Lindy Lee wanted to see Gabe again? *This* was an interesting development, as well as an unexpected one. Her employer wasn't the motherly type—to put it mildly. Lindy Lee was all about Lindy Lee.

Grabbing her coat and purse, Holly rushed over to Finley's, calling Caroline Krantz en route. The store was crowded, and by the time she reached the third floor Holly felt as though she'd run a marathon. She saw Mrs. Miracle first, and the woman's eyes brightened the instant she noticed Holly.

"You don't have a thing to worry about, my dear. Gabe is perfectly safe with Jake."

"Aunt Holly!" Gabe raced to her side and Jake followed.

"You're in a lot of trouble, young man," she said sternly, hands on her hips.

Gabe hung his head. "I'm sorry," he whispered, his voice so low she could hardly hear it.

Customers thronged the toy department, several of them

carrying the boxes that held the SuperRobot. A line had already formed at the customer service desk, and she noted that a couple of extra sales associates were out on the floor today. Everyone was busy.

"You'll have to come back to the office with me," Holly told Gabe. "I'm warning you it won't be nearly as much fun as it would've been with Jonathan and his mother."

"I know," he muttered. "Am I grounded?"

"We'll discuss that once we're home."

"Okay, but nothing happened...."

"You mean nothing other than the fact that you nearly gave me a heart attack."

Jake murmured a quick goodbye and started to leave to help a customer but Mrs. Miracle stopped him. "I'll take care of them," she said. "Besides, I believe there was something you wanted to ask Holly?"

"There was?" He looked surprised, wrinkling his brow as if he couldn't recall any such question.

"The Christmas party," Mrs. Miracle said under her breath. "You mentioned asking Holly to go with you."

Jake's mouth sagged open. "I'd thought about it, but I didn't realize I'd said it out loud." Now, instead of looking surprised, he seemed confused. "My father and I usually just make a token appearance."

"This year is different," the older woman insisted. "You need to be there for your staff. After all, the toy department's the busiest of the whole store at Christmastime. And," she continued sagely, "I predict record sales this year. Your staff needs to know you appreciate them."

"But..."

"I can't go," Holly said, resolving the issue. "There's no one to watch Gabe."

"Oh, but there is, my dear," Mrs. Miracle told her.

Holly frowned. Finding someone to stay with Gabe had always been a problem. She didn't want to impose on Caroline any more than she already did, especially since her neighbor wouldn't take any payment. With Jake they'd managed to work around it, which was easy enough, since Jake had mostly come to her apartment.

"I'll be more than happy to stay with Gabe while the two of you attend the party," Mrs. Miracle said.

It was generous of her to offer, but Holly couldn't accept. She shook her head. "You should be at the party yourself, Mrs. Miracle."

"Oh, heavens, no. After a full day on my feet I'll look forward to sitting in that comfy blue chair of yours. The one your parents gave you."

Before she could question how Mrs. Miracle knew about her chair, Jake asked, "Would you like to go to the party with me?" His eyes met hers, and she found herself nodding.

"Yes," she whispered. "When is it?"

"Wednesday night, after the store closes."

"Wednesday," she repeated.

"I'll pick you up at nine-thirty. I know that's late but—"

"I'll be ready."

"I'll come over a bit earlier," Mrs. Miracle added. "The two of you will have a *lovely* evening." She spoke with the utmost confidence, as if no other outcome was possible.

Holly and Gabe left a few minutes later, and Jake walked them to the elevator. "I'll see you Wednesday," he said as he pressed the button.

"Listen, Jake, you don't need to do this. I mean, it's fairly obvious you didn't intend to ask me and—"

"I'd really like it if you'd come to the party with me," he said, and she couldn't doubt his sincerity.

"Then I will," she murmured. "I'll look forward to it."

In the elevator, Holly remembered Mrs. Miracle's comment. The woman had never been to her apartment and yet somehow she knew about the chair her parents had given her. Furthermore, she seemed to know her address, too.

Oh, well. Gabe had probably told her. He obviously felt comfortable with the older woman and for that Holly could only be grateful.

Thirteen

On Wednesday at nine-fifteen, Emily stood at Holly's
door, her large purse draped over one arm and her knitting bag in the other hand. Holly answered, smiling in welcome. She absolutely sparkled. In her fancy black dress and
high heels, her hair gathered up and held in place with a jew-
eled comb, she looked stunning.

"Mrs. Miracle, I can't thank you enough." Holly stepped
aside so Emily could enter the apartment. "Tonight wouldn't
be possible if not for you."

"The pleasure's all mine," she said. She put down her bags,
then unwrapped the knitted scarf from around her neck and
removed her heavy wool coat. Holly hung them in the hallway closet as Emily arranged her bags by the chair, prepared
to settle down for the evening. The toy department had kept
her busy all day and she was eager to get off her feet.

Holly followed her into the small living room. "I feel bad
that you won't be attending the party."

"Oh, no, my dear." Emily dismissed her concern. "I'm

not a party girl anymore." She chuckled at her own humor. "Besides, I intend to have a good visit here with my young friend Gabe."

"He's been pretty subdued since the episode on Monday. He's promised to be on his best behavior."

"Don't you worry. We'll have a grand time together." And they would.

"Hi, Mrs. Miracle."

She was surprised to see Jake standing on the other side of the room. He'd arrived early, she thought approvingly, and he looked quite debonair in his dark suit and red tie. She'd seen an improvement in his attitude toward Christmas, mostly due to Holly and Gabe. And she had it on excellent authority that it would improve even more before the actual holiday.

"Gabe's on the computer," Holly said, pointing at the alcove between the living room and kitchen. "He's had his dinner and he can stay up until ten tonight."

Gabe twisted around and waved.

Emily waved back. "I'll make sure he's in bed by ten."

Jake held Holly's coat and the young woman slipped her arms into the sleeves. "I appreciate your volunteering to watch Gabe," he said with a smile for Emily.

"As I told Holly, I'm delighted to do it." She walked over to where Gabe sat at the small desk and put her hand on his shoulder. "Now, you two go. Have fun."

Holly kissed the top of Gabe's head. "Be good."

"I will," the boy said without taking his eyes from the screen.

Holly and Jake left, and Emily had to grin as she glanced over Gabe's shoulder at the message he was emailing his father.

From: "Gabe Larson" <gabelarson@msm.com>
To: "Lieutenant Mickey Larson" <larsonmichael@goarmy.com>

Sent: December 22
Subject: Me and Aunt Holly

Hi, Dad,

I made Aunt Holly cry. Instead of going to Jonathan's house like I was supposed to, I went to see the robot. I was afraid the store would run out before
Santa got my Intellytron. Aunt Holly came and picked me up and when we
were outside she started to cry. When I asked her why she was crying she
said it was because she was happy I was safe.

Are you mad at me? I wish Aunt Holly had gotten mad instead of crying. I felt awful inside and got a tummy ache. She took me back to her office and made me sit quiet all afternoon. But that was okay because I knew
I didn't do the right thing. Her boss is real pretty. I don't think she's around
kids much because she talked to me like I was in kindergarten or something.
I think she's nice, though.

You said you had a gift coming for me for Christmas. It isn't here yet. I
know I was bad, so you don't have to send it if you don't want. I'm sorry I
made Aunt Holly cry.

Love,

Gabe

Emily sank down in the big comfortable chair, rested her
feet on the matching ottoman and took out her knitting. She
turned on the television and had just finished the first row
when Gabe joined her. He didn't say anything for a long time,
but Emily could see his mind working.

After a while he said, "My dad's going to be mad at me."

"It was brave of you to tell him you did something you
weren't supposed to," she murmured.

Gabe looked away. "I told him he doesn't need to send me
anything for Christmas. He said there was a special gift on
the way but it hasn't come. He probably won't send it now."

"Don't be so sure." She pulled on the skein of yarn as she continued knitting.

"What if Santa finds out what I did?" His face crumpled in a frown. "Do you think maybe he won't bring me the robot 'cause I went to Finley's by myself and I didn't tell anyone where I was going?"

"Well, now, that remains to be seen, doesn't it?"

Gabe climbed onto the sofa and rested his head against the arm. "I didn't think Aunt Holly would be so worried when I didn't go to Jonathan's house after school. She got all weird."

"Weird?"

"Yeah. When we were still at her office, all of a sudden she put her arms around my neck and hugged me really hard. Isn't that weird?"

Emily shrugged but didn't answer. "Are you ready for Christmas?" she asked instead.

Gabe nodded. "I made Aunt Holly an origami purse. A Japanese lady came to my school and showed us how to fold them. She said they were purses, but it looks more like a wallet to me, all flat and skinny." He sighed dejectedly. "I wrapped it up but you can't really see where the wrapping stops and the gift starts."

"I bet Holly will really like the purse because you made it yourself," Emily said with an encouraging smile.

"I made my dad a gift, too. But Aunt Holly and I mailed off his Christmas present a long time ago. They take days and days to get to Afghanistan so we had to go shopping before Thanksgiving and wrap up stuff for my dad. Oh, we mailed him the picture of me and Santa, too. And I made him a key ring. And I sent him nuts. My dad likes cashews. I've never seen a cashew in the shell, have you?"

"Why, yes, as a matter of fact I have," she said conversationally.

Gabe sat up. "What do they look like?"

"Well, a cashew is a rather unusual nut. My goodness, God was so creative with that one. Did you know the cashew is both a fruit *and* a nut?"

"It is?"

"The fruit part looks like a small apple and it has a big stem."

The boy's eyes were wide with curiosity.

"The stem part is the nut, the cashew," she explained.

"Wow."

"And they're delicious," she said. "Good for you, too," she couldn't resist adding.

"What are you doing for Christmas?" Gabe asked.

"I've been invited to a party, a big one with lots of celebrating. I'll be with my friends Shirley, Goodness—"

"Goodness? That's a funny name."

"Yes, you're right. Anyway, the party preparations have already begun. It won't be long now."

"Oh." Gabe looked disappointed.

"Why the sad face?"

"I was going to ask you to come here for Christmas."

Emily was touched by his invitation. "I know you'll have a wonderful Christmas with Holly," she said.

"I invited Aunt Holly's boss, too."

She had to make an effort to hide her smile. This was all working out very nicely. Very nicely, indeed.

"Lindy didn't say she'd come for sure but she might." He paused. "She said to call her Lindy, not Ms. Lee like Aunt Holly said I should."

"Well, I hope she comes."

"Me, too. I think she's lonely."

"So do I," Emily agreed. The boy was very perceptive for his age, she thought.

"I asked her what she wants for Christmas and she said she didn't know. Can you *believe* that?"

In Emily's experience, many people walked through life completely unaware of what they wanted—or needed. "I brought along a book," she said, changing the subject. "Would you like to read it to me?" She'd put the children's book with its worn cover on the arm of her chair.

Gabe considered this. "I'm not in school now. Can you read it to me?"

"The way your dad used to when you were little?" she asked.

Gabe nodded eagerly. "I used to sit on his lap and he'd read me stories until I fell asleep." His face grew sad. "I miss my dad a lot."

"I know you do." Emily set aside her knitting. "Would you like to sit in my lap?"

"I'm too big for that," he insisted.

Emily could see that despite his words he was mulling it over. "You're not too big," she assured him.

Indecision showed on his face. Gabe wanted to snuggle with her, yet he hesitated because he was eight now and eight was too old for such things.

"What book did you bring?" he asked.

"It's a special one your grandma Larson once read to your dad and your aunt Holly."

"Really? How'd you know that?"

"Oh, I just do. It's the Christmas story."

"I like when the angels came to announce the birth of Baby Jesus to the shepherds."

She closed her eyes for a moment. "It was the most glorious night," she said. "The sky was bright and clear and—"

"And the angels sang," Gabe finished enthusiastically. "Angels have beautiful voices, don't they?"

"Yes, they do," Emily confirmed. "They make music we know nothing about here on earth… I'm sure," she added quickly. "Glorious, heavenly music."

"They do?" He cocked his head to one side.

"You'll hear it yourself one day, many years from now."

"What about you? When will you hear it?"

"Soon," she told him. He climbed into her lap and she held him close. He really was a sweet boy and would become a fine young man like his father. He'd be a wonderful brother to his half brother and half sister, as well—but she was getting ahead of herself.

"Tell me more about the angels," Gabe implored. "Is my mom an angel now?"

"No, sweetheart. Humans don't become angels. They're completely separate beings, although both were created by God."

"How come you know so much about angels?"

"I read my Bible," she said, and he seemed to accept her explanation.

"I never knew my mom," he said somberly. "Dad has pictures of her at the house. I look at her face and she smiles at me but I don't remember her."

"But you do understand that she loved you very much, right?"

"Dad said she did, and before she died she made him promise that he'd tell me every night how much she loved me."

"I know," she whispered.

"Do you think there are lots of angels in heaven?" Gabe asked.

"Oh, yes, and there are different kinds of angels, too."

"What kinds are there?"

"Well, they have a variety of different tasks. For instance,

Gabriel came to Mary as a messenger. Other angels are war-riors."

"When I get to heaven, I want to meet the warrior angels."

"And you shall."

"Do you think I was named after the angel Gabriel?" he asked.

Emily pressed her cheek against the top of his head, inhaling the clean, little-boy scent of his hair. "Now, that's something you'll need to ask your father when you see him."

"Okay, I will."

"Gabriel had one of the most important tasks ever assigned," Emily said. "He's the angel God sent to tell Mary about Baby Jesus."

He yawned. "Can people see angels?"

Emily's mouth quivered with a smile she couldn't quite suppress. "Oh, yes, but most people don't recognize them."

Gabe lifted his head. "How come?"

"Not all angels show their wings," she said.

"They don't?"

"No, some angels look like ordinary people."

"How come?"

"Well, sometimes God sends angels to earth. But if people saw their wings, they'd get all excited and they'd miss the les-son God wanted to teach them. That's why angels are often disguised."

"Are they always disguised?"

"No, some are invisible. Other times they look like ordi-nary people."

"Do angels only come to teach people a lesson?"

"No, they come to help, too."

Gabe yawned again. "How do angels help?"

"Oh, in too many ways to count."

He thought about that for a while, his eyelids beginning to droop.

"Are you ready for me to read you the story?" Emily asked.

"Sure." He rested his head against her shoulder as she opened the book. She read for a few minutes before she noticed that Gabe had fallen asleep. And she hadn't even gotten to the good part.

Fourteen

The Christmas party was well under way by the time Holly and Jake arrived. When they entered the gala event, the entire room seemed to go still. Holly kept her arm in Jake's, self-conscious about being the center of attention.

"Why's everyone looking at us?" she whispered.

Jake patted her hand reassuringly. "My father and I usually show up toward the end of the party, say a few words and then leave. No one expected me this early."

He'd mentioned that before. Still, she hadn't realized his arrival would cause such a stir. Jake immediately began to walk through the room, shaking hands and introducing Holly. At first she tried to keep track of the names, but soon gave up. She was deeply impressed by Jake's familiarity with the staff.

"How do you remember all their names?" she asked when she had a chance.

"I've worked with them in each department," he explained.

"My father felt I needed to know the retail business from the mail room up."

"You started in the mail room?"

"I did, but don't for a minute consider the mail room unimportant. I made that mistake and quickly learned how vital it is."

"Your father is a wise man."

"He is," Jake said. "And a generous one, too. But he'd describe himself as *fair*. He's always recognized the value of hiring good people and keeping them happy. I believe it's why we've managed to hold on to the company despite several attempts to buy us out."

It went without saying that Jake intended to follow his father's tradition of treating employees with respect and compensating them generously.

Ninety minutes later Holly's head buzzed with names and faces. They sipped champagne and got supper from the buffet; the food was delicious. Numerous people commented happily on seeing Jake at the party.

His father appeared at about midnight and immediately sought out his son and Holly.

"So this is the young lady you've talked about," J. R. Finley said, slapping Jake jovially on the back.

"Dad, meet Holly Larson."

J.R. shook her hand. "I'm pleased to meet you, young lady. You've made a big impression on my son."

Holly glanced at Jake and smiled. "He's made a big impression on me."

J. R. Finley turned to his son. "When did you get here?"

"Before ten," Jake said.

His father frowned, then moved toward the microphone. As was apparently his practice, he gave a short talk, handed out dozens of awards and bonuses and promptly left.

The party wound down after J.R.'s speech. People started to leave, but almost every employee, singly and in groups, approached Jake to thank him for attending the party. Holly couldn't tell how their gratitude affected Jake, but it had a strong impact on her.

"They love you," she said when they went to collect their coats.

"They're family," Jake said simply.

She noticed that he didn't say Finley's employees were *like* family but that they *were* family. The difference was subtle but significant. J.R. had lost his wife and daughter and had turned to his friends and employees to fill the huge hole left by the loss of his loved ones. Jake had, too.

As they stepped outside, Holly was thrilled by the falling snow. "Jake, look!" She held out her hand to catch the soft flakes that floated down from the night sky. "It's just so beautiful!"

Jake wrapped his scarf more securely around his neck. "I can't believe you're so excited about a little snow."

"I love it…. It's so Christmassy."

He grinned and clasped her hand. "Do you want to go for a short walk?"

"I'd love to." It was cold, but even without boots or gloves or a hat, Holly felt warm, and more than that, *happy*.

"Where would you like to go?" Jake asked.

"Wherever you'd like to take me." Late though it was, she didn't want the night to end. Lindy Lee had never thrown a Christmas party for her staff. Maybe she'd talk to Lindy about planning one for next December; she could discuss the benefits—employee satisfaction and loyalty, which would lead to higher productivity. Those were the terms Lindy would respond to. Not appreciation or enjoyment or fun. Having worked with Lindy as long as she had, Holly suspected her employer wasn't a happy person. And she wasn't someone who cared about the pleasure of others.

"I thought this would be a miserable Christmas," Holly confessed, leaning close to Jake as they moved down the busy sidewalk. They weren't the only couple reveling in the falling snow.

"Why?" Jake asked. "Because of your brother?"

"Well, yes. It's also the first Christmas without my parents, and then Mickey got called up for Afghanistan so there's just Gabe and me."

"What changed?"

"A number of things, actually," she said. "Meeting you, of course."

"Thank you." He bent down and touched his lips to hers in the briefest of kisses.

"My attitude," she said. "I was worried that Gabe would resent living with me. For months we didn't really bond."

"You have now, though, haven't you?"

"Oh, yes. I didn't realize how much I loved him until he went missing the other day. I… I don't normally panic, but I did then."

Holly was still surprised by how accommodating her employer had been during and after that crisis. First Lindy Lee had allowed Gabe to come to the office and then she'd actually chatted with him. Holly didn't know what the two of them had talked about, but her employer had seemed almost pleasant afterward.

"Remember the other night when you and Gabe decorated your Christmas tree?" Jake asked.

"Of course."

"Gabe asked me about mine."

"Right." It'd been an awkward moment. Gabe had been full of questions. He couldn't understand why some people chose not to make Christmas part of their lives. No tree. No presents. No family dinner. The closest Jake and his father got to celebrating the holidays was their yearly sojourn to the Virgin Islands.

Holly knew this was his father's way of ignoring the holiday. Jake and J.R. left on Christmas Eve and didn't return until after New Year's.

She was sure they'd depart sooner if they could. The only reason they stayed in New York as long as they did was because of the business. The holiday season made their year financially. Without the last-quarter sales, many retailers would struggle to survive. Finley's Department Store was no different.

"You told Gabe you didn't put up a tree," Holly reminded him.

"I might've misled him."

"You have a tree?" After everything he'd said, that shocked her.

"You'll see." His stride was purposeful as they continued walking. She soon figured out where they were headed.

"I can't wait," she said with a laugh.

When they reached Rockefeller Center, they stood gazing up at the huge Christmas tree, bright with thousands of lights and gleaming decorations. Jake gestured toward it. "*That's* my Christmas tree," he said.

"Gabe's going to be jealous that I got to see it again—with you."

Music swirled all around them as Jake slipped his arm about her waist. "When I was young, I found it hard to give up the kind of Christmas I'd known when my mother and sister were alive. Dad refused to have anything to do with the holidays but I still wanted the tree and the gifts."

Holly hadn't fully grasped how difficult those years must've been for him.

"Dad said if I wanted a Christmas tree, I could pick one in the store and make it my own. Better yet, I could claim the one in Rockefeller Center and that's what I did."

Instinctively she knew Jake had never shared this information with anyone else.

"Well, you've got the biggest, most beautiful Christmas tree in the city," she said, leaning her head against his shoulder.

"I do," he murmured.

"Jake," she said carefully. "Would you consider having Christmas dinner with Gabe and me?"

He didn't answer, and she wondered if she'd crossed some invisible line by issuing the invitation. Nevertheless she had to ask.

"I know that would mean not joining your father when he leaves for the Caribbean, but you could fly out the next day, couldn't you?" Holly felt she needed to press the issue. If he was ever going to agree, it would be tonight, after he'd witnessed how much it meant to Finley's employees that he'd attended their party.

"I could fly out later," he said. "But then I'd be leaving my father alone on the saddest day of his life."

"I'd like to invite him, too."

Jake's smile was somber and poignant. "He'll never come, Holly. He hates anything to do with Christmas—outside of the business, anyway."

"Maybe so, but I'd still like to ask him." She wasn't sure why she couldn't simply drop this. It took audacity to invite two wealthy men to her small apartment, when their alternative was an elaborate meal in an exotic location.

She was embarrassed now. "I apologize, Jake. I don't know what made me think you'd want to give up the sunshine and warmth of a Caribbean island for dinner with me and Gabe."

"Don't say that! I want to be with you both."

"But you don't feel you can leave your father."

"That's true, but maybe it's time I started creating traditions of my own. I'd be honored to spend Christmas Day with the two of you," he said formally.

Holly felt tears spring to her eyes. "Thank you," she whispered.

She turned to face him. He smiled as she slid her hands up his chest and around his neck. Standing on the tips of her toes with a light snow falling down on them, she pressed her mouth to his.

Jake held her tight. Holly sensed that they'd crossed a barrier in their relationship and established a real commitment to each other.

"When I come, I'll bring the robot for Gabe and hide it under the tree so it'll be a real surprise."

"I'll give you the money on Friday—Christmas Eve."

Christmas Eve.

"Okay." She knew he'd rather not take it, but there was no question—she had every intention of paying.

Jake called his car service, and a limousine met them at Rockefeller Center fifteen minutes later. When he dropped her off at the apartment Mrs. Miracle was sound asleep, still in the blue chair. Jake helped her out to the car, then had the driver take her home. Holly was touched by his thoughtfulness.

Even after Jake had left, Holly had trouble falling asleep. Her mind whirled as she relived scenes and moments of what had been one of the most memorable evenings of her life. When the alarm woke her early Thursday morning, she couldn't get up and just dozed off again. She finally roused herself, horrified to discover that she was almost half an hour behind schedule.

She managed to drag herself out of bed, gulp down a cup of coffee and get Gabe up and dressed and over to the Krantzes'.

Filled with dread, Holly rushed to work. As she yanked off her coat, she heard her name being called. Breathless, she flew into Lindy Lee's office; as usual, Lindy looked pointedly at her watch.

Holly tried to apologize. "I'm sorry I'm late. I'll make up the twenty-five minutes, I promise."

Lindy Lee raised one eyebrow. "Make sure you do."

Holly stood waiting for the lecture that inevitably followed. To her astonishment, this time it didn't. "Thank you for understanding."

"See to it that this doesn't happen again," her employer said, dismissing Holly with a wave of her hand.

"It won't… I just couldn't seem to get moving this morning." Thinking she'd probably said too much already, she started to leave, then remembered her resolve to discuss a Christmas party with Lindy Lee.

Aware that Holly was lingering, Lindy Lee raised her head and frowned. "Was there something else?"

"Well, yes. Do you mind if I speak freely?"

"That depends on what you have to say." Lindy Lee held her pen poised over a sheet of paper.

"I was at the employees' party for Finley's Department Store last evening," she said, choosing her words carefully. "It was a wonderful event. The employees work together as a team and…and they feel such loyalty to the company. You could just tell. They feel valued, and I doubt there's anything they wouldn't do to help the company succeed."

"And your point is?" Lindy Lee said impatiently.

"My point is we all need to work as a team here, too, and it seemed to me that maybe we should have a Christmas party."

Lindy Lee leaned back in her chair and crossed her arms. "In a faltering economy, with flat sales and an uncertain future, you want me to throw a *Christmas party?*"

"It's…it's just an idea for next year," Holly said, and regretted making the suggestion. Still, she couldn't seem to stop. "The future is always uncertain, isn't it? And there'll always be ups and downs in the economy. But the one constant is the fact that as long as you're in business you'll have a staff, right? And you need them to be committed and—"

"I get it," Lindy Lee said dryly.

Holly waited.

And waited.

"Let me think about it," Lindy Lee finally mumbled.

She'd actually agreed to think about it. Now, this was progress—more progress than Holly had dared to expect.

Fifteen

THE BEST VITAMIN FOR A CHRISTIAN IS B1.

—MRS. MIRACLE

Jake Finley was in love. Logically, he knew, it was too soon to be so sure of his feelings, and yet he couldn't deny his heart. Love wasn't about logic. He'd been attracted to Holly from the moment he met her, but this was more than attraction. He felt…connected to Holly, absorbed in her. He thought about her constantly. Over the years he'd been in other relationships, but no woman had made him feel the way Holly did.

When he arrived at work Thursday morning, he went directly to his father's office. Dora Coffey seemed surprised to see him.

"Is my father in yet?" Jake asked her.

"Yes, he's been here for a couple of hours. You know your father—this store is his life."

"Does he have time to see me?" Jake asked next. "No meetings or conference calls?"

"He's free for a few minutes." She left her desk and announced Jake, who trailed behind her.

When Jake entered the office, his father stood. "Good

morning, son. What can I do for you?" He gestured for Jake to take a seat, which he did, and settled back in his own chair.

Jake leaned forward, unsure where to start. He should've worked out what he was going to say before coming up here.

"I suppose you want to gloat." J.R. chuckled. "You were right about that robot. Hardly anyone else forecast this trend. I turned on the TV this morning and there was a story on Telly the SuperRobot. Hottest toy of the season, they said. Who would've guessed it? Not me, that's for sure."

"Not Mike Scott, either," Jake added, although he didn't fault the buyer.

"True enough. And yet Mike was the first to admit he didn't see this coming."

So Scott had mentioned it to J.R. but not to him. Still, it must've taken real humility to acknowledge that he'd been wrong.

"I'm proud of you, son," J.R. continued. "You went with your gut and you were right to do it."

Jake wondered what would've happened if Finley's had been stuck with four hundred leftover robots. Fortunately, however, he wouldn't have to find out.

"I checked inventory this morning, and we have less than twenty of the robots in stock."

Jake didn't need to point out the benefits of being the only store in the tristate area with *any* robots in stock. Having a supply—even a rapidly dwindling supply—of the season's most popular toy brought more shoppers into the store and created customer loyalty.

"They're selling fast. The entire quantity will be gone before Christmas."

"Good. Good," his father said. He grinned as he tilted back in his high leather chair. "Oh, I enjoyed meeting your lady friend last night."

"Holly enjoyed meeting you."

"She's special, isn't she?"

Jake was astonished that his father had immediately discerned his feelings for Holly. "Yes, but... What makes you say that?" He had to ask why it had been so obvious to his father.

J.R. didn't respond for a moment. Finally he said, "I recognized it from the way you looked at her. The way you looked at each other."

Jake nodded but didn't speak.

"I remember when I met your mother." There was a faraway expression in his eyes. "I think I fell in love with Helene as soon as I saw her. She was the daughter of one of my competitors and so beautiful I had trouble getting out a complete sentence. It's a wonder she ever agreed to that first date." He smiled at the memory.

So rarely did his father discuss his mother and sister that Jake kept quiet, afraid that any questions would distract J.R. He craved details, but knew he had to be cautious.

"I loved your mother more than life itself. I still do."

"I know," Jake said softly.

"She wasn't just beautiful," he murmured, and the same faraway look stole over him. "She had a heart unlike anyone I've ever known. Everyone came to her when they needed something, whether it was a kind word, a job, some advice. She never turned anyone away." His face, so often tense, relaxed as he sighed. "I felt that my world ended the day your mother and Kaitlyn died. Since then you've been my only reason for going on."

"Well, I hope your grandchildren will be another good reason," Jake teased, hoping to lighten the moment.

J.R. gave a hearty laugh. "They certainly will. So... I was right about you and Holly."

"It's too early to say for sure," Jake hedged. Confident

though he was about his own feelings, he didn't want to speak for Holly. Not yet...

"But you *know*."

"It looks...promising."

Slapping the top of his desk, J.R. laughed again. "I thought so. I'm happy for you, Jake."

"Thanks, Dad." But he doubted J.R. would be as happy when he found out what that meant, at least as far as Christmas was concerned.

"Oh, before I forget," J.R. said with exquisite timing. "Dora's ordered the plane tickets for Christmas Eve. We leave JFK at seven and land in Saint John around—"

"Dad, I'll need to change my ticket," Jake said, interrupting his father.

That brought J.R. up short. "Change your ticket? Why?"

"I'll join you on the twenty-sixth," Jake explained. "Holly invited me to spend Christmas Day with her and her nephew."

J.R.'s frown was back as he mulled over that statement. "You're going to do it?"

"Yes. I told her I would."

J.R. stood and walked to the window, turning his back to Jake. "I don't know what to say."

"Holly invited you, too."

"You told her it was out of the question, didn't you?"

More or less. "You'd be welcome if you chose to come."

Slowly J.R. turned around. "Well," he said with a sigh, "I suppose it was unrealistic of me not to realize times are changing." He paused. "I look forward to our vacation every year."

Jake had never thought of their trip to the Caribbean as a getaway. His father always brought work with him and they spent their week discussing trends, reading reports and forecasting budgets. It was business, not relaxation.

"You call it a *vacation?*" Jake asked, amused.

"Well, yes. What would you call it?" J.R. frowned in confusion.

Jake hesitated, then decided to tell the truth, even if his father wasn't ready to hear it. "I call it an escape from reality—but not from work. A vacation is supposed to be fun, a break, a chance to do nothing or else do something completely out of the ordinary. Not sit in a hotel room and do exactly the same thing you'd be doing here."

J.R.'s frown deepened.

"Admit it, Dad," Jake said. "You don't go to the islands to lounge on the beach or snorkel or take sightseeing trips. Far from it. You escape New York because you can't bear to be here over Christmas."

J.R. shook his head.

Jake wasn't willing to let it go. "From the time Mom and Kaitlyn died, you've done everything possible to pretend there's no Christmas.

"As a businessman you need the holidays to survive financially but if it wasn't for that, you'd ban anything to do with Christmas from your life—and mine."

J.R. glared at Jake. "I believe you've said enough."

"You need to accept that Christmas had nothing to do with the accident. It happened, and it changed both our lives forever, but it was a fluke, a twist of fate. I wish with everything in me that Mom and Kaitlyn had stayed home that afternoon, but the fact is, they didn't. They went out, and because their cab collided with another one, they were killed."

"Enough!" J.R. shouted.

Jake stood. "I didn't mean to upset you, Dad."

"If that's the case, then you've failed. I *am* upset."

Jake regretted that; nevertheless, he felt this had to be said. "I'm tired of running away on Christmas Eve. You can do it if you want, but I'm through."

"Fine. Spend the day with Holly if you prefer. It's not going to bother me."

"I wish you'd reconsider and join us."

J.R. tightened his lips. "No, thanks. You might think I'm hiding my head in the sand, but the truth is, I enjoy the islands."

Jake might have believed him if J.R. had walked along the beach even once or taken any pleasure in their surroundings. Instead, he worked from early morning to late evening, burying himself in his work in a desperate effort to ignore the time of year—the anniversary of his loss.

"Yes, Dad," Jake said rather than allow their discussion to escalate into a full-scale argument.

"You'll come the next day, then?"

Jake nodded. He'd make his own flight arrangements. They always stayed at the same four-star hotel, the same suite of rooms.

"Good."

Jake left the office and hurried down to the toy department. He was surprised to see Mrs. Miracle on the floor. According to the schedule she wasn't even supposed to be in. That was his decision; since she'd volunteered to watch Gabe, he'd given her the day off.

"I didn't expect to see you this morning," he said.

"Oh, I thought I'd come in and do a bit of shopping myself."

"I didn't realize you had grandchildren," he said. In fact, he knew next to nothing about Mrs. Miracle's personal life, including her address. He'd offered to have the driver take her home and she'd agreed, but only on the condition that he be dropped off first. For some reason, he had the impression that she lived close to the store....

"So how'd the meeting with your father go?" she asked, disregarding his remark about grandchildren.

"How did you know that's where I was?" Jake asked, peering at her suspiciously.

"I didn't, but you looked so concerned, I guessed it had to do with J.R."

"It went fine," he said, unwilling to reveal the details of his conversation with an employee, even if she'd become a special friend. He didn't plan to mention it to Holly, either. All he'd say was that he'd extended the dinner invitation to his father and J.R. had thanked her but sent his regrets.

"I'm worried about J.R.," Mrs. Miracle said, again surprising him.

"Why? He's in good health."

"Physically, yes, he's doing well for a man of his age."

"Then why are you worried?" Jake pressed.

Instead of answering, the older woman patted his back. "I'm leaving in a few minutes. Would you like me to wrap Gabe's robot before I go?"

"Ah, sure," he said.

"You *are* taking it with you when you go to Holly's for Christmas, aren't you?"

"Yes."

"Then I'll wrap it for you. I'll get some ribbon and nice paper from the gift-wrapping kiosk."

"Thank you," Jake said, still wondering what she'd meant about J.R.

The older woman disappeared, leaving Jake standing in the toy department scratching his head. He valued Mrs. Miracle as an employee and as a new friend, and yet every now and then she'd say something that totally confused him. How did she know so much about him and his father? Perhaps she'd met his parents years ago. Or…

Well, he couldn't waste time trying to figure it out now.

Jake was walking to the customer service counter when his cell phone rang. Holly. He answered immediately.

"Can you talk?" she asked. "I know it's probably insane at the store, but I had to tell you something."

"What is it? Everything okay?"

"It's my boss, Lindy Lee. Oh, Jake, I think I'm going to cry."

"What's wrong?" he asked, alarmed.

"Nothing. This is *good*. Lindy just called me into her office. I spoke with her this morning about a Christmas party. I saw what a great time your employees had. I thought it would help morale, so I mentioned it to Lindy Lee."

"She's going to have a party?"

"No, even better than that. I can have a real Christmas dinner now with a turkey and stuffing and all the extras like I originally planned. I... I'd decided to make fried chicken because I couldn't really afford anything else, and now I can prepare a traditional meal."

"You got your bonus?"

"Yes! And it's bigger than last year's, so I can pay for the robot now."

"That's fabulous news!"

"It is, Jake, it really is." She took a deep breath. "If you don't mind, I'd like to call your father and invite him personally."

Jake's smile faded. "I should tell you I already talked to Dad about joining us on Christmas Day."

"I hope he will."

"Don't count on it." Jake felt bad about discouraging her. "I think he'd like to, but he can't let go of his grief. He feels he'd dishonor the memory of my mother and sister if he celebrated Christmas. For him, their deaths and Christmas are all tied together."

"Oh, Jake, that's so sad."

"Yes..." He didn't say what he knew was obvious—that, until now, the same thing had been true of him.

"I'm looking forward to spending the day with you," Jake said, and he meant every word. "Can you meet me for lunch this afternoon?" he asked, not sure he could wait until Christmas to see her again.

When she agreed, he smiled, a smile so wide that several customers looked at him curiously...and smiled back.

Sixteen

HAPPIEST ARE THE PEOPLE WHO GIVE THE MOST
HAPPINESS TO OTHERS.

—MRS. MIRACLE

That same morning Lindy Lee called Holly into her office
again. Saving the document she was working on, Holly
grabbed a pad and pen and rushed inside. Gesturing toward
the chair, Lindy invited her to sit. This was unusual in itself;
Lindy Lee never went out of her way to make Holly comfortable. In fact, it was generally the opposite.

"I've given your suggestion some thought," she said crisply.

"You mean about the Christmas party for next year?"

Lindy Lee's eyes narrowed. "Of course I mean the Christmas party. I want you to organize one for tomorrow."

"*Tomorrow?* But—"

"No excuses. *You're* the one who asked for this."

"I'll need a budget," Holly said desperately. It was a little late
to be organizing a party. Every caterer in New York would've
been booked months ago. Finding a restaurant with an opening the day before Christmas would be hopeless. What was she
thinking when she'd suggested the idea to Lindy Lee? Hadn't

she emphasized that she was talking about the *following* year? Not this one? Holly hardly knew where to start.

Lindy Lee glared at her. "I'm aware that you'll require a budget. Please wait until I'm finished. You can ask your questions then."

"Okay, sorry." Holly wasn't sure how she was supposed to manage this on such short notice.

Lindy explained that she'd close the office at two, that she wanted festive decorations and Christmas music, and that attendance was mandatory. "You can bring your nephew if you like," she added, after setting a more than generous budget.

"In other words, the family of staff is included?"

"Good grief, no."

"But Gabe's family."

"He's adorable. He even—" Lindy Lee stopped abruptly.

Holly was in complete agreement about Gabe's cuteness, but it wouldn't go over well if Gabe was invited and no one else's children were. "The others might get upset," Holly said, broaching the subject cautiously. "I mean, if I bring Gabe and no other children are allowed, it might look bad."

Lindy Lee sat back and crossed her arms, frowning. "If we invite family, then the place will be overrun with the little darlings," she muttered sarcastically. She sighed. "*Should* we include them?"

Holly shook her head. "There are too many practical considerations. People with kids would have to go home and pick them up and... Well, I think it's too much trouble, so let's not."

"Okay," Lindy said with evident relief.

"I'll get right on this."

"You might invite Gabe to the office again," Lindy Lee shocked her by saying. "Maybe in the new year."

Holly wondered if she'd misunderstood. "You want me to bring Gabe into the office?"

"A half day perhaps," her boss said, amending her original thought.

"Okay." So Gabe had succeeded in charming Lindy Lee, something Holly had once considered impossible.

Lindy Lee turned back to her computer, effectively dismissing Holly. Head whirling with the difficulty of her assignment, Holly returned to her own desk. She immediately got a list of nearby restaurants and began making calls, all of which netted quick rejections. In fact, the people she spoke with nearly laughed her off the phone. By noon she was growing desperate and worried.

"How's it going?" Lindy Lee asked as she stepped out of her office to meet someone for lunch. "Don't answer. I can tell by the look on your face."

"If only we'd scheduled the party a bit sooner..."

"You shouldn't have waited until the last minute to spring it on me," she said, laying the blame squarely on Holly.

That seemed unfair and a little harsh, even for Lindy Lee.

"We could have our event here in the building," Lindy Lee suggested, apparently relenting. "The sixth floor has a big open space. Check with them and see if that's available."

"I'll do it right away."

"Good," Lindy said, and turned to leave.

"I'll make this party happen," Holly promised through gritted teeth.

"I'll hold you to that," Lindy Lee tossed over her shoulder on her way out the door.

As soon as she'd left, Holly called the sixth floor. As luck would have it, the only time available was the afternoon of Christmas Eve—exactly what she needed. That solved one problem, but there was still an equally large hurdle to jump. Finding a caterer.

Despite the urgency of this task, Holly kept her lunch date

with Jake. These last days before Christmas made getting away for more than a few minutes difficult for him. Yet he managed with the help of his staff who, according to Jake, were determined to smooth the course of romance. Mrs. Miracle, God bless her, had spearheaded the effort.

Holly picked up a pastrami on rye at the deli and two coffees, and walked to Finley's; that was all they really had time for. Now that she'd been assured of her Christmas bonus, Holly had resumed the luxury of buying lunch. When she arrived at the store, white bag in hand, Jake was busy with a customer.

Mrs. Miracle saw her and came over to greet Holly. "My dear, what's wrong?"

Once again Holly was surprised at how readable she must be. "I'm on an impossible mission," she said.

"And what's that?" the older woman asked.

Holly explained. As soon as she'd finished, Mrs. Miracle smiled. "I believe I can help you."

"You can?" she asked excitedly.

"Yes, a friend of mine just opened a small restaurant in the Village. She's still getting herself established, but she'd certainly be capable of handling this party. What are you planning to serve? Sandwiches? Appetizers? Cookies? That sort of thing?"

"The party will be in the early afternoon, so small sandwiches and cookies would be perfect. It doesn't have to be elaborate." At this point she'd accept almost anything.

"I'll get you my friend's number."

"Yes, please, and, Mrs. Miracle, thank you so much."

"No problem, my dear. None whatsoever." The older woman beamed her a smile. "By the way, I've set up a table in the back of the storeroom for you and Jake to have your lunch."

"How thoughtful."

"You go on back and Jake'll be along any minute. Meanwhile, I'll get you that phone number."

"Thanks," she said again. "Could you tell me your friend's name?"

"It's Wendy," she said. "Now don't you worry about a thing, you hear?"

Feeling deeply relieved, Holly went to the storeroom. Sure enough, Mrs. Miracle had set up a card table, complete with a white tablecloth and a small poinsettia in the middle. Holly put down the sandwich, plus a couple of pickles and the two cups of coffee.

Jake came in a few minutes later, looking harassed. He kissed her, then took his place. "It's crazy out there," he said, slumping in his chair.

"I can tell." She noticed that the rest of the staff was diligently avoiding the storeroom, no doubt under orders from Mrs. Miracle.

He reached for his half of the massive sandwich. "I sold the last of the robots this morning."

"That's wonderful!"

"It is and it isn't," he said between bites. "I wish I'd ordered another hundred. We could've sold those, as well. Now we have to turn people away. I hate disappointing anyone."

"Is there any other store in town with inventory?"

"Nope, and believe me, I've checked. Another shipment is due in a week after Christmas but by then it'll be too late."

Holly hated to bring up the subject of Gabe's Intellytron, but she needed Jake's reassurance that the one he'd set aside hadn't been sold in the robot-buying frenzy. "You still have Gabe's, don't you?"

Still chewing on his sandwich, Jake nodded. "Mrs. Miracle wrapped it herself. It's sitting right over there." He pointed to a counter across from her. The large, brightly decorated package rested in one corner.

"I'm so grateful you did this for me," she told him. Meeting Jake had been one of the greatest blessings of the year—in so many ways.

"Thank Mrs. Miracle, too," he said. "She wasn't even supposed to be in today, but she ended up staying to help us out."

The few minutes they'd grabbed flew by much too quickly. Jake stood, kissed her again, and they left the storeroom together. As they stepped onto the floor, Mrs. Miracle handed her a slip of paper. "The name of the restaurant is Heavenly Delights and here's the number."

"Heavenly Delights," Holly repeated. "I'll give your friend a call as soon as I'm back at my desk."

"You do that."

Holly tucked the paper in her coat pocket and nearly danced all the way to the office. With a little help from Mrs. Miracle, she'd be able to pull off a miracle of her own—she'd organize this Christmas party, regardless of the difficulties and challenges.

Once at her desk, Holly reached for the phone and called the number Mrs. Miracle had written down for her.

"Hello." A woman answered on the third ring.

"Hello," Holly returned brightly. "Is this Wendy?"

"Yes. And you are?"

"I'm Holly Larson, and I'm phoning on behalf of Lindy Lee."

"Lindy Lee, the designer?" Wendy sounded impressed.

"Yes," Holly answered. "I know I'm probably calling at the worst time, but I felt I should contact you as soon as possible." She assumed the restaurant would be busy with the lunch crowd.

"No, no, this is fine."

"I was given your phone number by Emily Miracle."

"Who?"

"Oh, sorry. Her badge says Miracle, but that's a mistake. Rather than cause a fuss, she asked that we call her Mrs. Miracle, although that's not actually her name. I apologize, but I can't remember what it is. I'm so accustomed to calling her Mrs. Miracle." Holly hoped she wasn't rambling.

"Go on," Wendy urged without commenting on all the confusion about names.

"Long story short, she suggested I call you about catering Lindy Lee's Christmas party for her employees."

"She did?"

"Yes… She highly recommended you and the restaurant."

"What restaurant?"

"Heavenly Delights," Holly said. Wendy must own more than one. "The location in the Village."

"Heavenly Delights," Wendy gasped, then started to laugh. "Heavenly Delights?"

"Yes." Holly's spirits took a sharp dive; nevertheless, she forged ahead. "I'm wondering if you could work us into your schedule."

"Oh, dear."

Holly's spirits sank even further. "You can't do it?"

"I didn't say that."

Her emotions went from hopeful to disheartened and back again. "Then you could?"

"I… I don't know what to say." The woman seemed completely overwhelmed.

Yes, I can do it would certainly make Holly's day, but the words weren't immediately forthcoming.

"Unfortunately, the party's scheduled for tomorrow afternoon—Christmas Eve." Holly suspected that, by then, practically everyone in the restaurant business would be closing down and heading home to their families. As an incentive, she mentioned the amount she could offer. The catering would take up most of the budget, with a little left over for decorations.

"That sounds fair," Wendy said.

"Would you be able to accommodate us?" she asked hopefully. "We're talking about forty people, give or take."

"I..."

Holly closed her eyes, fearing the worst.

"I think I could. However, there's something you should know."

"What's that?"

"First, I can't imagine who this Mrs. Miracle is."

"As I said, that isn't her real name. But I can find out for you, if you like."

"No, it doesn't matter. What I wanted to tell you is that I don't have a restaurant."

"No restaurant?" Holly's mouth went dry.

"The thing is, I've been talking with my daughter about opening one. She's attending culinary school. I've been praying about it, too. However, a lot of problems stand in the way— one of which is money."

"Oh."

"When I applied for a loan, the bank officer asked me what we intended to call the restaurant. Lucie and I have gone over dozens of names and nothing felt right. Our specialty would be desserts.... I like the name Heavenly Delights. If you don't mind, I'll borrow it."

"I... That's the name Mrs. Miracle gave me."

"Well, if *she* doesn't mind, we'll definitely use it." She paused. "Maybe I know her, but right now I can't figure out who she is."

"Um, so if you don't have a restaurant yet, you can't cater the event?"

"I can't," Wendy agreed. "But perhaps Lucie and her friends from culinary school could."

"Really?" Holly asked excitedly.

"Give me your number and I'll call her to see if we can make this happen."

"Great!"

Holly fidgeted until Wendy called back five minutes later. "We'll do it," Wendy told her. "Lucie talked to several of her colleagues and they're all interested. I can promise you'll *love* their menu. Lucie's already working on it."

"Fabulous. Thank you! Oh, thank you so much." Her relief was so great that she felt like weeping.

She disconnected just as Lindy returned from lunch.

"The party's all set," Holly said happily.

"Really?" She'd impressed Lindy Lee, which was no small feat.

"Christmas Eve from two to four."

Her employer nodded. "Good job, Holly."

Holly closed her eyes and basked in the glow of Lindy Lee's approval.

Seventeen

WE DON'T CHANGE GOD'S MESSAGE.
HIS MESSAGE CHANGES US.

—MRS. MIRACLE

Jake glanced at his watch and felt a surge of relief. Five-thirty on Christmas Eve; in half an hour, the store would close its doors for the season.

Finley's would open again on the twenty-sixth for the year-end frenzy. He felt good that toy sales for this quarter were twenty percent higher than the previous year. He attributed the boost in revenue to Intellytron the SuperRobot. Jake felt vindicated that his hunch had been proven right. He'd be proud to take these latest figures to his father. While the robot alone didn't explain the increase, the fact that it was available at Finley's had brought new customers into the store.

Holly was occupied with her boss and the Christmas party, which she'd arranged for Lindy Lee at the last moment. The poor girl had worked herself into a nervous state to pull off the event, and Jake was confident that the afternoon had gone well. He knew Holly had obsessed over each and every detail.

No doubt exhausted, she'd go home to her Brooklyn apartment as soon as she was finished with the cleanup. Jake would come by later that evening to spend time with her and Gabe. The three of them would enjoy a quiet dinner and then attend Christmas Eve services at her church.

It felt strangely luxurious not to be rushing away from the city with his father, although Jake was saddened that he hadn't been able to convince J.R. to join them on Christmas Day.

His cell chirped, and even before he looked, Jake knew it was Holly.

"Hi," he said. "How'd the party go?"

"Great! Wonderful. Even Lindy Lee was pleased. The caterers did a fabulous job, above and beyond my expectations. Wendy told me that Heavenly Delights plans to specialize in desserts and they should. Everything was spectacular."

"I'm glad."

"Don't forget to bring over Gabe's gift tonight," she said in a tired voice. As he'd expected, Holly was worn-out.

"Sure thing."

"We'll hide it in my bedroom until he goes to sleep, and then we can put it under the tree. That way it'll be the first thing he sees Christmas morning."

"Sounds like a plan."

"I'll distract him when you arrive so you can shove it in my closet."

"Okay."

She hesitated. "Are you sure you can't talk your father into coming for Christmas dinner?"

"I don't think so, Holly. He isn't ready to give up his…vacation." He nearly choked on the word.

"Ask him again, would you?" she said softly.

"I will," he agreed with some reluctance, knowing it wouldn't have any effect.

"And thank Mrs. Miracle for me. She saved the day with this recommendation."

"Of course. Although I believe she's already left."

"She'll be back, won't she?"

"As seasonal help, she'll stay on until the end of January when we finish inventory." The older woman had been a real success in the department. She'd reassured parents and entertained their kids. If she was interested, Jake would like to offer her full-time employment.

He ended his conversation with Holly and went into the storeroom to pick up Gabe's robot.

He stopped short. The package that had lain on the counter, the package so beautifully wrapped by Mrs. Miracle, was missing.

Gone.

"Karen," Jake said, walking directly past a customer to confront one of the other sales associates. If this was a practical joke, he was not amused. "Where's the robot that was on the counter in the storeroom?" he demanded, ignoring the last-minute shopper she was assisting.

Karen blinked as though he was speaking in a foreign language. "I beg your pardon?"

"The wrapped gift in the storage room?" he repeated.

"I… I don't have a clue."

"You know what I'm talking about, don't you?"

Her face became flushed. "I'm not sure."

"It was wrapped and ready for delivery and now it's missing." Jake couldn't believe anyone would steal the robot. He knew his employees, and there wasn't a single one who was capable of such a deed. He'd stake his career on it.

"Did you ask John?"

"No." Jake quickly sought out the youngest sales associate. John had just finished with a customer and looked expectantly at Jake.

"The robot's missing," he said without preamble.

John stared back at him. "The one in the storeroom?"

"Are there any others in this department?" he snapped. If there were, he'd grab one and be done with it. However, no one knew better than Jake that there wasn't an Intellytron to be had.

"I saw it," Gail said, joining them.

Relief washed over Jake. Someone had moved it without telling him; that was obviously what had happened. The prospect of facing Holly and telling her he didn't have the robot didn't bear thinking about.

That morning, the moment she'd received her Christmas bonus, Holly had rushed over to Finley's to pay for the toy. Her face had been alight with happiness as she described how excited Gabe would be when he found his gift under the Christmas tree. That robot meant so much to the boy. If Jake didn't bring it as promised, Holly might not forgive him. He hoped that wouldn't happen, but the thought sent a chill through him nonetheless.

Frances, another sales associate, came over, too. "Mrs. Miracle had it," she said.

"When?"

"This morning," Frances explained. "She didn't mention it to you?"

"No." Jake shook his head. "What did she do with it?"

Frances stared down at the floor. "She sold it."

"*Sold* it?" Jake exploded. This had to be some kind of joke—didn't it? "How could she do that? It was already paid for by someone else." That robot belonged to Gabe Larson. She knew that as well as anyone.

"Why would she sell it?" he burst out again, completely bewildered.

"I… I don't know. You'll have to ask her," Frances said. "I'm so sorry, Mr. Finley. I'm sure there's a logical explanation."

There'd better be. Not that it would help now.

Sick at heart, Jake left the department and went up to his father's office. Dora had already gone home; the whole administrative floor was deserted. He didn't know what he'd tell Holly. He should've taken the robot to his apartment and kept it there. Then he could've been guaranteed that nothing like this would happen. Still, berating himself now wouldn't serve any useful purpose.

Preparing for his flight, J. R. Finley was busy stuffing paperwork in his computer case when Jake entered the office. J.R. looked up at him. "What's the matter with you? Did you decide to come with me, after all?"

"No. Have you decided to stay in New York?" Jake countered.

"You're kidding, right?"

Jake slumped into a chair and ran his fingers through his hair. "Gabe's robot is missing," he said quietly. "Emily Miracle, or whatever her name is, sold it."

"Mrs. Miracle?" J.R.'s face tightened and he waved his index finger at Jake. "I told you that woman was up to no good, butting into other people's business. She's a troublemaker. Didn't I tell you that?"

"Dad, stop it. She's a sweet grandmotherly woman."

"She's ruined a little boy's Christmas and you call that *sweet?*" He made a scoffing sound and resumed his task of collecting papers and shoving them into his case.

"Do you have any connections—someone who can locate a spare Intellytron at the last minute?" This was Jake's only hope.

Frowning, his father checked his watch. "I'll make some phone calls, but I can't promise anything."

Jake was grateful for whatever his father could do. "What about your flight?"

J.R. looked at his watch again and shrugged. "I'll catch a later one."

Jake started to remind his father that changing flights at this point might be difficult, but stopped himself. If J.R. was going to offer his assistance, Jake would be a fool to refuse.

"I'll shut down the department and meet you back here in twenty minutes," Jake said.

His father had picked up his phone and was punching out numbers. One thing Jake could be assured of—if there was a single Intellytron left in the tristate area, J.R. would locate it and have it delivered to Gabe.

He hurried back to the toy department and saw that the last-minute customers were being ushered out, bags in hand, and the day's sales tallied. The store was officially closed. His staff was waiting to exchange Christmas greetings with Jake so they could go home to their families.

"Is there anything we can do before we leave?" John asked, speaking for the others.

"No, thanks. You guys have been great. Merry Christmas, everyone!"

As soon as they'd left, he got Mrs. Miracle's contact information and called the phone number she'd given HR. To his shock, a recorded voice message informed him that the number was no longer in service. That wasn't the only shock, either—she'd handed in her notice that afternoon.

He groaned. Mrs. Miracle was unreachable and had absconded with precious information regarding the robot—like why she'd sold it and to whom.

Jake returned to his father's office to find him pacing the floor with the receiver pressed to his ear. J.R. glanced in Jake's direction, then quickly looked away. That tight-lipped expression told Jake everything he needed to know—his father hadn't been successful.

He waited until J.R. hung up the phone.

"No luck," Jake said, not bothering to phrase it in the form of a question.

J.R. shook his head. "Everyone I talked to said as far as they knew we're the only store in five states to have the robot."

"*Had*. We sold out."

"Apparently there isn't another one to be found anywhere till after Christmas."

Jake had expected that. A sick feeling attacked the pit of his stomach as he sank into a chair and sighed loudly. "I appreciate your help, Dad. Thanks for trying."

"I'm sorry I couldn't do more." J.R. nodded and placed a consoling hand on Jake's shoulder. "I know how you feel."

Jake doubted that but he wasn't in the mood to argue.

"Holly's special," J.R. said. "I've known that since the first time you mentioned her."

"She is." Jake was in full agreement there.

"If it'd been your mother who needed that thing, I would've moved heaven and earth to make sure she got it."

He reconsidered. Maybe his father *did* know what he was feeling. He'd done his utmost to keep Holly and Gabe from being disappointed. Unfortunately, nothing he or J.R. did now would make any difference. It was simply too late.

"Every Intellytron in New York State and beyond is wrapped and under some youngster's tree," J.R. said.

Jake rubbed his face. "I'll come up with something to tell Holly and Gabe," he said, thinking out loud.

"Is there anything else the boy might like?" his father asked.

The only toy Gabe had referred to, at least in Jake's hearing, was the robot. He'd even risked Holly's wrath and traveled into the city on his own just to see it again and watch it in action.

"What about a train set?" his father suggested. "Every little boy wants a train set."

Jake had. He'd longed for one the Christmas his mother and sister had died. But there'd been no presents the next morning or any Christmas morning since the accident.

"He might," Jake said. "But—"

"Well, we have one of those."

Jake wondered what his father was talking about. As head of the toy department Jake was well aware of the inventory left in stock and there were no train sets. This season had been record-breaking in more ways than one; not only the robot but a number of other toys had sold out. The trains, a popular new doll, a couple of computer games... "Exactly where is there a train set?" he asked. "Unless you mean the one in the window..."

"Not the display train. A brand-new one. Except that it's twenty-one years old." J.R. swallowed visibly. "I have it," he said. "It's still wrapped in the original paper. Your mother bought it for you just before..." He didn't need to finish the sentence.

"Mom bought me the train set I wanted?" Jake asked, his voice hoarse with emotion.

J.R. grinned. "You were spoiled, young man. Your mother loved you deeply. And your little sister adored you."

A sense of loss hit him hard and for a moment that was all Jake could think about. "You kept the train set all these years?" he finally asked.

J.R. nodded solemnly. "I always meant to give it to you but I could never part with it. In a way, holding on to it was like...having your mother still with me. I could pretend it was Christmas Eve twenty-one years ago and she hadn't died. Don't worry, I didn't *actually* believe that, but I could indulge the fantasy of what Christmas should've been. That train set made the memory so real...."

"And you're willing to give it up for Gabe?"

"No" was his father's blunt reply. "I'm willing to give it up for *you*."

Jake smiled and whispered, "Thanks, Dad."

"You're welcome. Now we've got a bit of digging to do. I don't remember where I put that train set but I know it's somewhere in the condo. Or maybe the storage locker. Or..."

"Do we have time? Did you change your flight?"

"Flight?" J.R. repeated, then seemed to remember he was scheduled to fly out that evening. Shaking his head, he muttered, "It's fine. I'll catch one tomorrow if I have to."

Jake didn't want to pressure his father, but he'd promised Holly he'd invite J.R. to dinner at her apartment. Although he'd already tried once, he'd ask again. If he was going to disappoint her on one front, then the least he could do was surprise her on another.

"Since you're apparently staying over..." he began.

"Yes?"

"Have Christmas dinner with Holly and Gabe and me tomorrow afternoon. Will you do that, Dad?"

His father took a long moment to consider the invitation. Then, as if the words were difficult to say, he slowly whispered, "I believe I will. Something tells me your mother would want me to."

Eighteen

GOD ISN'T POLITICALLY CORRECT. HE'S JUST CORRECT.

—MRS. MIRACLE

H olly set the phone down and forced herself to keep the smile on her face. Gabe's robot was missing. Because Gabe was in earshot, she couldn't ask Jake the questions that clamored in her mind. He'd said something about Mrs. Miracle, but Holly had been too disheartened to remember what followed.

Adding to her distress, Jake had said there was something he needed to do with his father, which meant he'd have to renege on dinner that night. In addition to the bad news about the missing robot, Jake had passed on some good news, too. Evidently his father had changed his plans and would be joining them on Christmas Day, after all, which delighted Holly and greatly encouraged her. She recognized that this was no small concession on J.R.'s part.

"Isn't Jake coming for dinner?" Gabe asked, looking up from his handheld video game. He lay on the sofa as he expertly manipulated the keys.

"I... No. Unfortunately, Jake has something else he has

to do," Holly explained, doing her best to maintain an even voice. "Something really important," she emphasized.

Gabe frowned and sat up. "What's more important than Christmas Eve?"

Again Holly made an effort to pretend nothing was wrong. "We'll have to ask when we see him tomorrow," she said airily.

Her nephew slouched back onto the sofa. His downcast look prompted Holly to sit beside him. She felt as depressed as Gabe did, but was trying hard not to show it. In the larger scheme of life, these disappointments were minor. Nevertheless, she'd hoped to give Gabe a very special gift this year. And she'd hoped—so had Gabe—to spend Christmas Eve with Jake.

"Did Jake promise to come tomorrow?"

"He'll be here."

"But he said he'd come for dinner tonight, too—and he didn't."

"We'll have a wonderful time this evening, just the two of us." She slipped her arm around his small frame and squeezed gently.

Gabe didn't seem too sure of that. "Can I email my dad?"

"Of course." Holly would come up with ways to keep them both occupied until it was time to walk to church for the Christmas Eve service. They could watch a Christmas movie; Gabe might enjoy *The Bishop's Wife,* Holly's favorite, or *A Christmas Carol* with Alastair Sim as the ultimate Scrooge. Still cheering herself up, she headed into her kitchen to start frying the chicken, which had been marinating in buttermilk since six that morning. They'd have turkey tomorrow, but tonight she'd make the meal she associated with her mother... with comfort.

Gabe leaped up from the sofa and hurried into the kitchen. "Can we invite Mrs. Miracle for dinner?" he asked excitedly.

"Oh, Gabe, I wish we'd thought of that sooner."

"I like Mrs. Miracle."

"I like her, too." The older woman had never mentioned whether she had family in the area, which made Holly wonder if she was spending this evening by herself.

Gabe returned to writing his email. "Dad's surprise didn't come, did it?" he said in a pensive voice.

Holly suddenly realized it hadn't. This complicated everything. Not only wouldn't she be able to give her nephew the only toy he'd requested for Christmas, but the gift his father had mailed hadn't arrived, either.

"He might be mad at me for going into the city by myself," Gabe murmured.

"Oh, sweetie, I'm positive that's not it."

Before she could finish her reassurances, the doorbell chimed. Hoping, despite everything, that it was Jake, Holly answered the door, still wearing her apron. To her astonishment, Emily Miracle was standing in the hall.

"I hope you don't mind me dropping in unexpectedly like this."

"Mrs. Miracle! Mrs. Miracle!" Gabe rushed to the door. "We were just talking about you." He grabbed her free hand and tugged her into the apartment. "Can you stay for dinner? Aunt Holly's making fried chicken and there's corn and mashed potatoes and cake, too. You can stay, can't you? Jake said he was coming and now he can't."

"Oh, dear," Emily said, laughing softly. "I suppose I could. I came by to bring you my Christmas salad. It's a family favorite and I wanted to share it with you."

"That's so nice of you, Emily," Holly said, adding a place setting to the table. Her mood instantly lightened.

"Jake *said* he'd come," Gabe pouted.

"He's doing something important," Holly reminded her nephew.

"I'm sure he is," Emily said, giving Holly a covered ceramic bowl and removing her coat. "It isn't like Jake to cancel at the last moment without a good reason. He's a very responsible young man—in his personal life and in business, too. He'll do his father proud." She held out her hands for the bowl.

"You mean *does* his father proud," Holly corrected, passing it back. She had every confidence that Jake would one day step up to the helm at Finley's, but that was sometime in the future. Jake seemed to think it might take as long as five years, and he said that suited him fine.

"Yes, that's what I mean. I've enjoyed working with him this Christmas season." Emily made her way into the kitchen and put her salad in the refrigerator.

"Can you come to church with us?" Gabe asked, following her. "It's Christmas Eve, and there's a special program and singing, too."

"I'd like that very much, but unfortunately I already have other plans."

"We're grateful you could have dinner with us," Holly said. She waited until Gabe had left the room before she asked Emily about the robot.

"Do you have any idea what happened to the you-know-what Jake put aside?" She spoke guardedly because the apartment was small and she wanted to ensure that Gabe didn't hear anything that would upset him.

Mrs. Miracle was about to answer when he dashed into the kitchen again.

Grasping the situation, she immediately distracted him. "Do you want to help me fill the water glasses?" she asked.

"Okay," Gabe agreed.

Emily poured water into the pitcher, which she handed to Gabe. Holding it carefully, he walked over to the dining area, which was actually part of the living room. The older woman turned to Holly. "I think there was a misunderstanding between Jake and me," she said in a low voice. "I'll clear everything up as soon as I can."

"Please do," Holly whispered. She tried to recall her conversation with Jake. He seemed to imply that Emily had sold the robot to someone else. That didn't seem possible. She'd never do anything to hurt a little boy; Holly was convinced of it.

The fried chicken couldn't have been better; in fact, it was as good as when her mother had prepared this dish. Holly had wanted tonight's meal to be memorable for Gabe, and because Mrs. Miracle was with them, it was.

During dinner, Emily entertained them with story after story of various jobs she'd taken through the years. She'd certainly had her share of interesting experiences, working as a waitress, a nanny, a nurse and now a salesperson.

All too soon, it was time to get ready for church. Holly reluctantly stood up from the table.

"Everything was lovely," Mrs. Miracle told her with a smile of appreciation. "I've never had chicken that was more delicious." She carried her empty dessert plate to the kitchen sink. "And that coconut cake…"

"I liked the sauce best," Gabe chimed in, putting his plate in the sink, too.

"I loved the salad," Holly said, and was sincere. "I hope you'll give me the recipe."

"Of course. I'll be happy to write it out for you now if you'll get me some paper and a pen."

Holly tore a page from a notebook and grabbed Gabe's Santa pen; minutes later, Mrs. Miracle handed her the recipe with a flourish. "Here you go." Then she frowned at her watch. "Oh, my. I hate to run, but I'm afraid I must."

"No, no, don't worry," Holly assured her. "We have to

leave for church, anyway. I'm just glad you could be with us this evening. It meant a lot to Gabe and me."

The older woman bent down and kissed the boy's cheek. "This is going to be a very special Christmas for you, young man. Just you wait. It's one you'll remember your whole life. Someday you'll tell your grandchildren about the best Christmas of your life."

"Do you really think so?" Gabe asked, eyes alight with happiness.

She reached for her coat and put it on before she hugged Holly goodbye. "It's going to be a special Christmas for you, as well, my dear."

Holly smiled politely. Maybe Mrs. Miracle was right, but it definitely hadn't started out that way.

Gabe woke at six o'clock Christmas morning. He knocked on Holly's bedroom door and shouted, "It's Christmas!" Apparently he suspected she might have forgotten.

Holly opened one eye. Still half-asleep, she sat up and stretched her arms above her head.

"Can we open our presents?" Gabe asked, leaping onto her bed.

"What about breakfast?" she said.

"I'm not hungry. You aren't, either, are you?" The question had a hopeful lilt, as though any thought of food would be equally irrelevant to her.

"I could eat," she said.

Gabe's face fell.

"I could eat…later," she amended.

His jubilant smile reappeared.

"Shall we see what Santa brought you?" she asked, tossing aside her covers. She threw on her housecoat and accompanied him into the living room, where the gifts beneath the small tree awaited their inspection.

Gabe fell to his knees and began rooting through the packages she'd set out the night before, after he'd gone to sleep. He must've known from the size of the wrapped boxes that the robot wasn't among them. He sat back on his heels. "Santa didn't get me Intellytron, did he?"

"I don't know, sweetie. I hear Santa sometimes makes late deliveries."

"He does?" Hope shone in his face. "When?"

"That I can't say." Rather than discuss the subject further, Holly hurried into the kitchen.

While she put on a pot of coffee, Gabe arranged the gifts in two small piles. Most of them had been mailed by Holly's parents, and Gabe's didn't take long to unwrap. He was wonderful, sweetly expressing gratitude and happiness with his few gifts. A number of times Holly had to wipe tears from her eyes.

"I hope you're not too disappointed," she said when she could speak. "I know how badly you wanted the robot—and I'm sure Santa has one for you but it might be a little late."

Gabe looked up from the new video game she'd purchased on her way home from work. "I bet I'll still get Intellytron. Mrs. Miracle said this was going to be my best Christmas ever, remember? And it wouldn't be without my robot." He jumped up and slid his arms around Holly's neck and gave her a tight hug.

She opened her gifts after that—a book from her parents, plus a calendar and a peasant-style blouse. And the origami purse from Gabe, which brought fresh tears to her eyes.

They had a leisurely breakfast of French toast and then, while Gabe played with his new video game, Holly got the turkey in the oven. The doorbell rang around eleven o'clock.

Jake and his father came in, carrying a large wrapped box

between them. Holly's heartbeat accelerated. It must be In-tellytron, although the box actually seemed too big.

"Merry Christmas," Jake said, and held her close. "Don't get excited—this isn't what you think it is," he whispered in her ear just before he kissed her.

"Merry Christmas, young man," J.R. said, and shook Gabe's hand.

"What's that?" Gabe asked, eyeing the box Jake had set on the carpet.

"Why don't you open it and see?" J.R. suggested.

Jake stood at Holly's side with his arm around her waist. "I'm sorry I had to cancel last night," he said in a low voice.

"It's fine, don't worry."

"Mrs. Miracle came over," Gabe said as he sat on the floor beside the box.

"Emily Miracle?" Jake frowned. "Did she happen to deliver something?" he asked, his eyes narrowing.

"She brought a Christmas salad for dinner," Gabe told him, tearing away the ribbon. He looked up. "We didn't eat it all. Do you want to taste it?" He wrinkled his nose. "For green stuff, it was pretty good."

"I wouldn't want to ruin my dinner," J.R. said, smiling down at him. "Go ahead, young man, and let 'er rip."

Gabe didn't need any encouragement. He tore away the wrapping paper. "It's a train set," he said. "That was the second thing on my Christmas list, after Intellytron. Can we set it up now?"

"I don't see why not," Jake told him and got down on his knees with Gabe. "I wanted one when I was around your age, too."

"Did you get one?" Gabe asked.

Jake looked at his father, who sat on the sofa, and nodded. "I certainly did, and it was the best train set money could buy."

Gabe took the engine out of the box. "Wow, this is heavy."

"Let's lay out the track first, shall we?"

Holly sat on the sofa next to Jake's father. "I'm so glad you could have dinner with us."

"I am, too." A pained look came over him and he gave a slight shake of his head. "I was sure I'd never want to celebrate Christmas again, but I've decided it's time I released the past and started to prepare for the future."

"The future?" she repeated uncertainly.

"Grandchildren," J.R. said with a sheepish grin. "I have the distinct feeling that my son has met the woman he's going to love as much as I loved his mother."

Embarrassed, Holly looked away. With all her heart she hoped she was that woman.

"Jake would be furious with me if he knew I'd said anything. It's too soon—I realize that. He probably isn't aware of how strongly he feels, but I know. I've seen my son with other women. He's in love with you, the same way I was in love with Helene."

Holly was about to make some excuse about dinner and return to the kitchen when the doorbell chimed again. Everyone looked at her as if she knew who it would be.

"I... I wonder who that is," she murmured, walking to the door.

"It could be Mrs. Miracle," Gabe said hopefully.

Only it wasn't.

Holly opened the apartment door to find her brother standing there in his army fatigues, wearing a smile of pure happiness. In his arms he held a large wrapped box.

"Mickey!" she screamed. He put down the box and hugged her fiercely.

"Dad!" Gabe flew off the floor as though jet-propelled and launched himself into his father's arms.

Eyes closed, Mickey held the boy for a long, long time.

Merry Christmas, Holly thought, tears slipping down her face. Just as Emily Miracle had predicted, this was destined to be the best Christmas of Gabe's life.

Baby Arugula Salad with Goat Cheese, Pecans and Pomegranate Seeds

(from Debbie Macomber's Cedar Cove Cookbook).

This salad is a lively blend of sharp arugula, tangy goat cheese, mellow pecans and tart pomegranates. If you can't find arugula, substitute any delicate salad green.

1 small shallot, minced
3 tablespoons balsamic vinegar
1 teaspoon Dijon mustard
Salt and pepper, to taste
1/2 cup extra-virgin olive oil
10 to 12 cups baby arugula (about 10 ounces)
1 cup pomegranate seeds (from one pomegranate)
1/2 cup toasted pecans, chopped
1 cup crumbled goat cheese

1. In a measuring cup, whisk shallot, vinegar, mustard, salt and pepper until combined. Slowly pour oil in a stream until blended.

2. In a large serving bowl, combine arugula, pomegranate seeds and pecans. Add dressing; toss to coat. Top salad with cheese; toss once.

Tip: Extra-virgin olive oil, which comes from the first cold pressing of the olives, has a stronger, purer flavor than virgin olive oil. Since it is more expensive, most cooks prefer to use it only for salad and other uncooked dishes. Virgin olive oil is better for sautéing.

Serves 8.

Nineteen

Mickey stepped into the apartment, still holding Gabe, and extended his hand to Jake. "You must be Jake Finley."

"And you must be Holly's brother, Mickey."

"I am."

"What's in there?" Gabe asked, looking over his father's shoulder at the large box resting on the other side of the open door.

"That's a little something Santa asked me to deliver," Mickey told his son.

Gabe squirmed out of his arms and raced back into the hallway. He stared at Holly and his grin seemed to take up his whole face. "I think I know what it is," he declared before pushing the box inside. "Aunt Holly told me Santa sometimes makes deliveries late."

No one needed to encourage him to unwrap the gift this time. He tore into the wrapping paper, which flew in all directions. As soon as he saw the picture of Intellytron on the outside of the box, Gabe gave a shout of exhilaration.

"It's my robot! It's my robot!"

"Wherever did you find one?" J.R. asked Mickey. The older man stepped forward and extended his hand. "J. R. Finley," he said.

"He bought it at Finley's," Jake answered in a confused tone.

"Our department store?" J.R. sounded incredulous. "When?"

"My guess is that it was late on Christmas Eve." Again, Jake supplied the answer.

"And how do you know all this?" Holly had a few questions of her own.

"Because that's the gift wrap Mrs. Miracle used."

"But…who sold it to him?" J.R. appeared completely befuddled by this latest development.

"Mrs. Miracle," Jake and Holly murmured simultaneously.

"He's right," Mickey said as he sat on the couch next to his son, who remained on the floor. "I remember her name badge. Mrs. Miracle. We talked for a few minutes."

Thankfully, Gabe was too involved with his robot to listen.

"I had a chance to go into the city yesterday," Mickey told them.

"Wait." Holly held up her hand. "You've got some splainin' to do, Lieutenant Larson. Why are you in New York in the first place?"

Mickey laughed. "Don't tell me you don't want me here?"

"No, no, of course I do! But you might've said something."

"I couldn't."

"Security reasons?" Holly asked.

"No, just that I wasn't sure I'd get the leave I was hoping for. I've been sent back for specialized training—I'll be at Fort Dix for the next six weeks. I didn't want to say anything to Gabe yet, in case it fell through. I could tell from his emails that he was starting to adjust to life here with you. It would've been cruel to raise his hopes, only to have Uncle Sam dash them. Turns out I was on duty until nine this morning...so here I am. I thought I'd bring Gabe his Christmas surprise."

"You might've mentioned it to *me*," Holly said with more than a little consternation.

"True, but I had to take your poor track record with keeping secrets into consideration."

"I can keep a secret," she insisted.

"Oh, yeah? What about the time you told Candi Johnson I had a crush on her?"

"I was twelve years old!"

Jake chuckled and she sent him a stern look. If Mickey had asked her not to say anything about his possible visit, she wouldn't have uttered a word. Then it occurred to her that he'd hinted at it when he referred to the surprise he was sending Gabe. Fantastic, stupendous, *exhilarating* though this was, a Christmas visit was the last thing she'd expected.

"But why buy the robot?" Holly asked. "I told you I'd get it for Gabe."

"Yes, but you were going without lunches—"

"True," she interrupted, whispering so Gabe wouldn't hear. "Then Lindy Lee had a change of heart and decided to give me a Christmas bonus, after all."

Mickey shrugged. "You didn't say anything to me. Not that it matters because *I* wanted to get this for Gabe."

"I didn't tell you I received my bonus?"

"You've done enough for the two of us," Mickey told her, his eyes warm with appreciation. "I didn't want to burden you with the added expense of Christmas."

"Hey, Holly, that means Finley's owes you two hundred and fifty dollars," Jake said. "Plus tax. By the way, Mickey, did you tell Mrs. Miracle who you were?" he asked, approaching the two of them. He slipped his arm around Holly's waist and she casually leaned against him.

Mickey shook his head. "Should I have?"

Jake and Holly exchanged a glance, but it was Jake who voiced their question. "How did she know?"

"Know what?" Mickey asked.

"That it was you," Holly said.

"Look, Dad!" Gabe cried out.

Mickey turned his attention to the robot, who walked smartly toward him, stopped and asked in a tinny voice, "When…do…you…go…back…to…Afghanistan?"

Mickey's eyes widened. "How'd you make him say that?"

J.R., who'd been working with Gabe, grinned at Mickey. "I programmed him," Gabe announced proudly. "Mr. Finley helped, but he said I can do it on my own now that I know how."

"You managed to get the robot to do that already?"

"He does all kinds of cool tricks, Dad. Watch."

While Mickey and Gabe were engaged in programming the robot, Jake and Holly stepped into the kitchen.

"She *couldn't* have known Mickey was Gabe's father." Jake's face was clouded with doubt. "Could she?"

Holly didn't have an answer.

Jake continued, still frowning. "I tried to reach her, but the phone number she listed with HR wasn't in service."

"Then ask her when you see her again," Holly said. Jake had mentioned that, as seasonal help, Emily Miracle would be working until after inventory had been completed in January.

"I won't be able to," Jake told her. "When I went to HR for her personal information, I discovered that she'd handed in her notice. Christmas Eve was her last day."

"But…" Holly wanted to argue. Surely Mrs. Miracle would've said *something* at dinner the night before. Things didn't quite add up.... And yet, this wonderful woman had done so much to brighten their Christmas.

Before she could comment, the doorbell rang again. Holly chuckled, not even daring to guess who it might be *this* time. Her apartment was turning into Grand Central Station. If she had to guess, the last person to cross her mind would've been...

"Lindy!" Her employer's name shot out of Holly's mouth the second she opened the door.

Lindy Lee smiled hesitantly. "I hope I'm not intruding."

"You came, you came." Gabe bounded up from the floor and raced to Lindy Lee's side, taking her hand.

Lindy gave Holly an apologetic look. "Gabe invited me and since I, uh, didn't have any commitments, I thought I'd stop by for a few minutes and wish you all a merry Christmas." She glanced about the room. "I see you already have a houseful."

"I'm Gabe's father," Mickey said, stepping forward. "Holly's brother." He set his hands on Gabe's shoulders.

"She's the lady I wrote you about," Gabe said, twisting around and looking up at his father. "Isn't she pretty?"

"Yes, she is...." Mickey seemed unable to take his eyes off Lindy Lee.

Holly wouldn't have believed it possible, but Lindy actually blushed.

"Thank you," the designer murmured.

"Make yourself at home," Holly said. "I was just about to serve some eggnog. Would you like a glass?"

"Are you sure it won't be any bother?"

"She's sure," Gabe said, dragging Lindy Lee toward the couch. "Here, sit next to my dad." He patted an empty space on the sofa. "Dad, you sit here."

Mickey smiled at Lindy Lee. "I guess we've got our orders."

"Yes, sir," Lindy joked, winking at Gabe.

"You know what she said to me, Dad?"

"What?"

"I said," Lindy Lee supplied, "that I need a little boy in my life. A little boy just like Gabe."

Holly wondered if she'd heard correctly. This woman who looked identical to her employer sounded nothing like the Lindy Lee she knew. Gone was the dictatorial, demanding tyrant who ran her fashion-design business with military precision. She'd either been taken over by aliens or Lindy Lee had a gentle side that she kept hidden and revealed only on rare occasions. Like Christmas…

An hour later, during a private moment in the kitchen, Jake gave Holly a gift—a cameo that had once belonged to his mother. He said J.R. had given it to him for this very purpose the night before. Holly was thrilled, honored, humbled. She held her breath as he put the cameo on its gold chain around her neck. Holly didn't have anything for him, but Jake said all he wanted was a kiss, and she was happy to comply.

Two hours after that, the small group gathered around the table laden with Christmas fare, including several bottles of exceptional wine brought by Jake and his father. Gabe sat between Mickey and Lindy Lee and chatted nonstop, while J.R. and Jake sat with Holly between them. They took turns saying grace, then took turns again, passing serving dishes to one another.

Amid the clinking of silverware on china and the animated conversation and laughter, Gabe's voice suddenly rose.

"Mrs. Miracle was right," he declared after his first bite of turkey. "This is the *best* Christmas ever."

Emily Merkle reached for her suitcase and started down the long road. Her job in New York was finished, and it had gone even better than she'd expected. Holly and Jake were falling in love. J.R. had more interest in anticipating the future than reliving the pain of the past. Mickey had met Lindy Lee, and Gabe had settled in nicely with his aunt Holly.

Emily hadn't walked far when she was joined by two others, a beautiful woman and a ten-year-old girl. Kaitlyn skipped gracefully at her mother's side, holding Helene's hand.

"All is well," Emily told the other woman. "J.R. and Jake will celebrate Christmas from now on. It was a big leap for J.R., but once the grandchildren arrive, he will lavish them with love."

"Jake will marry Holly?" she asked.

Emily nodded. "They'll have many years together."

"You chose well for my son."

Emily nodded in agreement. Jake and Holly were a good match and they'd bring out the best in each other.

The other woman smiled contentedly. "Thank you," she whispered.

"It was my pleasure," Emily told her.

And it truly was.

★ ★ ★ ★ ★

The Christmas Basket

To
Laurie and Jaxon Macomber
And
in memory of our son Dale

Noelle McDowell's
Journal

December 1

I did it. I broke down and actually booked the flight to Rose. I have a ticket for December 18—Dallas to San Francisco to Portland and then the commuter flight to Rose.

All my excuses are used up. I always figured there was no going back, and yet that's exactly what I'm doing. I'm going home when I swore I never would. Not after what happened... Not after Thom Sutton betrayed me. I know, I know, I've always been dramatic. I can't help that—it's part of my nature.

When I was a teenager I made this vow never to return. I spoke it in the heat of passion, and no one believed me. For that matter, I didn't believe me, not really. But it proved to be so easy to stay away.... I hardly had to invent excuses. While I was in college I had an opportunity to travel to Europe two years in a row. Then in my junior year I had a summer job and was a bridesmaid in a Christmas wedding. And when my senior year rolled around, I was working as an intern for the software company, and it was impossible to get time off. After that...well, it was just simpler to stay away. Without meaning to, my family made it convenient. I didn't need to visit them; they seemed willing enough to come to Dallas.

All of that is about to end. I'm prepared to face my past. I joined Weight Watchers. If I happen to see Thom Sutton, I want him to know exactly what he's missing. I've already lost five of the ten pounds I need to get rid of, and by next week he'll hardly recognize me—if we even run into each other. We won't, of course, but just on the off-chance, I plan to be prepared.

Good ol' Thom Sutton. I wonder what he's doing now. Naturally I could ask, but no one dares mention the name Sutton to my family. It's the Hatfields and McCoys or the Montagues and Capulets all over again. Except that it's our mothers who started this ridiculous feud.

If I really wanted to know about Thom, I could ask Megan or Stephanie. They're the only two girls out of my entire high school class who still live in Rose. But I wouldn't do that. Inquiring about Thom would only invite questions from them about what happened between the two of us. As far as I'm concerned, the fewer people who know, the better.

He's bound to be married, anyway. Good. I want him to be happy. No, I don't.

If I can't be honest in my journal, then I shouldn't keep one. Okay, I admit it—what I really want is for him to have suffered guilt and regret all these years. He should have pined for me. His life should be a bleak series of endless days filled with haunting memories of me. It's what he deserves.

On a brighter note, I'm thrilled for Kristen. I'll return home, help her plan her wedding, hold my head high and pray that Thom Sutton has the opportunity to see me from afar, gorgeous and thin. Then I want him to agonize over all the might-have-beens.

One

It would be the wedding of the year. No—the wedding of the century.

Sarah McDowell intended to create the most exquisite event possible, a wedding worthy of *Vogue* magazine (or at least a two-page spread in the Rose, Oregon, *Gazette*). The entire town would talk about her daughter's wedding.

The foundation for Sarah's plans rested squarely on booking the Women's Century Club for the reception. It was why she'd maintained her association with the club after *that* woman had been granted membership. She was outraged that such a fine institution would lower itself to welcome the likes of Mary Sutton.

Sarah refused to dwell on the sordid details. She couldn't allow herself to get upset over something that had happened almost twenty years ago. Although it didn't hurt any to imagine Mary hearing—second- or third-hand, of course—about Kristen's wedding. As Sarah understood it, Mary's daughter had eloped. Eloped, mind you, with some riffraff hazelnut farmer. Sarah didn't know that for sure because it was her

Christian duty not to gossip or think ill of others. However, sometimes information just happened to come one's way....

Pulling into the parking lot of the Women's Century Club, Sarah surveyed the grounds. Even this late in the year, the rose garden was breathtaking. Many of the carefully tended bushes still wore their blooms, and next June, when the wedding was scheduled, the garden would be stunning. The antique roses with their intoxicating scents and the more recent hybrids with their gorgeous shapes and colors would make a fitting backdrop for the beautiful bride and her handsome groom. It would be *perfect,* she thought with satisfaction. Absolutely perfect.

Sarah had stopped attending the Women's Century Club meetings three years ago. Well, there wasn't any need to obsess over the membership committee's sorry lapse in judgment. For many years Sarah had chaired that committee herself. The instant she stepped down, Mary Sutton had applied for membership to the prestigious club—and received it. Now the only social event Sarah participated in was the annual Christmas dance. Mary Sutton had robbed her of so much already, but Sarah wasn't letting her ruin that, too.

Sarah did continue to meet with other friends from the club and managed to keep up with the news. She understood that Mary had become quite active in the association. Fine. Good for her. It gave the woman something to write about in her column for the weekly *Rose Gazette.* Not that Sarah read "About Town." Someone had told her it was fairly popular, though. Which didn't bother her in the least. Mary was a good writer; Sarah would acknowledge that much. But then, what one lacked in certain areas was often compensated in others. And Mary was definitely lacking in the areas of generosity, fairness, ethics.... She could go on.

With a click of her key chain, Sarah locked her car and

headed toward the large, two-story stone structure. There was a cold wind blowing in from the ocean, and she hurried up the steps of the large veranda that surrounded the house. A blast of warm air greeted her as she walked inside. Immediately in front of her was the curved stairway leading to the ballroom on the second floor. She could already picture Kristen moving elegantly down those stairs, her dress sweeping grandly behind her. Today, evergreen garlands were hung along the mahogany railing, with huge red velvet bows tied at regular intervals. Gigantic potted poinsettias lined both sides of the stairway. The effect was both festive and tasteful.

"Oh, how lovely," she said to Melody Darrington, the club's longtime secretary.

"Yes, we're very pleased with this year's Christmas decorations." Melody glanced up from her desk behind the half wall that overlooked the entry. The door to the office was open and Sarah heard the fax machine humming behind her. "Are you here to pick up your tickets for the Christmas dance?"

"I am," Sarah confirmed. "And I'd like to book the club for June seventh for a reception." She paused dramatically. "Kristen's getting married."

"Sarah, that's just wonderful!"

"Yes, Jake and I are pleased." This seriously understated her emotions. Kristen was the first of her three daughters to marry, and Sarah felt as if the wedding was the culmination of all her years as a caring, involved mother. She highly approved of Kristen's fiancé. Jonathan Clark was not only a charming and considerate young man, he held a promising position at an investment firm and had a degree in business. His parents were college professors who lived in Eugene; he was their only son. Whenever she'd spoken with Jonathan's mother, Louise Clark had sounded equally delighted.

Melody flipped the pages of the appointment book to June. "It's a good idea to book the club early."

Holding her breath, Sarah leaned over the half wall and stared down at the schedule. She relaxed the instant she saw that particular Saturday was free. The wedding date could remain unchanged.

"It looks like June seventh is open," Melody said.

"Fabulous." Sarah's cell phone rang, and she reached inside her purse to retrieve it. She sold real estate, but since entering her fifties, she'd scaled back her hours on the job. Jake, who was head of the X-ray department at Rose Hospital, enjoyed traveling. Sarah no longer had the energy to accompany Jake and also maintain her status as a top-selling agent. The number displayed on her phone was that of her husband's office. She'd call him back shortly. He was probably asking about the time of their eldest daughter's flight. Jake and Sarah were going to meet Noelle at the small commuter airport later in the day. What a joy it would be to have all three of their girls home for Christmas, not to mention Noelle's birthday, which was December twenty-fifth. This would be the first time in ten years that Noelle had returned to celebrate *anything* with her family. Sarah blamed Mary Sutton and her son for that, too.

"Should I give you a deposit now?" she asked, removing her checkbook.

"Since you're a member of the club, that won't be necessary."

"Great. Then that's settled and I can get busy with my day. I've got a couple of houses to show. Plus Jake and I are driving to the airport this afternoon to pick up Noelle. You remember our daughter Noelle, don't you?"

"Of course."

"She's living in Dallas these days, and has a high-powered job with one of the big computer companies." What Sarah didn't add was the Noelle had become a workaholic. Getting her twenty-eight-year-old daughter to take time off work was nearly impossible. Sarah and Jake made a point of visiting her once a year and sometimes twice, but this couldn't go on. Noelle had to get over her phobia about returning to Rose—and the risk of seeing Thom Sutton. Oh, yes, those Suttons had done a lot of damage to the McDowells.

With Kristen announcing her engagement and inviting the Clarks to share their Christmas festivities, Sarah had strongly urged Noelle to come home for the celebration. This was an important year for their family, and it was absolutely necessary that Noelle be there with them. After some back-and-forth discussion, she'd finally capitulated.

"Before you leave, there's something you should know," Melody said hesitantly. "There's been a rule change about members using the building."

"Yes?" Sarah tensed, anticipating a roadblock.

"The new rule states that only members who have completed a minimum of ten hours' community service approved by the club will be permitted to lease our facilities."

"But I'm an active part of our community already," Sarah complained. She provided plenty of services to others.

"I realize that. Unfortunately, the service project in question must be determined by the club and it must be completed by the end of December to qualify for the following year."

Sarah gaped at her. "Do you mean to say that in addition to everything else I'm doing in the next two weeks, I have to complete some club project?"

"You haven't been reading the newsletters, have you?" Melody asked, frowning.

Obviously not. Sarah refused to read about Mary Sutton, whose name seemed to appear in every issue these days.

"If you attended the meetings, you'd know it, too." Melody added insult to injury by pointing out Sarah's intentional absence.

Despite her irritation, Sarah managed a weak smile. "All right," she muttered. "What can I do?"

"Actually, you've come at an opportune moment. We need someone who's willing to pitch in on the Christmas baskets."

Sarah was trying to figure out how she could squeeze in one more task before the holidays. "Exactly what would that entail?"

"Oh, it'll be great fun. The ladies pooled the money they raised from the cookbook sale to buy gifts for these baskets. They've made up lists, and what you'd need to do is get everything on your list, arrange all the stuff inside the baskets and then deliver them to the Salvation Army by December twenty-third."

That didn't sound unreasonable. "I think I can do that."

"Wonderful." A smile lit up Melody's face. "The woman who's heading up the project will be grateful for some help."

"The woman?" That sounded better already. At least she wouldn't be stuck doing this alone.

"Mary Sutton."

Sarah felt as though Melody had punched her. "Excuse me. For a moment I thought you said *Mary Sutton.*"

"I did."

"I don't mean to be catty here, but Mary and I have...a history."

"I'm sure you'll be able to work something out. You're both adults."

Sarah was stunned by the woman's lack of sensitivity. She wanted to argue, to explain that this was unacceptable, but she couldn't think of exactly what to say.

"You did want the club for June seventh, didn't you?"

"Well, yes, of course, but—"

"Then be here tomorrow morning at ten to meet with Mary."

Numb and speechless, Sarah slowly turned and trudged toward the door.

"Sarah," Melody called. "Don't forget the dance tickets."

Dance. How could she think about the dance when she was being forced to confront a woman who detested her? The feeling might be mutual but that didn't make it any less awkward.

One across. A four-letter word for fragrant flower. Rose, naturally. Noelle McDowell penciled in the answer and moved to the next clue. A prickly feeling crawled up her spine and she raised her head. She disliked the short commuter flights. This one, out of Portland, carried twenty-four passengers. It saved having to rent a vehicle or asking her parents to make the long drive into the big city to pick her up.

The feeling persisted and she glanced over her shoulder. She instantly jerked back and slid down in her seat as far as the constraints of the seat belt allowed. It couldn't be. *No, please,* she muttered, closing her eyes. *Not Thom.* Not after all these years. Not now. But it was, it had to be. No one else would look at her with such complete, unadulterated antagonism. He had some nerve after what he'd done to her.

Long before she was ready, the pilot announced that the plane was preparing to land in Rose. On these flights, no carry-on bags were permitted, and Noelle hadn't taken anything more than her purse on board. Her magazines would normally go in her briefcase, but that didn't fit in the compact space beneath her seat, so the flight attendant had stowed it. She had a *Weight Watchers* magazine and a crossword puzzle book marked *EASY* in large letters across the top. She wasn't going to let Thom see her with either and stuffed them in the outside pocket of her purse, folding one magazine over the other.

Her pulse thundered like crazy. The man who'd broken her heart sat only two rows behind her, looking as sophisticated as if he'd stepped off the pages of GQ. He'd always been tall, dark and handsome—like a twenty-first-century Cary Grant. Classic features that were just rugged enough to be interesting and very, very masculine. Dark eyes, glossy dark hair. An impeccable sense of style. Surely he was married. But finding out would mean asking her sister or one of her friends who still lived in Rose. Coward that she was, Noelle didn't want to know. Okay, she did, but not if it meant having to ask.

The plane touched down and Noelle braced herself against the jolt of the wheels bouncing on tarmac. As soon as they'd coasted to a stop, the Unfasten Seat Belt sign went off, and the people around her instantly leaped to their feet. Noelle took her time. Her hair was a fright. Up at three that morning to catch the 6:00 a.m. out of Dallas/Ft. Worth, she'd run a brush through the dark tangles, forgoing the usual routine of fussing with mousse. As a result, large ringlets fell like bedsprings about her face. Normally, her hair was shaped and controlled and coerced into gentle waves. But today she had the misfortune of looking like Shirley Temple in one of her 1930s movies—and in front of Thom Sutton, no less.

When it was her turn to leave her seat, she stood, looking staunchly ahead. If luck was with her, she could slip away unnoticed and pretend she hadn't seen him. Luck, however, was on vacation and the instant she stepped into the aisle, the handle of her purse caught on the seat arm. Both magazines popped out of the outside pocket and flew into the air, only to be caught by none other than Thom Sutton. The crossword puzzle magazine tumbled to the floor and he was left holding the *Weight Watchers* December issue. As his gaze slid over her, she immediately sucked in her stomach.

"I read it for the fiction," she announced, then added, "Don't I know you?" She tried to sound indifferent—and to look thin. "It's Tim, isn't it?" she asked, frowning as though she couldn't quite place him.

"Thom," he corrected. "Good to see you again, Nadine."

"Noelle," she said bitterly.

He glared at her until someone from the back of the line called, "Would you two mind having your reunion when you get off the plane?"

"Sorry," Thom said over his shoulder.

"I barely know this man." Noelle wanted her fellow passengers to hear the truth. "I once thought I did, but I was wrong," she explained, walking backward toward the exit.

"Whatever," the guy behind them said loudly.

"You're a fine one to talk," Thom said. His eyes were as dark and cold as those of the snowman they'd built in Lions' Park their senior year of high school—like glittering chips of coal.

"You have your nerve," she muttered, whirling around just in time to avoid crashing into the open cockpit. She smiled sweetly at the pilot. "Thank you for a most pleasant flight."

He returned the smile. "I hope you'll fly with us again."

"I will."

"Good to see you, Thom," the pilot said next.

Placing her hand on the railing of the steep stairs that led to the ground, Noelle did her best to keep her head high, her shoulders square—and her eyes front. The last thing she wanted to do was trip and make an even worse fool of herself by falling flat on her face.

She was shocked by a blast of cold air. After living in Texas for the last ten years, she'd forgotten how cold it could get in the Pacific Northwest. Her thin cashmere wrap was completely inadequate.

"One would think you'd know better than to wear a sweater here in December," Thom said, coming down the steps directly behind her.

"I forgot."

"If you came home more often, you'd have remembered."

"You keep track of my visits?" She scowled at him. A thick strand of curly hair slapped her in the face and she tossed it back with a jerk of her head. Unfortunately she nearly put out her neck in the process.

"No, I don't keep track of your visits. Frankly, I couldn't care less."

"That's fine by me." Having the last word was important, no matter how inane it was.

The luggage cart came around and she grabbed her briefcase from the top and made for the interior of the small airport. Her flight had landed early, which meant that her parents probably hadn't arrived yet. At least her luck was consistent—all bad. One thing was certain: the instant Thom caught sight of her mother and father, he'd make himself scarce.

He removed his own briefcase and started into the terminal less than two feet behind her. Because of his long legs, he quickly outdistanced her. Refusing to let him pass her, Noelle hurried ahead, practically trotting.

"Don't you think you're being a little silly?" he asked.

"About what?" She blinked, hoping to convey a look of innocence.

"Never mind." He smiled, which infuriated her further.

"No, I'm serious," she insisted. "What do you mean?"

He simply shook his head and turned toward the baggage claim area. They were the first passengers to get there. Noelle stood on one side of the conveyor belt and Thom on the other. He ignored her and she tried to pretend he'd never been born.

That proved to be impossible because ten years ago Thom Sutton had ripped her heart right out.

For most of their senior year of high school, Thom and Noelle had been in love; they'd also managed to hide that fact from their parents. Sneaking out of her room at night, meeting him after school and passing notes to each other had worked quite effectively.

Then they'd argued about their mothers and the ongoing feud between Sarah and Mary. They'd soon made up, however, realizing that what really mattered was their love. Because they were both eighteen and legally entitled to marry without parental consent, they'd decided to elope. It'd been Thom's suggestion. According to him, it was the only way they could get married, since the parents on both sides would oppose their wishes and try to put obstacles in their path. But once they were married, he said, they could bring their families together.

Noelle felt mortified now to remember how much she'd trusted Thom. But their whole "engagement" had turned out to be a ploy to humiliate and embarrass her. It seemed Thom was his mother's son, after all.

She'd been proud of her love for Thom, and before she left to meet him that fateful evening, she'd boldly announced her intentions to her family. Her stomach twisted at the memory. Her parents were shocked as well as appalled; she and Thom had kept their secret well. Her mother had burst into tears, her father had shouted and her two younger sisters had wailed in protest. Undeterred, Noelle had marched out the door, suitcase in hand, to meet the man she loved. The man she'd defied her family to marry. Except that he didn't show up.

At first she'd assumed it was a misunderstanding—that she'd

mistaken the agreed-upon time. Then, throwing caution to the wind, she'd phoned his house and asked to speak to him, only to learn that Thom had gone bowling.

He'd gone *bowling?* Apparently some friends from school had phoned and off he'd gone, leaving her to wait in doubt and misery. The parking lot at the bowling alley confirmed his father's words. There was Thom's car—and inside the Bowlerama was Thom, carousing with his friends. Noelle had peered through the window and seen the waitress sitting on his lap and the other guys gathered around, joking and teasing. Before she went home, Noelle had placed a nasty note on his windshield, in which she described him as a scum-of-the-earth bastard. Their supposed elopement, their so-called love had all been a fraud, a cruel joke. She figured it was revenge what for her mother had done, losing Thom's grandmother's precious tea service. Not *losing* it, actually. She'd borrowed it to display at an open house for another real estate agent—and someone had taken it. That was how the feud started and it had escalated steadily after that.

To make matters worse, she'd had to return home in humiliation and admit that Thom had stood her up. Like the heroine of an old-fashioned melodrama, she'd been jilted, abandoned and forsaken.

For days she'd moped around the house, weeping and miserable. Thom hadn't phoned or contacted her again. It was difficult to believe he could be so heartless, but she had all the evidence she needed. She hadn't seen or talked to him since. For ten years she'd avoided returning to the scene of her shame.

The grinding sound of the conveyor belt gearing up broke Noelle from her reverie. Luggage started to roll out from the black hole behind the rubber curtain. Thom stepped forward, in a hurry to claim his suitcase and leave, or so it seemed.

Noelle was no less eager to escape. She'd rather wait in the damp cold outside the terminal than stand five feet across from Thomas Sutton.

The very attractive Thomas Sutton. Even better-looking than he'd been ten years ago. Life just wasn't fair.

"I would've thought your wife would be here to pick you up," she said without looking at him. She shouldn't have spoken at all, but suddenly she had to know.

"Is that your unsubtle way of asking if I'm married?"

She ground her teeth. "Stood up any other girls in the last ten years?" she asked.

His eyes narrowed. "Don't do it, Noelle."

"You're the one who shouldn't have done it."

The man from the back of the plane waltzed past Noelle and reached for his suitcase. "Why don't you two just kiss and make up," he suggested, winking at Thom.

"I don't think so," Noelle said, sending Thom a contemptuous glare. She was astonished to see his anger, as though *he* had something to be angry about. *She* was the injured party here.

"On that I'll agree with you," Thom said. He caught hold of a suitcase and yanked it off the belt with enough force to topple a second suitcase. Without another word, he turned and walked out the door.

No sooner had he disappeared than the glass doors opened and in walked Noelle's parents.

Noelle's youngest sister held a special place in her heart. Carley Sue was an unexpected surprise, born when Noelle was fifteen and Kristen twelve. She'd only been three when Noelle left for college. Nevertheless, all three sisters remained close. Or as close as email, phone calls and the occasional visit to Dallas allowed.

Sitting on Noelle's bed, Carley rested her chin on one hand

as Noelle unpacked her suitcase. "You don't mind that I have your old room, do you?" she asked anxiously.

"Heavens, no. It's only right that you do."

Some of the worry disappeared from Carley's eyes. "Are you really going to be home for two whole weeks?"

"I am." Noelle had tentatively planned a discounted cruise with a couple of friends. Instead, she was vacationing with her parents, planning her sister's wedding and trying not to think about Thom Sutton.

"You're going to the Christmas dance, aren't you?"

"Not if I can get out of it." Her mother was the one who insisted on these social outings, but Noelle would live the rest of her life content if she never attended another dance. They reminded her to much of those long-ago evenings with Thom....

"Mom says you're going."

Noelle sat down on the end of the bed and sighed. "I'll tell her I don't have anything to wear."

"Don't do that," Carley advised. "She'll buy you a pink dress. Mom loves pink. Not just any old pink, either, but something that looks exactly like Pepto-Bismol. She actually wanted Kristen to choose pink for her wedding colors." She grimaced. Reaching down for her feet, Carley curled her fingers over her bare toes and nodded vigorously. "You'd better come to the dance."

This was one of the reasons Noelle found excuse after excuse to stay away from Rose. Admittedly it wasn't the primary reason—Thom Sutton and his mother were responsible for that. But as much as she loved her family, she dreaded being dragged from one social event to the next. She could see her mother putting her on display—in Pepto-Bismol pink, according to Carley. If that wasn't bad enough, Sarah had an embarrassing tendency to speak as though Noelle wasn't in the room, bragging outrageously over every little accomplishment.

"Hey, you want to go to the movies tomorrow?" Noelle asked her sister.

Carley's eyes brightened. "Sure! I was hoping we'd get to do things together."

The doorbell chimed and Carley rolled onto her stomach. "That's Kristen. She's coming over without Jonathan tonight."

"You like Jonathan?" Noelle asked.

"Yeah." Carley grinned happily. "He danced with me once and no one asked him to or anything."

This was encouraging. Maybe he'd dance with her, too.

"Noelle!" Kristen called from the far end of the hallway. She burst into the room, full of energy and spirit. Instantly Noelle was wrapped in a tight embrace. "I can't believe you're here—oh, sis, it's so good to see you."

Noelle hugged her back. She missed the chats they used to have; discussions over the phone just weren't the same as hugs and smiles. "Guess who I ran into on the plane?" Noelle had been dying to talk about the chance encounter with Thom.

Some of the excitement faded from Kristen's eyes. "Don't tell me. Thom Sutton?"

Noelle nodded.

"Who's Thom Sutton?" Carley asked, glancing from one sister to the other.

"A guy I once dated."

"Were you lovers?"

"Carley!"

"Just curious." She shrugged as if this was information she was somehow entitled to.

"Where?" Kristen demanded.

"He was on the same flight as me."

"He still lives here, you know. He's some kind of executive

for a mail-order company that's really taken off in the last few years. Apparently he does a lot of traveling."

"How'd you know that?" They'd always avoided the topic of Thom Sutton in their telephone and email communications.

"Jon told me about him. I think Thom might be one of his clients."

"Oh." Not only was Thom Sutton gorgeous, he was successful, too. "I suppose he's engaged to someone stunningly beautiful." That was to be expected.

"I hear—again from Jon—that he dates quite a bit, but there's no one serious."

Noelle shouldn't be pleased, but she couldn't help it. She didn't want to examine that reaction too closely.

"I want to know what happened," Carley demanded, rising to her knees. "I'm not a kid anymore. Tell me!"

"He was Noelle's high school sweetheart," Kirsten explained.

"The guy who left you at the altar?"

"Who told you that?" Noelle asked, although the answer was obvious. "And he didn't leave me at the altar." *Just being accurate,* she told herself. *I'm not defending him.*

"Mom told me 'cause she wants me to keep away from those Suttons. When I asked her why, she said you learned your lesson the hard way. She said a Sutton broke your heart and jilted you."

"There's more to it than that," Kirsten told her.

"I want to know *everything*," Carley pleaded. "How can I hate them if I don't know what they did that was so awful?"

"You shouldn't hate anyone."

"I don't, not really, but if our family doesn't like their family, then I should know why."

"It's a long story."

Carley sat back on her heels. "That's what Mom said."

"God help me," Kristen murmured, covering her eyes with one hand. "Don't tell me I already sound like Mom. I didn't think this would happen until I turned thirty."

Noelle laughed, although she wasn't sure how funny it was, since she herself was only days from her twenty-ninth birthday.

"Did you love him terribly?" Carley asked with a faraway look in her eyes.

Noelle wasn't sure how to respond. She felt a distant and remembered pain but refused to let it take hold. "I thought I did."

"It was wildly romantic," Kristen added. "They were madly in love, but then they had a falling-out—"

"That's one way to put it," Noelle said, interrupting her sister. Thom had apparently fallen out of love with her. He'd certainly fallen out of their plans to elope.

"This is all so sad," Carley said with an exaggerated sigh.

"Our parents not getting along is what started this in the first place."

"At least you and Thom didn't kill yourselves, like Romeo and Juliet—"

"No." Noelle shook her head. "I've always been the sane, sensible sister. Remember?" But even as she spoke, she recognized her words for the lie they were. Staying away for ten years was a pretty extreme and hardly "sensible" reaction. Even she knew that. The fact was, though, something that had begun as a protest had simply become habit.

"Oh, sure," Kristen teased. "Very sensible. You work too hard, you don't date nearly enough and you avoid Rose as though we've got an epidemic of the plague."

"Guilty, guilty, not guilty." She wasn't *purposely* avoiding Rose, she told herself, at least not anymore and not to the extent that Kristen implied. Noelle's job was demanding and it was difficult to take off four or five days in a row.

"I've never met Thom, and already I don't like him," Carley announced. "Anyone who broke your heart is a dweeb. Besides, if he married you the way he said he would, you'd be living in Rose now and I could see you anytime I wanted."

"Well put, little sister," Kristen said. She shrugged off her coat, then joined Carley at the foot of the bed.

Noelle smiled at her two sisters and realized with a pang how much she missed them. Back in Texas it was all too easy to let work consume her life—to relegate these important relationships to fifteen-minute conversations on the phone.

"Look," Kristen said and stretched out her arm so Noelle could see her engagement ring. It was a solitaire diamond, virtually flawless, in a classic setting. A perfect choice for Kristen. "Jon and I shopped for weeks. He wanted the highest-quality stone for the best price." Her eyes softened as she studied the ring.

"It's beautiful," Noelle whispered, overcome for a moment by the sheer joy she saw in her sister's face.

"You'll be my maid of honor, won't you?"

"As long as I don't have to wear a dress the color of Pepto-Bismol."

"You're safe on that account."

"If you ask me to be the flower girl, I think I'll scream," Carley muttered. "Why won't anyone believe me when I tell them I'm not a little kid anymore? I'm almost fourteen!"

"Not for ten months," Noelle reminded her.

"But, I'm *going* to be fourteen."

Kristen brushed the hair away from Carley's face. "Actually, I intended to ask you to be a bridesmaid."

"You did?" Carley shrieked with happiness. "Well, then, I'll tell you what I overheard Mom tell Dad." Her voice dropped to a whisper as she detailed a conversation between their parents regarding Christmas baskets.

"Mom's meeting with *Mrs. Sutton* tomorrow morning?" Noelle repeated incredulously.

"That's what she said. She didn't sound happy about it, either."

"I'll just bet she didn't."

"This should be interesting," Kristen murmured.

Yes, it should, Noelle silently agreed. *It should be very interesting, indeed.*

Noelle McDowell's
Journal

December 19
(2:00 a.m.)

So I saw him before I even got back to town. Of all the flights I could've taken…

Seeing Thom after all these years was probably the most humbling experience of my life, except for the last time I was with him. Correction. Wasn't with him. Why did this have to happen to me? Or did I bring it on myself because of my obsession over seeing him again?

Okay, the thing to do is look at the positive aspect of this. It's over. I saw him, it was worse than I could have imagined, but now I don't need to worry about it anymore. Thom made it clear that he wasn't any happier to see me than I was about running into him. At least the feeling's mutual. Although I'm kind of confused by that, since I'm the offended one. He jilted me. Unfortunately, after this latest run-in, he doesn't have any reason to regret that. I behaved like an idiot.

On a brighter note—and I'm always looking for brighter notes!—it's good to be home. I shouldn't have stayed away for ten years. That was foolish and I'm sorry about it. I walked all through the house, stopping in each room. After a while, I got all teary as I looked around. Nothing's really changed and yet everything's different. I didn't realize how much I've missed my home. Mom's got the house all decorated for Christmas, including those funny-looking cotton-ball snowmen I made at camp a thousand years ago. When I commented on that, she told me it was tradition. She puts them out every Christmas. She got all choked up and I did, too. We hugged, and I promised I'd never stay away this long again. And I won't.

Carley Sue (she hates it when I use her middle name) is so much fun. Seeing her here, in her own space (even if it is my old room), is like discovering an entirely different side of her. She's freer, more relaxed, and so eager to share the camaraderie between me and Kristen.

Speaking of Kristen—she's on cloud nine. We sat up and talked for hours, and she told me all about meeting and falling in love with Jonathan. I'd heard it before, but the story felt brand-new as I listened to her tell it in person. It's so romantic, meeting her future husband in a flower shop when he's there to pick up a dozen red roses for another woman. I give him credit, though; Jonathan knew a real flower when he saw one. It was Kristen who walked out with those roses.

Carley warned me that Mom's going to be looking for company when she has to meet Mrs. Sutton in the morning. We've already thwarted her. We sisters have our ways....

Two

Sarah would have preferred a root canal to meeting with Mary Sutton. A root canal without anaesthetic.

Her husband lingered over his morning coffee before leaving for the hospital. "You're really stressed about this, aren't you?"

"Yes!" Sarah wasn't afraid to admit it. "The last time I spoke to Mary was the day she wrote that dreadful article about me in her column."

"You think that article was only about you," Jake said. "But it could've been about any real estate agent. Maybe even a bunch of different ones." His voice drifted off.

Sarah didn't understand why her husband was arguing when they both knew the entire dreadful piece titled *The Nightmare Real Estate Agent,* was directed solely at *her.* Although she hadn't committed any of sins Mary had described, she'd been guilty of the one crime Mary hadn't mentioned. Never once had she misrepresented a home or hidden a defect. Nor had she ever low-balled a client. But Sarah had borrowed something she couldn't return.

"Was that *before* or *after* you planted the OPEN HOUSE sign in her front yard?" Jake asked.

"Before, and she deserved it."

Her husband chuckled. "Go on, meet with her and don't for a moment let her know you're upset."

"You sound like a commercial for deodorant."

"Yes, dear." He kissed her cheek and headed out the door to work.

Tightening the belt of her housecoat, Sarah gazed out the front window as he drove away. *Meet with her...* Easy for him to say. He wasn't the one coming face-to-face with Mary after all these years.

Yawning, Noelle wandered into the kitchen and poured a cup of coffee. Sarah's spirits lifted immediately. It was so good to have her daughter home—and even better that she'd arrived at such an opportune moment. Noelle could act as a buffer between her and that demented newspaper writer who'd once been her friend. True, there was the business with the Sutton boy, but if nothing else, that unfortunate bit of history would distract them all from this current awkwardness. She felt a twinge of guilt at the idea of involving her daughter. Still, she needed reinforcements, and surely Noelle was long over her infatuation with Thom.

"Good morning, dear," Sarah said, mustering a cheerful greeting. "I was wondering if you'd like to come with me this morning." Try as she might, she couldn't keep the plea out of her voice.

Her daughter leaned against the kitchen counter, holding the mug with both hands. "I promised to take Carley shopping and to the movies."

"Oh. That won't be until later, will it?"

"Mom," Noelle said, sighing loudly. "I'm *not* going to let you use me as a buffer when you meet Mrs. Sutton."

"Who told you I was meeting…" She didn't bother to finish the question, since the answer was obvious. Jake! Dumping the rest of her coffee down the sink, she reluctantly went to her room to dress. She'd be entering the lion's den alone, so she wanted to look her best.

"I don't think she's nearly the monster you make her out to be," Noelle called after her.

That her own daughter, her oldest child—the very one who'd been jilted by Thom Sutton—could say such a thing was beyond Sarah. As far as she was concerned, there was too much forgiveness going on here. And if Noelle thought Mary was so wonderful, then she should be willing to come along.

Didn't Noelle grasp the unpleasantness of this situation? Clearly not. Even Jake didn't take it seriously. He seemed to think this was some kind of joke! Well, she, for one, wasn't laughing.

Despite her bad feelings about the meeting with Mary Sutton, Sarah arrived at the Women's Century Club twenty minutes early. This was the way she'd planned it. As she recalled, Mary possessed a number of irritating habits, one of which was an inability to ever show up on time. Therefore, Sarah considered it advantageous to be early, as though that would highlight Mary's lack of responsibility and basic courtesy.

"Good morning, Melody," she said as she stepped briskly into the entry.

"Morning," came Melody's reply. The phone rang just then, and she reached for it, still standing in front of the copy machine.

While she waited, Sarah checked her appearance in the lobby restroom. She'd taken an inordinate amount of time with her makeup that morning. Her hair was impeccably styled, if she did say so herself, and her clothes looked both businesslike and feminine. Choosing the right outfit was of the utmost importance; in the end, after three complete changes, she'd chosen navy-blue wool slacks, a white cashmere sweater and a silk scarf with a pattern of holly and red berries.

Melody finished with the phone. "Sorry, it's crazy around here this morning. Everyone's getting ready for the dance."

Of course. In her dread, she'd nearly forgotten about the annual dance.

The door opened, and with a dramatic flair—all swirling scarves and large gestures—Mary Sutton entered the building. Did the woman think she was on stage, for heaven's sake? "Hello, Melody," she said, her voice light and breezy. Then—as if she'd only now noticed Sarah—she turned in her direction, frowned slightly and then acknowledged her with a curt nod.

"Good to see you, too," Sarah muttered.

"I'm here for the list. The Christmas basket list," Mary said, walking over to the half wall behind which Melody stood.

"That's why I'm here," Sarah said and forced herself into the space between Mary and the wall.

The two jockeyed for position, elbowing each other until Melody stared at them aghast. "What's *wrong* with you two?" she asked.

"As I explained earlier, we have a *history*," Sarah said, as though that should account for everything.

"A very long and *difficult* history," Mary added.

"You'll have to work together on this." Melody frowned at them both. "I'd hate to see these needy families deprived because you two can't get along." The phone rang again and Melody scooped up the receiver.

"You're impossible to work with," Mary said, practically shoving Sarah aside.

"I won't stand here and be insulted by the likes of you," Sarah insisted. Talk about impossible!

"This isn't going to work."

"You're telling me!" She was ready to walk out the door. But then she realized that was exactly what Mary wanted her to do. She'd been provoking Sarah from the moment she'd made that stagy entrance. This was a low, underhanded attempt to prevent her from holding Kristen's wedding reception at the club. Somehow Mary had found out about the wedding and hoped to thwart the McDowells' plans. That had to be it. But Sarah refused to let a Sutton—especially *this* Sutton—manipulate her.

"There are ways of doing what needs to be done without tripping over each other's feet," Sarah murmured, trying to sound conciliatory. She could only hope that Kristen truly appreciated the sacrifice she was making on her behalf. If it wasn't for the wedding, she wouldn't be caught dead working on a project with Mary Sutton, charity or not!

"What do you mean?"

"There *must* be a way." She personally didn't have any ideas, but perhaps the club secretary could think of something. "Melody?"

Another line rang, and Melody put the first caller on hold in order to answer the second. She placed her palm over the mouthpiece and said, "Why don't you two go talk this out in the lobby?" She waved them impatiently away. "I'll be with you as soon as I can."

Sarah took a few steps back, unwilling to voluntarily give up hard-won territory. This was more of a problem than she'd expected. For her part, she was willing to make the best of it, but she could already tell that Mary had her own agenda.

"The Christmas decorations are lovely this year, aren't they?" Sarah said, making an effort to start again. After all, she was stuck with the woman.

"Yes," came Mary's stilted reply. "I'm the chair of the decorating committee."

"Oh." She studied the staircase again and noticed a number of flaws apparent on closer inspection. Walking to the bottom step, she straightened a bow.

"Leave my bows alone!"

"A little possessive, are we?" Sarah murmured.

"You would be, too, if you'd spent twenty minutes making each of those velvet bows."

"I could have done it in ten."

"Next year, I'll let you." Then, as if she was bored with the subject, Mary said, "I understand Noelle's in town."

"Yes, and I'd appreciate if you'd keep your son away from her."

"My son!" Mary cried. "You don't need to worry about *that*. Thom learned his lesson as far as your daughter's concerned a long time ago."

"On the contrary, I believe your son broke my daughter's heart."

"Ladies!" Melody came out from behind the counter, shaking her head. "I thought we were discussing ways you two can work together to fill those Christmas baskets."

"I don't think I *can* work with her," Mary said, crossing her arms. She presented Sarah with a view of her back.

"Then divide the list," Melody suggested. "One of you can shop for the gifts and the other can buy the groceries. Arrange a day to meet and assemble the baskets, and then you'll be done with it."

Sarah didn't know why she hadn't thought of that earlier. It made perfect sense and would allow them to maintain a healthy distance from each other.

"Divide the list," Mary instructed with a dramatic wave of her hand.

"By all means, divide the list," Sarah said and mimicked Mary's gesture.

"All right," Melody said. She went back to her office, with the two women following, and slipped the list into the photocopier. The phone rang again, and she answered it, holding the receiver between her shoulder and ear. Melody retrieved the original and the copy, reached for the scissors and cut both lists in two. Still talking, she dropped the papers, then picked them up and handed half of the original list to Mary and half to Sarah. The copies of each woman's list went into a file on her desk.

Sarah glanced over her list and tucked it inside her purse. "When do you suggest we meet to assemble the baskets?"

"The twenty-third before noon. That way, we'll be able to drop them off at the Salvation Army in plenty of time. They'll distribute the baskets on Christmas Eve."

"Fine." That settled, Sarah charged out the door without a backward glance. This wasn't the best solution, but it was manageable. She'd do her share of the work, and she wasn't about to let anyone suggest otherwise.

"This is so cool," Carley said as they left the mall late Thursday afternoon, their arms loaded with bags and packages. Noelle smiled fondly at her youngest sister. That summer, Carley had spent two weeks with her in Texas while their parents were on a cruise. She'd matured noticeably in the six months since then.

"Mom's not selling much real estate anymore," her sister told her as they climbed into the car. "I think she's bored with it, but she won't admit it."

"Really?"

"She's totally involved in Kristen's wedding. It's all she thinks about. She's read a whole bunch of books and magazine articles and has everything set in her mind. Just the other day, she said that what this town really needs is a wedding planner."

"And you think Mom would enjoy that?"

"Are you kidding?" Carley said. "She'd *love* it."

Their mother was extremely sociable, which was one of the reasons she was such a successful real estate agent, Noelle mused. Sarah knew nearly everyone in town and had wonderful connections. Perhaps Carley was right.

"The Admiral really hasn't changed," Noelle murmured. She'd spent a lot of time at the old downtown theater, back in high school. It was there, in the balcony, that Thom had first kissed her. To this day—as much as she wanted to forget it—she remembered the thrill of that kiss.

The Admiral was a classic theater built sixty years earlier. The screen was huge and the second-floor balcony held the plush loge seats—always Noelle's favorite place to sit.

They purchased the tickets, a large bucket of popcorn and drinks.

"Do you want to go up to the balcony?" Carley asked.

"Where else would we sit?" Noelle was already halfway up the winding staircase that led to the second floor. She went straight to the front row and plopped down on a cushioned seat. Carley plopped down beside her. The main feature was a Christmas release, an animated film starring the voices of Billy Crystal and Nathan Lane.

"I'm not a kid anymore, but I'm glad you wanted to see this movie, too," her sister confided.

Noelle placed the bucket of popcorn between them. "Thanks for giving me the excuse." She leaned forward and looked at the audience below. The theater was only half-full and she wondered if she'd recognize anyone.

"Oh, my goodness," she whispered. This couldn't be happening! Thom Sutton sat almost directly below her. If that wasn't bad enough, a blonde sat in the seat beside him and—to Noelle's disgust—had her hands all over him.

"What?" Carley demanded.

"It's Thom." Heaven help her, Noelle couldn't keep from watching. The blonde's hand lingered at the base of his neck; she was stroking his hair with all the tenderness of a long-time lover.

"Not Thom Sutton? The son of the enemy?" Carley asked.

Noelle nodded. Sad and shocking though it was, he obviously still had the power to hurt her. No, not hurt her—infuriate her!

Carley reached for a kernel of popcorn and tossed it down.

Noelle gasped, grabbing her sister's hand. The last thing she wanted was to call attention to the balcony. "Don't do that!"

"Why not? He jilted you and now he's here with another woman." She hurled another kernel in his direction.

Noelle glanced down and saw the blonde nibbling on his earlobe. That did it. She scooped out a handful of popcorn and threw it over the balcony railing. Noelle and her sister leaned back and smothered their giggles. A few minutes later, unable to resist, Noelle looked down again.

"Oh, no," Carley muttered under her breath as she sent a fresh shower of popcorn over the edge. She jerked back instantly.

"What?" Noelle asked.

"I think we're in trouble. He just turned around and looked up here and I don't think he's pleased."

Fine, the management could throw her out of the theater if he complained. Noelle didn't care.

"I want to know about you and him," Carley said. "I wasn't even born when his mom and our mom had their big fight."

Noelle was reluctant to describe all this old history, but she supposed her sister had a right to know. "Well, Mom had just started selling real estate and was making new friends. She claims Mary was jealous of those friends, especially one whose name was Cheryl. Cheryl had been working at the agency for a while and was kind of showing Mom the ropes. She was holding an open house and wanted something elegant to set off the dining room. Mom knew that Mary had this exquisite silver tea service—the perfect thing. But Mom also knew that if she asked Mary to lend it to Cheryl, Mrs. Sutton would turn her down. Instead, Mom asked to borrow it for herself, which was a fib."

Carley frowned. "So that's why Mrs. Sutton blamed Mom? Because Mom lied—I mean fibbed—and then the expensive silver tea service got stolen? Oh, I bet Mom was just sick about it."

"She felt awful. According to Mrs. Sutton, the tea service had belonged to her grandmother and was a family heirloom. It was irreplaceable."

"What did Mom do?"

"She called the police and offered a reward for its return, but the tea service didn't turn up. She went to every antiques store in the area, looking for something similar. Finally there was nothing more she could do. She tried to repair the damage to the friendship, but Mrs. Sutton was angry—and really, you can't blame her. She was hurt because Mom had misled her. They got into this big argument about it and everything escalated from there. Mrs. Sutton did some petty things and Mom retaliated. Next thing you know, a grudge developed that's gone on to this day."

"Retaliated?" Carley asked. "How?"

"When it became clear that Mrs. Sutton wasn't going to forgive and forget, Mom tried another tactic. She thought she'd be funny." Noelle smiled at the memory. "Mrs. Sutton got her hair cut, and Mom sent her flowers and a sympathy card. Then Mrs. Sutton ordered pizza with double anchovies and had it delivered to Mom. You know how Mom hates an- chovies—and furthermore she had to pay for it." She shook her head. "It's sad, isn't it? That a good friendship should fall apart for such a silly reason."

"Yeah," Carley agreed. "They acted pretty childish."

"And my relationship with Thom was one of the casualties."

"When did you fall in love with him?" Carley wanted to know.

"We became good friends when we were kids. For a long time, our families got along really well. We often went on picnics and outings together. Thom and I were the closest in age, and we were constant companions—until the argument."

"What happened after the argument?"

"Mrs. Sutton sent Thom and his older sister to a private school, and I didn't see him again for about six years. He came back to public school when we were sophomores. We didn't have a lot in common anymore and hardly had anything to do with each other until we both were assigned to the same English class in our senior year."

"That was when you fell in love?" Carley's voice rose wist- fully.

Noelle nodded, and the familiar pain tightened her stom- ach. "Apparently I fell harder than Thom."

Noelle carefully glanced down again. Talking about Thom and her romance—especially while she was sitting in this theater—brought up memories she'd prefer to forget. Why wouldn't the stupid movie start? It was two minutes past the scheduled time.

The boy who'd rung up the popcorn order marched down the side aisle toward Noelle and Carley. He wore a bored but determined look. "There's been a complaint from the people down below about you throwing popcorn," he said accusingly.

Noelle could feel the heat build up in her cheeks. "I'm sorry—that was, uh, an accident."

The kid's expression said he'd heard it all before. "Make sure it doesn't happen again, okay?"

"It won't," Noelle promised him.

"Sorry," Carley said in a small voice as the boy left.

"It was my fault. I encouraged you."

"But I started it."

"You think you're the one who invented throwing popcorn? Hey, I've got fifteen years on you."

"I want to fall in love one day, too," Carley said, leaning back in her seat, which rocked slightly.

"You will," Noelle said, hoping her sister had better luck in that department than she'd had.

The lights dimmed then and with a grand, sweeping motion the huge velvet curtains hanging over the screen slowly parted. Soon, they were watching previews for upcoming features. Noelle absently nibbled on popcorn and let her mind wander.

Thom had changed if the blonde down below was the type of woman he found attractive. That shouldn't surprise her, though. Time changed a lot of things in life. Some days, when she felt lonely and especially sorry for herself, she tried to imagine what would've happened if she *had* married Thom all those years ago. Getting married that young rarely worked out. They might've been divorced, she might've ended up a single mother, she might never have completed her education.... All kinds of difficult outcomes were possible. In all honesty, she told herself, it was for the best that they hadn't run off together.

Carley slid forward and peeked over the railing. Almost immediately she flopped back. "You wouldn't *believe* what they're doing now."

"Probably not."

"They're—"

Noelle gripped her sister's elbow. "I don't want to know."

Carley's eyes were huge. "You don't want me to tell you?"

"No."

Her sister stared at her in utter amazement. "You really don't care?"

Noelle shook her head. That wasn't the whole truth—or even part of it. But she didn't want to know if Thom had his arm around the blonde or if he was kissing her—or anything else. It was a lot less painful to keep her head buried in a popcorn bucket. Forget Weight Watchers. Sometimes fat grams were the only source of comfort.

"Are you going to confront him after the movie?" Carley asked excitedly.

Noelle snickered. "Hardly."

"Why not?"

"Just watch the movie," she advised.

Carley settled in her seat and and began to rock back and forth. Another time, the action might have annoyed Noelle, but just then she found it oddly comforting. She wanted a special someone to put his arm around her and gently rock her. To create a private world for the two of them, the way Thom had once done in this very theater, on this very balcony. He'd kissed her here and claimed her heart. It'd been a pivotal moment in their fledgling romance. From that point onward, they knew—or at least Noelle had known. She was in love and willing to make whatever sacrifices love demanded.

All too soon, the feature had ended and the lights came back on. "That was great," Carley announced.

Caught up in wistful memories, Noelle got to her feet, gathering her coat and purse. She took pains not to glance below, although her curiosity was almost overwhelming.

"We meet again," an all-too-familiar voice said from behind her.

"Thom?" She turned to see him two rows back, with a four- or five-year-old boy at his side.

Noelle's reaction was instantaneous. She looked below and discovered the blonde beauty with her male friend, who just happened *not* to be Thom Sutton. "I thought—"

"*You're* Thom?" Carley asked, glowering with righteous indignation.

"Don't tell me you're Carley," he returned, ignoring the girl's outrage. "My goodness, you've grown into a regular beauty."

Carley's anger died a quick death. "Do you really think so?"

"I sure do. Oh, this is my nephew Cameron."

"Hello, Cameron," Noelle said. "Did you enjoy the movie?"

The boy nodded. "Yeah, but the best part was when the man came up and told you not to throw any more popcorn. Uncle Thom said you got in trouble." The kid sounded far too smug for Noelle's liking.

So Thom had heard and seen the whole thing.

Oh, great.

Friday morning, Sarah dressed for her Christmas basket shopping adventure. She felt as though she was suiting up for an ordeal, some test or rite of passage. The hordes of shoppers were definitely going to try her patience; she'd finished her own shopping months ago and failed to see why people waited until the very last week. Well, the sooner she purchased the things on her half of the list, the better. With Christmas only five days away, she didn't have a minute to waste.

She wasn't getting any help from her family—not that she'd really expected it. Jake was at work, and Noelle was driving Carley to her friend's house and then meeting Kristen for lunch.

She was on her own.

Wanting to get the most for her buying dollar, Sarah drove to the biggest discount store in Rose. The Value-X parking lot was already filled. After driving around repeatedly, she finally found a space. She locked her car and hunched her shoulders against the wind as she hurried toward the building. The sound of the Salvation Army bell-ringer guided her to the front entrance. She paused long enough to stick a dollar bill in his bucket, then walked into the store.

Sarah grabbed a cart and used the booster seat to prop up her purse. The list was in the side pocket of her bag, and she searched for the paper as she walked. She hadn't gone more than a few feet from the entrance when she nearly collided with another woman obtaining a cart.

"I'm sorry," she said automatically. "I—" The words froze on her lips.

"I should've known anyone that rude must be you," Mary Sutton muttered sarcastically.

Although her heart was pounding, Sarah made a relatively dignified escape and steered the cart around Mary. With purpose filling every step, she pushed her cart toward the toy department. Her list was gifts, which meant Mary had the grocery half. Hmph. It didn't surprise her that Mary Sutton bought her family's Christmas gifts at a discount store—or that she waited until the last minute.

The first part of the list directed her to purchase gifts for two girls, ages six and seven. The younger girl had requested a doll. Having raised three daughters, Sarah knew that every little girl loved Barbie. This late in the season, she'd be fortunate to find the current Barbie.

Almost right away she saw that the supplies were depleted,

just as she'd suspected. But one lone Firefighter Barbie stood on the once-crowded shelf. Sarah reached for it at the precise moment someone else did.

"I believe I was first," she insisted. Far be it from her to allow some other person to deprive a poor little girl longing for a Barbie on Christmas morning.

"I believe you're wrong."

Mary Sutton. Sarah glared at her with such intensity that Mary must have realized she was not about to be dissuaded.

"Fine," Mary said after a moment and released her death grip on the Barbie.

"Thank you." Sarah could be gracious when called upon.

With her nose so high in the air she was in danger of hitting a light fixture, Mary stomped off in the opposite direction. Feeling satisfied with herself, Sarah studied the list again and noticed the name of a three-year-old boy. A small riding toy would do nicely, she decided and headed for that section of the department.

As she turned the corner she ran into Mary Sutton a third time. Mary stopped abruptly, her eyes narrowed. "Are you following me?" she demanded.

"Following *you?*" Sarah faked a short, derisive laugh. "You've got to be joking. I have no desire to be within ten feet of you."

"Then I suggest you vacate this aisle."

"You can't tell me where to shop or in what aisle!"

"Wanna bet?" Mary leaned forward and, intentionally or not, her cart rammed Sarah's.

Refusing to allow such an outrage to go unanswered, Sarah retaliated by banging her cart into Mary's.

Mary pulled back and hit her again, harder this time.

Soon they were throwing stuffed French poodles at each other, hurling them off the shelves. A German shepherd sailed over Sarah's head. That was when she reached for the golden retriever, the largest of the stuffed animals.

"Ladies, ladies." A man in a red jacket hurried toward them, his arms outstretched. His name badge read Michael and identified him as the store manager.

"I'm so sorry, Michael," Sarah said, pretending to recognize him. "This little, uh, misunderstanding got completely out of hand."

"You're telling me!" Mary yelled.

"This woman is following me."

"Oh, puh-leeze." Mary groaned audibly. "This woman followed *me*."

"I don't think it's important to know who followed whom," the manager said in a conciliatory voice. "But we need to—"

"She took the last Barbie," Mary broke in, pointing an accusing finger at Sarah. "I got it first—the doll was *mine*. Any jury in the land would rule in my favor. But I kindly offered it to her."

"Kindly, nothing. I had that Barbie and you know it!"

"Ladies, please…" The manager stood between them in an effort to keep them apart.

"There's only so much of this I can take," Mary said, sounding close to tears. "I'm here—"

"It isn't important why you're here," Sarah interrupted. She wasn't about to let Mary Sutton come off looking like the injured party. The woman had purposely rammed her cart. "She assaulted me."

"I most certainly did not!"

"You should check the front of my cart for damage, and if there is any, I suggest that you, as manager, charge this woman," Sarah said.

Two security officers arrived then, dressed in blue uniforms.

"Officer, officer…"

Mary turned soft and gentle. "Thank you for coming."

"Oh, give me a break," Sarah muttered. "Is it within your power to arrest this woman?" she demanded.

"Ladies," the manager said, trying once more, it seemed, to appeal to their better natures. "This is the season of good-will toward men—and women. Would it be possible for you to apologize to each other and go about your business?"

Mary crossed her arms and looked away.

Sarah gestured toward the other woman as if to say Mary's action spoke for itself. "I believe you have your answer."

"Then you leave me no choice," the manager said. "Offi-cers, please escort these two ladies from the store."

"What?" Mary cried.

"I beg your pardon?" Sarah said, hands on hips. "What is this about?"

The larger of the two security guards answered. "You're being kicked out of the store."

Sarah's mouth fell open.

The only person more shocked was Mary Sutton. "You're evicting me from Value-X?"

"You heard the manager, lady," the second officer said. "Now, come this way."

"Could I pay for the Barbie doll first?" Sarah asked, clutch-ing the package to her chest. "It's for a little girl and it's all she wants for Christmas."

"You should've thought of that before you threw the first poodle," the manager said.

"But—"

Dramatically, he pointed toward the front doors. "Out."

Mortified to the marrow of her bones, Sarah turned, taking her cart with her. One wheel was now loose and it squeaked and squealed. Just when she figured things couldn't get any worse, she discovered that a crowd had gathered in the aisle to witness her humiliation.

"Merry Christmas," she said with as much bravado as she could manage.

The officer at her side raised his hand. "We're asking that everyone return to their shopping. What happened here is over."

With her dignity intact but her pride in shreds, Sarah made her way to the parking lot, still accompanied by the officer.

She could see the "About Town" headline already. *Manager Expels Sarah McDowell From Value-X After Cat Fight*. Although technically, she supposed, it should be Dog Fight.

She had no doubt that Mary Sutton would use the power of the press to complete her embarrassment.

Noelle McDowell's
Journal

December 19
11:30 p.m.

I can't believe it! Even now, when it's long past time for bed, I'm wide-awake and so furious, any chance of falling asleep is impossible. I doubt if anyone could do a better job of looking like a world-class idiot. Right there in the theater, with my little sister at my side, I behaved like a juvenile.

I've worked hard to be a positive influence on Carley. I take my role as oldest sister very seriously. Then I go and pull a stunt like this. Adding insult to injury is the fact that I then had to face Thom, knowing he was completely aware of what a fool I'd made of myself.

Speaking of Thom...no, I don't want to think about him. First the airplane and now this! I'd sincerely hoped he'd be married with a passel of kids. I wanted him to be so completely out of the picture that I'd never need to think about him again. Instead—just my luck—he's single, eligible and drop-dead handsome. Life can be brutally unfair.

One good thing that came from all this is the long conversation I had with Carley after the movie. She's young and idealistic, much the same way I was at her age. We talked some more about Mom and Mrs. Sutton. It's really a very sad feud. I told her what good friends our two families used to be. The telling brought up a lot of memories. At one time, our families did everything together.

Thom was the first boy ever to kiss me. We were both sixteen. Wow! I still remember how good it felt. I don't remember what movie was playing and I doubt Thom does, either. That kiss was really something, even though we had no idea what we were doing. There was a purity to it, an innocence. His lips stayed on mine for mere seconds, but somehow we knew. I certainly did, and I thought Thom did, too.

It's funny how much it hurts to think about the way he deceived me. I try not to dwell on it. But I can't help myself, especially now....

Three

"I've never been so humiliated in my life!" Thom's mother sagged into the chair across from his desk as if she were experiencing a fainting spell. The back of her hand went to her forehead and she closed her eyes. "I'll never be able to look those people in the eye again," she wailed. "Never!"

"Mother, I'm sure no one recognized you," Thom said, hoping to calm her down before she caused a second scene by retelling the first. He hadn't really appreciated his mother's flair for drama until now. This was quite a performance, and he could only imagine the show she'd put on at the store.

"Of *course* I was recognized," Mary insisted, springing to life. "My picture's right there by my news column each and every week. Why, I could be fired from the newspaper once the editor gets wind of this." She swooned again and slumped back in the chair. "Where's your father, anyway? He should've known something like this was bound to happen. It seems every time I need him, he's conveniently in court." Greg Sutton was the senior partner in a local law firm.

Thom managed to hold back a smile. As far as he was concerned, his father possessed impeccable timing. Unfortunately, that meant his mother had sought solace from him.

"I'll sue Sarah McDowell," his mother said, as if she'd suddenly come to that decision. "Assault and besmirching my reputation and…and—"

"Mother," Thom pleaded. He stood and leaned forward, his hands on the edge of his desk. "Take a couple of deep breaths and try to calm down." Dragging a lawyer—most likely someone from his father's firm—into the middle of this feud would only complicate things.

"Do you believe it's remotely possible to calm down after this kind of humiliation?"

Perhaps she was right. "Why don't I take you to lunch and we can talk about it," Thom suggested. It was the Friday before Christmas and he could spare the time.

"The Rose Garden?" His mother raised pleading eyes to him. The Rose Garden was the most elegant dining room in town.

"If you like." It was more a "ladies who lunch" kind of place, but if that was what it took to make his mother listen to reason, then he'd go there.

"At least the day won't be completely ruined," she mumbled, opening her purse. "Let me put on some lipstick and I'll be ready to go." She took out her compact and gasped when she saw her reflection in the mirror.

"What?" Thom asked.

"My hair." Her fingers worked feverishly to repair the damage. "Why didn't you say something?"

Mainly because he hadn't been able to get a word in edgewise from the moment she'd stormed into his office. At first, Thom had assumed she'd been in some kind of accident. His mother had spoken so fast it was hard to understand what she was saying—other than the fact that she'd been kicked out of the Value-X because of Sarah McDowell.

"This must have happened when she hurled a French poodle at me."

"Mrs. McDowell threw a dog at you?" He gazed at her in horror.

"A stuffed one," she qualified. "It hit me on the head." Her hand went back to her hair, which she'd more or less managed to straighten.

Thom could picture the scene—two grown women acting like five-year-olds fighting in a schoolyard. Once again, he struggled to hide his amusement. His mother had tried to give him the impression that she was an innocent victim in all this, but he strongly suspected she'd played an equal role.

"I think I might be getting a bruise on my cheek," she said, peering closely into the small compact mirror. She lowered it and angled her face for him to get a better look.

"I don't see anything," he told her.

"Look harder," she said.

To appease her, he did but saw nothing. "Sorry," he said and reached for his overcoat. "Ready for lunch?"

"I'm starving," his mother told him. "You know how hungry I get when I'm angry."

He didn't, and felt this was information he could live without. The Rose Garden was only a block from his office, so they decided to walk. His mother chattered the whole way, reliving the incident and her outrage all over again, embellishing it in the retelling. Thom listened politely and wondered what Noelle would think when she heard *her* mother's version of the incident. He quickly pulled himself up. He didn't want to think about Noelle; that was something his self-esteem could do without.

As he'd expected, The Rose Garden bustled with activity.

Christmas was only a few days away, and shoppers taking a welcome lunch break now filled the restaurant. Thom glanced about the room as they were waiting to be seated. He recognized a few associates, who acknowledged him with nods. Two women sitting by the window gave him an appreciative glance and he warmed to the attention. That was when he caught sight of another pair of women.

Noelle and her younger sister Kristen. Wouldn't you know it? He nearly groaned aloud. He hadn't seen or heard from her in ten years and yet in the last three days she seemed to turn up every place he went.

This wasn't good. In fact, if his mother were to see them, she might very well consider it her duty to create a scene and walk out of the restaurant. Worse yet, she might find it necessary to make some loud and slanderous comment about their mother. Staring in their direction was a dead giveaway, but for the life of him, he couldn't stop. Noelle. The years had matured her beauty. He'd been in love with her as a teenager and she'd become the greatest source of pain in his life. For a long time, he'd convinced himself that he hated her. Eventually he'd realized it wasn't true. If anything, he was as strongly drawn to her now as he had been back then. More so, and he detested his own weakness. The woman had damn near destroyed him. In spite of that, he couldn't look away.

"I can seat you now," the hostess said.

Thom hesitated.

"Thom," his mother said, nudging him, "we can be seated now."

"Yes, sorry." He could only hope it wouldn't be anywhere close to Noelle.

The hostess escorted them to a table by the window. He pulled out his mother's chair, making sure her back was to Noelle and Kristen. Unfortunately, that meant *he* was facing them. Kristen had her back to him, which left him with an excellent view of Noelle. She apparently noticed him for the first time because her fork froze halfway to her mouth. For the longest moment, she stared at him, then caught herself and averted her eyes.

"Do you see someone you know, dear?" his mother asked, scrutinizing the menu.

"Yes...no," he corrected. He lifted the rather large menu and pretended to read over the offerings. The strategy of entertaining his mother in order to get her mind off the events of that morning was about to backfire.

In the years since Noelle, Thom had been in several relationships, two of which had grown serious. Both times he'd come close to suggesting marriage and then panicked. It was little wonder after what Noelle had done to him, but he couldn't blame her entirely.

When the moment came to make a commitment, he couldn't. He simply couldn't. And he knew why—although the reason baffled and frustrated him. He didn't love either Caroline or Brenda with the same intensity he'd loved Noelle. Perhaps it was impossible to recapture the emotional passion of that youthful episode; he didn't know. What he did know was that the feelings he'd had for other women hadn't been enough. He'd found them attractive, enjoyed their company... but he needed more than that.

He needed what he'd had with Noelle.

As he thought about the scene at the theater, he started to grin. It couldn't have worked out better had he planned it. Just thinking about her tossing popcorn at some poor, unsuspecting moviegoer's head was enough to keep him laughing for years. He'd listened in while she talked about their mothers—and about them. But the most priceless part of all was the astonished look on her face when she'd realized he was sitting right behind her and had heard every word.

"What is so amusing?" his mother asked.

"Oh, I was just thinking about something that happened recently."

"What? Trust me, after the morning I've had, I could use a good laugh."

Thom shook his head. "It'll lose something in the translation."

"Oh." She sounded disappointed, then sighed. "I do feel better. This was an excellent idea."

The waitress came by and his mother ordered a glass of wine. "For my nerves," she explained to the woman. "Ordinarily I don't drink during the day, but…well, suffice it to say I've had a very difficult morning."

"I understand," the waitress told her in a sympathetic voice. She glanced at Thom and gave him a small coy smile.

"What a nice young woman," his mother commented as the waitress walked off.

"I suppose so," he said with little interest. He looked up, straight into Noelle's steady gaze.

"Perhaps now isn't the right moment to broach the subject, but both your father and I think it's time you considered settling down."

She was right; the timing could be better. However, a little appeasement seemed in order. "I've been thinking the same thing myself," he said, forcing himself to focus on his mother.

"Really?" Her face lit up. "Is there someone special?"

"Not yet." Involuntarily he stared at Noelle again. As if against her will, her eyes met his and held. Then she looked away—but she quickly looked back.

Kristen turned around and glanced at him over her shoulder.

"Did you know Kristen McDowell is getting married?" his mother said.

Thom nearly choked on his glass of water. "Now that you mention it, I remember hearing something about that." It also explained why his mother had brought up the subject of his settling down. She didn't want Sarah McDowell to outdo her in the married children department.

"Now," his mother said, eagerly leaning forward, "tell me about your lady friend."

"What lady friend?"

"The one you're going to propose to."

"Propose?" He'd only proposed to one woman, the one watching him from two tables away. "I told you already—I'm not seeing anyone."

"You were never able to keep a secret from me, Thomas. I'm your mother."

He stared at her blankly, not knowing how to respond. "What makes you think I've met someone?"

"It isn't *think,* Thom, I know. I told your father, too. Ask him if you don't believe me. I noticed it the day you came home from your business trip to California. It was the sparkle in your eyes."

"California?" Thom tried to recall the trip. It had been a quick one, and strictly business. But on the return flight, he'd bumped into Noelle McDowell.

Noelle got home after lunch with Kristen to discover her mother sitting in the family room, stocking feet propped up on the ottoman. She leaned back against the sofa cushion and held an icepack to her forehead.

"Mom?" Noelle whispered. "Are you ill?"

"Thank goodness someone's finally home," her mother said, lowering the bag of ice.

"What's wrong?"

"Never in all your life could you guess the kind of morning I had." She clutched Noelle's arm as she spoke.

"What happened?"

Sarah closed her eyes. "I can't even tell you about it. I have never been more humiliated."

"Does this have something to do with Mrs. Sutton?"

Her mother's eyes sprang open in sheer terror. "You heard about it? Who told you?"

"Ah..."

"She's going to report it in the newspaper, I just know she is. I wouldn't put it past her to use her news column to smear my good name. It was *her* fault, you know. She followed me, and then purposely rammed her cart into mine. And that was only the beginning."

An ugly picture began to take shape in Noelle's mind. A Sutton/McDowell confrontation would explain the fierce looks Thom had sent her way during lunch. The fact that he'd showed up at The Rose Garden—with his mother in tow— was a coincidence she could have done without.

Kristen had invited her to lunch, and then after a few minutes of small talk, her sister had immediately turned to the subject that happened to be on Noelle's mind: Thom Sutton. Noelle had described the disaster at the movies the day before and reluctantly confessed her part. To her consternation, Kristen had thought the incident downright hilarious. Noelle, however, had yet to recover from the embarrassment of knowing that Thom had seen her resort to such childish behavior.

Now their mother had been involved in another confrontation with Mary Sutton. If her present state of mind was anything to go by, Sarah had come out of it badly. Judging by what Noelle had seen of Mrs. Sutton at the restaurant, *she* wasn't the least bit disturbed.

"The police took down our names and—"

"The *police?*"

"Value-X Security, but they wear those cute blue uniforms and look just like regular policemen."

"They took your names? What for?"

Her mother covered her face with both hands. "I can't talk about it."

The door off the garage opened and in walked Noelle's father. "Dad," she said, hoping to prepare him. "Something happened to Mom this morning."

"Oh, Jake…" Her mother languished in her seat as though she lacked the energy to even lift her head.

"Sarah?"

"Apparently Mom and Mrs. Sutton tangled with security at the Value-X this morning."

"We more than tangled," her mother insisted, her voice rising, "we were…banished. The officer who escorted me out told me I won't be allowed inside the store for three months." She bit her lip and swallowed a loud sob. "I don't know if I misunderstood him, but I think I might be permanently banned from all blue-light specials."

"No!" Her father feigned outrage.

"Jake, this is serious."

"Of course it is," he agreed. "I take it this is Mary's doing?"

Her mother's fist hit the sofa arm. "I swear to you she started it!"

"You don't need to tell me what happened," Jake said. "I can guess."

So could Noelle.

"From here on out, I absolutely refuse to be in the same room as that woman." She sat straighter, jaw firm, head back. "For years I've had to deal with her…her malice, and I won't put up with it anymore!"

Jake reached for Sarah's hand and gently patted it. "You're absolutely right—you shouldn't."

Her mother's eyes narrowed suspiciously. "How do you mean? Are you being sarcastic?"

"Of course not, dear," he said reassuringly. "But there's no need to rehash old history, is there?"

"No-o-o." Noelle heard her mother's hesitation.

"Not going to the Christmas dance will show Mary Sutton that she won't have you to kick around anymore."

As far as Noelle was concerned, missing the Century Club Christmas dance was far from a tragedy. The only reason she'd agreed to attend was to placate her mother. This mysterious incident at the Value-X was a blessing in disguise; it seemed her father saw it in the same light. She just hoped he hadn't overplayed his hand with that last ringing pronouncement.

"Who said anything about not going to the dance?" her mother demanded.

"You did." Her father turned to Noelle for agreement, which she offered with a solemn nod.

"Yes, Mom, you just said you won't be in the same room with that woman ever again."

"I did?"

"Yes, sweetheart," Noelle's father said. "And I agree whole-heartedly. Missing the dance is a small price to pay if it means protecting your peace of mind."

"We aren't going to the dance?" Carley asked, entering the room. She looked disappointed, but then Noelle's little sister was too young to understand what a lucky escape she'd just had.

"No," Jake said. "We're going to skip the dance this year, and perhaps every year from now on. We won't let Mary Sutton hurt your mother's feelings or her reputation again!"

"We're going," her mother insisted.

"But, sweetheart—"

"You're absolutely right, Jake, Mary Sutton's done enough to me. I refuse to allow her to ruin my Christmas—and Noelle's birthday—too. We're going to show up at the dance and hold our heads high. We have nothing to be ashamed of."

"But…" Her father cleared his throat. "What if Mary mentions the incident at the Value-X?" He lowered his voice, sounding as though that would be a horrible embarrassment to them all. Noelle had to give her father credit; he was good at this.

"She won't say a word," her mother said with complete confidence. "Mary wouldn't dare bring up the subject, seeing that she was tossed out on her ear, right along with me."

Her resolve clearly renewed, Sarah stood and placed her hands on her hips. Nothing would thwart her now. "We're attending the dance tomorrow night, and that's all there is to it."

Her father made a small protesting noise that echoed Noelle's sentiments. She was stuck going to this dance when it was the very last thing she wanted.

Dressed in a floor-length pink formal that had once been worn by Kristen in high school, Noelle felt like last year's prom queen. Her enthusiasm for this dance was on a par with filing her income tax return.

"You look positively lovely," her mother told her as they headed out the door.

How Noelle looked had little to do with how she felt. Her father brought the car out of the garage and held open the doors for Noelle and Carley, then helped their mother into the front seat beside him.

"How did I get so lucky—escorting three beautiful women to the biggest dance of the year?"

"Clean living," Noelle's mother said with authority. "And

a clear conscience." Noelle didn't know whether to laugh at that remark or shrug in bewilderment. Leaning forward in order to look out the front window, Sarah added, "I think it's going to snow."

Hearing "Jingle Bells" on the car radio, Noelle suspected her mother was being influenced by the words of the song.

"We're more prone to ice storms than snow this time of year," her father said mildly.

Noelle had forgotten about the treacherous storms, although she'd experienced a number of them during the years she'd lived in Rose. They created astonishing beauty—and terrible dangers.

"Kristen and Jonathan are meeting us at the dance, aren't they?" Carley asked.

"That's what she said," Noelle answered. Carley was dressed in a full-length pale blue dress with cap sleeves and she wore matching low-heeled shoes. She looked lovely and so mature it was all Noelle could do not to cry. Her baby sister was growing up.

"Do you think *she'll* be there?" her mother asked, lowering her voice.

"Mrs. Sutton's probably asking the same thing about you," Noelle said.

Her mother gave an exaggerated sigh. "I'll say one thing about Mary Sutton—she never did lack nerve."

The Century Club was festive, with Christmas music and evergreen swags and large red bows. The ballroom was on the second floor, the cloakroom, a bar and buffet on the first. Couples lingered on the wide staircase, chatting and sipping champagne.

Noelle glanced toward the upstairs, and her stomach tensed. Thom was there. She didn't need to see him to feel his presence. Why did he have to show up everywhere she did? Was this some kind of cosmic joke?

"Kristen!" her mother called. "Yoo hoo!" Anyone might think it'd been weeks since she'd last spoken to her daughter. "Hello, Jonathan." She hugged her soon-to-be son-in-law.

"Hi, Mom. Hi, Dad." Kristen paused in front of Carley, feigning shock. "This isn't my little sister, is it? It can't be."

Carley rolled her eyes, but couldn't hide her pleasure. "Of course it's me. Don't be ridiculous."

"Shall we go upstairs?" her mother suggested.

Noelle recognized the order disguised as a request. They were to mount the stairs on guard, as a family, in case they ran into the dreaded Mary Sutton.

Kristen cozied up to Noelle. "He's here," she whispered in her ear.

"I know."

"Who told you?"

"No one." She couldn't explain how she'd recognized Thom's presence. She just did. Like it or not.

The ballroom was crowded, and although this wasn't the kind of social activity Noelle would have attended on her own, she couldn't help getting caught up in the spirit of the evening. A six-piece orchestra was playing a waltz, the chandeliers glittered and she saw that it had indeed begun to snow; flakes drifted gently past the dark windows. On the polished dance floor, the women in their long shimmery gowns whirled around in the arms of their dashing partners. The scene reminded her of a Victorian Christmas card.

"Would you care to dance?" Jonathan asked.

Surprised, Noelle nodded. She'd only spoken once or twice to this man who was marrying her sister, and was anxious to know him better. "Thank you. That would be very nice."

Just as Noelle and Jonathan stepped onto the dance floor,

Kristen's gaze met her fiancé's. Noelle could have sworn some unspoken message passed between them. She didn't have time to question her sister before Jonathan loosely wrapped her in his arms.

"I assume you heard what happened at the Value-X store," she said, searching for a subject of conversation.

"Did you have as much trouble not laughing as I did?"

"More," Noelle confessed with a grin.

"I've done business with the Suttons. They're good people."

"This feud between our mothers is ridiculous." Out of the corner of her eye, she noticed Kristen, who was dancing, too—her partner none other than Thom Sutton. It didn't take a genius to put two and two together, especially when she noticed that Kristen was steering Thom in her direction. Noelle marveled at her sister's courage in asking Thom to dance with her. And of course she had. Thom would never have sought Kristen out, especially for a dance in the Women's Century Club Ballroom with both mothers present.

The two couples made their way toward the center of the polished floor. When they were side by side, Jonathan stopped.

"I believe you're dancing with the wrong partner," he said.

Noelle didn't need to look over her shoulder to guess Jonathan was speaking to Thom.

"I believe you're with the wrong woman," Noelle heard Kristen tell her partner.

Jonathan released Noelle, and Kristen stepped out of Thom's embrace and sailed into her fiancé's waiting arms, leaving Thom and Noelle standing alone in the middle of the crowded dance floor.

Slowly, dread dictating every move, Noelle turned and came face-to-face with Thom. He didn't look any happier than she felt at this sudden turn of events. "I didn't plan this," she said in clear, even tones.

His expression implied that he didn't consider her comment worthy of a response.

"Are you two going to dance or are you just going to stand there and stare at each other all night?" Jonathan asked.

Thom shrugged, implying that he could do this if he had to. Reluctantly Noelle stepped into his arms. She wasn't sure what to expect. Actually, she hadn't expected to feel anything, certainly not this immediate deluge of emotion. He kept her at arm's length and gazed into the distance.

To Noelle's horror, tears filled her eyes as all the old feelings came flooding back. She was about to turn and walk off the dance floor when his fingers dug into her upper arms.

"You're not running away from me again."

"Me?" she cried, furious at the accusation.

"Yes, you."

His words made no sense, she thought grimly, but said nothing. The dance would be over soon and she could leave him behind. Or try to. Kristen would answer for this.

No, she decided, she had only herself to blame. Over lunch, Noelle had confided in her sister. Kristen, being idealistic and in love, had plotted to bring Noelle and Thom back together. She didn't understand that reconciliation wasn't always possible.

"I'd like to ask you a question," she said when she could tolerate the silence no longer.

"Fine."

"Why'd you do it? Did you want revenge for your mother so badly it was worth using me to get it?"

He stopped dancing and frowned at her. "What?"

"You heard me." She couldn't keep the pain out of her voice.

He continued to frown, as if he still didn't understand the question.

"Don't give me that injured look," she said, clenching her jaw. "Too many years have passed for me to be taken in by that."

"You were the one who stood *me* up."

"Yeah, right," she said with a mocking laugh. "After I made an idiot of myself in front of my parents, too. That must've given you a real kick."

"I don't know what you're talking about."

"Thom, I waited in that park for two miserable hours and you didn't show."

Not an inch separated them now as his icy glare cut into her. Dancing couples swirled around them, but Noelle was barely conscious of anyone else. For all she knew or cared, they were alone on the dance floor.

"I waited hours for you, too."

His lying to her now was almost more than she could stand. "I beg to differ," she said stiffly.

"Noelle, listen to me! I was there."

"You most certainly were not." Then, to prove that she wasn't going to accept a lie, no matter how convenient, she added, "You think I just waited around? I was sure something had gone wrong, sure there was some misunderstanding, so I phoned your home."

"I wasn't there because I was waiting for you!"

He persisted with the lie and that irritated her even more.

"You were gone, all right," she said, spitting out the words. "You were with your buddies bowling."

His eyes narrowed and he began to speak.

But the music stopped just then, which was all the excuse Noelle needed to get away from him. He reached for her hand and pulled her back. "We need to talk."

"No. It happened years ago. Some things are better left alone."

"Not this time," he insisted, unwilling to budge.

"What do you hope to accomplish by going through all of this now? It's too late." They'd gain nothing more than the pain of opening old wounds. Any discussion was futile. It'd been a mistake to let herself get drawn into this silly drama—just one very big mistake.

"I'm not hoping to accomplish one damn thing," he told her coldly.

"I didn't think so."

Thom released her hand. "Just a minute," he said as she turned from him.

Noelle hesitated.

"I *was* there. I stood there for two hours and waited. You were the one who never showed."

"That's not true!"

They stood glowering at each other, both refusing to give in. Noelle wasn't going to let him lie his way out of this, though—not after what his deception had cost her.

"Hey, you two, this is Christmas," someone called out.

The voice ended Noelle's resolve. Whatever had happened in the past didn't matter anymore. Certainly not after all these years.

"If you find comfort in believing a lie, then do so," he said, "but don't involve me." He walked away, his face hard and impassive.

Left alone in the middle of the dance floor, Noelle stared at him in amazement. Of all the nerve! He'd stopped her from leaving and now *he'd* taken off!

Picking up her skirt, she raced after him. "All right! You want to talk this out, then we will."

"When?" He continued walking, tossing the question over his shoulder.

With Christmas so close, her time was booked solid. "I… soon."

"Tonight."

"All right." She swallowed hard. "When and where?"

"After the dance. In the park, same place as before."

That seemed fitting, since it was where they were originally going to meet the day they'd planned to elope.

"What time is the dance over?"

"Midnight." He glanced at his watch. "So make it one."

"I'll be there."

He shot her a look. "That was what you said the *last* time."

NOELLE MCDOWELL'S
JOURNAL

December 21
5:00 p.m.

Everyone's getting ready for the big dance, but my head's still spin-ning and I've learned that it helps me sort through my emotions if I write everything down. I ran into Thom again. It's as though we're being drawn together, as though we're trapped in some magnetic field and are being pulled toward each other from opposite directions. I can tell he doesn't like it any better than I do.

It happened yesterday when I met Kristen for lunch at The Rose Garden. No sooner had our order arrived when in walked Thom and his mother.

Try as I might, I couldn't keep my eyes off him. He apparently suf-fered from the same malady. Every time I glanced up, he was staring at me—and frowning. His mother was with him and I could see that he was trying to keep her distracted so she wouldn't notice Kristen and me. I didn't completely understand why until we arrived home and discovered that Mom and Mrs. Sutton had had another run-in while shopping for the Christmas baskets. That must have been something to see, although I'm grateful I didn't!

After we left the restaurant, Kristen and I had a long talk about Thom. I told her far more than I meant to. I don't think I've thought or talked this much about Thom in years, and I found myself expe-

riencing all those pathetic emotions all over again. Kristen confessed that she's been hurt and upset with me for staying away, and now that I'm home, I can understand her disappointment. It's ironic, because after I told her how devastated I was when Thom and I broke up, she said she could understand why I'd stayed away. She even said she'd probably have done the same thing.

When I got back to the house, Mom was in quite a state. For a moment I thought she might have talked herself out of attending the dance, but our hopes were quickly dashed. Dad and I should've realized Mom has far too much pride to let Mary Sutton get the upper hand.

This Christmas-basket project is driving her nuts, but Mom's determined to make Kristen's wedding one this town will long remember, and she's willing to make whatever sacrifice is necessary. I do admire her determination.

It's time to get ready for the dance. Wouldn't you know it? Mom came up with a dress, and just as Carley predicted, it's pink. Pepto-Bismol pink. I can only hope Thom doesn't show up, but at the rate my luck is running...

Four

The rest of the Christmas dance passed in a blur for Noelle. She danced with a constant stream of attractive men. She greeted longtime family friends and socialized the evening away, but not once did she stop thinking about Thom. They were finally going to settle this. Only she wasn't a naive eighteen-year-old anymore and she wouldn't allow his lies to go unchallenged. Thom claimed he'd been waiting for her in the park, but she knew otherwise.

At the end of the evening, the families trooped down the wide sweeping staircase. Noelle, Carley and their mother waited while Jake stood in line to collect their coats. No more than three feet away from them was Mary Sutton, who also appeared to be waiting for her coat. Noelle had to hand it to the woman; she did a marvelous job of pretending not to see them.

"Good evening, Mrs. Sutton," Noelle greeted her, refusing to ignore Thom's mother.

Sarah's onetime friend opened and then closed her mouth, as if she didn't know how to respond.

"Noelle." Her mother elbowed her sharply in the ribs. "What's the matter with you?"

"Nothing. I'm greeting an old family friend."

"*Former* friend," her mother insisted. "We haven't been friends in almost twenty years."

"But you once were."

Her mother sighed wearily. "I was younger then, and I didn't have the discretion I have now. You see, back then I took friendship at face value. I trusted in goodwill and forgiveness."

"Hello, Noelle," Mary Sutton said, moving closer. "I, too, was once young and I, too, believed in the power of friendship. But I was taught a painful lesson when the woman I assumed was my dearest friend lied and deceived me and entrusted a priceless family heirloom to another. But that was a very long time ago. Tell me," she said, turning a cold shoulder to Noelle's mother. "How are *you?*"

"Very well, thank you."

Her mother clasped Carley's arm and stepped back as though to protect her youngest daughter.

"You're looking lovely," Thom's mother said, and her eyes were kind.

"Thank you," Noelle said, although she could feel her mother's gaze burning into her back.

Mary Sutton lowered her voice. "I couldn't help overhearing your mother's comments just now about friendship. I probably should've stayed out of it—but I couldn't."

"It's so sad that the two of you have allowed this nonsense to go on for all these years."

"Let me assure you, my grandmother's tea service is not nonsense. It was all I had to remind me of her. Your mother lied to me about using it, and then lost it forever." Her downcast eyes clearly said that the loss of her grandmother's legacy still caused her pain. "You're right, though. It's unfortunate this has dragged on as long as it has."

That sounded encouraging, and Noelle was ready to leap on what she considered a gesture of peace.

"However," Mrs. Sutton continued, "there are certain things no friendship can overcome, and I fear your mother has crossed that line too many times to count. Regrettably, our friendship is unsalvageable."

"But—"

"Another thing," Mrs. Sutton said, cutting Noelle off. "I saw you dancing with Thom this evening. You two were once sweet on each other, but you hurt him badly. I hope for both your sakes that you're not thinking of renewing your acquaintance."

"I... I..." Noelle faltered, not knowing how to answer.

Noelle's mother stepped forward. "I suggest your son stay away from our daughter."

"Mom, keep out of this, please," Noelle cried, afraid of what would happen if the two women started in on each other—particularly after the Value-X incident. This was the town's biggest social event of the year, and a scene was the last thing either family needed.

Mr. Sutton returned with the coats, and Noelle's father followed shortly afterward. The McDowells headed immediately for the parking lot, careful to avoid any and all Suttons. Everyone was silent on the drive home, but Noelle knew she'd upset her mother.

Fifteen minutes later as they walked into the house, she decided she should be the one to compromise. "Mom, I wish now that I hadn't spoken to Mrs. Sutton," she said quietly. And she meant it; she should have restricted her remarks to "Hello" and maybe "Merry Christmas."

"I do, too," her mother said. "I know your intentions were

good, but it's best to leave things as they are. I tried for a long time to make up with her, but she refused to accept a replacement set and she refused my apology." Sadness crept into her voice. "Mary did make one good point, though."

Noelle mentally reviewed the conversation.

"She said it's a good idea for you to stay away from Thom, and she's right." She sighed, then briefly placed her palm against Noelle's cheek. Her eyes were warm with love. "The two of you have a history you can't escape."

"Mom, it isn't like that. We—"

"Sweetheart, listen please. I know you once had strong feelings for that young man, and it hurt me deeply."

"It hurt *you?*"

Her mother nodded. "Very much so, because I knew you'd be forced to make a choice between your family and Thom. I couldn't bear the thought of you married to him or sharing my grandchildren with Mary Sutton. You saw for yourself how she feels about me. There's no forgiveness in her. Really, is this the kind of woman you want in your life and the lives of your children? That's the history I mean." She kissed Noelle on the cheek and headed down the hallway to her room. "Good night now."

Noelle shut her eyes and sagged against the wall. She'd been just a moment away from explaining that she was going to meet Thom in order to talk things out. Her mother sounded as though she'd consider it a personal affront if Noelle so much as looked at him. It was like high school all over again.

The only thing left to do now was sneak out the same way she had as a teenager. She couldn't leave him waiting in the cold, that was unthinkable. Besides, this might be her one and only chance to sort out what had really happened, and she wasn't going to throw it away. She didn't intend any disrespect toward her mother or his, but she *had* to be there. If she didn't show up, she'd confirm every negative belief he already had about her.

Carley was in bed asleep as Noelle passed her room. She went in to drop a kiss on her sister's forehead, then softly closed the door. Noelle changed out of her party dress, choosing wool slacks and a thick sweater to wear to the park. Sitting on the edge of the bed, she waited for the minutes to tick past. With luck, her parents would be exhausted and both go directly to bed. Then Noelle could slip away undetected.

Finally the house was dark and quiet. The only illumination came from the flashing Christmas lights that decorated the roofline.

Opening her bedroom door, Noelle was horrified by the way it creaked. On tiptoe, she carefully, silently crept down the narrow corridor.

"Jake." Her mother was instantly awake. "I heard something."

"Go to sleep, honey."

"There's someone in the house," her mother insisted.

Noelle froze. She could hardly breathe. Just imagining what her mother would say was enough to paralyze her.

"Jake, I'm serious."

"I don't hear anything," her father mumbled.

"I did. We could all be murdered in our beds."

"Sarah, for the love of heaven."

"Think of the children."

Noelle nearly groaned aloud. She was trapped. She'd have to pass her parents' bedroom in order to steal back into her own. They were sure to see her. She couldn't go forward and she couldn't go back.

"All right, all right," her father muttered as he climbed out of bed.

"Take something with you," her mother hissed.

"Like what?"

"Here, take a wooden hanger."

"So I can hang him out to dry if I happen on a burglar?"

"Just do it, Jake."

"Yes, dear."

Noelle had made it safely into the kitchen by the time her father came upon her. "Dad," she whispered, hiding in the shadows, "it's me."

"Why didn't you say so?" he whispered back.

"I couldn't. I'm sneaking out of the house."

"This late? Where are you going?"

He wouldn't like the answer, but she refused to lie. "I'm meeting Thom Sutton in the park. We're going to talk."

Her father didn't say anything for a long moment. Then it sounded as if he was weeping.

Noelle felt dreadful. "Dad? I'm sorry if this upsets you."

"Upsets me?" he repeated. "I think it's hilarious."

"You...do?"

"Go ahead and meet your young man and talk all you want. This thing is between Sarah and Mary. Greg and I have been friends for years."

This was news to Noelle. "You're still friends?"

"Of course. He's the best golfing partner I ever had."

"You and Mr. Sutton are golf partners?" Noelle thought perhaps she'd slipped into another dimension.

"Shhh." Her father raised a finger to his lips. "Your mother doesn't know."

"Mom doesn't know." This was more unbelievable by the moment.

"Scoot," her father ordered, and reaching for the keys on the peg outside the garage door, he said, "Here, take my car. It's parked on the street."

Noelle clutched the set of keys and leaned forward to kiss his cheek. "Thanks, Dad."

He coughed loudly as she opened the back door. "You're hearing things, Sarah," he called out. "There's nothing." He gave her a small wave and turned back toward the hallway.

As soon as she was out the door, Noelle sprinted toward her dad's car. It took her a moment to figure out which key she needed and then another to adjust the mirror and the seat. When she glanced at her watch, she was shocked to see the time. It was already ten minutes past one.

Thom would assume she wasn't coming. He'd think she'd stood him up...when nothing could be further from the truth.

Thom expelled his breath into the cold, and it came out looking like the snort of a cartoon bull. An *angry* cartoon bull. That was exactly how he felt. Once again, he'd allowed his heart to rule his head and he'd fallen prey to Noelle Mc-Dowell.

He should have known better. Everything he'd learned about heartache, Noelle had taught him. And now, fool that he was, he'd set himself up to be taken again. Noelle McDowell was untrustworthy. He knew it and yet he'd still risked disappointment and worse.

Slapping his hands against his upper arms to ward off the cold, he paced the area beneath the trees across from the pool at Lions' Park. This had been their special meeting place. It was here that Thom had kissed Noelle for the second time. Here, they'd met and talked and shared their secrets. Here, he'd first confessed his love.

A car door slammed in the distance. Probably the police coming to check out his vehicle, which was parked in a lot that was closed to the public at this time of night. He deserved to get a ticket for being enough of an idiot to trust Noelle.

He didn't know why he'd hung around as long as he had. Looking at his watch he saw that it was twenty after one. She'd kept him waiting nineteen minutes too long. Her non-appearance was all the proof he'd ever need.

"Thom... Thom!" Noelle called out as she ran across the lawn.

Angry and defiant, he stepped out from beneath the shadow of the fifty-foot cedar tree.

"Thank goodness you're still here," she cried and to her credit, she did sound relieved. She was breathless when she reached him. "I had to sneak out of the house."

"Sneak out? You're almost thirty years old!"

"I know, I know. Listen, I'm so sorry." She pushed back the sleeve of her coat and squinted at her watch. "You waited— I can't believe you stayed for twenty extra minutes. I prayed you would, but I wouldn't have blamed you if you'd left."

The anger that had burned in him moments earlier evaporated so fast it shocked him.

"When did they turn Walnut into a dead-end street?"

"Years ago." Of course she'd drive down the same street they'd used as teenagers. He'd forgotten the changes made over the last decade; it hadn't occurred to him that she wouldn't know. "You're here now."

"Yes...listen, I know I shouldn't do this, but I can't help myself." Having said that, she slipped her arms around his waist and hugged him hard. His own arms went around her, too, tentatively and then with greater strength.

Closing his eyes and savoring the feel of her was a mistake, the first of many he knew he'd be making. She smelled like Christmas, somehow, and her warmth wrapped itself around him.

"Why'd you do that?" he asked gruffly as she released him

and took a step back. He was trying to hide how damn good it'd felt to hold her.

"It's the only way I could think of to thank you for staying, for believing in me enough to wait."

"I wasn't exactly enumerating your good points while I stood here freezing."

"I know, I wouldn't, either—I mean, well, you know what I mean."

He did.

Clearing off a space on the picnic table, Noelle climbed up and sat there just as she had when they were teenagers. "All right," she said, drawing in a deep breath. "Let's talk. Since you were the one to suggest we do this, you should go first."

So she'd become a take-charge sort of woman. That didn't surprise him. She'd displayed leadership qualities in high school, as well, serving on the student council and as president of the French Club. "All right, that's fair enough." She might be able to sit, but Thom couldn't. He had ten years of anger stored inside and that made it impossible to stand still for long. "We argued, remember?"

"Of course I do. The argument had to do with our mothers. You said something derogatory about mine and I defended her."

"As I recall, you had a less-than-flattering attitude toward *my* mother."

"But you were the first..." She paused. "None of that's important now. What we should be discussing is what happened afterward."

Once again she was right. "We made up, or so I thought."

"We made up because we refused to allow the ongoing feud between our mothers to come between us. Later that day, you wrote me a note and suggested we elope."

Her voice caught just a little. He wanted so badly to believe her. It was a struggle not to. "I loved you, Noelle."

She smiled, but he saw pain in her eyes and it shook him. For years he'd assumed that she'd used his love against him. That she'd stood him up just to hurt him. To humiliate him. He'd never really understood why. Was it vindication on behalf of her mother?

"We were going to confront our parents, remember?" Noelle said.

"Yes. I made a big stand, claiming how much I loved you and how I refused to let either of our mothers interfere in our lives. You should've heard me."

"I did, too!" she declared. "I spilled out my guts to them. Can you imagine how humiliating it was to have to go back and confess that you'd tricked me—that you'd jilted me?"

"Me!" he shouted. "You were the one—"

Noelle held up both hands and he let his anger fade. "Something happened. It must have." She pressed one hand to her heart. "I swear by all I consider holy that I've never lied to you."

"You're assuming I did?" he challenged.

"Yes. I mean no," she cried, confused now. "Something *did* happen, but what?"

"I don't know," he said. "I was here at three, just like I wrote you in the note."

She frowned, and he wondered if she was going to try to tell him she hadn't gotten his note. He knew otherwise because he'd personally seen Kristen hand it to her at school.

"The note said eight."

"Three," he insisted. Now it was his turn to look perplexed. "I wrote down three o'clock."

"The note said…" She brought her hand to her mouth. "No, I refuse to believe it."

"You think Kristen changed the time?"

"She wouldn't do that." She shook her head. "I know my sister, and she'd never hurt me like that."

"How do you explain the discrepancy then?"

"I have no idea." She squeezed her eyes shut. "I remember it vividly. You'd sent it to me after your math class."

His defenses were down. Time rolled back, and the events of that day were starting to focus in his mind. The fog of his pain dissipated. Finally he was able to look at the events with a clear head and an analytical eye.

"Kristen spilled soda on it," Noelle said thoughtfully. "Do you think that might have smudged the number?"

"It might explain part of it—but not the nasty note you left on my windshield."

She had the grace to blush at the reminder. "After waiting until after ten o'clock, I didn't know what to do. It was pretty dark by then, and I couldn't believe you'd just abandon me. I was positive something must've happened, so I phoned your house."

He nodded, encouraging her to go on.

"Your father said you were out with your friends bowling. I went to the alley to see for myself." Her voice tightened. "Sure enough, you were in there, boozing it up with your buddies."

"Don't tell me you actually thought I was having a good time?"

"Looked like it to me."

"Noelle, I was practically crying in my beer. I felt... I felt as if I'd just learned about some tragedy that was going to change my whole life."

"Why didn't you call me? How could you believe I'd stand you up? If you loved me as much as you said, wouldn't you make some effort to find out what happened?"

"I did." To be fair, it'd taken him a day, but he had to know, had to discover how he could've been so mistaken about No-elle. "I waited until the following afternoon. Your mother an-swered the phone and said I'd already done enough damage. She hung up on me."

"She never told me," Noelle whispered. "She never said a word."

"Why would she?" Thom murmured. "Your mother as-sumed I'd done you wrong, just the way everyone else in your family did."

"I left that horrible note on your car and you still phoned me?"

He nodded.

"I can only imagine what you must have thought."

"And you," he said.

They both grew quiet.

"I'm so sorry, Thom," she finally said. "So very sorry."

"So am I." He was afraid to touch her, afraid of what would happen if she came into his arms.

Noelle brushed the hair back from her face and when he glanced at her, he saw tears glistening in her eyes.

"It all worked out for the best, though, don't you think?" he asked. He had to say *something*.

She nodded. Then after a moment she spoke in a voice so low he had to lean closer to hear. "Do you really believe that?"

"No." He reached for her then, crushing her in his arms, lifting her from the picnic table and holding her as if his very life depended on keeping her close to his heart.

His mouth found hers, and her lips were moist and soft, her body melting against his. Their kisses were filled with hunger and passion, with mingled joy and discovery. This sense of *rightness* was what had been missing from every re-lationship he'd had since his breakup with Noelle. Nothing had felt right with any other woman. He loved Noelle. He'd always loved her.

She buried her face in his shoulder and he kissed the top of her head. Her arms circled his neck and he ran his fingers through her hair, gathering it in his hands as he closed his eyes and let his emotions run free—from anger to joy. From joy to fear. From fear to relief.

"What happens now?" he asked. They didn't seem to have many options. Each had made a life without the other.

She didn't answer him for a long time, but he knew she'd heard the question.

"Noelle," he said as she raised her head. "What do we do now?"

She blinked back tears. "Do we have to decide this minute? Can't you just kiss me again?"

He smiled and lowered his mouth to hers. "I think that could be arranged."

Fresh from Sunday services—where she'd been inspired by a sermon on giving—Mary Sutton drove to the local Walmart store. She refused to show up the following day and not have the items on her list. No doubt Sarah McDowell assumed she'd arrive at the club empty-handed, but Mary fully intended to prove otherwise.

As soon as Greg had settled in front of the television set watching the Seahawks' play-off game, she was out the door. Shopping this close to Christmas went against every dictate of common sense. Usually she was the organized one. Christmas gifts had been purchased, wrapped and tucked away soon after Thanksgiving. But, with these six Christmas baskets, she had no choice. She had to resort to last-minute shopping.

The parking lot at Walmart was packed. Finding a space at the very rear of the lot, Mary trudged toward the busy store.

She dreaded dealing with the mob of shoppers inside. On the off chance she might have a repeat of that horrible scene in Value-X, she surveyed the lot—looking up one row and down the next—in search of Sarah's vehicle. She sighed with relief when she didn't see the other woman's car.

List in hand, Mary grabbed a cart and headed straight for the toy section. She hoped the store would have Barbie dolls left on the shelf. She hated the thought of a single child being disappointed on Christmas morning. Fortunately, the shelves appeared to have been recently restocked.

Reaching for a Firefighter Barbie doll, she set it inside her basket. With a sense of accomplishment, she wheeled the cart around the corner to the riding toys. To her horror and dismay, she discovered Sarah McDowell reading the label on a toddler-sized car. This was her worst nightmare.

"No," she muttered, not realizing Sarah would hear her.

Her bitterest enemy turned and their eyes locked. "What are *you* doing here?" Sarah demanded.

"The same thing you are."

Sarah gripped her cart with both hands, as if she was prepared to engage in a second ramming session. Frankly, Mary had suffered all the humiliation she could stand and had no desire to go a second round.

"Can't you buy your grandson's gifts some other time?"

"How dare you tell me when I can or cannot shop." Mary couldn't believe the gall. She would shop when and where she pleased without any guidance from the likes of Sarah McDowell.

"Mary, hello."

Mary wanted to groan out loud. Janice Newhouse, the pastor's wife, was easing her cart toward them. "This must be Sarah McDowell. I've seen your photo on a real estate brochure." She smiled warmly at the woman who had caused Mary so much pain. "I'm Janice Newhouse."

"Hello." Sarah's return greeting was stiff.

"I've heard so much about you," Janice said, apparently oblivious to the tension between the two women.

"I'll just bet you have." Sarah said this as though to suggest that Mary was a gossipmonger, when nothing could be further from the truth. For years, she'd quietly refused to get drawn into any discussion involving Sarah. It wouldn't do either of them any good. The same could not be said for Sarah McDowell. She'd taken delight in blackballing Mary's membership in the Women's Century Club. She'd dragged Mary's name and reputation through the mud. Mary, on the other hand, had chosen the higher ground—with the exception, perhaps, of that newspaper column on the perfidy of real estate agents, and that certainly hadn't been a personal attack.

"I understand the Willis family bought their home through you," Janice said, making polite conversation.

"You know the Willises?"

"Yes, they're members of our church. So are Mary and her husband."

Sarah's expression was glacial. "Oh."

"Sarah and I are buying gifts for the charity baskets," Mary said.

"We divided the list and now we're each getting half," Sarah went on to explain. "Tomorrow we're assembling the baskets and taking them to Salvation Army headquarters."

That was much more than Janice needed to know, Mary thought irritably. Sarah was just showing off.

"That's wonderfully charitable of you both," Janice murmured.

"Thank you." Sarah added a pull toy to her basket.

Mary reached for one herself.

Next Sarah took down a board game; Mary took two. Sarah grabbed a skateboard.

"How generous you are," Janice commented, eyes widening as she observed their behavior. "Both of you appear to be very...zealous."

"I believe in giving back to the community," Mary said.

"As do I," Sarah insisted. By now her cart was so full she couldn't possibly cram anything else into it.

"Leave something for me to buy," Mary challenged, doing her best to keep the smile on her face from turning into a scowl.

"I'm the one who has the little girl who wants a Firefighter Barbie on my list," Sarah said, staring pointedly at the doll in Mary's cart.

"*I'm* the one with the gift list," Mary countered. "Besides, there are plenty of Barbie dolls."

"You aren't even supposed to be buying toys. That was *my* job." Sarah's eyes narrowed menacingly.

"Ladies, I don't think there's any reason to squabble here." Janice raised both hands in a calming gesture. "Let me look at your lists."

"Fine," Sarah snapped.

"Good idea," Mary added in a far more congenial tone. She opened her purse and dug out the list Melody Darrington had given her.

Janice examined both pages. She ran down Sarah's first and then Mary's. She frowned. "Here's the problem," she said, handing them back. "You have the same list."

"That's impossible," Mary protested.

"Let me see." Sarah snatched Mary's from her hand with such speed it was a wonder Mary didn't suffer a paper cut.

"That's what I think happened," Janice said. "You were accidentally given one list instead of two."

Sarah glanced over each page. "She's right."

Mary wanted to weep with frustration. "Do you mean to say we're actually working from the same list?" It made sense now that she thought about it. Melody had been so busy that morning, and the phone was ringing off the hook. It was no wonder the secretary had been distracted.

"You were supposed to pick up the grocery items," Mary said.

"I most certainly was not. That was *your* job."

If Sarah was trying to be obtuse and irritating, she was succeeding.

Janice glanced from one to the other. "Ladies, this is for the Christmas baskets, remember?"

Mary smiled benevolently at the pastor's wife, who was new to the area. Janice couldn't know. But then, a twenty-year-old feud wasn't something Mary was inclined to brag about.

"She's right," Sarah said again. "We're both behaving a bit childishly, don't you think?"

Mary was staying away from that question.

"I'll call Melody in the morning and pick up the second half of the list."

"No, you won't," Mary told her. "I'll do it."

"I said I would," Sarah said from between clenched teeth.

"You don't need to, I will."

"Would you ladies prefer that I do it?" Janice volunteered.

"No way," Sarah muttered.

"Thank you, but no," Mary said more politely.

Janice looked doubtful. "You're sure?"

"Yes."

"Yes." Sarah's voice blended with Mary's.

"All right, ladies, I'll leave you to your good works then."

Out of the corner of her eye, Mary watched Janice stroll away.

As soon as the pastor's wife was out of earshot, Sarah said, "You can pick up the list if you want." She made it sound as though she was making a big concession.

Naturally, she'd agree now. Mary sighed; this problem with the list complicated everything. "I'll need time to shop for the groceries."

"And your point is?"

"Shouldn't it be obvious?" Clearly it wasn't. "We'll need to meet on the morning of the twenty-fourth now."

"Christmas Eve?"

"Yes, the twenty-fourth is generally known as Christmas Eve," Mary told her a bit sarcastically.

"Fine. Let's meet at the club at nine and deliver the baskets to the Salvation Army from there."

"Fine."

"In the meantime," Sarah suggested, "let's do the sensible thing and divide up the toys on this list. Why don't I get the girls' stuff and you get the boys'?"

Wordlessly, they each returned half of their purchases. Mary hated to follow Sarah's lead, but for once the woman had come up with a reasonable idea. "I'll see you Tuesday morning at nine," she finally said.

Sarah gave a curt nod.

Mary wheeled her cart to the front of the store. All the cashiers were busy, so she found the shortest line and waited her turn. Not until a few moments later did she notice that Sarah stood in the line beside hers.

Mary took a magazine from the stand, leafed through it and tossed it into her cart.

Sarah placed two magazines in hers.

Mary decided to splurge and buy a candy bar. As she put it in the cart, she glanced at Sarah. The other woman grabbed one of every candy bar on the rack. Refusing to be outdone, Mary reached for two.

Sarah rolled her eyes and then emptied the entire container of candy into her cart.

Mary looked over and saw two men staring at them. A woman was whispering to her companion, pointing in her and Sarah's direction.

Once again, they'd managed to make spectacles of themselves.

Noelle McDowell's Journal

December 22

I just got back from church, and it was lovely to attend services with Mom and Dad and Carley. The music was stirring and brought back so many memories of Christmases spent in Rose. I wish I'd paid closer attention to the sermon, but my mind refused to remain focused on the pastor's message. All I could think about was Thom.

Now that we've talked, I think we've actually created more problems than we've solved. We're going to get together again later in the day, but that's not until one. We both realize we can't leave things as they are, yet neither one of us knows where to go from here.

Still, it's wonderful to know my faith in him was justified. That makes this decision even harder, though. I'm afraid I'm falling in love with him again—if I ever stopped!—but there are so many complications. In fact, I wonder if our best choice would be simply to call it quits. But I'm not sure we can, because we made a mistake last night. We kissed.

If we hadn't done that, I might've found the courage to shake Thom's hand, claim there were no hard feelings and walk away. But we did kiss and now...well, now we're in a quandary. I wish his kisses didn't affect me, but they do. Big-time. Oh boy, nothing's changed in that department. It's as if I was sixteen all over again, and frankly, that's a scary feeling.

I felt Thom's kisses all the way through me, from head to toe. Thom felt them, too, and I think he's just as confused as I am. Things got intense very quickly, and we both recognized we had to stop. Now it's decision time.

Thom withdrew from me, physically and emotionally, and I did from him, too. We both tried to play it cool—as if this was all very nice and it was good to clear the air. He acted as if we should just get on with our lives. I played along and was halfway back to the car when he stopped me. He wanted to know if we could meet at the mall today to talk again.

God help me, I jumped at the invitation. Maybe I should've been more nonchalant, but I couldn't do it. I was just happy for the chance to see him again.

Five

Shopping was the perfect excuse to get out of the house on Sunday afternoon, and Noelle used it. Her mother was gone, her father was absorbed in some televised football game and Carley was in her room checking *Buffy* websites on her computer.

"I'm going out for a while," Noelle said casually.

Her father's eyes didn't waver from the television screen. "Are you meeting Thom?"

"Ah…"

Her father raised his hand. "Say no more. What do you want me to tell your mother if she asks?"

"That I've gone shopping… We're meeting at the mall."

"That's all she needs to know."

Noelle kissed her father on the cheek. His eyes didn't leave the screen as he reached inside his pants pocket and handed her his car keys. "Why don't you take my car again?"

"Thanks, Dad."

"Don't mention it." Then her father did look away from

the television and his gaze sought hers. "You have feelings for this young man?"

Noelle nodded. It was the truth, much as she hated to acknowledge it, even to herself.

Her father nodded, too. "I was afraid of that."

His words lingered in Noelle's mind as she drove to the Rose Mall on the west side of town. She'd lived for this moment ever since she and Thom had parted the night before. They'd resolved what both had considered a deception, but so many questions were still unanswered. They needed time to think, to consider the consequences of becoming involved a second time. Nothing had changed between their families— or more specifically, their mothers—but other things *were* different. Noelle wasn't the naive eighteen-year-old she'd been ten years ago; neither was Thom.

It took a good twenty minutes to find a parking space, and the mall was equally crowded. Carolers dressed in Victorian costumes stood in front of the JCPenney store, cheerfully singing "Silver Bells." Noelle wished she could listen for a while, but fearing she might be late, she paused only a moment to take in the sights and the sounds of the holiday season.

She hurried through the overheated mall and found Thom at a table in the food court, just the way they'd agreed. He stood as she approached.

"I haven't kept you waiting, have I?" she asked.

"No, no. It occurred to me that with Christmas this close we might have trouble finding a table so I grabbed one early."

He'd always been thoughtful. As he put down his coffee and pulled out her chair, she shrugged out of her coat and threw it on the back of the seat. "Would you like to get some lunch?"

She shook her head. "You should have something, though." Her stomach had been upset all morning.

"Are you ill?"

"No—it's guilt." He might as well know. She'd been anxious since last night, since their first moonlit kiss… All through church services and afterward, she'd repeatedly told herself how ridiculous it was to sneak around behind her mother's back. Her father had apparently been doing it for years, but secretive actions truly bothered Noelle.

"Guilt?"

"I don't like being dishonest."

"Then tell your mother." Thom made it sound so easy, but he didn't need an excuse every time he stepped out the front door. He didn't even live at home, and he wasn't visiting his family for Christmas the way she was. He wasn't accountable to his parents for every minute spent outside their presence.

"Did you let your parents know we were meeting?" she asked.

He half grinned, looking sheepish. "No."

"That's what I thought."

"How about coffee?" he asked in an all-too-obvious effort to change the subject. "I could use a refill."

She gave a quick nod. She'd been counting the minutes until they could talk again. After their meeting in the park, she'd barely slept. She'd relived their conversation—and their kisses—over and over. It seemed a miracle that they'd finally learned what must have happened that day ten years ago. Truly a Christmas miracle. Now, if only their mothers would miraculously reconcile…

Thom left and returned a few minutes later with two steaming cups of coffee.

Noelle held her cup with both hands, letting the heat warm her palms. She hadn't felt chilled before, but she did now. "I—I don't know where to start."

"Why didn't you ever come home?" he asked bluntly. "Start by telling me that."

"It was just too painful to come back here. I made excuses at first and it got easier after a while. Plus, Mom and Dad and my sisters were always willing to visit Texas. It's beautiful in a way that's completely different from the Northwest. Oh, and the shopping is excellent."

He laughed. "Is there anyone special in your life?"

"I have a number of good friends."

"Male or female?"

She hesitated. "Female."

Thom visibly relaxed. "You don't date much, then?"

"Of course I date—I've gone out lots. Well, maybe not as much as I'd like, but I *was* engaged for a while. How about you?"

"I came close to getting engaged. Twice."

Without knowing a single detail, Noelle was instantly jealous. "Who?"

He seemed pleased by her reaction. He leaned back in his chair, stretched out his legs and crossed his ankles. "No one you know. Besides, I'm the one asking the questions here. You can drill me later."

"No way! In other words, you became some kind of ladies' man after you dumped me?"

His face suddenly grew serious and he reached across the table for her hand. "I didn't dump you, Noelle."

She'd meant to tease him but realized her remark was insensitive—not to mention plain wrong. "I know. I apologize. Chalk it up to a bad choice of words."

Thom squeezed her hand. "Do you think that's what happened with our mothers?" he asked. "A bad choice of words?"

"How do you mean?"

"Think about it. Just now, you reverted to your old thought pattern—your assumption that you'd been betrayed. It wasn't until after you spoke that you remembered what had really happened."

He was right. The words had slipped out easily, thoughtlessly.

"Our mothers are probably behaving in the same way. After all these years, they're caught in this pattern of disparaging each other, and they can't break the habit."

Noelle wasn't sure she agreed with him. For one thing, she knew her mother had desperately tried to end the feud. Every attempt had been rebuffed. "I don't think it's a good idea to discuss our mothers."

"Why not?"

"Because we argue. You want to defend your mother and I want to defend mine, and the two of us end up fighting. Besides, weren't we talking about the women in your life after I left Rose?"

He chuckled. "You make it sound like there were hordes of them."

"There weren't?" She pretended to be shocked.

He shook his head. "Not really. Two I considered marrying and a few others I saw for a while. What about you?"

"You keep asking. All right, I was serious once. Paul was a computer programmer, and we both worked for the same company, developing new software. It was an exciting time in the business and we got caught up in the thrill of it all." Paul was actually very sweet and very brilliant, but their romance wasn't meant to be. Noelle had been the first to realize it. She'd ended their brief engagement, and they'd parted on good terms, remaining friends to this day. "After the launch of Curtains, our new operating system, well…it was curtains for our marriage plans, too," she said, smiling at her own feeble pun.

"Just one guy?" Thom asked.

"Don't sound so disappointed." Noelle had told him far

more than necessary. He hadn't said a word about either of the women he'd loved.

"Listen, what I said earlier regarding our mothers—I wonder if—"

"I don't want to discuss our mothers, Thom."

"We can't avoid it forever."

"Maybe not," she agreed, "but does it have to be the first thing we talk about?"

"It's not," he argued.

"Look at us," she said. "I haven't been with you fifteen minutes and already we're both on the defensive. This isn't going to work." She was ready to give up and go home, but Thom stopped her.

"Okay, we'll leave our mothers out of the conversation."

Now it seemed neither one had anything to say.

"I kept waiting to hear that you were married," she said after a silence. "But I refused to ask. That's silly I suppose." It was like waiting for the dentist's drill; when it happened there'd be pain and she hadn't been in a hurry to experience it.

"I assumed you'd get married first," he said.

Noelle grinned, shaking her head. "There's something else we need to talk about," she murmured. "What are we going to do now?" She began with the least palatable option—which was also the easiest. "I mean, we could shake hands and say it's great to have this cleared up, then just go back to our respective lives." She waited, watching for a response from him.

His face revealed none of his thoughts. "We could do that," he said. "Or..." He looked at her.

"Or we could renew our friendship."

Thom leaned back in his chair. "I like that option."

So did Noelle. "But, as you said, there's still the situation with our mothers." Now she was the one bringing it up, although she'd hoped to avoid any mention of their mothers' feud. It was futile, she realized. They *couldn't* avoid it, no matter how hard they tried.

"If your mother hadn't borrowed my great-grandmother's tea service," Thom began, "she—"

"My mother?" Noelle cried. "I agree she made a mistake, but she was the first to admit it. Your mother refused to forgive her, and that says a lot about the kind of person she is."

Thom's eyes were flinty with anger. "Don't paint *your* mother as the one who was wronged because—"

Noelle was unwilling to listen to any more. "Listen, Thom, this isn't going to solve anything. I think it'd be best if we dropped the subject entirely."

"That isn't the only thing you want to drop, is it?"

It was a question she didn't want to answer. A question that implied it would be best for all concerned if they simply walked away from each other right now. Their circumstances hadn't changed, not really; the business with their mothers would always be an obstacle between them. They could ignore it, but it would never disappear.

She stood and gathered her purse, pulled on her coat. This time Thom didn't try to stop her.

"So, you're walking away at the first sign of difficulty," he said.

"No. As a teenager my heart was open to you and your family, but I'm older now."

"What's that got to do with anything?" he demanded.

"This time, my eyes are open, too."

He looked as if he wanted to continue their argument. But she didn't have the heart for it. Obviously Thom didn't, either, because he let her go without another word.

"Help me carry everything in, Greg," Mary Sutton said as she stepped into the house. Her arms were loaded with plastic bags bursting at the seams.

Mary had never understood or appreciated football, and she didn't mind saying so. Her husband's gaze reluctantly left the television screen, where a bunch of men in tight pants and large helmets chased after an oddly shaped ball. As far as she was concerned, it was ridiculous the way they grunted and called out a few numbers now and then and groped their privates right on national television.

"Greg, are you going to help me or not?"

Her husband slowly stood up, his eyes still on the TV. "Honey, it's third down and inches."

He might as well be speaking Greek, but she wasn't going to argue with him. From the sudden reaction of the crowd, something had happened. Greg muttered, shaking his head in a disparaging manner. Mary pretended not to hear and walked back out to the car.

A moment later, he met her in the garage. "We're losing."

"Sorry, darling." She hoped she sounded sympathetic, but she didn't try very hard. Men and their football.

"What on earth did you buy?" he complained, lifting the last of the blue plastic bags from the car's trunk.

"Oh, various things," she said dismissively. "This Christmas basket project hasn't been a positive experience," she went on, following her husband into the house.

"Why not?"

Distressed and angry, she blurted out, "You won't believe this. Sarah McDowell was there!"

"At Walmart?" Even Greg sounded surprised. "Don't tell me we've lost our shopping privileges there, too?"

"Very funny." The incident at the Value-X would haunt her forever.

"So you got along better?"

"I wouldn't say that, but I did discover the problem. We had the same list."

"For the Christmas baskets?"

"Yes." Mary set her load on top of the kitchen counter.

The football game ended, and Greg reached for the remote control to turn off the television set. He opened the first sack and seemed pleasantly surprised to find a stash of candy bars. "For me?" he asked. Without waiting for her to respond, he peeled the wrapper halfway down a Baby Ruth bar and took a bite.

"You can have them all." She threw herself onto the sofa.

Her husband walked into the family room and sat down. "You'd better tell me exactly what happened."

"What makes you think anything did?"

Greg chortled. "I haven't been married to you all these years without knowing when something's bothering you."

"Oh, Greg," she moaned. "I behaved like such an idiot." She longed to cover her face with her hands.

"What went wrong this time?"

She shook her head, unwilling to reveal how low she'd sunk. One thing she'd discovered years ago was still true: Sarah McDowell brought out the very worst in her. It never failed. Mary became another person whenever Sarah was around— a person she didn't like.

"Do you want to talk about it?"

"No. I want to crawl into bed and hide my head in shame." The most embarrassing part of all was that the pastor's wife had seen the whole thing.

"Tomorrow morning, I need to go back to the club."

"For what?"

"I need the second half of the list."

"What's on the list?"

"I won't know until I see it, now will I?" She didn't mean to be short-tempered, but this afternoon hadn't been one of her best.

"I don't know if I want you driving. There's an ice storm forecast."

"Greg, I have to get that list. I told Sarah I'd take care of this. It's my responsibility."

"Then I'll drive you."

"You will?" Mary felt better already.

"Of course. Can't have you out on icy roads." Her husband finished off the candy bar and returned to the kitchen, where he rummaged through the bags on the counter. "You never did say why you bought all this candy."

Mary looked over at the ten plastic bags that lined her kitchen counter and shuddered. Half of them were filled with candy bars. "You don't want to know."

Greg didn't respond, but she caught him sneaking more Baby Ruth bars into his pockets and the sleeves of his sweater. He wasn't fooling her, but some things were best ignored.

On the other hand, certain things had to be faced. "Greg," she said thoughtfully. "I'm worried about Thom."

"Why?"

"Did you see him with Noelle last night? The two of them were dancing."

"Yes, dear, I saw them."

"Doesn't that concern you?" she asked.

"No." He added a couple of candy bars to his pants pockets, as though she wasn't going to see them protruding.

"Well, it should. Noelle is a sweet girl, but she's her mother's daughter. She's not to be trusted."

"Thom is an adult. He's fully capable of making his own decisions. My advice is to stay out of it."

Mary couldn't believe her husband would say such a thing to her. "You don't mean that! After what happened the last time—"

"You heard me. Stay out of it."

"But Thom is—"

Greg just shook his head. She wanted to say more but swallowed the words. Fathers weren't nearly as caring and concerned about matters of the heart; they lacked sensitivity. Greg hadn't spent time with Thomas the way she had that fateful summer ten years earlier. The McDowell girl had crushed him.

Her husband started toward the garage.

"Greg," she said.

"Yes, dear?"

"Put the candy bars back. I'm adding them to the charity baskets."

He muttered something under his breath, then said, "Yes, dear."

When Thom returned from the mall, he was suffering a full-blown case of the blues. His apartment had never seemed emptier. The small Christmas tree he'd purchased already decorated looked pitiful in the middle of his coffee table. Some Christmas this was turning out to be.

The light on his answering machine blinked, demanding his attention, and for half a heartbeat he thought it might be Noelle. But even as he pressed the Play button, he realized she wouldn't phone.

"Hey, Thom, this is Jonathan Clark," the message said. "Give me a call when you've got a moment."

Thom reached for the phone and punched in the number the investment broker had left. He knew Jonathan but didn't consider him a close friend. He was a business associate and Kristen McDowell's fiancé. This was the first time Jonathan had sought him out socially; Thom hoped it had something to do with Noelle.

After a brief conversation, they agreed to meet at a local pub. Jonathan didn't say why, but it didn't matter. The way

Thom felt, he was grateful for any excuse to get out of the house. The walls were closing in around him. Some jovial guy-talk and loud music was exactly what he needed. Although Jonathan was about to marry into the other camp, Thom knew he'd be objective.

Jon was sitting at the bar nursing a dark ale when Thom joined him. The music in the background was Elvis Presley's "Blue Christmas"—appropriate under the circumstances. They exchanged pleasantries and then Jonathan got right to the point.

"I wanted to make sure there weren't any hard feelings about last night."

"You mean finagling it so I ended up dancing with Noelle? No problem."

"I didn't really want to do it, but Kristen seemed to think it was important."

Thom pulled out his wallet and paid for his beer when the bartender delivered it. "Like I said, it wasn't a big deal."

"So you and Kristen's sister were once an item?"

"Once."

"But no more?"

Thom took a deep swallow of the cold beer. "There's trouble between our families."

"Kristen told me about it."

"You're lucky, you know." Jonathan faced none of the challenges he did.

"Very," Jonathan agreed.

There was a pause, not an uncomfortable one. Jon seemed willing to discuss the situation further, but he wouldn't force it. He'd left it up to Thom.

"Noelle and I talked after the dance," he finally ventured.

Jonathan swiveled around on his stool in order to get a better look at Thom. "How'd it go?"

"Last night? Good." His blood warmed at the memory of their kisses. It'd taken every ounce of self-control he'd possessed to let her go. That was one of the reasons he'd suggested they meet at the mall today; it was neutral ground.

"Did you two work everything out?"

"We tried." He waited, half hoping Jonathan would question him about it. Jonathan didn't. Thom sighed, feeling a little discouraged. Now that he'd started, he wanted to talk. "I think we're both leery of getting involved a second time," he continued. "Her home's in Texas now and I live here."

"Right, got ya."

"But it's more than logistics." He tipped back the mug and took another swallow of beer. "We have...this situation. She wants to defend her mother. I want to defend mine."

"Only natural." Jonathan glanced at his watch.

Thom shut up. He had the feeling he was boring the other man. Perhaps he had someplace he needed to be.

Jonathan's next remark surprised him. "Kristen and I were making out our guest list and I put down your name. You'll come, won't you?"

"Sure," Thom answered almost flippantly, and then it occurred to him that if he accepted the invitation, he'd see Noelle again. He found himself eager for the opportunity. "Speaking of the wedding—" well, not really, but he didn't know how else to introduce the topic "—did Kristen ever mention her sister being involved with a guy named Paul?"

Jonathan considered it for a moment, then shook his head. "Not that I can remember. Why?"

"Just curious." And jealous. And worried. Noelle had said it was over between her and this Paul character, but Thom had to wonder. She seemed far too willing to walk away from their conversation this afternoon. Maybe the relationship with Paul wasn't as dead as she'd led him to believe.

"Paul," Jonathan repeated slowly. "Did she give you a surname?"

Thom shook his head.

The door to the pub opened, and Kristen McDowell walked inside. Jonathan glowed like a neon light, he was so pleased to see her. "Over here, sweetheart," he called, waving his hand.

Kristen walked to the bar and slipped her arm around her fiancé's waist. "Hello, Thom," she said as naturally as if they saw each other every day. "How's it going?"

"All right. I understand congratulations are in order."

Kristen smiled up at Jonathan and nodded.

Thom felt like an intruder. Reaching for his overcoat, he was getting ready to go when Kristen stopped him.

"There's no need to rush off."

He was about to pretend he had people to see, places to go, but then decided not to lie. "You sure?"

"Of course I'm sure."

Thom was eager to learn what he could about Noelle, so he lingered and ordered another beer. Jon did, too; Kristen had a glass of red wine.

Thom paid for the second round. The three of them sat on bar stools with Kristen in the middle, talking about Christmas plans for a few minutes. "She had me call you," Jonathan confessed suddenly.

Kristen elbowed her fiancé in the ribs. "You weren't supposed to tell him."

The second beer had loosened Thom's tongue. "She damn near knocked me off my feet when I first saw her."

"Kristen?" Jonathan asked, sounding worried.

"No, Noelle."

"Really?" This appeared to please Noelle's younger sister. "So you're still stuck on her, after all these years."

"Damned if I know," Thom muttered. He did know but he wasn't willing to admit it. "We decided it's not going to work."

"Why not?" Kristen sounded outraged.

"We met and talked this afternoon," Thom informed them both.

Jonathan frowned. "I thought you met last night after the dance."

"We did."

"So you've talked twice in the past twenty-four hours."

"Yeah, and like I said, we both realized there are too many complications."

Kristen raised her hand for the bartender. "We need another round."

"I think we've already done enough damage," Jonathan protested.

"Coffee here," she said, pointing at her fiancé. "Same as before over here." She made a sweeping gesture that included Thom.

The bartender did as requested. As soon as the wine and beer arrived, Kristen turned to face Thom. "I thought you loved my sister."

"I did once." He was still working on his second beer.

"But not now?"

Thom didn't want to answer her. Hell, the last time he'd admitted to loving Noelle he was just a kid. But he'd stood up to his parents and been willing to relinquish everything for Noelle. To say he'd loved her was an understatement. He'd been crazy about her.

"Well?" Kristen pressed. "Don't you have an answer?"

"I do," Thom said, picking up his beer. "I just don't happen to like it."

"What's that mean?" Jonathan asked Kristen.

"I think it means he still has feelings for Noelle." Then,

as though she'd suddenly remembered, she said, "Hey! Her birthday's on Christmas Day, you know."

Like he needed a reminder. Not a Christmas passed that Thom forgot.

"She doesn't feel the same way about me," he murmured.

"Yeah, right," Kristen said, exaggerating the words. It took only two beers for him to bare his soul—and it was all for nothing because Noelle didn't love him anymore. It took only two beers to make him maudlin, he thought sourly.

"Yeah, right," Kristen said again.

"It's true," Thom argued. "Did you ask her?"

"Did you?" Kristen asked.

NOELLE MCDOWELL'S
JOURNAL

December 22
Afternoon

I blew it. I had the perfect chance to have a rational conversation with Thom. We had a chance to settle this once and for all without the angst and emotion. It didn't happen. Instead I let the opportunity slip through my fingers. Naturally I have a wealth of excuses, the first one being that I didn't sleep more than a couple of hours all night. This situation between Thom and me was on my mind and I couldn't seem to let it go. My feelings swung from happiness to dread and from joy to fear, and then the whole cycle repeated itself. I kept thinking about what I wanted to say when we saw each other again. Then I started worrying what would happen if he kissed me.

How is it that I can develop complicated software programs used all over the world, but when it comes to Thom Sutton I'm hopeless?

Mom's home from shopping, and when Carley asked if she'd gotten everything she needs for the Christmas baskets, it looked as if Mom was about to burst into tears. She said she had a headache, and went to bed. Apparently I wasn't the only one suffering from too little sleep. I have a feeling that something happened with Mrs. Sutton again, which is bad news all the way around.

Kristen wasn't home when I tried to phone, although she hadn't said she was going out. I'd hoped to discuss this with her, get her per-

spective. She's heard just about everything else that's gone on between Thom and me since I arrived. I could use a sympathetic ear and some sisterly advice.

Everything fell into place so naturally between her and Jonathan, but it sure hasn't been that way with me. I actually considered talking to Carley, which is a sign of how desperate I'm beginning to feel.

I'm not going to see Thom again. We left the mall and nothing more was said. It's over, even though I don't want it to be. It was within my power to change things, and I didn't have the courage to do it. I could've run after him and begged him not to let our relationship end this way, not after we'd come so far. But I didn't, and I'm afraid this is something I'm going to regret for a long time to come.

Six

"You don't need to worry about the dishes," Sarah Mc-Dowell protested.

Noelle continued to load the dishwasher. "Mom, quit treating me like a guest in my own home." The menial task gave her something to do. Furthermore, she hoped it would help take her mind off her disastrous meeting with Thom at the mall. She'd reviewed their conversation a dozen times and wished so badly it had taken a different course. Their second attempt at a relationship had staggered to a halt before it had really begun, she thought with regret as she rinsed off the dinner plates and methodically set them inside the dishwasher.

"Thank you, dear. This is a real treat," her mother said, walking into the family room to join her dad.

Sarah had returned from her shopping trip in a subdued mood. Noelle didn't ply her with questions, mainly because she wasn't in a talkative mood herself. Even Carley Sue seemed to be avoiding the rest of the family. Except for dinner, her sister had spent most of the day in her room, first on her computer, and then wrapping Christmas presents.

As Noelle finished wiping the counters, her youngest sister entered the kitchen. Carley glanced into the family room, where her parents sat watching television. Their favorite courtroom drama was on, and they seemed to be absorbed in it.

"Wanna play a game of Yahtzee?" Noelle asked. It was one of Carley's favorites.

Her sister shook her head, then motioned for Noelle to come into her room. Carley nodded toward their parents, then pressed her finger to her lips.

"What's going on?" Noelle asked, drying her hands on a kitchen towel.

"Shh," Carley said, tiptoeing back toward her room.

"What?" Noelle asked impatiently.

Carley opened her bedroom door, grabbed Noelle's hand and pulled her into the bedroom. To her shock, Thom stood in the middle of the room, wearing his overcoat.

"Thom!"

"Shh," both Thom and Carley hissed at her.

"What are you *doing* here?" she whispered.

"When did you trade bedrooms with your sister?" he asked.

"A long time ago." She couldn't believe he was in her family's home. Years ago, he'd come to the house and tapped on her bedroom window, and she'd leaned out on the sill and they'd kissed. Amazingly, her parents hadn't heard—and the neighbors hadn't reported him. "Why are you here?"

"I came to see you."

Okay, that much was obvious. But she still didn't understand why he'd come.

"It was a bit of a surprise to bump into your little sister."

"I didn't mind," Carley said. "But he scared me like crazy when he knocked on the window."

"Sorry," Thom muttered.

"You said he broke your heart," Carley said, directing her

remarks at Noelle. "We threw popcorn at him, remember? At least, we thought it was him, but then it wasn't."

Noelle didn't need any further reminders of that unfortunate incident. "I broke his heart, too. It was all a misunderstanding."

"Oh." Carley clasped her hands behind her back and leaned against the door, waiting. She was certainly in no hurry to leave and seemed immoderately interested in what Thom had to say.

Thom glanced at her sister, who refused to take the hint, and then said, "We need to talk."

"Now? Here?"

He nodded and touched her face in the gentlest way. "Listen, I'm sorry about this afternoon. We didn't even talk about what's most important—and that's you and me."

"I'm sorry, too." Unable to resist, Noelle slipped her arms around his waist and they clung to each other.

"This is so-o-o romantic," Carley whispered. "Why don't you two sit down and make yourselves comfortable. Can I get you anything to drink?"

Her little sister was as much of a hostess as their mother, Noelle thought with amusement. "No, but thanks."

Thom shrugged. "I should leave, but—"

"No, don't," Noelle pleaded with him. It might make more sense to meet Thom later, but she didn't want him out of her sight for another second.

Thom sat on the edge of the bed and Noelle sat beside him. He took both her hands in his. "I've been doing a lot of thinking about us."

"I have, too," she said hurriedly.

"I don't want it to end."

"Oh, Thom, I don't, either! Not the way it did this afternoon—and for all the wrong reasons." Noelle was acutely aware of her sister, listening in on their conversation, but she didn't care.

"Noelle, I know what I want, and that's you back in my life."

"Oh, Thom." She bit her lower lip, suddenly on the verge of tears.

Carley sighed again. "This is better than any movie I've ever seen."

Noelle ignored her. "What are we going to do about our families?" They couldn't pretend their relationship wouldn't cause problems.

"I've been thinking about that, but I'm just not sure." Thom stroked the side of her face, and his hand lingered there.

"Oh, this *is* difficult," Carley agreed.

Her little sister was absorbing every word. Had Carley left the room, Noelle was sure Thom would be kissing her by now. Then they'd be lost in the kissing and oblivious to anything else.

"Is there a solution for us? One that doesn't involve alienating our families. Or our mothers, at any rate." Thom didn't look optimistic.

"What about the tea service?" Noelle said, mulling over an idea. "You said there's no replacing it, but maybe if we found a similar one, your mother would be willing to accept it."

"I don't know," he said. "This wasn't just any tea service. It was a family heirloom that belonged to my great-grandmother. We'll never find one exactly like it."

"I know, but finding one even remotely similar would be a start toward rebuilding the relationship, don't you think?"

He didn't seem convinced. "Perhaps."

"Could you find out the style and type?"

Thom shook his head doubtfully. "I could try."

"Please, Thom. And see if there are any photos."

They hugged again and Noelle closed her eyes, savoring the feel of his strong arms around her, inhaling his clean, outdoorsy scent.

Everything had changed for her. The thought of returning to Texas and her life there held little appeal. For years, she'd stayed away from her hometown because it represented a past that had brought her grief, and now—now she knew this was where her future lay.

There was a knock on Carley's door.

Noelle and Thom flew apart and a look of panic came into Carley's eyes.

"The closet," Noelle whispered, quickly ushering Thom inside. No sooner had she shut the door than her little sister admitted their mother into the room.

Noelle figured they must look about as guilty as any two people could. Carley stared up at the bedroom ceiling and Noelle was tempted to hum a catchy Yuletide tune.

"I thought I'd turn in for the night," her mother said. She obviously hadn't noticed anything out of the ordinary.

"Good idea," Carley told her mother.

"You don't want to wear yourself out," Noelle added, letting her arms swing at her sides. "With Christmas and all…"

Her mother gave them a soft smile. "It does my heart good to see the two of you together. You were like a second mother to Carley when she was a baby."

"Mom!" her little sister wailed.

"I always thought you'd have a house full of your own children one day," she said nostalgically. "Don't you remember how you used to play with all your dolls?"

Noelle wanted to groan, knowing that Thom was listening in on the conversation.

"You'd make a wonderful mother."

"Thank you, Mom," she said. "'Night now. See you in the morning."

"'Night." She stepped out the door.

Noelle sighed with relief and so did Carley. She was about to open the closet when her mother stuck her head back inside the room. "Noelle, do you have plans for the morning?"

"No, why?" she asked, her voice higher than normal.

"I might need some help."

"I'll be glad to do what I can."

"Thank you, sweetheart." And with that she was gone. For good this time.

After a moment, Thom opened the closet door and peered out. "Is it safe?"

"I think so."

"Do you want me to keep watch?" Carley asked. "You know, so you guys can have some privacy." She smiled at Thom. "He's been wanting to kiss you ever since you got here." She lowered her voice. "I think he's kinda cute."

"So do I," Noelle confessed. "And yes, some privacy would be greatly appreciated."

Carley winked at Thom. "I think I'll go out and see what Dad's doing."

The instant the door closed, Thom took her in his arms and lowered his mouth to hers. Noelle groaned softly, welcoming him. Together, they created warm, moist kisses, increasing in intensity and desire. Other than the brief episode in the park, it'd been years since they'd kissed like this. Yet his touch felt so familiar....

"It's always been you," he whispered.

She heard the desperation in his voice. "I know—it's always been you," she echoed.

He kissed her again with a hunger and a need that reflected her own.

"Oh, Thom, what are we going to do?"

"We're going to start with your suggestion and find a silver tea service," he said firmly. "Then we're going to give it to my mother and tell her it's time to mend fences."

"What if we *can't* find one?" She frowned. "Or what if we do and they still won't forgive each other?"

"You worry too much." He kissed the tip of her nose. "And you ask too many questions."

Sarah was sitting up in bed reading a brand-new and highly touted mystery when her husband entered their room.

"You've been quiet this evening," Jake commented as he unbuttoned his shirt.

"Have I?" She gazed at the novel, but her attention kept wandering. She'd read this paragraph at least six times and she couldn't remember what it said. Every word seemed to remind her of a friend she'd lost twenty years ago.

"You haven't been yourself since you got back from shopping."

Sarah decided to ignore his words. "I stopped in and said good-night to the girls before I went to bed. Isn't it nice that Noelle and Carley get along so well?"

"You're changing the subject," Jake said. "And not very subtly."

Sarah set aside the book. In her present frame of mind, she was doing the author and herself a disservice. She reached for the light, but instead of flicking it off, she fell back against her pillows.

"I ran into Mary this afternoon," she told her husband.

"Again?"

"Again," she confirmed. "This meeting didn't go much better than the one at Value-X."

"That bad?"

"Almost. I can't even begin to tell you how horribly the two of us behaved."

Jake chuckled, shaking his head. "Does this have anything to do with the two hundred or so candy bars I found in the back of the big freezer?"

"You saw?"

He nodded. "What is it with you two?"

"Oh, honey, I wish I knew. I *hate* this. I've always hated this animosity. It would've been over years ago if Mary had listened to reason."

Her husband didn't respond.

"Everything was perfectly fine until we were forced to work on this Christmas project. Until then, she ignored me and I ignored her."

"Ignored her, did you?" he asked mildly.

Sarah pretended not to hear his question. "I think Melody Darrington might have planned this." The scheme took shape in her mind. "Melody *must* have."

"Isn't she the club secretary?"

"You know Melody," Sarah snapped. "She's the cute blonde who sold me the tickets to the dance."

"I wasn't there when you picked up the tickets," Jake reminded her as he climbed into bed.

"But you know who I mean."

"If you say so."

"You do. Now listen, because I think I'm on to something here. Melody's the one who told me we couldn't rent the hall for Kristen's wedding unless I performed a community service for the club."

"Yes, I remember, and that's how you got involved in the Christmas basket thing."

"Melody's also the one who assigned me to that project," she went on. "There had to be dozens of other projects I could've done. Plus, she insisted I had to fulfill those hours this year. That makes no sense whatsoever."

"Why would Melody do anything like that?"

"How would I know?"

Her husband looked skeptical. "I think you might be jumping to conclusions here."

"Melody gave us half of the same list, too." Outrage simmered just below the surface as Sarah sorted through the facts. She tossed aside the covers and leaped out of bed. Hands on hips, she glared at her husband. Of course. It all added up. Melody definitely had a role in this, and Sarah didn't like it.

"Hey, I didn't do anything," Jake protested.

"I'm not saying you did." Still not satisfied, she started pacing the area at the foot of the bed. "This is the lowest, dirtiest trick anyone's ever played on me."

"Now, Sarah, you don't have any real proof."

"Of course I do! Why did Melody make a copy of that list, anyway? All she had to do was divide it."

"Sounds like an honest mistake to me. Didn't you tell me the office was hectic that morning? Melody was dealing with you, the phones and everything else when she gave you and Mary the lists."

"Yes, but that's no excuse for what happened."

"You're angrier with yourself than Melody."

Sarah knew the truth when she heard it. The outrage vanished as quickly as it had come, and she climbed back into bed, next to her husband.

For a long time neither spoke. Finally Jake turned on their bedside radio and they listened to "Silent Night" sung by a children's choir. Their pure, sweet voices almost brought tears to Sarah's eyes.

"In two days, it'll be Christmas," she said in a soft voice.

"And Noelle's birthday." Her husband smiled. "Remember our first year? We could barely afford a Christmas tree, let alone gifts. Yet you managed to give me the most incredible present of all, our Noelle."

"Remember the next Christmas, when I'd just found out I was pregnant with Kristen?" she said fondly. "Our gift to each other was a secondhand washer." In the early years of their marriage, they'd struggled to make ends meet. Yet in many ways, those had been the very best.

Jake smiled. "We were poor as church mice."

"But happy."

"Very happy," he agreed, sliding his arm around her shoulders. "I thought it was clever of you to knit Christmas stockings for the girls the year Noelle turned four. Or was it five?"

"I didn't knit them," Sarah said sadly. "Mary did."

"Mary?"

"Don't you remember? She knit all the kids' stockings, and I baked the cookies and we exchanged?"

"Ah, yes. You two had quite a barter system worked out."

"If we hadn't traded babysitting, none of us would've been able to afford an evening out." Once a month, they'd taken the girls over to their dearest friends' home for the night; Mary and Greg had done the same. It'd been a lifesaver in those early years. She and Jake had never been able to afford anything elaborate, but a night out, just the two of them, had been heaven. Mary and Greg had cherished their nights, as well.

"I miss her," Sarah admitted. "Even after all these years, I miss my friend."

"I know." Jake gently squeezed her shoulder.

"I'd give anything never to have borrowed the silver tea service."

"You were trying to help someone out."

"That's how it started, but I should've been honest with

Mary. I should've told her the tea service wasn't for my open house, but for Cheryl's."

"Why didn't you?"

She'd had years to think about the answer to that question. "Because Mary didn't like Cheryl. I assumed she was jealous. Now... I don't know."

Sarah remembered the circumstances well. She'd recently begun selling real estate and Cheryl Carlson had given her suggestions and advice. Cheryl had wanted something to enhance the look of the dining room for her open house, and Sarah had volunteered to bring in the tea service. When she'd asked Mary, her friend had hesitated, but then agreed. Sarah had let Mary assume it was for her own open house.

"You were so upset when you found out the tea service had been stolen."

To this day her stomach knotted at the memory of having to face Mary and confess what had happened. Soon afterward, Cheryl had left the agency and hired on with another firm, and Sarah had lost touch with her.

"I'd always hoped that one day Mary would find it in her heart to forgive me."

"I did, too."

"I'm so sorry, sweetheart," Sarah whispered, resting her head against her husband's shoulder.

"Why are you apologizing to me?"

"Because you and Greg used to be good friends, too."

"Oh."

"Remember how you used to golf together."

"Yes."

"I wonder if Greg still plays."

"I see him out at the club every now and then," Jake told her.

"Does he speak to you?"

"Yes."

Sarah was comforted knowing that. "I'm glad."

"So am I," her husband said, then kissed her good-night.

On December twenty-third, Thom's office was running on a skeleton crew. His secretary was in for half a day and he immediately handed her the assignment of locating every antiques store in a hundred-mile radius.

He'd called his father before eight that morning. "Tell me what you know about Mom's old tea service."

"Tell you what I know?" he repeated. "It was stolen, remember?"

"I realize that," Thom said impatiently.

"What makes you ask?"

"I thought I'd buy her a replacement for Christmas."

"Don't you think you're leaving your shopping a little late?"

"Could be." Thom didn't feel comfortable sharing what this was really about, but he was going to do whatever he could to replace that damn tea service.

"I think we might have a picture of it somewhere."

Thom perked up.

"For years your mother looked for a replacement, you know. We hadn't actually taken a picture of the tea set, but it was in the background of another photograph."

Thom remembered now. His parents had the photo enlarged in order to get as much detail as possible.

"Do you still have the photograph? Or better yet, the enlargement?"

"I think it might be around here somewhere. I assume you need this ASAP."

"You got it."

"Well, I promised to drive your mother out to the Women's

Century Club this morning and then to the grocery store. You're welcome to stop by the house and look."

"Where do you figure it might be?"

His father considered that for a moment. "Maybe the bottom drawer of my desk. There are a few old photographs there. That's my best suggestion."

"Anyplace else I should look?"

"Your mother's briefcase. Every once in a while she visits an antiques store, but for the most part she's given up hope. She's still got her name in with several of the bigger places. If anything even vaguely similar comes in, the stores promised to give her a call."

"Has she gotten many calls?"

"Only two in all these years," his father told him. "Both of them excited her so much she could barely sleep until she'd checked them out. They turned out to be completely the wrong style."

Thom didn't know if he'd have any better success, but he had to try.

"Good luck, son."

"Thanks, Dad."

As soon as he hung up, Thom called Noelle's cell phone. She answered right away.

"Morning," he said, warming to the sound of her voice. "I hope you're free to do a bit of investigating."

"I am. I canceled out on Mom—told her I was meeting an old friend."

"Did she ask any questions?"

"No, but I could tell she was disappointed. I do so hope we're successful."

"Me, too. Listen, I've got news." Thom told her about the old photograph and what his father had said earlier. He hoped it would encourage Noelle, but she seemed disheartened when she spoke again.

"If your parents searched all these years, what are the chances of us finding a replacement now?"

"We'll just keep working on it. I'm not giving up, and I'm guessing you feel the same way."

"I do—of course."

"Good. How soon before we can meet?"

"Fifteen minutes."

"I'll wait for you at my parents' place."

On his way out the door, Thom grabbed the list Martha, his secretary, had compiled and when he read it over, he knew why he paid this woman top dollar. Not only had she given him the name and address of every store in the entire state, she'd also listed their websites and any other internet information.

"Merry Christmas," he said, then gave her the rest of the day off with pay.

Noelle was already parked outside his parents' house when Thom arrived. She got out of her car and joined him as he pulled into the driveway.

"Hi," she said softly.

Thom leaned over and kissed her. "Hi." The key to the house was under a decorative rock. He unlocked the door and turned off the burglar alarm. Holding Noelle's hand, he led her into his parents' home.

Noelle stopped in the entryway and glanced around. It'd been many, many years since she'd walked into this house. It wasn't really familiar—everything had been redecorated and repainted since she was a little girl—but the place had a comfortable relaxed feel. Big furniture dominated the living room, hand-knit stockings hung on the fireplace and the mantel was decorated with holly. The scent of the fresh Christmas tree filled the air.

"Your mother has a wonderful eye for color and design," she commented, taking in the bright red bows on the tree and all the red ornaments.

Still holding her hand, Thom led her into his father's den. The oak rolltop desk sat in the corner, and Thom immediately started searching through the bottom drawer. He found the stack of photographs his father had mentioned and sorted through them with Noelle looking over his shoulder. She leaned against him, and he wondered if she realized how good it felt to have her pressed so close to him. Or how tempting it was to turn and kiss her...

"That's it," she cried triumphantly when he flipped past a black-and-white picture. She grabbed it before he had a chance to take a second look. Examining the print, she murmured, "It really was exquisite, wasn't it?" She passed it back to him.

"It *is* beautiful," he said, emphasizing the present tense. Thom wasn't sure why he insisted on being this optimistic about finding a replacement. He suspected that wanting it so badly had a lot to do with it.

Reaching into his coat pocket, he pulled out the list Martha had compiled for him.

"Now that we have a picture," Noelle said, "I'll go home and scan it into Carley's computer. Then I'll send it out to these addresses and see what comes back."

"Great. But before you do, I'll get a copy of this photograph and start contacting local dealers. They might be able to steer me in a different direction."

"Oh, Thom, it'd mean so much to me if we could bring our mothers back together."

They kissed, and it would've been the easiest thing in the world to become immersed in the wonder of having found each other again. Her mouth was warm, soft to the touch. She enticed him, fulfilled him and tempted him beyond any woman he'd ever known or loved. He didn't know much about her present life. They'd spoken very little of their accomplishments, their friends, their jobs. It wasn't necessary. Thom *knew* her. The girl he'd loved in high school had matured into a capable, beautiful and very desirable adult.

"It's hard to think about anything else when you kiss me," she whispered.

"It is for me, too."

Before leaving the Sutton home, Thom put everything back as it was, and remembered to reset the burglar alarm.

After making a photocopy at his office, Thom gave her the original, thinking that would scan best.

"I'll go back to the house now and plead with Carley to let me on the computer," she told him.

"Okay, and I'll see what a little old-fashioned footwork turns up."

Noelle started to get into her car, then paused. "What'll happen if we don't find a replacement before I return to Texas?"

Thom didn't want to think about that yet. "I don't know," he had to admit.

"Want to meet in the park at midnight?" she asked.

Thom chuckled. "I'm a little old to be sneaking around to meet my girlfriend."

"That didn't stop you from climbing in my bedroom window last night."

True, but his need to see her had overwhelmed his caution, not to mention his good sense.

"I love you, Noelle." There, he'd said it. He'd placed his heart in her hands, to accept or reject.

Tears glistened in her eyes. "I love you, too—I never stopped loving you."

"Even when you hated me?"

She laughed shakily. "Even then."

NOELLE McDOWELL'S
JOURNAL

December 23
11:00 a.m.

I feel as if I'm on an emotional roller coaster. One moment I'm feeling as low as I can get, and the next I'm soaring into the clouds. Just now, I'm in the cloud phase. Thom found the picture of the tea set! We're determined to locate one as close to the original as possible. As I said to Thom, I'm hoping for a Christmas miracle. (I never knew I was such a romantic.) Normally I scoff at things like miracles, but that's what both Thom and I need. We've already had one miracle—we have each other back.

Before we parted this morning, Thom said he loved me. I love him, too. I've always loved Thom, and that's what made his deception—or what I believed was his deception—so terribly painful.

Now all we've got to do is keep our mothers out of the picture until we can replace the tea service. I know it's a challenging task, but we're up to it.

As of right now, we each have our assignments. Carley's using the computer for ten more minutes and then it's all mine. My job is to scan in the picture he found at his parents' house and send it to as many online antiques dealers as I can. Thom is off checking local dealers and has some errands to run. We're going to meet up again later.

I had to cancel a lunch date with Kristen and Jonathan, but my sister understood. She's excited about Thom and me getting back to-gether. Apparently she's had more of a hand in this than I realized. I really owe her.

Finding a tea service to replace the one that was stolen is turning out to be even harder than I expected—but we have to try. I believe in miracles. I was a doubter less than a week ago, but now I'm convinced.

Seven

"How many turkeys did you say we had to buy?"

"Six," Mary said, checking the list to make sure she was correct. December twenty-third, and the grocery store was a nightmare. The aisles were crowded, and many of the shelves needed restocking. The last thing Mary wanted to do was fight the Christmas rush, but that couldn't be helped. Next year, she'd leave the filling of these Christmas baskets to someone else.

"Get six bags of potatoes while you're at it," she told her husband as they rolled past a stack of ten-pound bags.

"Getting a little bossy, aren't you?" Greg muttered.

"Sorry, it's just that there are a hundred other things I'd rather be doing right now."

"Then you should've given the task to Sarah McDowell. Didn't you tell me she offered?"

Mary didn't want to hear the other woman's name. "I don't trust her to see that it's done properly."

"Don't you think you're being a little harsh?"

"No." That should be plain enough. The more she thought about her last encounter with Sarah McDowell, the more she realized how glad she'd be when they'd completed this project. "Being around Sarah has dredged up a whole slew of bad memories," she informed her husband.

Greg dutifully loaded sixty pounds of potatoes into the cart. As soon as he'd finished, Mary headed down the next aisle.

"My Christmas has been ruined," she said through gritted teeth.

"How's that?"

"Greg, don't be obtuse." She reached for several cans of evaporated milk and added them to the food piled high in their cart. "I've had to deal with *her*."

"Yes, but—"

"Never mind," Mary said, cutting him off. She didn't expect Greg to understand. Her husband had never really grasped the sense of loss she'd felt when Sarah destroyed their friendship with her deception. The silver tea service was irreplaceable; so was the friendship its disappearance had shattered.

"Hello, Mary." Jean Cummings, a friend who edited the society page, pulled her cart alongside Mary's. "Merry Christmas, Greg."

Her husband had the look of a deer caught in the headlights. He no more knew who Jean was than he would a stranger, although he'd attended numerous social functions with the woman.

"You remember Jean, don't you?" she said, hoping to prompt his memory.

"Of course," he lied. "Good to see you again."

"It looks like you're feeding a big crowd," Jean said, surveying the contents of Mary's cart.

Mary didn't bother to explain about the Christmas baskets. "Is your family coming for the holidays?" she asked.

"Oh, yes, and yours, too, I imagine?"

"Of course." Mary was eager to get about her business. She

didn't have time to dillydally. As soon as she was finished with the shopping, she could go back to planning her own family's Christmas dinner. Greg would need to order the fresh Dungeness crabs they always had on Christmas Eve; he could do that while they were here.

"Tell me," Jean said, leaning close to Mary and talking in a stage whisper. "Am I going to get the scoop on Thom?"

"Thom?" Mary didn't know what she was talking about.

"I saw him just now in Mendleson's."

It was well known that the jeweler specialized in engagement rings.

"Thom's one of the most eligible bachelors in town. I know plenty of hearts will be broken when he finally chooses a bride."

Mary was speechless. She'd had lunch with her son on Friday and although he'd hinted, he certainly hadn't said anything that suggested he was on the verge of proposing. She didn't even know who he was currently seeing.

"I'm sure Thom would prefer to do his own announcing," Greg said coolly, answering for Mary.

"Oh, drat," Jean muttered. "I was hoping you'd let the cat out of the bag."

"My lips are sealed," Mary said, recovering. "Have a wonderful Christmas."

"You, too." Jean pushed her cart past them.

As soon as the society page editor was out of earshot, Mary gripped her husband's forearm. "Has Thom spoken to you lately?"

"This morning," Greg told her. "But he didn't say anything about getting engaged."

"Who could it be?" Mary cried, aghast that she was so completely in the dark. As his mother, she should know these things.

"If he was serious about any woman, we'd know."

Mary wasn't buying it.

"Let's not leap to conclusions just because our son happened to walk into a certain jewelry store. I'm sure there's a perfectly logical reason Thom was in Mendleson's and I'll bet it hasn't got a thing to do with buying an engagement ring."

"This is all Sarah's fault," she murmured.

Her husband looked at her as though she were speaking in a foreign language.

"I mean it, Greg. I've been so preoccupied with the whole mess Sarah's created about these baskets, I haven't had time to pay attention to my son. Why, just on Friday when we had lunch..." Suddenly disheartened, Mary let her words fade.

"What's wrong?" Greg asked.

All the combativeness went out of her. "I can't blame Sarah entirely—I played a role in this, too."

"What role?"

Once again, she was amazed by her husband's obliviousness. "This business with Thom. Now that I think about it, I'm convinced he wanted to talk over his engagement with me, only I was so rattled by the Value-X incident I didn't give him a chance. Oh, Greg, how could I have been so self-absorbed?"

"What makes you think he was going to tell you he was getting engaged? Why don't we call and ask him when we get home?" Greg suggested.

"And let him think we're interfering in his life? We can't do that!"

"Why not?"

"We'd ruin his surprise, if indeed there is one."

Greg merely sighed as they wheeled the cart to the checkout counter.

Ten minutes later, once everything was safely inside the trunk, Mary turned to him. "I just don't know what I'll do if *she's* the one he's interested in. I couldn't stand it if he married into *that* family."

"I don't think we need to worry about it," he told her as they started back to the house. "There's no evidence whatsoever."

"He *danced* with Noelle McDowell!"

"He danced with lots of girls."

The engine made a coughing sound as they approached the first intersection. "What's that?" Mary asked.

"It's time for an oil change," her husband said. "I'll have the car looked at after the holidays."

She nodded. She trusted the upkeep of their vehicles to her husband and immediately put the thought out of her mind. Car troubles were minor in the greater scheme of things.

By the end of the day, when clouds thickened the sky and the cold swept in, fierce and chilling, Thom finally had to admit that replacing the silver tea service wasn't going to be easy.

He'd tried everything he could think of, called friends and associates who might know where he could find an antiques dealer who specialized in silver—anyone who might lead him to his prize. Far more than a gift lay in the balance. It was possible that his and Noelle's entire future hinged on this.

At seven, after an exhaustive all-day search, he went home. The first thing he did was check his answering machine, hoping to hear from Noelle. Sure enough, the message light was flashing. Without waiting to remove his coat, he pushed the button and grabbed paper and a pen.

A female voice, high and excited, spilled out. "It's Carley Sue. Remember me? I'm Noelle's sister. Anyway, Noelle asked me to call you. She'd call you herself, but I asked if I could do it, 'cause it was my bedroom window you knocked on. And my computer Noelle used."

Thom laughed out loud, almost missing the second half of the message.

"Anyway, Noelle wanted to know if you could meet her at the park tomorrow morning. She said you should be there early. She said six o'clock 'cause you have to drive all the way to Portland. She said you'd know why, but she wouldn't tell me. When you see Noelle, please tell her it's not nice to keep secrets from her sister, will you?" She giggled. "Never mind, I could get it out of her if I really wanted to. Bye."

Thom smiled, feeling a surge of energy. Obviously Noelle had had better luck than he did.

A second message followed the first.

"Thom, it's me. I wasn't sure Carley got the entire message to you. When we meet at the park, come with a full tank of gas. If this conflicts with your Christmas Eve plans, call me on my cell phone." There was a short pause. "I don't want you to get your hopes up. I found a tea service that's not *exactly* like your grandmother's, but I'm looking for a Christmas miracle. We'll need to compare it to the picture. The dealer's only keeping his store open until noon, which is why we need to leave here so early. I'm sorry I can't see you tonight. I wish I could, but I've got family obligations. I know you understand."

He did understand—all too well. A third message started; he was certainly popular today. It was his mother and she sounded worried.

"It's Mom… I ran into a friend from the newspaper this morning and she mentioned seeing you at Mendleson's Jewelers. Were you…buying an engagement ring? Thom, it isn't that McDowell girl, is it? Call me, will you? I need reassurance that you're not about to make a big mistake."

This was what happened when you lived in a small town.

Everyone knew your business. So, his mother had heard, and even with the wrong facts, she'd put together the right answer. Yes, he'd been at Mendleson's. And yes, it *was* "that McDowell girl."

Thom decided he had to talk about all of this with someone who understood the situation and knew all the people involved. Someone discreet, who had his best interests at heart. Someone with no agenda, hidden or otherwise.

The one person he could trust was his older sister. Suzanne was three years his senior, married and living ten miles outside of town; she and her husband, Rob, owned a hazelnut orchard. Thom didn't see Suzanne often, but he was godfather to his five-year-old nephew, Cameron.

A brief phone call assured him that his sister was available and eager to see him. Off he went, grabbing a chunk of cheese and an apple to eat on the way. Maybe his sister would have some wisdom to share with him.... How quickly life can change, he mused, and never more so than at Christmas.

Suzanne had a mug of hot cider waiting when he arrived. Rob was out, dealing with some late deliveries. His family owned the orchard and leased it to him. Rob worked long hours making a success of their business, and so did Suzanne. Both his sister and brother-in-law were honest, hardworking people, and he trusted their advice.

"This is a surprise," Suzanne said, pulling out a chair at the large oak table in the center of her country kitchen.

"Cameron's in bed already?" Thom asked, disappointed to miss seeing his nephew.

"He thinks if he goes to bed early Santa will come sooner." She gave a shrug. "Never mind that this is only the twenty-third. I guess he's hoping he can make time speed up," she said with a smile. "By the way, he had a ridiculous tale about you and some woman at the movies the other day. Throwing popcorn was a big theme in this story."

"I don't know what he told you, but more than likely it's true. We bumped into Noelle McDowell and her little sister at the theater."

"Noelle. Oh, no." Suzanne was instantly sympathetic. "That must've been uncomfortable."

"Yes and no." He hesitated, wondering to what extent his sister's attitude was a reflection of their parents'. "It was difficult at first, because we didn't exactly part on the best of terms."

"At first?"

His sister had picked up on that fast enough. "We've talked since and resolved our difficulties."

"Resolved them, did you?" Suzanne raised her eyebrows.

"I love Noelle." There, he'd said it.

"Who's Noelle?" Rob asked as he walked in through the kitchen door, shedding hat, scarf and gloves.

"I'll explain later," Suzanne promised, ladling a cup of cider from the pot on the stove. "Here, honey."

"Our families don't get along," Thom explained.

"Do Mom and Dad know?" his sister asked.

"Not yet, but Mom got wind of me going to Mendleson's. She must have her suspicions, since she left a message on my machine practically begging me to tell her I'm not seeing Noelle."

"Did you buy a ring?"

"That's not the point."

"Okay," his sister said slowly. "What *do* you plan to tell Mom and Dad?"

"I don't know."

Suzanne sipped her cider, then put down the mug to focus

on him. "You're going to wait until Christmas is over before you say anything, right?"

Thom didn't know if he could. His mother was already besieging him with questions and she'd keep at him until she got answers—preferably the answers she wanted. He needed an ally and he hoped he could count on Suzanne.

"Let me play devil's advocate here a moment," his sister suggested.

"Please."

"Put yourself in Mom's place. Noelle's family has hurt our family. And now you're asking Mom to welcome Noelle into our lives and our hearts."

"Noelle is already in my heart."

"I know," Suzanne told him, "but there's more than one person involved in this. How does her family feel about you, for instance?"

That was a question Thom didn't want to consider. This wouldn't be easy for Noelle, either. Kristen and Carley were obviously supportive, but Sarah McDowell—well, she was another matter.

"We were ready to defy everyone as teenagers," he said, reminding his sister of the difficult stand he'd taken at eighteen.

"You were a kid."

"I was in love with her then, and I'm still in love with her."

"Yes," Suzanne said, "but you're more responsible now."

"I can't live my life to suit everyone else," he said, frustrated by her response.

"He's got a point," Rob said. "I don't understand the family dynamics here, but I have a fairly good idea what you're talking about. I say if Thom feels this strongly about Noelle after all these years, he should go for it. He should live his own life."

Thom felt a rush of gratitude for his brother-in-law's enouragement.

"That's what you wanted to hear, isn't it?" Suzanne said, smiling. "For what it's worth, I agree with my husband."

"Thanks," Thom said. "That means a lot, you guys." He shook his head. "Noelle and I are well aware of the problems we face as a couple. We'd hoped to come to our parents with a solution."

"What kind of solution?"

"I've been pounding the pavement all day, checking out antiques stores and jewelry stores for a replacement tea service. Noelle's been doing an internet search."

His sister frowned. "I don't want to discourage you, but you're not going to find one."

She certainly had a way of cutting to the chase. "Thank you for that note of optimism. Anyway, how can you be so sure? Noelle thinks she might have a lead."

"Hey, that's good," Rob said. "It's worth trying to find... whatever this thing is that you're looking for."

"An antique silver tea service—I'll fill you in later, Rob." She turned to her brother. "I don't want to be pessimistic. It's just that Mom and Dad looked for years. They've given up now, but for a long time they left no stone unturned."

"If we find one, we'll consider it a Christmas miracle."

"Definitely," Suzanne agreed. "And I'd consider it a lucky omen, too."

"But you don't think we'll succeed."

"No," his sister told him. "I don't think so, but who knows?"

"If I ask Noelle to be part of my life, will you accept her?"

"Of course." Suzanne didn't hesitate. "But I'm not the one whose opinion matters. However, Rob's right, you've got to live your own life, and we'll support you in whatever choice you make."

He visited with his sister a while longer and assured her

that no matter what he decided, he'd meet the family for the annual Christmas Eve dinner, followed by church services.

The next morning Noelle was waiting in the park at the appointed time and place when he got there. His heart reacted instantly to the sight of her. She looked like an angel in her long white wool coat and cashmere scarf. A Christmas angel. He smiled at the thought—even if he *was* getting sentimental in his old age.

"Merry Christmas," he said.

"Merry Christmas, Thom." Her eyes brightened as he approached.

Thom folded her in his arms and their kisses were deep and urgent. His mouth lingered on hers, gradually easing into gentler kisses. Finally he whispered, "Ready to go?"

"I hope this isn't a wild-goose chase," Noelle told him as she leaned her head against his shoulder.

"I do, too." But if it was, at least he'd be spending the day with her.

If they couldn't carry out their quest, they'd simply have to find some other way to persuade both mothers to accept the truth—that Thomas Sutton and Noelle McDowell were in love.

It was Christmas Eve, nine in the morning, and Sarah McDowell was eager to finish with the Christmas baskets. She'd skillfully wrapped each gift to transport to the Salvation Army.

"You're coming with me, aren't you?" she asked her husband.

Jake glanced up from the morning paper, frowning. "I can't."

"Why not?" Sarah didn't know if she could face Mary alone—not again. She'd assumed Jake would drive with her.

"I've got errands of my own. It's Christmas Eve."

"What about you, Carley?" she said, looking hopefully toward her daughter.

"Can't, Mom, sorry."

But not nearly sorry enough, Sarah thought. Her family was abandoning her in this hour of need. "Where's Noelle?" she asked. Surely she could count on Noelle.

"Out," Carley informed her.

"She's left already?"

Carley nodded.

Sarah thought she saw Jake wink at Carley. Apparently those two were involved in some sort of conspiracy against her.

At least Jake helped her load up the car, shifting his golf clubs to the backseat, but he disappeared soon afterward. Grumbling under her breath, Sarah drove out to the Women's Century Club.

Mary's car was already in the lot when she arrived. So, Mary Sutton was breaking a lifelong habit of tardiness in her eagerness to finish this charity project. For that, Sarah couldn't blame her. She, too, had reached her limit.

The cold air cut through her winter coat the instant she climbed out of the car. The radio station had mentioned the possibility of an ice storm later in the day. Sarah only hoped it wouldn't materialize.

"Merry Christmas," Melody called out as Sarah struggled through the front door, carrying the largest and most awkward of the boxes.

Sarah muttered a reply. Her Christmas Eve was *not* getting off to a good start.

"Mary's waiting for you," Melody told her. "I understand there was a mix-up with the lists. I'm so sorry. It was crazy that morning, wasn't it?"

Sarah wasn't fooled by the other woman's cheerful attitude. Melody Darrington had done her utmost to manipulate the two of them into working on this project together, and Sarah, for one, didn't take kindly to the interference. It was clear that Mary hadn't realized anything was amiss, but then Mary Sutton wasn't the most perceptive person in the world. Still, Sarah wasn't going to make a federal case of it, on the off chance that it *had* all been an innocent mistake as Melody was implying.

Sarah made her way into the meeting room, where Mary had the six baskets set up on a long table, as well as six large boxes, already filled with the makings for Christmas dinner.

"Is that everything you've got?" Mary asked, peering into Sarah's carton. Her tone insinuated that Sarah had contributed less than required.

"Of course not," she snapped. "I have two more boxes in the car."

Neither woman leaped up to help her carry them inside, although Melody did make a halfhearted offer when Sarah headed out the front door.

"No thanks—you've already done enough," she said pointedly.

"You're sure you don't need the help?" Melody asked.

Shaking her head, Sarah brought in the second of the boxes and set it on the table.

"I thought you'd bring one of the girls with you," Mary said in that stiff way of hers.

"They're busy." She started back for the last of the cartons.

"Noelle isn't with Thom, is she?"

The question caught her off guard. No one had said where Noelle had gone, but it couldn't be to meet Thom Sutton. Could it? No, she wouldn't do that. Not her daughter.

"Absolutely not," Sarah insisted. Noelle had already learned her lesson when it came to the Suttons.

"Good," Mary said.

"Noelle's with friends," Sarah returned and then, because she had to know, she asked a question of her own. "What makes you ask?"

"Oh—no reason."

Sarah didn't believe that for a moment. "You tell your son Noelle's under no illusions about him. She won't be so easily fooled a second time."

"Now just one minute—"

"We both know what he did."

"You're wrong, Sarah—but then you often are."

Melody stepped into the meeting room and stopped abruptly. With a shocked look, she regarded both women. "Come on, you two! It's Christmas."

"And your point is?" Sarah asked.

"My point is that the least you can do is work together on this. These baskets need to get to the Salvation Army right away. They're late already, and my husband just phoned and said there's definitely an ice storm coming, so you shouldn't delay."

"I'll get them there in time," Mary promised. "If we could get the baskets filled…"

"Fine," Sarah said. "I'll bring in the last box."

"We wouldn't be this late if you'd—"

Sarah ignored her and hurried out the door, only to hear Melody mutter something about an ice storm developing right in this room.

She knew that the minute she left, Melody and Mary would talk about her. However, she didn't care. Right after Kristen's wedding, she was letting her membership in the Women's Century Club lapse.

Once the third box was safely inside, Sarah placed the gifts in the correct baskets. Then both women sorted through the family names by checking the tag on each present. Sarah had spent a lot of time wrapping her gifts, wanting to please the recipients…and, to be honest, impress Mary and Melody with her talents. Given the opportunity, she could have decorated the clubhouse to match Mary's efforts. No, to exceed them.

"You did get that Firefighter Barbie doll, didn't you?" Mary asked.

"Of course I did," she answered scornfully.

They attached ribbons to each basket, then prepared everything—gifts and groceries—for transport.

"Would you like help loading up your car?" Sarah asked. Since Mary was driving and this was a joint project, she felt constrained to offer.

Mary seemed surprised, then shook her head. "I can manage. But…thanks."

Sarah had wanted to make a quick getaway, but Melody stopped her at the door, appointment book in hand.

"I have a few questions about Kristen's wedding."

"What do you need to know?"

Melody flipped open the book. "Will you require the use of our kitchen?"

"I'm not sure because we haven't picked the caterer yet, but we'll do that right after the first of the year."

"I have a list, if you'd like to look at it."

"I would." Sarah wanted to make her daughter's day as special as she could. But as she answered Melody's questions, her mind drifted to Noelle. Mary had brought up a frightening possibility. Noelle had been absent from the house quite a bit since the dance on Saturday night. She was at the mall on Sunday, and then on Monday—oh, yes, she'd worked on Carley's computer most of the day. Reassured now, Sarah relaxed. Mary's fears about her son and Noelle were unfounded.

She glanced around the lot; Mary's car was gone. She'd apparently left for the Salvation Army already. She must have moved her vehicle to the side entrance in order to load up the baskets and boxes more easily and Sarah hadn't seen her drive off. That was just fine. Maybe this was the last she needed to see of Mary Sutton.

Now she could enjoy Christmas.

"Merry Christmas, Melody," she said. "I'm sorry for the way I snapped at you earlier."

Melody accepted her apology. "I realize this was hard on both of you but what's important are the Christmas baskets."

"I couldn't agree with you more."

Sarah's spirits lifted considerably as she walked to her car or rather, Jake's. He'd insisted she take his SUV, and she was glad of it. If possible, it seemed even colder out; she drew her coat more closely around her and bent her head as she trudged toward the car.

As she turned out of the parking lot, she saw that the roads were icing over. The warning of an ice storm had become a reality, and even earlier than expected. This weather made her nervous, and Sarah drove carefully, hoping she wouldn't run into any problem.

She hadn't gone a mile when she noticed a car pulled off to the side of the road. She slowed down and was surprised to see Mary Sutton in the driver's seat. Mary was on her cell phone; she looked out the passenger window as Sarah slowed down. Mary's eyes met hers, and then she waved her on, declining help before Sarah could even offer it.

A Note From Noelle McDowell

Christmas Eve

Dear Carley Sue,

Good morning. I'll be gone by the time you read this. I'm meeting Thom in the park and we're driving to an antiques store outside Portland to check out a tea service. Kristen knows I'm with Thom, but not why.

I'm asking you to keep my whereabouts a secret for now. No, wait—you can mention it to Dad if you want. Mom's the only one who really can't know. I don't think she'll ask, because she's got a lot to do this morning delivering the Christmas baskets.

This whole mix-up with those baskets has really got her in a tizzy. I find it all rather humorous and I suspect Dad does, too.

I'm trusting you with this information, little sister. I figured you (and your romantic heart) would want to know.

Love,
Noelle

Eight

The car had made a grinding noise as soon as Mary started it—the same sound as the day before. Greg had said he'd look into it after the holidays, but she'd assumed it was safe to drive. Apparently not.

The car had slowed to a crawl, sputtered and then died. That was just great. The Salvation Army was waiting for these Christmas baskets, which, according to Melody, were already late. If Mary didn't hurry up and deliver them to the organization's office before closing time, six needy families would miss out on Christmas. She couldn't let that happen.

Reaching for her cell phone, she punched in her home number and hoped Greg was home. She needed rescuing, and soon. Greg would know what to do. The phone had just begun to ring when Sarah McDowell drove past.

Mary bit her lip hard. Pride demanded that she wave her on. She didn't need that woman's help. Still, she felt Sarah should've stopped; it was no less than any decent human being would do.

Well, she should know better than to expect compassion or concern from Sarah McDowell. Good Christian that she professed to be, Sarah had shown not the slightest interest in Mary's safety.

Mary clenched her teeth in fury. So, fine, Sarah didn't care whether *she* froze the death, but what about the Christmas baskets? What about the families, the children, whose Christmas depended on them? The truth was, Sarah simply didn't care what happened to Mary *or* the Christmas baskets.

The phone was still ringing—where on earth was Greg? Suddenly an operator's tinny voice came on with a recorded message. "I'm sorry, but we are unable to connect your call at this time."

"*You're* sorry?" Mary cried. She punched in Thom's number and then Suzanne's and got the same response. She tossed the phone back in her purse and waited. The Women's Century Club was on the outskirts of Rose. On Christmas Eve, with an ice storm bearing down, the prospect of a Good Samaritan was highly unlikely.

"Great," she muttered. She might be stuck here for God knows how long. Surely *someone* would realize she wasn't where she was supposed to be. Still, it might take hours before anyone came looking for her. And even more hours before she was found.

With the engine off, the heater wasn't working, and Mary was astonished by how quickly the cold seeped into the car's interior. She tried her cell phone again and got the same message. There was obviously trouble with the transmitters; maybe it would clear up soon. She struggled to remain optimistic, but another depressing thought overshadowed the first. How long could she last in this cold? She could imagine herself still sitting in the car days from now, frozen stiff, abandoned and forgotten on Christmas Eve.

Trying to ward off panic, she decided to stand on the side of the road to see if that would help her cell phone reception. That way, she'd also be ready to wave for assistance if someone drove by.

She retrieved her phone, climbed out of the car and immediately became aware of how much colder it was outside. Hands shaking, she tried the phone. Same recorded response. She tucked her hands inside her pockets and waited for what seemed like an eternity. Then she tried her cell phone again.

Nothing. Just that damned recording.

Resigned to waiting for a passerby, she huddled in her coat.

Five minutes passed. The icy wind made it feel more like five hours. The air was so frigid that after a few moments it hurt to breathe. Her teeth began to chatter, and her feet lost feeling, but that was what she got for wearing slip-on loafers instead of winter boots.

A car appeared in the distance and Mary was so happy she wanted to cry. Greg was definitely going to hear about this! Once she got safely home, of course.

Stepping into the middle of the road, she raised her hand and then groaned aloud. It wasn't some stranger coming to her rescue, but Sarah McDowell. Desperate though she was, Mary would rather have seen just about anyone else.

Sarah pulled up alongside her and rolled down the window. "What's wrong?"

"Wh-what does it l-look like? M-my car broke down." She wished she could control the chattering of her teeth.

"Is someone coming for you?"

"N-not yet... I c-can't get through on my cell phone."

"I'm here now. Would you like me to deliver the Christmas baskets?"

Mary hesitated. If the gifts were to get to the families in time, she didn't really have much choice. "M-maybe you should."

Sarah edged her vehicle closer to Mary's and with some difficulty they transferred the six heavy baskets and the boxes of groceries from one car to the next.

"Thanks," Mary said grudgingly.

Sarah nodded curtly. "Go ahead and call Greg again," she suggested.

"Okay." Mary punched out the number and waited, hoping against hope that the call would connect. Once again, she got the "I'm sorry" recording.

"Won't go through."

"Would you like to use my phone?" Sarah asked.

"I doubt your phone will work if mine doesn't." It was so irritating—Sarah always seemed to believe that whatever she had was better.

"It won't hurt to try."

"True," Mary admitted. She accepted Sarah's phone and tried again. It gave her no satisfaction to be right.

"Go ahead and deliver the baskets," Mary said, putting on a brave front.

"I'm not going to leave you here."

Mary hardened her resolve. "Someone will come by soon enough."

"Don't be ridiculous!" Sarah practically shouted.

"Oh, all right, you can drive me back to the club. And then deliver the baskets."

Sarah glared at her. "Aren't you being a little stubborn? I could just as easily drive you home."

Mary didn't answer. She intended to make it clear that she preferred to wait for Greg to rescue her rather than ride to town with Sarah.

"Fine, if that's what you want," Sarah said coldly.

"I'm grateful you came back," Mary told her—and she was. "I don't know how long I could've stood out here."

This time Sarah didn't respond.

"What's most important is getting these baskets to the families."

"At least we can agree on that," Sarah told her.

Mary climbed into the passenger side of Sarah's SUV and nearly sighed aloud when Sarah started the engine. A blast of hot air hit her feet and she moaned in pleasure.

Sarah was right, she decided. She *was* being unnecessarily stubborn. "If you don't mind," she said tentatively, "I would appreciate a ride home."

Sarah glanced at her as she started down the winding country road. "That wasn't so hard, now was it?"

"What?" she asked, pretending not to understand.

Just then, Sarah hit a patch of ice and the vehicle slid scarily into the other lane. With almost no traction, Sarah did what she could to keep the car on the road. "Hold on!" she cried. She struggled to maintain control but the tires refused to grip the asphalt.

"Oh, no," Mary breathed. "We're going into the ditch!" At that instant the car slid sideways, then swerved and went front-first into the irrigation ditch.

Mary fell forward, bracing her hands against the console. The car sat there, nose down. A frozen turkey rolled out of its box and lodged in the space between the two bucket seats, tail pointed at the ceiling. Sarah's eyes were wide as she held the steering wheel in a death grip.

Neither spoke for several moments. Then in a slightly breathless voice, Sarah asked, "Are you hurt?"

"No, are you?"

"I'm okay, but I think I broke three nails clutching the steering wheel."

Mary couldn't keep from smiling. Sarah had always been vain about her fingernails.

"Do you think we should try to climb out of the car?" Sarah murmured.

"I don't know."

"One of us should."

"I will," Mary offered. After all, Sarah would've been home by now if she hadn't come back to help.

"No, I think I should," Sarah said. "You must be freezing."

"I've warmed up—some. Listen, I'll go get Melody."

"It's at least a mile to the club."

"I know how far it is," Mary snapped. Sarah argued about everything.

"Why can't you just accept my help?"

"I'm in your car, aren't I?" She resisted the urge to remind Sarah that she hadn't actually been much help. Now they were both stuck, a hundred feet from where she'd been stranded. The charity baskets were no closer to their destination, either.

"Maybe another car will come by."

"Don't count on it," Mary told her.

"Why not?"

"Think about it. We're in the middle of an ice storm. It's Christmas Eve. Anyone with half a brain is home in front of a warm fireplace."

"Oh. Yes."

"I'll walk to the club."

"No," Sarah insisted.

"Why not?"

Sarah didn't say anything for a moment. "I don't want to stay here alone," she finally admitted.

Mary pondered that confession and realized she wouldn't want to wait in the car by herself, either. "Okay," she said. "We'll both go."

"Tell me what you found out about the tea service," Thom said as they headed toward the freeway on-ramp.

"The internet was great. Your secretary's list was a big help, too. I scanned in the photograph you gave me and got an immediate hit with the man we're going to see this morning."

"Hey, you did well."

"I have a good feeling about this." Noelle's voice rose with excitement.

Thom didn't entirely share her enthusiasm. "I don't think we should put too much stock in this," he said cautiously.

"Why not?"

"Don't forget, my mom and dad searched for years. It's unrealistic to think we can locate a replacement after just one day."

"But your parents didn't have the internet."

She was right, but not all antiques stores were online. Under the circumstances, it would be far too easy to build up their expectations only to face disappointment. "You said yourself this could be a wild-goose chase."

"I know." Noelle sounded discouraged now.

Thom reached out and gently clasped her fingers. "Don't worry—we're going to keep trying for as long as it takes." The road was icy, so he returned his hand to the steering wheel. "Looks like we're in for a spell of bad weather."

"I heard there's an ice storm on the way."

Thom nodded. The roads were growing treacherous, and he wondered if they should have risked the drive. However, they were on their way and at this point, he wanted to see it through as much as Noelle did.

What was normally a two-and-a-half-hour trip into Portland took almost four. Fortunately, the roads seemed to improve as they neared the city.

"I'm beginning to wonder if we should've come," Noelle said, echoing his thoughts as they passed an abandoned car angled off to the side of the road.

"We'll be fine." They were in Lake Oswego on the outskirts of Portland already—almost there.

"It's just that this is so important."

"I know."

"Maybe we should discuss what we're going to do if we don't find the tea service," Noelle said as they sought out the Lake Oswego business address.

"We'll deal with that when we have to, all right?"

She nodded.

The antiques store was situated in a strip mall between a Thai restaurant and a beauty parlor. Thom parked the car. "You ready?" he asked, turning to her.

Noelle smiled encouragingly.

They held hands as they walked to the store. A bell above the door chimed merrily when they entered, and they found themselves in a long, narrow room crammed with glassware, china and polished wood furniture. Every conceivable space and surface had been put to use. A slightly moldy odor filled the air, competing with the piney scent of a small Christmas tree. Thom had to turn sideways to get past a quantity of comic books stacked on a chest of drawers next to the entrance. He led Noelle around the obstacles to the counter, where the cash register sat.

"Hello," Noelle called out. "Anyone here?"

"Be with you in a minute," a voice called back from a hidden location deep inside the store.

While Noelle examined the brooches, pins and old jewelry beneath the glass counter, Thom glanced around. A collection of women's hats filled a shelf to the right. He couldn't imagine his mother wearing anything with feathers, but if she'd lived in a different era...

He studied a pile of old games next, but they all seemed to be missing pieces. This looked less and less promising.

"Sorry to keep you waiting." A thin older man with a full crop of white hair ambled into the room. He was slightly stooped and brushed dust from his hands as he walked.

"Hello, my name is Noelle McDowell," she said. "We spoke yesterday."

"Ah, yes."

"Thom Sutton." Thom stepped forward and offered his hand.

"Peter Bright." His handshake was firm, belying his rather frail appearance. "I didn't know if you'd make it or not, with the storm and all."

"We're grateful you're open this close to Christmas," Noelle told him.

"I don't plan on staying open for long. But I wanted to escape the house for a few hours before Estelle found an excuse to put me to work in the kitchen." He chuckled. "Would you like to take a look at the tea service?"

"Please."

"I have it back here." He started slowly toward the rear of the store; Thom and Noelle followed him.

Noelle reached for Thom's hand again. Although he'd warned her against building up their expectations, he couldn't help feeling a wave of anticipation.

"Now, let me see..." Peter mumbled as he began shifting boxes around. "You know, a lot of people tell me they're coming in and then never show up." He smiled. "Like I said, I didn't really expect you to drive all the way from Rose in the middle of an ice storm." He removed an ancient Remington typewriter and set it aside, then lifted the lid of an army-green metal chest.

"I've had this tea service for maybe twenty years," Peter explained as he extracted a Navy sea bag.

"Do you remember how you came to get it?"

"Oh, sure. An English lady sold it to me. I displayed it for a while. People looked but no one bought."

"Why keep it in the chest now?" Noelle asked.

"I didn't like having to polish it," Peter said. "Folks have trouble seeing past the tarnish." He straightened and met Thom's gaze. "Same with people. Ever notice that?"

"I have," Thom said. Even on short acquaintance, he liked Peter Bright.

Nodding vigorously, Peter extracted a purple pouch from the duffel bag and peeled back the cloth to display a creamer. He set it on the green chest for their examination.

Noelle pulled the photograph from her purse and handed it to Thom, who studied the style. The picture wasn't particularly clear, so he found it impossible to tell if this was the same creamer, but there was definitely a similarity.

The sugar bowl was next. Peter set it out, waiting for Thom and Noelle's reaction. The photograph showed a slightly better view of that.

"This isn't the one," Noelle said. "But it's close, I think."

"Since you drove all this way, it won't hurt to look at all the pieces."

Thom agreed, but he already knew it had been a futile trip. He tried to hide his disappointment. Against all the odds, he'd held high hopes for this. Like Noelle, he'd been waiting for a Christmas miracle but apparently it wasn't going to happen.

Bending low, Peter thrust his arm inside the canvas bag and extracted two more objects. He carefully unwrapped the silver teapot and then the coffeepot and offered them a moment to scrutinize his wares.

The elaborate tray was last. Carefully arranging each piece on top of it, Peter stepped back to give them a full view of the service. "It's a magnificent find, don't you think?"

"It's lovely," Noelle said.

"But it's not the one we're looking for."

He accepted their news with good grace. "That's a shame."

"You see, this service—" she held out the picture "—was

stolen years ago, and Thom and I are hoping to replace it with one that's exactly the same. Or as much like it as possible."

Peter reached for the photograph and studied it a moment. "I guess I should've looked closer and saved you folks the drive."

"No problem," Thom said. "Thanks for getting back to us."

"Yes, thank you for your trouble," Noelle said as they left the store. "It's a beautiful service."

"I'll give you a good price on it if you change your mind," the old man said, following them to the front door. "I'll be here another hour or so if you want to come back."

"Thank you," Thom said, but he didn't think there was much chance they'd be back. It wasn't the tea service they needed.

"How about lunch before we head home," he suggested. The Thai restaurant appeared to be open.

"Sure," Noelle agreed.

Thom shared her discouragement, but he was determined to maintain her optimism—and his own. "Hey, we've only started to look. It's too early to give up."

"I know. You're right, it was foolish of me to think we'd find it so quickly. It's just that…oh, I don't know, I guess I thought it *would* be easy because everything else fell into place for us."

They were the only customers in the restaurant. A charming waitress greeted them and escorted them to a table near the window.

Thom waited until they were seated before he spoke. "I guess this means we go to Plan B."

"What about pad thai and—" Noelle glanced up at him over the menu. "What exactly is Plan B?"

Thom reached inside his coat pocket and set the jeweler's box in the middle of the table.

"Thom?" Noelle put her menu down.

This wasn't the way he'd intended to propose, but—as the cliché had it—there was no time like the present. "I love you, Noelle, and I'm not going to let this feud stand between us. Our parents will have to understand that we're entitled to our own happiness."

Tears glistened in her eyes. "Oh, Thom."

"I'm asking you to be my wife."

She stretched her arm across the table and they joined hands. "And I'm telling you it would be the greatest honor of my life to accept. I have a request, though."

"Anything."

"I want to buy that tea service. Not you. Me."

Thom frowned. "Why?"

"I want to give it to your mother. From me to her. I can't replace the original, but maybe I can build a bridge between our families with this one."

Thom's fingers tightened around hers. "It's worth a try."

"I think so, too," she whispered.

"I'm going to try my phone again," Sarah said. Technology had betrayed them, but surely it would come to their rescue. Eventually. Walking a mile in the bitter cold was something she'd rather avoid.

"Go ahead," Mary urged. She didn't seem any more eager than Sarah to make the long trek.

Sarah got her phone and speed dialed her home number. Hope sprang up when the call instantly connected, but was dashed just as quickly when she heard the recording once again.

"Any luck?" Mary asked, her eyes bright and teary in the cold.

She shook her head.

"Damn," Mary muttered. "I guess that means there's no option but to hoof it."

"Appears that way."

"I think we should have a little fortification first, though," Sarah said. Her husband's golf bags were in the backseat, and she knew he often carried a flask.

"Fortification?"

"A little Scotch might save our lives."

Mary's look was skeptical. "I'm all for Scotch, but where are we going to find any out here?"

"Jake." She opened the back door and grabbed the golf bag. Sure enough, there was a flask.

"I don't remember you liking Scotch," Mary said.

"I don't, but at this point I can't be choosy."

"Right."

Sarah removed the top and tipped the flask, taking a sizable gulp. Wiping her mouth with the back of her hand, she swallowed, then shook her head briskly. "Oh my, that's strong." The liquor burned all the way down to her stomach, but as soon as it hit bottom, a welcoming warmth spread through her limbs.

"My turn," Mary said.

Sarah handed her the flask and watched as Mary rubbed the top, then tilted it back and took a deep swallow. She, too, closed her eyes and shook her head. Soon, however, she was smiling. "That wasn't so bad."

"It might ward off hypothermia."

"You're right. You'd better have another."

"You think?"

Mary nodded and after a moment, Sarah agreed. Luckily Jake had refilled the flask. The second swallow didn't taste nearly as nasty as the first. It didn't burn this time, either. Instead it enhanced the warm glow spreading through her system.

"How do you feel?"

"Better," Sarah said, giving Mary the flask.

Mary didn't need encouragement. She took her turn with the flask, then growled like a grizzly bear.

Sarah didn't know why she found that so amusing, but she did. She laughed uproariously. In fact, she laughed until she started to cough.

"What?" Mary asked, grinning broadly.

"Oh, dear." She coughed again. "I didn't know you did animal impressions."

"I do when I drink Scotch."

Then, as if they'd both become aware that they were having an actual conversation, they pulled back into themselves. Sarah noticed that Mary's expression suddenly grew dignified, as though she'd realized she was laughing and joking with her enemy.

"We should get moving, don't you think?" Mary said in a dispassionate voice.

"You're right." Sarah put the flask back in the golf bag and wrapped her scarf more tightly around her neck and face. Fortified in all respects, she was ready to face the storm. "It's a good thing we're walking together. Anything could happen on a day like this."

They'd gone about the length of a football field when Mary said, "I'm cold again."

"I am, too."

"You should've brought along the Scotch."

"We'll have to go back for it."

"I think we should," Mary agreed solemnly. "We could freeze to death before we reach the club."

"Yes. The Scotch might make the difference between survival and death."

Back at the car, they climbed in and shared the flask again. Soon, for no apparent reason, they were giggling.

"I think we're drunk," Mary said.

"Oh, hardly. I can hold my liquor better than this."

Mary burst into peals of laughter. "No, you can't. Don't you remember the night of our Halloween party?"

"That was—what?—twenty-two years ago!"

"I know, but I haven't forgotten how silly those margaritas made you."

"You were the one who kept filling my glass."

"You were the one who kept telling me how good they were."

Sarah nearly doubled over with hysterics. "Next thing I knew, I was standing on the coffee table singing 'Guantanamera' at the top of my lungs."

"You sounded fabulous, too. And then when you started to dance—"

"I *what?*" All Sarah recalled was the blinding headache she'd suffered the next morning. When she woke and could barely lift her head from the pillow without stabbing pain, she'd phoned her dearest, best friend in the world. Mary had dropped everything and rushed over. She'd mixed Sarah a tomato-juice concoction that had saved her life, or so she'd felt at the time.

Both women were silent. "I miss those days," Sarah whispered.

"I do, too," Mary said.

Sarah sniffled. It was the cold that made her eyes water. Digging through her purse, she couldn't find a single tissue. Mary gave her one.

"I've missed you," Sarah said and loudly blew her nose.

"I've missed you, too."

The cold must have intensified, because her eyes began to water even more. Using her coat sleeve, she wiped her nose.

"Here," she said to Mary, handing her the flask. "I want you to have this. Take the rest."

"The Scotch?"

Sarah nodded. "If we're not found until it's too late—I want you to have the liquor. It might keep you alive long enough for the rescue people to revive you."

Mary looked as though she was close to bursting into tears. "You'd die for—me?" She hiccuped on the last word.

Sarah nodded again.

"That's the most beautiful thing anyone's ever said to me."

"But before I die, I need to ask you something."

"Anything," Mary told her. "Anything at all."

Sarah sniffled and swallowed a sob. Leaning her forehead against the steering wheel, she whispered, "Forgive me."

Mary placed her hand on Sarah's shoulder. "I do forgive you, but first you have to forgive *me* for acting so badly. You were right—I *was* jealous of Cheryl. I thought you liked her better than me."

"Never. She's one of those people who move in and out of a person's life, but you—you're my...my soul sister. I've missed you so much."

"We're idiots." Mary returned the flask. "I can't accept this Scotch. If we freeze, we freeze together."

Sarah was feeling downright toasty at the moment. The world was spinning, but that was probably because she was drunker than a skunk. The thought made her giggle.

"What's so funny?" Mary wanted to know.

"We're drunk," she muttered. "Drunk as skunks. Drunk as skunks," she recited in a singsong voice.

"Isn't it wonderful?"

They laughed again.

"Jake always insists I eat something when I've had too much to drink."

"We have lots of food," Mary said, sitting up straight.

"Yes, but most of it's half-frozen by now."

Mary's eyes gleamed bright. "Not everything. I'm sure the families would want us to take what we need, don't you think?"

"I'm sure you're right," Sarah said as Mary climbed over the front seat and into the back, her coat flipping over her head.

Sarah laughed so hard she nearly peed her pants.

Women's Century Club
Rose, Oregon

December 24

Dear Mary and Sarah,
Just a note to let you know how much the Women's Century Club appreciates the effort that went into preparing these Christmas baskets. You two did a splendid job. I could see from the number of gifts filling the baskets that you went far beyond the items listed on the sheet I gave you. Both of you have been generous to a fault.

Sarah, I realize it was difficult to come into this project at the last minute, but you are to be commended for your co-operation.

Mary, you did a wonderful job making all the arrangements, and I'm confident the baskets will reach the Salvation Army in plenty of time to be distributed for the holidays.

If you're both willing to take up the task again next year, I'd be happy to recommend you for the job.

Sincerely,
Melody Darrington

Nine

Jake McDowell glanced at the kitchen clock and frowned. "What time did your mother say she'd be home?"

"I don't know." His youngest daughter was certainly a fount of information. Carley lay flat on her stomach in front of the Christmas tree, her arms outstretched as she examined a small package.

"She should be back by now, don't you think?" Jake asked, looking at the clock again.

"I suppose."

"When will Noelle be home?"

Unconcerned, Carley shrugged.

Jake decided he wasn't going to get any answers here and tried Sarah's cell for perhaps the fiftieth time. Whenever he punched in the number, he received the same irritating message. "I'm sorry. We are unable to connect your call...."

Not knowing what else to do, he phoned his golfing partner. Greg Sutton answered on the first ring.

"I thought you were Mary," he said, sounding as worried as Jake was.

"You haven't heard from Mary?"

"Not a word. Is Sarah back?"

"No," Jake said. "That's why I was calling you."

"What do you think happened?"

"No idea. I could understand if one of them was missing, but not both."

Greg didn't say anything for a moment. "Did you phone the Women's Century Club?"

"I did. Melody said they were there and left two hours ago. She told me the ice storm's pretty bad in her area. She's going to stay put until her husband can come and get her this afternoon."

"What did she say about Mary and Sarah?"

"Not much. Just that they got the baskets all sorted and loaded into Mary's vehicle. Melody did make some comment about Sarah and Mary being pretty hostile toward each other. According to her, they left at different times."

"That doesn't explain why they're both missing."

"What if one of them had an accident and the other stopped to help?" Greg suggested.

Jake hadn't considered that. "But wouldn't they have been back by now?"

"Unless they got stuck."

"Together?"

"I wouldn't know."

Jake laughed grimly. "If that's the case, God help us all."

"What do you think we should do?"

"We can't leave them out there."

"You're right," Greg said. "But I have to tell you the idea is somewhat appealing. If they *are* stuck with each other for a while, they just might settle this mess."

"They could murder each other, too." Jake knew his wife

far too well. When it came to Mary Sutton, she could be downright unreasonable. "I say we go after them—together."

Jake had no objection to that. Greg owned a large four-wheel-drive truck that handled better on the ice than most vehicles. "You want to pick me up?"

"I'm on my way," Greg said.

Sarah reached for another Christmas cookie. "What did you call these again?" she asked, studying the package. Unfortunately, the letters wouldn't quite come into focus.

"Pfeffernusse."

"Try to say *that* three times when you're too drunk to stand up."

Mary giggled and helped herself to one of the glazed ginger cookies. "They're German. One family on the list had a German-sounding name and I thought they might be familiar with these cookies."

Sarah was touched. Tears filled her eyes. "You're so thoughtful."

"Not really," Mary said with a sob. "I... I was trying to outdo you." She was weeping in earnest now. "How could I have been so silly?"

"I did the same thing." Sarah wrapped her arm around Mary's shoulders. "I was the one who got us thrown out of Value-X."

Mary sniffled and dried her eyes. "I'm never going to let anything come between us again."

"I won't, either," Sarah vowed. "I think this has been the best Christmas of my life."

"Christmas!" Mary jerked upright. "Oh, Sarah, we've got to get these baskets to the Salvation Army!"

"But how? We can't carry all this stuff."

"True, but we can't just sit here, either." She looked into

the distance, in the direction of the Women's Century Club. "We're going to have to walk, after all."

Her friend was right. They had to take matters into their own hands and work together. "We can do it."

"We can. We'll walk to the club and send someone to get the baskets. Then we'll call Triple A. See? We have a plan. A good plan. There isn't anything we can't do if we stick together."

Sarah felt the tears sting her eyes again. "Is there any Scotch left?"

"No," Mary said, sounding sad. "We're going to have to make it on our own."

Clambering out of the car, Sarah was astonished by how icy the road had become in the hour or so they'd dawdled over their comforting Scotch. Luckily, she was wearing her boots, whereas Mary wore loafers.

Her friend gave a small cry and then, arms flailing, struggled to regain her balance. "My goodness, it's slippery out here."

"How are we going to do this?" Sarah asked. "You can't walk on this ice."

"Sure I can," Mary assured her, straightening with resolve. But she soon lost her balance again and grabbed hold of the car door, just managing to save herself.

"It's like you said—we'll do it together," Sarah declared. "We have to, because I'm not leaving you behind."

With Mary's arm around Sarah's waist and Sarah's arm about Mary's shoulder, they started walking down the center of the road. The treacherous ice slowed them down, and their progress was halting, especially since both of them were drunk and weepy with emotion.

"I wonder how long it'll take Greg to realize I'm not home,"

Mary said. Her husband was in trouble as it was, leaving her a defective vehicle to drive.

"Probably a lot longer than Jake. I told him I wouldn't be more than an hour."

"I'm sure there's some football game on TV that Greg's busy staring at. He won't notice I'm not there until Suzanne and Thom arrive for dinner." Mary went strangely quiet.

"Are you okay?" Sarah asked, tightening her hold on her friend.

"Yes, but… Thom. I was thinking about Thom. He's in love with Noelle, you know."

"Noelle's been in love with Thom since she was sixteen. It broke her heart when he dumped her."

"Thom didn't dump her. She dumped him."

Sarah bristled. "She did not!"

"You mean to say something else happened?"

"It must have, because I know for a fact that Noelle's always loved Thom."

"And Thom feels the same about her."

"We have to do something," Sarah said. "We've got to find a way to get them back together."

"I think they might've been secretly seeing each other," Mary confessed.

Sarah shook her head, which made her feel slightly dizzy. "Noelle would've told me. We're this close." She attempted to cross two fingers, but couldn't manage it. Must be because of her gloves, she decided. Yes, that was it.

"We're drunk," Mary said. "Really and truly drunk. The cookies didn't help one bit."

"I don't care. We're best friends again and this time it's for life."

"For life," Mary vowed.

"We're on a mission."

"A mission," Mary repeated. She paused "What's our mission again?"

Sarah had to stop and think about it. "First, we need to deliver the Christmas baskets."

Mary slapped her hand against her forehead. "Right! How could I forget?"

"Then…"

"There's more?" Mary looked confused.

"Yes, lots more. Then we need to convince Noelle and Thom that they were meant to be together."

"Poor Thom," Mary said. "Oh no." She covered her mouth with her hand.

"What?"

"I left a message on his answering machine. I may not remember much right now, but I remember that. I told him I didn't think he should marry Noelle…."

"Why would you do that?"

"Well, because—oh dear, Sarah, I might have ruined everything."

"We'll deal with it as soon as we're home," Sarah said firmly.

A car sounded from behind them. "Someone's coming," Mary cried, her voice rising with excitement.

"We've got to hitch a ride." Sarah whirled around and held out her thumb as prominently as she could.

"That's not going to work," Mary insisted, thrusting out her leg. "Don't you remember that old Clark Gable movie?"

"Clark Gable got a ride by showing off his ankle?"

"No… Claudette Colbert did."

The truck turned the corner; Sarah wasn't willing to trust in either her thumb or Mary's leg, so she raised both hands above her head and waved frantically.

"It's Greg," Mary cried in relief.

"And Jake's with him." Thank God. Sarah had never been happier to see her husband.

To their shock and anger, the two men drove directly past them.

"Hey!" Mary shouted after her husband. "I am in no mood for games."

The truck stopped, and the driver and passenger doors opened at the same time. Greg climbed down and headed over to Mary, while Jake hurried toward Sarah.

"We're friends for life," Mary told her husband, throwing her arm around Sarah again.

"You're drunk," Greg said. "Just what have you been drinking?"

"I know exactly what I'm doing," she answered with offended dignity.

"Do *you?*" Jake asked Sarah.

"Of course I do."

"We're on a mission," Mary told the two men.

Jake frowned. "What happened to the car?"

"I'll tell you all about it later," Sarah promised, enunciating very carefully.

"What mission?" Jake asked.

Sarah exchanged an exasperated look with Mary. "Why do we have to explain everything?"

"Men," Mary said in a low voice. "Can't live with 'em, can't live without 'em."

Her friend was so wise.

The drive back to Rose took even longer than the trip into Portland. The roads seemed to get icier and more slippery with every mile. Keeping her eyes on the road, Noelle knew how tense Thom must be.

"Would you rather wait until after Christmas?" she asked as

they neared her family's home. It might be better if they got through the holidays before making their announcement and throwing their families into chaos. Noelle hated the thought of dissension on Christmas Day.

"Wait? You mean to announce our engagement?" Thom clarified. "I don't think we should. You're going to marry me, and I want to tell the whole world. I refuse to keep this a secret simply because our mothers don't happen to get along. They'll just have to adjust."

"But—"

"I've waited all these years for you. I'm not waiting any longer. All right?"

"All right." Noelle was overwhelmed by contradictory emotions. Love for Thom—and love for her family. Excitement and nervousness. Happiness and guilt.

"Do you know what I like most about Christmas?" Thom asked, breaking into her thoughts.

"Tell me, and then I'll tell you what I like."

"Mom has a tradition she started when Suzanne entered high school. On Christmas Eve, she serves fresh Dungeness crab. We all love it. She has them cooked at the market because she can't bear to do it herself, then Dad brings them home. Mom's got the butter melted and the bibs ready and we sit around the table and start cracking."

"Oh, that sounds delicious."

"It is. Does your family have a Christmas Eve tradition?"

"Bingo."

"Bingo?"

"Christmas Bingo. We play after the Christmas Eve service at church. The prizes aren't worth more than five dollars, but Mom's so good at getting neat stuff. I haven't been home for Christmas in years, but Mom always makes up for it by mailing me three or four little Bingo gifts."

"My favorite carol is 'What Child Is This,'" he said next. "Mine's 'Silent Night.'"

"What was your favorite gift as a kid?"

"Hmm, that's a toss-up," she said. "There was a Christmas Barbie I adored. Another year I got a set of classic Disney videos that I watched over and over."

Thom smiled. "As a little boy, I loved my Matchbox car garage. I got it for Christmas when I was ten. Mom's kept it all these years. She has Dad drag it out every year and tells me she's saving it to give to my son one day."

She sighed, at peace with herself and this man she loved. "I want to have your babies, Thom," she said in a soft voice.

His eyes left the street to meet hers. The sky had darkened and he looked quickly back at the road. "You make it hard to concentrate on driving."

"Tell me some of the other things you love about Christmas. It makes me feel good to hear them."

"It's your turn," he said.

"The orange in the bottom of my stocking. Every year there's one in the toe. It's supposed to commemorate the Christmases my great-grandparents had—an orange was a pretty special thing back then."

"I like Christmas cookies. Especially meringue star ones."

"Mexican tea cakes for me," she said. "I'll ask your mother for the recipe for star cookies and bake you a batch every Christmas."

"That sounds like a very wifely thing to do."

"I want to be a good wife to my husband." Noelle suddenly realized that she was genuinely grateful they hadn't married so young. Yes, the years had brought pain, but they'd brought wisdom and perspective, too. The love she and Thom felt for each other would deepen with time. They were so much more capable now of valuing what they had together.

"What's it like to be born on Christmas Day?" Thom asked.

"It's not so bad," Noelle said. "First, I share a birthday with Jesus—that's the good part. The not-so-good is having the two biggest celebrations of the year fall on the same day. When I was a kid, Mom used to throw me a party in June to celebrate my half-year birthday."

"I remember that."

"Do you remember teasing me by saying it really wasn't my birthday so you didn't need to bring a gift?"

Thom chuckled. "What I remember is getting my ears boxed for saying it."

Twenty minutes later, they were almost at her family's house. They'd decided to confront her parents first. Their laughter, which had filled the car seconds earlier, immediately faded.

"You ready?" Thom asked as he stopped in front of the house.

Noelle nodded and swallowed hard. "No matter what happens, I want you to remember I love you."

His hand squeezed hers.

Glancing at her family's home, Noelle noticed a truck parked outside. "Looks like we have company." She didn't know whether to feel relief or disappointment.

"Oh, no." Thom's voice was barely above a whisper.

"What is it?"

"That's my parents' truck."

Dread slipped over her. "They must've found out that we spent the day together. That's my fault—I left a note for Carley telling her I was with you." Noelle could imagine what was taking place inside. Her mother would be shouting at Thom's, and their fathers would be trying to keep the two women apart.

"Should we wait?" Noelle asked, just as she had earlier.

"For another time?" His jaw tensed. "No, we face them here and now, for better or worse. Agreed?"

Noelle nodded. "Okay…just promise me you won't let them change your mind."

He snorted inelegantly. "I'd like to see them try."

Thom parked behind the truck and turned off the engine. Together, holding hands, they approached the house. Never had Noelle been more nervous. If this encounter went wrong, she might alienate her mother, and that was something she didn't want to do. In high school, she'd self-righteously cast her family aside in the name of love. But if the years in Dallas had taught her independence, they'd also taught her the importance of home and family. Her self-imposed exile was over now, and she'd learned from it. Listening to Thom talk about his Christmas traditions, she'd realized that he'd find it equally hard to turn his back on his parents.

He was about to ring the doorbell when she stopped him. "Remember how I said I was looking for a Christmas miracle?"

Thom nodded. "You mean finding a tea service similar to my grandmother's?"

"Yes. But if I could be granted only one miracle this Christmas, it wouldn't be that. I'd want our families to rekindle the love and friendship they once had."

"That would be my wish, too." Thom gathered her in his arms and kissed her with a passion that readily found a matching fire in her. The kiss was a reminder of their love, and it sealed their bargain. No matter what happened once they entered the house, they would face it together.

"Actually, this is a blessing in disguise," Thom said. "We can confront both families at the same time and be done with it." He reached for the doorbell again, and again Noelle stopped him.

"This is my home. We don't need to ring the bell." Stepping forward, she opened the door.

Noelle wasn't sure what she expected, but certainly not the scene that greeted her. Her parents and two sisters, plus Thom's entire family, sat around the dining room table. Her mother and Mrs. Sutton, both wearing aprons, stood in the background, while her father and Thom's dished up whole Dungeness crabs, with Jonathan pouring wine.

"Thom!" his mother shouted joyfully. "It's about time you got here."

"What took you so long?" Sarah asked Noelle.

Stunned, Thom and Noelle looked at each other for an explanation.

"There's room here," Carley called out, motioning to the empty chairs beside her.

Noelle couldn't do anything other than stare.

"What...happened?" Thom asked.

"It's a long story. Sit down. We'll explain everything later."

"But…"

Thom put his arm around Noelle's shoulder. "Before we sit down, I want everyone to know that I've asked Noelle to be my wife and she's accepted."

"Nothing you say or do will make us change our minds," Noelle said quickly, before anyone else could react.

"Why would we want to change your minds?" her father asked. "We're absolutely delighted."

"You can fight and argue, threaten and yell, and it won't make any difference," Thom added. "We're getting married!"

"Glad to hear it," his father said.

A round of cheers followed his announcement.

Thom's mother and Noelle's mother embraced in joy.

"One thing this family refuses to tolerate anymore is fighting," his mother declared.

"Absolutely," her own mother agreed.

Both Thom and Noelle stared back at them, shocked into speechlessness.

"There's no reason to stand there like a couple of strangers," her mother said. "Sit down. You wouldn't believe the day we had."

Sarah and Mary put their arms around each other's shoulders. "At least the Christmas baskets got delivered on time," Mary said with a satisfied nod.

"And no one mentioned that the two of us smelled like Scotch when we got there," her mother pointed out.

They both giggled.

"What happened?" Noelle asked.

Her father waved aside her question. "You don't want to know," he groaned.

"I'll tell you later," her mother promised.

Thom leaned close to her and whispered, "Either we just walked into the middle of an *X-Files* episode or we got our Christmas miracle."

Noelle slipped an arm around his waist. "I think you must be right."

Sarah McDowell
9 Orchard Lane
Rose, Oregon

December 26

Dear Melody,
Mary and I found your note when we delivered the baskets
on Christmas Eve. We did have a wonderful time, and Mary
has agreed to head up the committee next year. I promised
I'd be her cochair.
   Now, about using the club for Kristen's wedding reception… Well, it seems there's going to be another wedding in
the family, and fairly soon. Mary and I will be in touch with
you about that right after New Year's.

Sincerely,
Sarah McDowell

⋆ ⋆ ⋆ ⋆ ⋆